Black Diamond

RACHEL INGALLS

Black Diamond

faber and faber
LONDON · BOSTON

First published in 1992
by Faber and Faber Limited
3 Queen Square London WC1N 3AU

Photoset by Wilmaset Ltd, Wirral
Printed in England by
Clays Ltd St Ives plc

A CIP record for this book is
available from the British Library

ISBN 0–571–16278–9

'Last Act: The Madhouse' was first published in the summer 1990 issue of *Esquire* Magazine, slightly edited and under the title 'Faces of Madness'.

Contents

Last Act: The Madhouse

Four other boys in William's class shared his name. At home he was Will. At school someone else was called Will; two were Bill and one went under a middle name. Only William was given the full, formal version.

His family had money. They owned a large house in town and a summer place at the beach. He was closer to his cousins – until they moved away – than to any of the boys and girls in his class. Everyone liked him, but he had no special companions. He had pets: as a child he'd kept mice, frogs, goldfish, and a dog his parents had bought for him when he was two. The dog lived to be almost thirteen and died of kidney disease. After that, William didn't want another pet. His energy went into the car he was learning to drive.

When he wasn't out on the road he'd spend his time playing phonograph records. He had hundreds, most of them highlights from Italian opera, though there were a few albums of Dixieland in his collection, and some blues and early jazz. He got interested in opera by listening to the radio. He liked the tunes. For years he knew nothing about the stories that were meant to accompany the music – in fact, he had no idea that the songs were intended to be played in any definite order. One day he decided to write down the name of a composer as it was announced at the end of a broadcast. He went to the library to find out more. He started to buy the records and to read about music in general.

Every once in a while his parents would take him along to a concert in the capital. They were glad to see that he wasn't completely brainwashed by the rock and roll everybody his age was dancing to, but they considered opera to be going a little too far. They drew the line at foreign languages, even the kind of French used in restaurants. The waiter could always tell you what things meant.

He began to pick up a few phrases in Italian. At school he was offered French, and Latin if he wanted it; he didn't want Latin because he thought he'd never need it. He did well in French. He even bought a couple of records of French opera, and some in German, but they failed to hold his attention. Already he was a specialist: it was the Italians or nothing.

He studied the stories from booklets that came with his boxed sets. The text included pictures of the singers in costume. And, on the back covers, photographs showed him how each scene would look to an audience. He read reviews in the papers. He subscribed to an opera magazine. As in many other matters, his acquaintance with opera was theoretical: imagined. He'd heard a lot, but seen nothing first-hand.

He knew the characters' names; he was familiar with their lives. The young men who sang the hero's part were soldiers or scholars, dukes and princes. Sometimes they were in disguise: that was the way life was then, apparently. And they loved. That hadn't changed. They were like real people to him. They were like himself. Of course they were also melodramatic and silly, but however inane the people and the plot, the music always won out. The music persuaded him so far that he even began to like the faults as well as the virtues of opera. He was captivated by the ludicrous misunderstandings, the eccentric motives and con-trived emotions, the coincidences that could never happen.

The stories were usually, as anyone could see, ridiculous. That wasn't important. You had to realize that certain conventions and situations were constant because they set the scene for a particular kind of music. There were arias of anger, forgiveness, longing, supplication; if you wanted to cram them all into one work, the story had to make room for them. Occasionally things got to the point where – because of the need to fit in all the songs – the plot no longer made sense. William didn't mind too much about that. He preferred an overcrowding of drama to a lack of excitement.

2

He also understood that sometimes the kind of voice a composer was writing for would determine the style of the music. In quite a few of these operas, for instance, there was a mad scene. When a coloratura soprano was in the cast, you could be fairly sure that before the last act she'd be crazy, although still able to hit a high E. Almost always the reason for her mental collapse was desertion or betrayal by her lover, whose black cloak (dark, anyway, according to the photographs) she would press to her heart as she trilled away at the high bits. The traditions of stage madness demanded that the more crazed a girl became, the higher she sang. Purity of tone would indicate the intensity of her love and pain. Another custom governed the color of her dress: it had to be white, and of a simple, shiftlike design. You were supposed to think it was her nightgown, and that she'd be too distracted to want to change her clothes, or perhaps to remember how to. Occasionally the nightdress resembled some sort of tattered bridal garment she'd put on under the impression that the hero would call for her in just a minute, to take her to church and make her his wife. Her complaint might not have been insanity as the twentieth century knew it, but more a kind of madness peculiar to the dictates of Romanticism.

As his knowledge and appreciation grew, William no longer felt that his greatest wish was to see an opera staged. What he longed for was the world the operas described: the emotions of other people, given to him by the music; the place where grand events took place, usually in the distant past or at the time when the music had been composed. That time too was gone. But all times in opera were equal; fictional and historical past occupied the same world. It was the world where William wanted to live. The time of Romance seemed more real to him than Korea, the Second World War, the Depression, the First World War, the Founding Fathers, and all the rest of it. A century or so made no difference to him, nor did the setting. People still felt the same, no matter where they were; love, hate, jealousy, the urge to kill, to die, to sacrifice, to capture beauty: emotions didn't change. But a small American town in 1958 wasn't an ideal stage on which to express emotion. You could get into trouble just trying to park at the side of the road with a girl.

He'd been out in his new car one night with a girl from the class above his, when a policeman had sneaked up and shone a flashlight at them through the window. William came home raving, asking his parents what kind of man would take a job like that – what kind of pervert? His father laughed. William said, 'Somebody old and ugly and envious; some slob that hates anyone young. He wanted to see my license and know all about the car, and – I bet he wasn't even on duty. He was probably one of those Peeping Toms. I'm going to report him.'

'Don't do that,' his father told him. 'He can say he was checking the car. To see if it was stolen, or if you'd had the brakes tested. Anything like that.'

'He wasn't checking the car. He was checking on us, to see if we were making out.'

'You wouldn't be able to prove that.'

William's mother said, 'It's part of their job, dear.' She was a generation younger than her husband. She'd been brought up primly and had always been cautious with younger men.

William shouted, 'How could that be anybody's job? It isn't anybody else's business what I want to do.'

'They just have to make sure you're not doing anything wrong,' she said.

William thought he was going to choke. He threw out his arms and stamped on the floor. 'Wrong?' he said. 'Jesus Christ!'

'Will, I don't want to have to keep asking you to watch your language.'

He marched up to the sideboard, back to the table and out of the room. His father called after him, 'That'll teach you to park a little farther out of town.'

He went down to the basement room his parents had let him make into a music studio. He put a record on the turntable. His anger and frustration flooded away on a tide of music. He couldn't understand how other people could hear the notes and not realize that opera was more beautiful, and better, than the kind of stuff they normally listened to. The music said every-

4

thing. It told you, without words, everything that was going on, and what it meant: what the people in the story felt. Even the plots, even the silly ones filled with coincidences, were marvelous: the violence, intimacy and commitment of the emotions they dealt with, the exaltation they allowed you; it was all wonderful. Small towns in America didn't leave any margin for that kind of uplifting experience. They didn't even let you try it out in your own car.

He was in his third year of highschool when he started going out with Jean. She was two years younger than he was. His mother didn't approve of that. She didn't trust Jean's parents, either, who were ordinary people no one had ever heard of. William's mother didn't associate with such families. She had sound instincts about that sort of thing; his father thought so, at any rate. Once William knew what his parents' attitude was going to be, he spent a lot of time in crowds: playing tennis, going to the movies, going out with seven or nine other people in his class. And he met Jean in secret.

Secrecy speeded up the affair, as did the knowledge that there were hindrances against them. They met and embraced in an isolation as charged with expectancy as any midnight assignation between soprano and tenor. All they needed to heighten their passion was an appreciation of danger. But the dangers were so obvious that they overlooked them.

Their conversation was all of abstract things. First of all they agreed on how wrong most people – especially the older generation – were about everything. Then they talked about love and about art. And poetry. They both wrote poems; they had written poetry long before they had anyone to write it to.

He'd have liked to listen to his records with her, but she was shy about coming to the house. She knew his parents still thought she wasn't the kind of girl he should be seeing: they didn't go out of their way to discourage the friendship – that might persaude their son to commit himself to the girl. They said instead that they felt sorry for her.

As for taking his records to her place: that wouldn't work, either. Her parents were definitely not the kind of people who

5

listened to opera. If he'd brought it into their house, they'd have thought he was showing off, or worse – that he considered them in need of extra education.

He played the records after seeing Jean, and before. He had Callas, he had Gobbi; he had everybody. He also had a car and good clothes and enough money to take a girl out dancing, to the movies, to restaurants. That should have been in his favor. What it actually meant was that Jean's parents suspected him of being unreliable: financial freedom leads to other freedoms. And although it might be possible in their town to conceal an aberrant or extravagant mind, any generosity or transgression of the body was found out immediately. Even when it wasn't true, illicit intercourse could be presumed: by the way people behaved, what they said, how they looked at each other. Hints, supposition, inference, couldn't harm a man; they hurt women and girls. There were many reasons for the parents of a daughter to feel mistrust. They would want her to refuse all physical advances in any case; but if she didn't, she'd have no control over what happened to her. Any power she had over her future would pass to the man she was with. A man, married or not, could buy contraceptives at the drugstore, whereas no unmarried woman of any age could legally ask a doctor to fit her with a diaphragm; a young girl who tried such a thing would be reported to her parents, or possibly to the police. That would be considered a question of morality. Jean was fifteen, William seventeen, which would have made it immorality. They thought it was love.

They made love outdoors at night and then in the daytime too. As his father had advised, William parked the car far enough away from the center of town not to attract attention. The fact that neither of them had sisters or brothers made it easy to keep their secret, although later it would mean that they'd have no allies against their parents' generation. And at school they hadn't found anyone to take the place of brothers and sisters. It seemed that all their lives they had been waiting for each other. William had his gang of pals, none of them very important to him. Jean was temporarily without anyone she wanted to confide in. She'd had two good friends, but both of them had left school. Her best friend had moved to another town the year before. She'd written letters for the first few months of their separation. After that, the correspondence became sporadic. She never mentioned William to the girl. She felt it would be a betrayal to talk about him behind his back, to share with anyone else the secret understanding they had; and as soon as they were lovers, there was no need for emotional corroboration from a third person: William had taken the place of best friend.

They wrote poems to each other and also letters. Sometimes they'd mail their poems, sometimes one of them would just slip a piece of paper to the other between classes. To exchange a look among a group of people, to brush by each other so that their hands touched, set them alight: to know, when nobody else knew.

They lost interest in schoolwork. When they weren't falling asleep over their books during the day, they'd want to laugh and joke. They liked sneaking into the back row of movie theaters to watch B-features while they fed each other popcorn and tried to see how much they could do with each other before anyone noticed.

At night he'd stand outside her house while she shinnied down the tree that grew in front of her bedroom window. Later on, he'd take up his post again as she climbed back. They blew kisses to each other. He'd take long walks or drive around for a while before returning to his parents' house. When he got back, he'd turn the volume down on the phonograph and play his records. He'd sink into the harmony – his breathing, his skin, his whole body aligned to the sound of passion in the voices: the delicious pain of love, the beauty, the intensity. To be able to sing like that, he thought, would be like being able to fly. And now that he was a lover himself, he understood: that was what it was all about – desire and suffering, betrayal and madness, rec-onciliation, the joy of being united in love.

Long ago opera had taken the place of a friend. Now that he had someone of his own, he hadn't lost his affection for it, but its use had changed. It supplemented his life, where before it had been a substitute. Jean had become his life. And he was living for the first time, as if he'd just woken up, having slept to his music all the time when he might have taken part in the world.

Eventually, after several months, Jean got pregnant. She didn't tell anyone. Even though her period had never come late before, she hoped and expected and prayed that it was late just this once, and it would come at any moment. When it was three weeks late she still hoped, doggedly and miserably. She threw up twice – once after she'd been drinking, so that didn't count. Her breasts began to hurt. But she told herself that if something had gone wrong with her period, she'd probably feel strange symptoms anyway.

Eleven days after she'd missed the second period, she told William she thought she might be pregnant. She might be; in fact, she was sure now: she was. She'd have to have an abortion straight away. How could she get one – what could they do?

William was so amazed that for a while he could only say, 'It's all right.' Then he told her he blamed himself for not trying to be more careful. He wasn't the one who'd get stuck, so he hadn't worried. He should have thought about her. Now that it had happened, he said, he wanted her to have the baby. It was his; he was proud of that. And it was natural. To do anything against that, he figured, would be somehow wrong. He was stunned by the idea of a new life that the two of them had made together. 'Because we loved each other,' he said. The only reason why she didn't want to have it was that all the people in town were such hyprocrites: wasn't it? She was afraid that they'd take it out on her, start talking about morality and do a lot of preaching at her. But everything was going to be all right. He wouldn't let them.

It wasn't going to be easy. He could imagine how bad things would be for her. He'd known for a long time how strongly society felt that any kind of love outside marriage, and sometimes within marriage, was bad. The physical expression was bad. In fact, the emotion itself, the idea, was suspect. Platonic love could sometimes be the worst, because it bound two souls together regardless of age, sex, color, belief or marital status. The

8

movies you could see in town were almost as repressed as real life; people were given their just deserts if they stepped out of line by a fraction. You only saw how beautiful love could be – the way everybody their age knew it had to be – if you could get to a foreign movie, where they showed people in their underwear and sometimes even, from far away, naked; at least, the women.

It would be bad for her, but it was going to be bad for him, too. Once people knew, the small town would close against him. It had never had anything in common with people like him, anyway.

As for her, she knew that what had happened to her was the end of a girl, unless she got married. Everybody knew what became of girls who got pregnant: everyone talked about them and the girls went away forever, or they came back later and no one talked about where they'd been. They were like women who had died.

If she got married, then it would be all right. She would escape from her parents, who were wrong about everything anyhow, and she'd be with William. He won her over. She'd do anything for him. He'd tell his parents. They wouldn't be able to fight it; they'd have to let him marry her in one of those states where the age-limit was lower. And if his father and mother accepted that, the rest of the town would, too.

He talked to her parents. They were impressed by him and by his family. 'As far as I'm concerned,' he said, 'we're married.' But Jean's mother thought, despite everything, it was a terrible shame – the ruin of at least two lives – for a girl to have a baby at such a young age: she'd be only just sixteen when it was born. And Jean's father got to thinking there should be some legal safeguard for his daughter, so that in three or four years' time, or even ten, she and the child would be provided for. Young men sometimes changed their minds.

'I'll see to all that,' William said. He was still only seventeen. He wouldn't be eighteen till the spring. He hadn't told his own parents anything yet. Knowing them and their views about who was or wasn't worthwhile, he'd prejudged their reactions and chosen, for the moment, not to speak out. In any case he'd

9

wanted to be with Jean when she had to face her mother and father. The money he'd have when he was eighteen wasn't much, but it was enough to start out on. If he had to, he could handle everything all by himself, though he'd rather have his parents' help. He'd rather have them understand, too.

He was still mulling over the wording of the speech that would overwhelm his parents, when he was beaten to the punch by Jean's father.

Her father had first of all let his daughter know what he thought of her. 'This is all the thanks we get,' he'd said. His wife backed him up. Jean ran upstairs, crying, and slammed her door, leaving her parents to talk about what should be done.

Her father decided there ought to be a discussion between all four parents on the matter of financial arrangements. He telephoned William's father. He assumed that the man knew what was going on.

Jean's father talked to William's father for twelve minutes. He brought up the subjects of rent, food, clothes, the price of babycarriages, hospitals, and so on.

William's father didn't say much, except that he'd remember all the points raised: he'd have to go over them with his wife before he could say anything definite. He left the office immediately. He went into conference at home with his wife. Together they greeted William on his return from school.

He opened his heart to them. They closed theirs to him. They told him that he had no idea how difficult it could be for a young couple with a baby – especially hard for a girl, who would have to become a mother before learning how to be a wife.

'We know that already,' William said. 'What it means to be man and wife. We don't need a piece of paper.'

'Without the piece of paper, and without being the right age, the child may not be legally yours,' his father told him. 'Or hers.'

'That can't be true.'

'You can prove you're not the father of a child, but it's impossible to prove that you are. You didn't know that, did you?'

'I guess so,' William said. 'Why does it matter?'

'She's still considered to be under the care of her parents. And now her father's trying to get money out of us. He called me up at the office, started talking about hospital bills and the price of maternity clothes and everything. He seemed to think I knew all about it.'

William was sorry about that, he said; he'd been racking his brains, wondering how to tell them: he'd known from the beginning that they didn't like Jean.

His parents denied it; they had nothing against the girl. Of course not. But as things stood now . . . Well, there were so many difficulties.

If they wanted to, his father told him, her parents could get really nasty. She was still a minor. If William were one year older, they could charge him with rape on the mere fact of her age, and send him to jail. Even as it was, they could put her into some kind of reform school until she was eighteen. For immorality.

'That's crazy,' William said. 'And disgusting.'

'It's the law.'

'Then the law is crazy. It ought to be changed.'

'Maybe so. But it isn't changed yet.'

William wanted to know what people were doing, passing laws like that: were they all religious bigots? Even bigots went to bed with each other; or did they just want to stop everybody else from doing it?

Laws, his father said, usually had some sense to them. This particular one was meant to protect people who had no defences: to prevent men from fooling around with young girls who didn't know how to take care of themselves and who wouldn't be able to raise a child on their own.

'But this isn't like that,' William said.

'Nothing is ever like the textbook case till somebody takes it to court, and then it's got to be argued like the book, because that's the only way you can figure out how to deal with it.'

'It doesn't have anything to do with other people.'

'Could you support a wife and child right now?'

'Yes,' William said, wanting to win the argument.

His father didn't tell him he was wrong. He simply pointed out how hard it would be, and added that the kind of salary and

11

career available to a college graduate was a lot better than what a man could hope to work up to after five years of living from hand to mouth. William thought that over. He saw that he'd have to have his parents' help. He knew he'd be able to count on them as long as he fell in with most of their advice.

He began to believe he might have been wrong about the way he'd handled the talk with Jean's parents. If that was the line they were going to take, they weren't worth considering, but naturally Jean would want to think there was an excuse for them. He also felt ashamed of not having trusted his own parents, who both appeared so reasonable, and so worried; they weren't angry at all.

His parents worked on him, in perfect counterpoint, until he agreed that he wouldn't see Jean for two weeks. It was an unsettling time for everybody, they said. Two weeks would be enough of a breathing-space to get everything straightened out. They asked him not to telephone Jean during that period; they wanted a free hand. They didn't put a ban on letters, since his mother had long ago searched his room and found the letters Jean had written to him. Nowhere in them had there been a hint of the pregnancy, but in one letter Jean had written something about the ornamental stone jar in which the two of them had started to hide their more fervent correspondence: the jar stood at a corner of the crumbling terrace wall that bounded three sides of the old Sumner house. The house had been shut up for years. Weeks before she could have known that the letters would make any difference to her life, William's mother knew the look of Jean's handwriting. She knew it nearly as well as she knew her son's.

William wrote a letter to Jean. In it he told her about the talk he'd had with his parents. Things would turn out all right – there was nothing any parent could do to keep them apart for long, but he didn't want her to imagine he'd stop thinking about her if they just didn't see each other for a few days. They were always going to be together in their thoughts. And he hoped she'd stay certain; even though they were close in spirit, he was a little afraid of her parents' influence. He was especially worried that she might be persuaded to think everything he and she had done together was bad.

He put the letter inside the terrace urn. His mother retrieved it. She then made a surprisingly good forgery of Jean's handwriting on paper she had bought that day. Each pale pink sheet was printed at the upper left-hand corner with a picture of forget-me-nots tied up in blue ribbon. The paper had been a lucky find: she'd bought a whole box; it was the same kind Jean wrote her letters on. William would never suspect his mother of using such paper.

The forged letter asked why his parents couldn't help out with the money, because her father was getting really mad about it and, actually, she was beginning to wonder, too; after all, he wasn't the one who was going to have the baby. Anyway, her father had told her that William's father had said something about her, something kind of insulting, so she realized that William had been *discussing her with his parents*. She thought that was a pretty cheap thing to do; in fact, it was measly.

William's mother was proud of her letter. She thought she'd hit the tone, the phrasing and the slang just right. Her pleasure was malicious, but her purpose wasn't. She believed that William had been maneuvered into fatherhood by a girl from a family of no background; and that if events were allowed to take their course, he'd hate the girl in a few years. It would be better to break up the affair now.

His father too was ready to protect William. He'd run across men like Jean's father before. He telephoned back and laid it on the line: he and his wife had no responsibility towards a girl who said she was pregnant by their son. Attempts to extort money out of their family – phoning him at his office, yes – could end in criminal prosecution. Naturally Jean's father was free to try to prove that some compensation was owed. But if there were to be a legal battle, money would win it in the end.

Jean's father felt a deep sense of unfairness and injury after the phone call; he felt it more and more as he continued to brood about it. Every time you tried to make excuses for people like that, he thought, they turned around and ran true to type. They had no respect for other families. They considered themselves better than other people. He couldn't quite bring himself to face the fact that it had been a disastrous move to raise the question of money, and that by doing so he had probably wrecked his daughter's hopes of marriage. He'd never really had anything against William, only against the double sin of sexual trespass and pregnancy. But he'd been intimidated. He didn't like the idea that somebody in his family could end up in a law court. They'd always been law-abiding – all of them.

He told his wife that it wasn't going to be the way they'd hoped; they couldn't expect any help from the boy's parents. They'd have to start thinking about those doctor and hospital bills, not to mention the embarrassment of having to go on living in the town afterwards. Jean's mother got scared. She had never done anything underhand or shameful; she'd worked hard and made a good home for her family. And if Jean didn't get married now, it would be her parents' lives that would be destroyed, not hers.

She had a little talk with her daughter. She told her that no matter how things went, Jean wasn't to worry: it still wasn't too late to do something about it.

Jean pretended to be reassured. She wrote a long letter to William, asking him what was going on at his house, and telling him that her mother had changed, and wanted her to get rid of the baby. She had to talk to him, she said.

She ran to the Sumner house, to the urn on the terrace. She left her note and hurried away with the letter she'd found addressed to her in an excellent facsimile of William's handwriting.

His mother saw her come and go. And she picked up the letter meant for William. If she or her husband had stopped to think, they might have said to themselves that many boys and young men will sleep with the wrong kind of girl because there's nobody else around, but that this affair wasn't like that: the two were in love. Traditionally, that was supposed to make all irregularities acceptable. Therefore, if the parents disapproved so violently, it might be because they actually wished to discourage the young from loving.

14

William's mother realized that she could keep up the letter game for only so long. It would be stupid to assume that one of them wouldn't catch her at her substitution; or, they might come across her while trying – in spite of their promises, and against their parents' wishes – to meet each other. Nor did she look forward to having her husband discover the exact extent of her interference. She could justify her actions if she had to: a mother has excuses not available to other people. But she'd rather not have to. All she had said in the beginning was that she was going to read the letters, in order to figure out the right way to approach William: as long as she was free to act on her own, everything would be fine. Of course, if her husband wanted to read their letters himself . . . No, he'd said; he didn't think it was necessary to read anyone's letters, but he'd leave the matter to her.

She was excited, frightened, and should have been worried about her rapid heartbeat. The thrill of participating in William's drama, of saving her son from making a mess of his life, kept her at fever-pitch. She was happy. She'd never had a real romance herself: the secret, stealthy, illicit going back and back again to temptation. She was having her romance now, fired by the heroic part she was playing – a woman rescuing her innocent son from ruin. She didn't blame the girl especially; it was just that a girl like Jean wasn't good enough. Girls like that wanted to get married. It didn't usually matter who was picked out to marry them. Jean would have to release her hold on William and find someone else.

Jean took her letter home and read it. She cried over it. Everything was going wrong: he was changing. If she could see him and try to talk to him, she wouldn't know what to say. His letter almost sounded as if he didn't love her any more. But that couldn't be true.

Her mother made an excuse to the school, to keep Jean at home for a while. She thought her daughter needed time to think. Besides, Jean was looking so unhappy that her classmates might start to ask her questions; or, she might just decide, out of a need to feel comforted, to talk to someone herself. Then, later, if she had to be sent away, everyone would know why. That wouldn't do. And William was there at school, too. Although he wouldn't be able to see Jean without cutting classes, he was there. He might wait around for her in the morning, or later in the afternoon.

At the same time, William's mother asked her husband to arrange for their son to take a break from school. She wanted to make sure that William and Jean didn't get a chance to plan anything on their own. She made the first suggestion herself: that William might like a change of scene for a short while, to get things clear in his mind; how about a trip somewhere nice for a couple of weeks? Nassau, perhaps; with his Uncle Bertram. William said no. He couldn't leave now. As soon as the time-limit was up, he'd get together with Jean. He already wished he hadn't given his word.

He couldn't bear the thought that Jean had lost faith in him. He broke his promise to his parents and went over to her house at night. He stood under her window, where the light was out. He threw small stones up at the panes. If he'd had a long, black cloak, he'd have felt safely disguised: covered by darkness, the lover's friend. On the other hand, it would have made throwing the stones even more difficult. It was impossible to hit anything in the dark. He might break the glass if he wasn't careful. He began to get mad enough to risk it. Her light went on. Then other lights came on too, one near her window and another downstairs; her parents had heard. He retreated. Maybe she hadn't even realized he'd been there.

He looked for her at school. He asked one of the girls in her class: where was she? 'She's sick,' the girl told him. But it wasn't anything serious, she said. Just a bad cold.

He stopped playing his records so often. He couldn't concentrate on them. The most beautiful parts upset him; and everything in between made him impatient. He wrote a letter to Jean, though he knew she wouldn't be able to go get it till she was better. He worried about her. She shouldn't be sick if she was carrying a child. He put his letter in the urn and took out the one that was waiting there for him.

His father had a long talk with him about money and compensation, college and law school. William was so distracted he could barely understand what was being said to him. The letter he had just read, and which he believed to be from Jean, told him in plain terms how little she thought of his conduct, said there were others who wouldn't have treated her so badly, talked about his petty-mindedness on the subject of money, sneered at his mother's fur coat, claimed she could sue him, and complained that he'd talked her into keeping the baby: now she was stuck with it while he was as free as a bird.

His mother was just in time to intercept his desperate answer. In its place she put a letter containing a key to a box at the post office. The letter said that William was afraid he might be followed or sent away, so it was safer to use the post office.

From then on, it was easy to deceive the young couple without danger. William protested when he was sent to the Caribbean, but he gave in; the fight was going out of him. He too had been given a key, to a post office box with a different number. His mother was therefore able to make her exchanges without fear that a letter would slip through. She could also use William's stamped and cancelled envelopes sent genuinely from the West Indies; a single numeral altered the box number. And she brought the affair to an end quickly. She sent Jean a letter that described William going to a party given by friends of his parents. These friends had a daughter he'd met years ago when they were children. He couldn't believe now, the letter said, how much they had in common. Although he'd always be fond of Jean, he thought they'd better both admit everything between them had been a big mistake. He felt pretty upset, but he had to be honest and say he wanted to do lots of things in life – starting with college and law school – that wouldn't be possible with a wife and child. He'd come to believe, from hearing some interesting theories on the subject recently, that it was better in every way not to start having children till you were about twenty-eight. He did realize, naturally, that in a certain sense he was to blame. But she couldn't deny that she'd said yes in the first place, and nice girls didn't – he knew that now: they just had

17

strong principles about the right way to behave in life. You had to have those high standards in order to become a mature human being. Of course he still liked her, but he thought she'd better take her parents' advice, except not about trying to get money out of his father, because that could land them in a lot of trouble, she'd better believe that.

The letter ended, *So I guess this is goodbye.*

Jean wrote back. She pleaded with him. She thought that he couldn't have meant to send her a letter like that. She asked him to read it over, and to think about what he felt, and to try to remember the way he'd known her. She enclosed his letter. She said she loved him; she'd wait for an answer.

He didn't answer. He hadn't seen her letter. She wrote again, almost immediately, telling him that her parents were taking her out of school for the rest of the year and sending her to live with her maiden aunt in the next state. She was going to have the baby there. She gave him the address and begged him to help her: if he didn't help, they could take the baby away from her as soon as it was born. That was what they wanted – for the baby to be adopted by somebody, so then nobody would know she'd had an illegitimate child.

William still knew nothing. His mother had written him a masterpiece of a letter, filled with accusation, silliness and platitudes. It also compared parents, saying that her father had worked all his life, which was more than you could say for his father, who spent all his time swindling people and called it big business: she didn't know why he was so stingy, either: William was going to be just the same when he grew up, which would probably be never. And she was taking her parents' advice, by the way, and having an operation because she didn't want to have anything more to do with him: she was hoping to get a steady job some day and meet a real man: and she was staying away from home for good, so he didn't need to write any more dumb letters to her.

A key was enclosed. His mother had had duplicates made. She hadn't worked out the details of her scheme at the beginning, but everything had seemed to go very well. She stopped writing any

18

letters herself. She merely collected and read theirs. At any moment she expected to find that William had written to Jean's parents – that would have spoiled everything: but he'd lost his trust in them. He stopped sending letters. He'd come to the conclusion, suddenly, that it was over between him and Jean. He hadn't done anything, or been able to do anything, to make a difference. She had changed; she was sorry about what had happened. She hadn't loved him, after all.

His Uncle Bertram said over the phone that William was desolate: he swam, and he went out in the boat with the rest of the gang, but he was so unhappy it was pitiful to see. And he'd gotten drunk one night and passed out cold. 'He's getting over it,' his father said.

When William returned to town and to school, Jean had gone. He finished his school year. His mother continued to collect the letters Jean was sending to the post office. At last a letter arrived that was much shorter than the others: it said simply that she loved him but she couldn't go on – she knew they were going to take the baby away, and she was tired of everything anyway. She'd decided to kill herself.

His mother didn't believe it. Girls tried that kind of threat all the time. She put the letter with the rest of them. She kept a regular check on the mailbox. Week after week there was nothing. Nothing for months. If Jean had killed herself, if she'd died – what could anyone do? It would be too late to go back. Long ago it was too late. But there was no question of suicide; that couldn't be. Obviously the girl had just given up, finally. There was no reason to wait for more letters. The keys could be turned in at the post office.

William did well at school. He drank at parties, but he stayed away from drugs like Benzedrine and Dexedrine, which had begun to make an impression on the college campuses of nearby states. He started to go around with a girl from his own graduating class, and then went out with her friend. He slept with both of them. He had fun. He didn't intend to get serious again. He began to feel better and to think of Jean with a sense of disappointment and revulsion. She had let him down. It seemed to him that all women would act the same way in the end. They didn't want love. Their sights were fixed on other things: safety, pride, interior decorating. He saw Jean's mother in town one day. They both turned away at the same time, instantly, as soon as they recognized each other.

He went away to college, where he also did well. And to law school. He came back briefly for his father's funeral and then, after he'd started work with a law firm, to visit his mother. She'd had a heart attack. She was only fifty-seven. William was horrified by the injustice of her illness. Because his father had been so much older, that death had seemed to come at a reasonable age. She was too young. He knew she still had hopes that he'd marry one of the girls she'd introduced him to. He hadn't come home so often as she'd have liked, either. He had been thoughtless. He'd neglected her.

She had a series of slight attacks and then the massive failure that carried her off. William phoned every relative he could think of. He asked them all to come to the funeral: stay at the house, be with him. He had nobody now. When the funeral was over, he sat downstairs with Uncle Bertram and his cousins from Kentucky. He told them he felt like the last of the dodos; for the first time in his life he thought it might be nice to have some brothers and sisters. 'Even though all of you turned up trumps,' he said. He thanked them for coming. They spent a long and raucous night reminiscing, but they were gone the next day.

Later there were the clothes to give away, the accounts to put in order, the question of what to do with the house when he was away – whether to sell it, or rent it, or leave it standing empty. There was a lot of junk to sort through. And his mother hadn't thrown out any of his father's clothes; she'd just left everything of his the way it had been.

William took a bottle of whiskey upstairs with him. He plugged in his father's portable phonograph and turned it on in the empty house. He put the volume way up. He played Verdi. He started with his father's study, moved to the attic and then to his mother's room. He was glad he was alone. He could cry without restraint.

He stuffed his parents' clothes into suitcases, laundry bags and cardboard boxes. He threw combs and brushes and shoes after them. He opened drawers containing half-used lipsticks and unopened perfume bottles. He discovered all his old school reports back to when he was six years old. And he found the box that held the pink, flowered notepaper, the sheets covered with repeated phrases scribbled as practice for the final draft. He saw the originals in his mother's handwriting, the bundle of letters he'd written himself, and the ones from Jean: all of them. He went out of his mind.

He smashed the empty whiskey bottle, the mirrors, the windows, the phonograph. His hands were cut and bleeding. He threw the unbreakable records out of the windows and snapped the others over his knee: all his precious collection of 78s. He picked up chairs and banged them down on the tables, threw vases against the walls. He screamed unceasingly, like a monkey in the forest. He slashed all the paintings in the house, even the ones he had known from his childhood and had loved most – the portrait of his grandparents as children, the view of the summer-house from the bay. He tore up all the photographs of himself and his parents, set fire to the Anatolian rug and walked out of the room while it was still smouldering. He took his father's bird guns from their cases, loaded them up and began to shoot into the walls, sideboards, ceilings, stairs. After a while people out in the street called the police, who came and broke down the back door. They got a doctor to give William an injection. He spent a couple of days asleep.

When he woke up, he didn't realize where he was. A private nurse had been left with him. She fed him some soup and said, 'You feeling better now?' She made it plain that she expected him to answer yes.

'It was the shock,' he said.

'That's right. You take it easy,' she told him.

He took it easy. He began to think. He thought for the first time in years about Jean; about how he and she had been tricked, treated with contempt; and how his parents' hatred – especially his mother's – had not been satisfied by merely frustrating his hopes and plans: they had had to destroy his chance of any kind of love for the rest of his life. Jean's chance, too. What had happened to Jean?

As soon as he was on his feet, he went to her parents' house. They were there but they wouldn't let him in. To begin with, they wouldn't even answer the door. His shouts and sobs convinced them that it would be better to talk him into being quiet than to have the neighbors hearing that old story dragged up again.

Her father opened the door a crack. The safety chain – a recent instalment – prevented entry. 'We don't want you here,' he said. 'Go away.'

William started to explain – fast, gasping, and doing his best not to yell – that his mother had written forgeries to Jean and to him too: she'd lied to both of them and now he had to find Jean, to ask her to forgive him and to make it up to her.

Her father said, 'We don't know where she is. That's the truth. And it's on account of you. She was staying with her aunt and she was five, almost six months to – you know. She couldn't stand the shame. She took some kind of poison.'

William stopped breathing for a moment.

'She nearly died,' her father said.

'But she didn't?'

'They had three doctors working on her for twenty-four hours. They couldn't save the baby: nobody in the family wasted any tears over that. They only just pulled her through. Soon as she was getting better, she ran off. Her aunt says she told Jeannie she'd better behave herself from now on, seeing as how what she did is a crime you can get put in jail for; and she would be, if anybody wanted to arrest her for it. It would be murder. I guess she took it the wrong way, got scared the police were going to come after her. That woman never treated her too kindly, from what I can make out.'

'Where is she?' William asked.

'Like I told you, we don't know. We haven't heard from her since that day. We haven't heard anything about her at all. All we know is, her aunt said her mind was a little unhinged from the time she took that poison. I reckon you'd better forget about her. That's what we had to do. It's like she was dead.'

William was about to ask some more questions when Jean's mother called out from the hallway, 'What are you telling him? Don't you say anything to him.' She sounded drunk. She raised her voice and screeched, 'You get away from us. Haven't you caused enough trouble? Go on, go away!' William turned and ran down the street.

He believed what her father had told him. He went back to his parents' house. All night long he howled and wept. He cursed his mother, he called on Jean, talking to her, explaining. He beat his head against the walls. He slept.

When he woke, his madness had developed into quiet conviction. He was no longer violent; the thought just kept repeating itself in his mind: that Jean was somewhere waiting for him, and that he had to find her. He'd find her if he had to search the world over. He had plenty of money: he could spend his life on it.

He got into his car and drove to the capital, where he hired a firm of private detectives. There were several clues, he told them: the hospital she'd been admitted to would have her name and address in its files. It would be in the same state where the aunt lived. He could let them have the aunt's address, but he didn't want them to go near her. They should concentrate on the medical register; there might even be a record of fingerprints.

He gave the agency approximate dates. Nothing could be learned from her parents, he said. It would be better not to disturb them: they might decide to get in touch with the aunt or somebody, and everyone would clam up. And maybe if the detectives got close to Jean or anyone who knew where she was, they ought to say they were looking for her because of a case that concerned distant relatives. They could pretend it was something to do with a legacy.

He couldn't understand why her mother and father hadn't tried to find her. Even though they wouldn't have had the money for detectives, they could have tried the police. It seemed to him that if you looked at the whole story, right through to where it stood at the moment, her parents hadn't behaved any better than his – maybe even worse, because Jean was their own child, whereas to his mother she'd been an outsider.

His detectives also had the clue of Jean's illness – her reported illness, anyway, which meant that she could have been in hospitals afterwards. Her father had specifically cited mental instability, so the investigation could start there, with a check on all the public asylums and private clinics in the general area. She might have changed her name; the detectives should concentrate on anyone who was the right age. He had photographs but he knew, as the agency men undoubtedly did too, that people sometimes changed radically in a short space of time, especially if they'd been sick. The expression of the face, the look in the eyes, could become like those of another person. A gain or loss in weight could also make someone unrecognizable. Thirty-five pounds either way was a better disguise than a wig and glasses.

William said, 'I guess maybe the thing for you to do is to go through all those places, get the possible names and then, if you think you're on the right track, I should go see for myself.'

One of the partners in the firm, a Mr McAndrew, presented William with a businesslike sheet of facts and figures, plus an estimate of costs. 'Those are the short-term calculations,' he explained. 'This could take a long time. But if it does, our charges would drop significantly. We believe in keeping our customers happy.'

William said that all sounded fine. He hoped they'd phone soon, because he was eager for news. He got up from his chair jerkily and lurched towards the door. Ever since finding the letters, his movements had become slightly uncoordinated. And he'd fallen into the habit of looking off into space, as if searching or remembering. Mr McAndrew might have considered William a fit subject for the clinics himself, if the princely retainer he'd pushed across the desktop hadn't proclaimed his sanity.

Weeks went by. William kept himself busy with the house. He couldn't decide whether or not to sell it. He took a leave of absence from the office. His hands healed. He hired painters to clean up the house, inside and out. And he got other workmen in to repair the damage he'd done.

Mr McAndrew found four patients in public wards whom he described as 'possible suspects'. Two of them were in the same hospital. If William wanted to go look for himself, one of their operatives could take him along. William said yes, he'd like that.

The detective called early. He was driving a company car. He was young, about thirty – only a couple of years older than William. He looked tough enough to deal with the rougher side of detective work, if he had to. He introduced himself as Harvey Corelli.

'Like the tenor?' William asked. 'Franco Corelli?'

'Don't know him. Call me Harvey, okay?'

'Sure. I'm Bill.'

'Yeah, but you're the client. You're supposed to be Mister.'

'If I call you Harvey, you call me Bill,' William said. People had started to call him Bill as soon as he got to college.

'Right,' Harvey said. 'That suits me fine.' He'd noticed the sudden far-off look his boss had mentioned. He got behind the wheel.

On that first trip they spent a week going from one hospital to another. Harvey handled the receptionists and doctors; William took a quick look at the patient and shook his head. Sometimes it was enough just to have her pointed out in the distance.

Two weeks later they started out on a second trip. They visited three institutions, all no good. While they were still travelling, McAndrew came up with some more names. Harvey passed on the information after he'd made his routine call to check in. 'You want to leave them till another time?' he asked.

William said no – he'd rather keep going, and follow up as many leads as possible. They could stay in motels and go down the whole list in a few days, unless Harvey had another case he was working on.

'Only this one at the moment,' Harvey said. One, to his mind, was usually one too many. He had always found it less easy to sympathize with his clients than with the people who had run out on them, cheated them, or otherwise let them have what they deserved. William was no exception to that rule, but he seemed like such an idiot that he actually had possibilities. Harvey knew the area. He could speed up the chase or slow it down. He figured that he could spin it out for a long time; he could be collecting a salary practically forever, if he played his hand right. He didn't like taking orders from McAndrew. He'd been bawled out in front of other people once: he hadn't appreciated that. He wasn't going to forget it. William, he thought, could turn out to be a pretty good meal ticket; he wasn't up to much in the way of fun, but Harvey knew the ropes: he'd get William interested somehow. It might be a good idea for all concerned to give old William something to think about besides his quest for the holy bride. There were a lot of moneybags in the family vault; Harvey could think of several uses for them.

William was lonely, so it wasn't hard, despite his mania, or obsession, or – as he preferred to think of it – love. One evening Harvey suggested that they call up a couple of girls: he knew one or two in the neighborhood. William said no, he didn't feel like it.

'Do you carry on like this all the time?' Harvey asked.

'Carry on?'

'No thanks, I don't feel like it?'

'Well, I don't.'

'Never?'

'I've got other things on my mind.'

'Mind isn't what I'm talking about, Bill. Come on.' He called up a woman he knew. He poured William a few drinks. When the woman arrived, she dropped her coat on the bed and said, 'Hey Harve, just like old times.' She then whipped off her dress and underclothes. William jumped to his feet. He intended to go to his own room, but he was too drunk. He fell over the corner of the bed. Harvey picked him up and slung him on top of the bedspread. The woman threw her arm over him. His buttons were being undone, his belt was being unbuckled. He heard Harvey going out of the room.

In the morning the woman was gone. Harvey knocked on the door. He dragged William into the bathroom and gave him two

Alka-Seltzers. He said, 'Now you've got the hang of it, you won't have to get so plastered. Next time, we'll have a party.'

'I feel god-awful,' William muttered. He had such a headache that he had to wear a pair of sunglasses all day, except for the moments when he looked at the hospital patients who might have been Jean, but weren't.

They kept traveling for another week. William talked to Harvey about his story. He explained why it was so important to find Jean. Harvey didn't seem to think the story was anything special. He said it was a tough break, but it happened all the time. 'You got to move on in life,' he told William. 'You got to move forward.'

William was sorry he'd said anything. That was another thing loneliness did to people – they'd spill out all the most secret, private details of their lives to complete strangers: they'd get drunk and try to obliterate themselves for a time, to get rid of the past and of themselves too, by transforming everything into talk. You could always change events by describing the truth another way, remembering it differently. It was a method of controlling your life, of understanding it.

Harvey, in his turn, talked. He had dozens of schemes for becoming famous, making money, cornering the market on something nobody else had thought of. He had ideas about travel, international finance, import–export. He wanted to buy a boat some day and trade between Florida and the islands, like everybody else: that was where the big money was.

William nodded and said, 'Yes, I see,' and, 'That's interesting.' He was looking into the distance again. Harvey phoned two girls. He wanted an evening where he'd trade girls with William; after they'd tried out their own, they'd swap. William said all right: he didn't mind.

'Picking up some tips, kid?' Harvey asked.

'I hope that's all I'm picking up,' William told him.

Harvey began to wonder how far he could push William. He'd gotten him in with the girls; the next step could be a couple of other, more expensive habits. He didn't want to take things too fast. William looked nearly ready to crack. Harvey thought hard about how to get him lined up just right.

Before he could do anything, they came to a sanatorium called Green Mansions. It wasn't green and it didn't look like a mansion: a three-story brick and concrete building that lacked the architectural charm of some of the older asylums. It was privately run.

There were three candidates for inspection – young women of the right age. Harvey saw at a glance that none of the three would fit the photographs. The women were seated around a table at the far end of a large hall that – on the evidence of the drawings, announcements and other pieces of paper tacked to the walls – was the patients' recreation room. It was the room where they'd be taught gymnastic exercises and would take part in dances. Scuffed linoleum covered the floor. There was a piano in one of the corners. The lid was down over the keyboard. In a place like that, it would have to be locked, too.

Right at the back, a line of folding chairs ran around three sides of the room. Patients and possibly nurses sat together in groups. There were no white uniforms. Many people were sitting quietly on their own, or standing. One man who tried to sit on the floor was immediately pulled to his feet by two other men: he didn't appear to be pleading for attention – it was as if he'd temporarily forgotten that people were supposed to sit on chairs instead.

A doctor led the way across the room. William followed, keeping pace with Harvey. When they were still several yards away from the three women, William said, 'No,' in a low voice. 'I don't think so.'

'Well, why don't we sit down?' the doctor suggested. 'I can tell you something about the work we do here.'

Harvey made a face at William. He saw the propaganda coming: *Our worthy cause, insufficient funds, these unfortunate people.* William ignored him. He told the doctor he'd be interested to hear what he had to say. Even if Jean wasn't at Green Mansions, she might be in a similar institution; he wanted to know about anything that could have a bearing on her life.

They sat. Harvey longed for a cigarette. Signs on the walls told him he couldn't have one. More than any of the hospitals and rest homes they'd seen, Green Mansions reminded him of a school he'd been sent to once. He'd stayed there for a year, and he'd hated every minute. It was one of those schools where they were supposed to straighten you out.

The doctor talked about state funds, federal grants and private subsidies. William nodded and looked out into the center of the floor. It was surprising how many people were just standing there, not talking to anyone – just standing alone, looking like machines that had been switched off: nothing registered on their faces. 'Do you use drugs?' he asked.

'In the case of a violent patient it's sometimes advisable,' the doctor answered.

'But not regular doses as a matter of policy?'

'No, of course not.'

Harvey turned his head to look at the doctor. Naturally they'd give drugs as a routine. It would make all the supervisory work easier. He was pretty certain that all those places did. If you weren't loony when you went in, they'd soon mess you up enough to pass for crazy.

William wasn't looking at the doctor. He was staring at one of the patients standing alone in the middle of the floor: a girl with straight, orange-blonde hair and a pale face that had a sweet, absent-minded look. 'Jean,' he whispered suddenly. He grabbed Harvey's arm. 'There,' he said. 'It's her.'

'It doesn't look like her,' Harvey said.

'It's Jean.'

'Doctor, who's the thin girl with the long hair?' Harvey asked.

'That's Coralee. She's been here eighteen months now. She'd be about five years younger than the girl you're looking for.'

'That's my girl,' William said.

'Her parents – '

Harvey said, 'She doesn't look like the photographs, Bill.'

'Well, she's changed. It's been years since those pictures were taken. And as for her name being different, I'd expected that.'

'Oh?' the doctor said.

Harvey put his hand on William's shoulder and told him they'd better talk things over. William agreed. He'd found Jean. Nothing else mattered.

He'd known that when, at last, they found each other, the healing power of love ought to cure her, although in an opera the heroine usually died at the moment of reuniting, having undergone too much. This was real life. Jean might never recover her reason, but they could live together as man and wife and be happy. He accepted the fact that she'd been committed under a different name and by people who claimed to be her relatives: naturally, if she were afraid of being sent to jail, she'd have made up a new name for herself. She might even have found a new home for a while. He was willing to marry her under any name at all.

While Harvey wrote down notes about the circumstances of her admission, William put questions about getting her out. He wanted to know what objections there might be from the authorities as well as from her family. He was hoping that both could be bought off: the clinic with money and proof of good intentions, the family with belief in his love.

Her parents – the doctor said – seeing that she seldom recognized them, had quickly found it too painful to continue their visits. They got into financial difficulties, stopped paying for her upkeep and moved away. Coralee was due to go into a state asylum at the end of the month.

'I know this story may sound unbelievable,' William said, 'but to me everything makes sense now that we're together again. I'd be glad to pay whatever Coralee owes the clinic.' He spoke for a long time. He was persuasive, partly because the doctor and his staff wanted to be persuaded, but also because his need inspired him. As he dug deeper into his fantasy, until he finally merged with it, his outer actions began to appear more normal and relaxed.

'I knew her before,' he said, 'and lost her. But I've been looking for her. And now I've found her, I want to take care of her.'

The doctor was favorably impressed by William's story, his future plans, his wealth and his ability to treat a madwoman with kindness for the rest of his life. He didn't consider the possibility that William himself was crazed. He promised to do what he could; and to meet again the next day. He introduced William to Coralee before escorting him and Harvey out of the sanatorium.

William took her hand in his. Her eyes moved back to the world where she was standing and where he stood, his hand touching hers. Her smile reflected the one he showed her. He told her his name, and said that he was going to see her the next day: she might not remember, but he had known her a long time ago. He'd loved her. He'd been looking for her, to rescue her, and he wanted to make her happy.

He talked to her slowly and clearly. For the first time in days she spoke. Her voice was feeble from lack of use. Later it would turn out that part of her disability was caused by deafness, for which she'd never been tested.

'Oh,' she said. 'I don't remember.'

'That's all right,' he told her. 'We'll get to know each other again from the beginning. We'll have a nice time.'

She smiled again. He let go of her hand. She looked after him as he walked to the door. He turned and waved. She came forward.

She walked up to him and put her hands on his jacket. 'What did you say your name was?' she asked.

'William,' he told her again. 'Will.'

The doctor was astounded. She'd never acted that way before.

She said, 'You come back soon, Will.'

'Tomorrow,' he promised.

As soon as they were in the car again Harvey said, 'Listen, Bill, it isn't the same one.'

'This is the happiest day of my life, Harvey. There's only going to be one happier one, and that's when Jean and I get married.'

'She doesn't look anything like the pictures.'

William smiled. He'd stopped staring strangely or seeming to go off into another dimension. Still smiling, he said, 'Her sufferings have changed her.'

'I just – you ought to think it over. You could be making a big mistake.'

31

'The mistake I made was to let you talk me into going with whores.'

'You liked it fine at the time.'

'I was so lonely, I couldn't stand it. Now I've found her, I'm never going to be lonely again.'

'Are you sure she's the same one?'

'I'm positive. She couldn't be anyone else.'

'But she is somebody else. Even if she wasn't goofy, she just isn't the right girl. Different age, different name – she's got a whole different face, man.'

'Unhappiness can practically destroy people. You don't know.'

'It can also prevent them from seeing what's right in front of them. I can't let you do it. Just think – maybe the real girl is still somewhere waiting for you. She'd have to wait forever, if you tie yourself up with this one.'

'I know you're worried,' William told him. 'I don't believe you're just thinking about the money and the case coming to an end.'

'What's that?'

'No. I know what worries you. It's love. It makes you uncomfortable. It isn't what you're used to. You see it, and you get scared.'

'Don't give me that horseshit.'

'Harvey, one day it's going to happen to you. Listen – one day you're going to find the right one: the only one for you. And then you'll be happy. Like me.'

'Christ,' Harvey muttered. He didn't trust himself to say anything more without losing his temper. He couldn't believe that William had ducked out from under so neatly, taken the first opportunity he saw, to escape: in the company of some jerk girl with a dopey smile, who wasn't even the one he'd been looking for.

William got on the telephone at the motel. He arranged through his lawyers to have people waiting for him at the house. He said that calls would be coming in soon, asking questions about him, but that everything would be all right.

And it was all right. Good credentials, his family's name, the record of their holdings, their history in the town they'd lived in for four generations, guaranteed William's fitness to remove a patient from Green Mansions. His money ensured speed.

The girl didn't mind. She'd taken a liking to William. When he spoke, she leaned into his face. He held her lightly by the hand and – once they were away from the clinic – by the arm. The drive home was made in almost total silence. At the house William helped her out of the car. He said, 'This is where I live, Coralee. I hope you'll be happy here.'

She looked pleased. She seemed to be taking in what was happening. 'Big house,' she said. William handed her over to the maid, housekeeper and cook he'd hired. That evening he asked her if she'd marry him. She said yes. In the morning he made plans for the wedding. He also asked a doctor to come on a house call to have a look at Coralee.

He phoned the detective agency and he went there, arriving just as Harvey was coming off work for his lunch hour. Harvey had registered a formal, written protest against the ending of the case. If anything were to go wrong with William's choice, Harvey wasn't going to be held responsible. Mr McAndrew had taken the matter calmly; he'd been content with a quick result, a large fee and a satisfied client who admitted to over-riding the objections of the agency.

'You're really going through with it?' Harvey asked.

William beamed. 'She's accepted me,' he said. 'She likes it here.'

'I bet she does. It's better than that place she was in.'

'I'm giving you a bonus. That's what I'd do anyway. But I also just wanted to say I appreciate the hard work you put in on the case, even when you didn't believe we were going to get anywhere. Well, you know what it's meant to me. It's saved my life. I want to thank you.' He handed over two checks, one for the firm and one made out to Harvey by name. They shook hands. William walked to the door, went down the steps and got back into his car.

Harvey looked at the amount on his check. He started to think about William and his search, the girl he'd discovered and the life they'd have together. They were both crazy, so what did it matter? And why should he be thinking about them? They might make out fine. There was no reason to feel that what had happened was such a terrible thing. And the check was for a lot, so what the hell?

Plans for the wedding went forward. Coralee had doctors' appointments to go to. William was told that she could live a normal life, but her mind would probably never develop. Everything had been left for too long. She didn't appear to have any mental illnesses – she was, as far as they could tell, just stupid, or – as they phrased it in that part of the world – slow. Of course she'd been sick, but that would leave her as she became accustomed to her new home. Some of her debility had undoubtedly been induced by her surroundings: first her family, then the institutions they'd put her in. With kindness and patience there would be some improvement; there always was. She might not become completely well, only enough recovered to believe everything William told her: to adopt his madness in place of her own.

She liked William. She was aquiescent, dreamy, vague. She was like someone asleep. He didn't mind. He liked her quietness. There was nothing to disturb his idea that deep down, under the different face and body, she was Jean.

He told her many times, simply and clearly, how they'd loved each other and been parted. Now that they were together again, their lives were going to be full of joy. He handed her the packet of letters his mother had kept tied with a ribbon. She held the letters to her face and smiled gently. Then she dropped them on the floor. He took her action to mean that as far as she was concerned, the past was over: they would get married and be happy.

The wedding was announced. Coralee was fitted for a wedding dress. The dressmaker called at the house to measure and alter. Coralee delighted in the fitting sessions; she played with the veil, she danced around, holding the partly completed skirt, she tried to sniff the artificial flowers. The dress was made with plenty of tucks that could be let out easily for extra width; Coralee had gained sixteen pounds since leaving Green Mansions and was still putting on weight. Apparently the inmates had been kept on a meagre diet.

He didn't try to reunite her with her parents, nor with the people who had had her committed under her new name. He didn't think they deserved a reconciliation of any kind – in fact, he didn't even send them an invitation.

The wedding was to be a small affair. Hardly anyone from his old days in the town went on the list of guests. He could have asked men and women he'd been to school with, but he hadn't kept up with them. He still said hello to people on the street when he ran into them – that was all: he'd made no effort to pick up old friendships again, and when pursued, he declined invitations. He didn't need anyone except Coralee.

He invited his lawyers, the local doctor, the dressmaker and her family, the women he'd hired to work in the house. He didn't bother to notify any of his aunts, uncles or cousins; he thought he'd write to them afterwards. As soon as Coralee got used to married life, they might take some trips, meet people; there would be time for everything. And then he'd get back to his job with the law firm. As an afterthought he picked up the phone and issued an informal invitation to Harvey.

Harvey said he'd really like to attend, but he just couldn't: he had too much work to do. It was nice of William to ask him, he said. His voice sounded right, but the truth was that after he'd banked his check, Harvey had begun to detest William and his love and the misery of it. He hated fools. He thought of them as people who had the sanction of the law to cause more damage than criminals. He didn't consider them funny or lovable.

William wouldn't have minded if nobody turned up but the preacher and a witness. He'd have had the whole business done in a registry office if he hadn't believed it would be more fun for Coralee, and more like a party, to have a church ceremony. When he saw the way she took to the white dress, with its train and veil and little crown of flowers, he knew he'd been right. She glowed with pleasure.

The dressmaker's two small nieces had been chosen to hold up the train. During the rehearsal Coralee kept turning around to peek at the children and then all three would laugh wildly. The cook's family arrived and sat proudly near the front, as William had told them to. Other people from around town were scattered among the pews. A bass and soprano sang to piano accompaniment. The pianist was a relic from William's schooldays; she was blind now and had almost cried with gratitude when William telephoned her. On the day of the wedding she did a good job; the singers too suddenly came into their own, delivering without affectation the simple old hymns about belief in the Savior, love of the Lord. *I believe*, they sang. *I believe*. William could feel that beside him Coralee had realized all at once where she was. He held his arm around her lightly, protectively. The singers' last words rang in the air, stopped, and echoed and left. The minister said afterwards that it was one of the most moving betrothals he could remember: sometimes it was like that – the spirit would seem to be fully present. The importance or grandeur of the family made no difference, nor the size of the congregation. Sometimes it was especially touching to have just a few witnesses there, when those few had love in their hearts.

To the people in the first three pews the church didn't seem empty; they sensed only good feeling and friendliness. There were even a few strangers who had wandered in and – seeing that there was a marriage ceremony in progress – had sat down to watch. The minister felt that their presence conferred additional blessings upon the happy pair: it was as if the extra observers stood for the rest of the world, who didn't know the couple being joined together, but wished them well.

Among the uninvited audience, almost on the aisle at about the midway point, was Jean. She'd seen the announcement in the papers.

She had changed: the shape of her body, the way she sat, her hair, the expression on her face where the action of the poison she'd taken had caused scarring. The damage to the skin was mild, but it was there; it made a slight difference to the overall facial look. If her parents had been at the wedding they would have known her. And Harvey would have recognized her from the many photographs he'd seen of her; he'd been trained to spot resemblances, even if a face had aged or been deliberately disguised.

She wasn't disguised, nor was she disfigured, although she looked old and clumsy. The doctors had told her that she was always going to have trouble with her health, and so maybe it was just as well that she didn't have a husband or children.

When she saw William with his bride, she knew it wasn't her health that was to blame for everything going wrong in her life – it was being without him. It was the fact that he hadn't wanted her.

She watched the whole ritual: the ring being put on, the kiss. She heard the promises: *till death*. And William turned around, his strange, vacant companion on his arm. He shook hands with people in the first rows; he pulled the bride along with him down the aisle, coming nearer. He bowed to a couple of women in front and to the left of Jean, then he looked at her: right into her eyes.

He moved forward, still looking at her face. He came closer, near enough to speak to her. Her lips parted, as if to shape his name: she almost said it out loud.

He smiled, his eyes going to the doorway beyond her. He passed on by. He didn't recognize her.

The Archaeologist's Daughter

The Norbert family had lived in Switzerland for generations. Although they had orginally come from farther north, by the 1830s, when Professor Norbert was born, his relatives had forgotten most of the habits and languages of their former homelands. He didn't try to find out about his ancestors; his interest lay in the distant past, among the great progenitors of humankind: their cities, statues, buildings, paintings and religions. He passed on his enthusiasm to his young daughter, Beatrice; she came to share his passion for lost civilizations because, from the very beginning of her life, the times when he was explaining the past to her were those when she was most certain of his paternal affection, pride and attention. She did not share his merry and inquisitive temperament. She was a quiet girl, serious even when she was happy, but often melancholy.

The house of Beatrice Norbert's childhood seemed to her to be set in a landscape that was reminiscent of the south – that is, the south of Europe. Later she would become acquainted with the sweltering countries of the equator, the deserts and plains, where people wrapped up their faces and bodies against the heat as if protecting themselves from a winter storm. Her parents took her along on their travels only once, when she was four years old; the journey so broke her sense of time that she forgot all of it but a few moments that she could call back like pictures out of a dream. What she remembered and thought of as her true life was home, in Switzerland.

The summers were hot and hazy, the parklands lush with flowering plants. Their house had a large garden that led down to a lake. And she remembered her mother as a lovely creature who was always wearing white dresses and standing under a blue sky. They had gone on picnics and boating parties together.

Her mother's name was Celeste; she had died young. Beatrice's memories for a few years on either side of the funeral were disrupted: she recalled staying in places where her mother, talking, had once walked with her, but to which her mother would never return. She remembered looking up for long periods at the sky and being confused between the words Celeste and celestial. Someone had foolishly told her that the dead went to heaven and became stars: that was why there was so many stars – innumerably, inconceivably many.

She was still a child when they moved away from the lake so that her father could be near town. He taught and lectured at the university. He wrote his books. And for a while he took her on his travels. They went to Turkey and Syria, to Petra; to Cairo, where Beatrice spent three years in a French school for French and English-speaking children. Most of the other girls were the daughters of diplomats, lawyers or bankers and they talked about the fashions and gossip of Paris, the theater and opera and the magnificent evenings – dinner and dancing in the ballrooms of palaces – for which they were destined: at which they would meet the men who were to become their husbands. She became enraptured by all things Parisian. She was sure that Paris had to be the center of the world. She listened avidly to the stories told by girls who had been there during the holidays. What was everyone wearing, she wanted to know; what had they had to eat? And the weather? Even the smallest scraps of information were enthralling.

It never occurred to her that there might be girls in Paris who would think Cairo exciting and exotic, and who would long to go there. For her – at that age – wherever she was, was normal. What most people considered ordinary had always seemed strange and marvelous to her, and unknown: the life of children who had both a mother and a father, and who stayed in one place until grown up. That was normal, but she couldn't imagine it.

She did well in school. Her father was proud of her. He'd made arrangements that she should study subjects not ordinarily taught by the school. Special tutors arrived to give her lessons in languages, architectural design, the natural sciences. Fortunately there was one other girl, Claudia Schuyler, who shared these extra classes with her. If Beatrice had been the only odd one, she might have been singled out by the other girls as hopelessly different and therefore perhaps an object of dislike. Claudia soon became her best friend, although she was a year younger than Beatrice. They studied together every afternoon, listening to the instruction of four different men – two of them quite young – who had been chosen to teach them. Mlle Dubourg, their chaperone, sat on guard at the back of the otherwise empty classroom. The high windows looked out on to the tops of palm trees.

Claudia's mother was half English, half Italian; her father, American. She had a younger sister at the school, one younger brother at home, an older one at a boys' school a few streets away, and another older brother who was just starting work in a bank. She invited Beatrice home for weekends and holidays.

Beatrice had dreamt for several years about the family that would one day be hers – when, of course, she found the right husband. But the desire for a husband had been prompted by her wish to have sisters, brothers and a mother. She didn't feel the need for a different father, despite the fact that her own father was so often away; he wrote regularly to her, and besides, was so loving and so willing to share his life with her when he did see her, that she was never without the sense that his presence was with her, nor that she was always in his mind and heart.

One day when Beatrice was staying with Claudia, Mrs Schuyler said, 'You know, I think I once met your father, many years ago. In Rome.'

Beatrice was too old to think it natural that somebody else should know everyone she knew. She had also passed the stage where it seemed an amazing coincidence that anyone should have thought the same thought or visited the same city, or loved the same person as someone else. But it did strike her as unusual that she and Claudia should be daughters of two people who had met years ago in another country; it seemed a good omen. She asked, 'Did you also meet my mother?'

Mrs Schuyler paused and then said no: she hadn't had that pleasure.

Beatrice was to remember the small hesitation when a week later she was in a shop with Mlle Dubourg to buy copybooks for the German class. A young man behind the counter was helping the chaperone to decide between different qualities of writing paper. The old woman who ran the shop was already occupied with a girl about five years older than Beatrice; the girl also had an older person with her – a man who was evidently her servant; he was Egyptian, whereas the girl herself had the look neither of an Egyptian, nor a European. Her eyes were light, her hair and skin – in striking contrast – palely brown. She resembled women Beatrice had seen in the south of France – light-complexioned dancers and singers from the West Indies and South America. As the girl turned to go, she looked briefly at Beatrice. The look said that Beatrice wasn't worth considering. She went through the doorway, followed by her servant, who carried all the packages.

The old woman shut the door behind them. She said to Beatrice in French, 'That was your sister.'

'I don't have a sister,' Beatrice told her.

'Maybe you don't,' the old woman muttered, 'maybe you do.' She started to walk away behind the counter.

Beatrice went after her. 'I've never seen that girl before in my life,' she said. 'Who is she?'

The woman pretended that she didn't understand French. When Beatrice changed to Arabic, she turned quickly and went through the curtains at the back of the shop, where the living quarters were.

'Is something wrong, Beatrice?' Mlle Dubourg asked.

'Did you see that girl? The one who was in here just a minute ago?'

'I didn't notice. Why? Have you lost something?'

Beatrice repeated what the old woman had told her. 'And she went behind there. She doesn't even know me. What did she mean?'

41

Mlle Dubourg called the young man over to them. But no amount of discussion could persuade him to make his grandmother come out again; she was ill, he said: forgetful, her thoughts not always completely collected. She often said things that made no sense. She was old.

The incident troubled Beatrice for days. If she'd been staring pointedly at the other girl, the old woman's remark might conceivably have been a rebuke – a way of saying that one girl was no better than another: all were alike. Such an explanation seemed far-fetched. And anyway, she hadn't been staring. She wanted to talk to someone about it, but she felt that Claudia wasn't the right person to go to. She needed someone who was grown up and who had lived in the city long enough to know who everyone was. Was it possible that her father had been in love with another woman before he'd married her mother? Perhaps if she'd had a sister, or even a brother, the idea wouldn't have made such an impression on her. As it was, her sleep became so disturbed that at last she was summoned to the office of Mme Bonnier, the principal of the school.

She stood by the desk. Madame sat on the other side; she was impeccably dressed, as usual, and looked as if she found life highly enjoyable. She told Beatrice to sit down, asked her the cause of her distress and said that it simply wouldn't do to drift around the schoolrooms, looking like a ghost and falling asleep over her lessons.

Beatrice told her. She described the girl from the shop and said, 'Do you know who she is?'

Mme Bonnier dismissed the story. The old woman, she said, wasn't right in the head; you wouldn't believe the things people muttered to themselves when they relaxed their concentration – even young, sane people.

'But who is she?'

The identity of the girl couldn't possibly be of importance, Madame said, because the old woman didn't know what she was talking about.

Mme Bonnier was embarrassed. Years later, Beatrice was to understand the nature and extent of the embarrassment: once

42

she'd realized that her father had been quite a ladies' man and that he'd know Mme Bonnier, as well as many other women. Beatrice might have had sisters and brothers over half the globe.

But at the time, her attention was trained on one person: the girl in the shop. And her worries were mainly theological. If the girl were a sister, she reasoned, that would mean that her father had been married twice. It followed that the other wife had to be still alive, otherwise the daughter would have stayed with him.

'And if that's true,' Beatrice said, 'then in the eyes of the Church, his second marriage, to my mother – you see what I mean? I might be the child of sin. One of us has to be.'

'Nonsense, Beatrice.'

'Well, is that girl's mother still living?'

'Yes.'

'Then she's the real daughter. And that makes me – '

'Your father,' Mme Bonnier said, 'was never married to this girl's mother. Nor, as far as I know, to anyone but your mother. Does that make you feel better?'

'Of course,' Beatrice said. 'It's a great relief.'

'Good. I'm glad to hear it. Now you can get some sleep.'

'But is it true? Is she my sister?'

'I've just told you.'

'No, Madame. You've just told me that they weren't married.'

'I see. In that case, I must say that to the best of my knowledge, no: she isn't. But her mother is one of those women who's always lived a very free life. So, people gossip about her.'

'And my father?'

'I've never heard anyone say a malicious thing about your father. He's always talked of with kindness. This is more the sort of tittle-tattle you'd expect to hear directed against a woman.'

'It was directed against me. She wanted to hurt me.'

'You know the kinds of people who gossip,' Mme Bonnier said. 'And you say she was old. Perhaps she didn't see well. There seemed to her to be two girls in her shop, both of them to her mind looking foreign. Do you understand? There's no great mystery about it.'

Beatrice had once heard her father say that when it was a

matter of something serious, it was always a good idea to get a second opinion. She went to Claudia's mother.

Mrs Schuyler knew the girl as soon as Beatrice described her. 'Ernestine,' she said. 'It's a peculiar family. They came here from Brazil. They were running away from something.' She appeared to think that the question had now been answered. She reached for another almond cake. The family was at the dining table for tea; one of the younger boys had broken a leg off the tea table: he'd been jumping on the top, but the parents weren't supposed to find out about that. Beatrice felt honored to be treated so completely as part of the family that she was expected to keep from one member of it the secrets of another.

'What were they running away from?' she asked.

'Oh, I don't know.'

'Something political,' her husband said, getting up from the table. 'In that part of the world.' He put down his napkin and took his teacup with him into his study.

Mrs Schuyler said that every country had its politics. However, in the case of the Cristo-Marquez family it was probably something simpler: debts, or a partnership that had fallen to pieces. 'There are lots of reasons why people leave a country. If the whole family has to get out, it's liable to be business, I suppose.'

'Or politics,' Claudia repeated.

'Yes, but they aren't that kind. The mother's a stay-at-home, the father's reserved and silent. They hardly talk to anyone. You see them out shopping with their servants and they never open their mouths. I don't think anyone in town has ever been inside their house.'

'Is it a very small house?' Beatrice asked. People who shared a small house with a staff of servants might not have room to ask anyone in.

'Enormous. Like a palace. One can't imagine what they find to do with themselves. Unless you believe the gossip, of course.'

'What does the gossip say?'

'We'd better not talk about that. One never learns much from gossip.'

44

'Could you tell me where the house is?' Beatrice said.

'Why?' Mrs Schuyler asked. 'Why do you want to know that?'

Beatrice couldn't think of any reason. Sometimes people didn't have reasons; or sometimes they didn't know exactly what their reasons were. She said, 'Just to know. A big house, like a palace – is it near the legation? The one with the two white pillars and the tiled roof?'

'No, that belongs to the medical institute. The Cristo-Marquez house is on the other side of town. About three streets away from the building they call the summer palace. It stands in part of the park there. It has a garden.'

'Are you sure?' Beatrice said.

'Of course, I'm sure. What a question, Beatrice.'

'It's just that if it's the same place, I remember driving past there one evening and all the lights were on – all of them. And it really is huge. I've always thought it was a hotel.'

'Exactly. That's the way they live. All the lights on, and the singing going on all night. That's why people talk.'

*

She was moved to a school in Constantinople, then to Athens and to Rome. In Rome she looked up Mrs Schuyler's sister, a Signora Arnoldi, whose address she'd been given.

The Arnoldis had three daughters, two of whom were already married. The third, Vittoria, was exactly the same age as Claudia: in fact – a fact considered magically propitious to everyone in the family – they had been born on the same day. She too, like Claudia, became a close friend. And though Beatrice was always being shunted on to other cities and countries, she never lost touch with Claudia herself. She thought of the Schuylers as her second family, although in some respects they were her only family. Other people had aunts and uncles, in-laws: she had only her father. There were no relatives left on her mother's side of the family, either; it was as if her parents had each been the last surviving member of a tribe, or a country, or a race.

Over the next few years the Schuylers too were on the move: to England, and afterwards to America, while Beatrice travelled with her father's expeditions. In his opinion she'd had enough of school; she was ready to do serious work.

They went to Afghanistan, Turkey, Mesopotamia. She kept the accounts, wrote up the day's findings and listened to her father's theories and stories.

When she was eighteen, she and her father joined a large expedition. At the base camp there were two wives and a woman described as a niece. There were difficulties with language, clashes over customs and habits and, above all, fights about who had the authority to do what. The general atmosphere of quarrel and intrigue was further complicated for Beatrice when she fell in love with a Canadian student named Paul, who had come out with the American team. He asked her to marry him. She was still pretending to think over her answer when one of the wives spoke to her father about him.

'I don't know what business it is of theirs,' Beatrice said.

'I think they probably have your interest at heart. You're so young.'

'They want to stop me having any romance in my life, just because they never had any.'

'I don't think it's that. Anyone can have romance, if he wants it. They may feel it's their duty, because you have no mother. For a woman, there's always the question of – '

'Morality? That's what they kept talking about in school. They nearly turned me into a religious fanatic.'

'Of pregnancy,' her father said. 'Of course, he's in the same field – you'd be able to help him with his studies for a while. When you had children, perhaps you'd leave them at home with someone. I was able to take you along with me because you were an only child, but it wasn't easy. If there'd been anyone to look after you, it would have been safer to leave you behind. And,' he added, 'you're a better archaeologist than he is. He's superficial. He doesn't know what to look for. He has no flair for the job.'

Beatrice's need for a romantic alliance with a man of her own age was so strong that if her father had been talking about a young man's character, she wouldn't have taken his word, but the indictment of his professional abilities made her question

46

Paul's integrity. Her father had a reputation. Paul was a new-comer. Her father was undoubtedly right. As for the rest, she recalled that among the stories circulating through the camp there was one about a girl back in Canada. And she knew for certain that Paul was writing to three women addressed as Miss: she'd seen the envelopes. She told him the next day, 'I've thought about what you asked me and I think we should get to know each other better.'

'But you love me, don't you?' he asked.

'Of course,' she said.

'Well, that's the main thing, isn't it?'

'I think we'd have a good start, because I've been trained for the same job. I could help you, even if we had a large family. But . . .' She thought she really ought to admit that despite her love, she didn't trust him. She trusted her father and Claudia and everyone in Claudia's family: if she were in trouble or ill or needed advice, she knew that they would help her, no matter what they had to sacrifice. But how long would Paul be patient or understanding? She had no idea; nor was she sure how long she'd be able to put him first if he didn't seem to be taking her wishes into consideration.

'I just think,' she repeated, 'that we should get to know each other better.'

'How long will that take?'

'Two years,' she said.

'This is a joke, isn't it?'

'I think we ought to be sure.'

'Because if it isn't, it's an insult. If you don't want to, Beatrice, just say so.'

'I don't even know you,' she burst out.

'That doesn't matter.'

'Don't be stupid,' she snapped. 'Of course it matters. We'd be living with each other for the rest of our lives.' They'd be one. The thought suddenly terrified her. She didn't know if she wanted to be one with anyone at all, ever.

'But that's all just going to happen as we go along. The important part is what we knew from the beginning.'

'I don't know.'

'Yes. That instant attraction.'

'I feel that way about lots of people,' she said.

'Oh?' He looked so scandalized that she didn't know how to explain: to say that the kind of emotion she meant was something that would come over her suddenly or, just as quickly, would go away; and it didn't seem to have much to do with who the man was, or whether he was likeable, or what the wives would have called 'possible'. Sometimes just seeing the way a man turned his shoulders as he lifted a load of stones or swung a pickax was enough to make her feel interest and excitement.

'I think it's better to find out what we're like,' she said.

'Is there any point? If you don't love me?'

'I love you, but why can't we wait?'

'That means no,' he said. He walked off.

She was so discouraged that she almost ran after him. A long time afterwards she realized that his abrupt departure was calculated. By then, she had also understood that he'd been right: whatever she'd said, she had meant no. But at the time, she didn't want to let go of him and of the idea of being wanted. She tried all through the evening meal to catch his eye. She stared at him across the table. He wouldn't lift his head. As soon as the company broke up, he rushed away.

She had almost made up her mind to go charging after him, when one of the wives called her back and, talking about inconsequential matters, took her arm and led her away from the others. 'When I was your age,' the woman said, 'I never imagined that I'd be part of a scholarly expedition. It's really most absorbing, despite the inconvenience. And the many discomforts. Yes – I know this one's a model of its kind, but you're used to it, my dear. You've had invaluable training, simply by being near your father. This life was new to me when I married. But now I see the familiar faces every year. And the young ones come and go. It's a shame that Paul won't be with us next year.'

'He hasn't resigned, has he?'

'Not at all. But his scholarship grant runs out at the end of the season. So, unless he can find some way of financing himself privately, I suppose he'll have to go back to Canada.'

'I see,' Beatrice said mildly. She hated the woman for telling her. Undoubtedly the action was meant kindly, although she didn't think so at the time. Later she would also wonder – after it was too late to ask him – whether her father had had a hand in the disillusionment: whether he'd asked the woman to speak to her. He might have felt that it was the sort of thing a real mother would do. Girls whose mothers were living, Beatrice knew, had to put up with that kind of interference all the time, and with the fear induced by constant protectiveness and warnings; whereas she had never had anything but the beauty of the dream she'd invented around the absence of her mother.

She kept quiet and waited. Paul tried to make up. He accused her of insincerity. She said to him, 'That's not true,' but she could tell that it was too late to go back to what she had felt before. She knew that he'd never loved her. She could hear it in his voice. She said that they'd better part and there was no reason why they shouldn't do it in a friendly way. Once more he left her abruptly and indignantly, this time calling her an obscene name: a word she didn't know the precise meaning of, although she could guess the general sense of it. That too was in his voice.

For the next few weeks she could feel that everyone was talking about her. The wives, unexpectedly, made an effort to keep her company. And her father was as easy to talk to as ever, as fun-loving and full of good conversation. She asked him, 'Have you ever thought of marrying again?' The question had come to her in a rush, as if it were in itself an attempt to get close to him. She'd never considered the idea before.

'I thought of it quite a lot when you were still small,' he said. 'Not that I had anyone in mind, but – it seemed to me that you needed a mother. You sometimes looked completely lost. It upset me a great deal. But then I talked it over with one or two friends. And they told me that things would be so much worse if you didn't take to a new mother.'

'I couldn't imagine it,' she said. 'I'm glad that you didn't. I only wondered for your sake. I wouldn't mind now, you know. I wouldn't have minded even when I was at school. It was just those six or seven years before.'

'It's impossible to repeat something like that,' he told her. 'I wouldn't want to try. Some people find happiness more than once. More than twice. We're all different. You'll find out what agrees with you. Just try to ask yourself if you're sure of what you want.'

'What kinds of people gossip, Papa?'

'Politicians, journalists, old women, old men. Girls. Boys. Everyone I can think of. Even your father, on occasion. Why? Are people gossiping about me again?'

'About me, I think. I can feel it in the air. And the way they all pretend not to be looking at me too closely.'

'Let them. Don't allow it to worry you.'

'If people tell me things about someone, and I don't know whether they're true or not – '

'You can ask the person. Or you can just think it over. Try to sort out the probable, the possible and the unlikely. It's part of the trade.'

'I might end up believing something bad of someone when it wasn't actually true.'

'You might. What would that show?'

'That I drew the wrong conclusion on lack of evidence.'

'Perhaps because other evidence predisposed you to think badly of the person.'

'What other evidence?'

'You tell me,' he said. 'You started this discussion.'

'I never really trusted him,' she said. 'I wanted him all the same. But not for too long. Not forever.'

He gave her a complicated assignment that entailed meticulous collations of original notes and translations. The work was harder than anything she had done before. The time passed quickly for her.

The next season saw a new set of students; and the next. She became invaluable to her father and – when he was away – to many of his colleagues, who used to consult her as if she were his partner and equal.

She presided over the house in Switzerland like a curator in a museum. She loved being there, even on her own, surrounded by her father's discoveries. She was always occupied with some work of hers or of his; she began to publish under her own name. And she traveled, sometimes with an expedition and sometimes merely to see friends. She made regular visits to the Arnoldis, in Rome; and to Paris, where the Schuylers went for Easter. She'd stay with Vittoria Arnoldi for a few weeks and then both of them would take the train to Paris, to join the Schuylers – 'my American cousins', as Vittoria called them. Beatrice began to remember Paul with less anger and blame. Ten years after the event, the hurt had gone. She thought of her old self as someone, like him, who shouldn't have been taken seriously, and who was too inexperienced to behave well.

She was happier than she had been when she was younger. She saw that she had a place in life and she liked it.

*

Her father had just come to the end of a stay in Palmyra and was back in Bagdad for a while, when he fell ill. The first indication Beatrice had of the fact was an official letter of condolence.

She was certain that whoever wrote the letter must have made a mistake; people got things mixed up all the time, even names. She wrote back, and then decided that that wasn't enough – she had to get out there and speak to the officials herself. Everyone tried to talk her out of it. They said that she wouldn't be able to help.

She made the journey anyway. How could she have stayed at home, when her father might be anywhere at all, and she wouldn't know about it? He could have written to her about plans to go on an expedition: it wasn't unknown for letters to be lost or delayed for months. He could be in danger, while some petty bureaucrat was entering his name in the wrong set of records. She remembered her father himself telling her that an acquaintance of his had had to travel all over the world as Mr Brown Gray simply because a clerk somewhere hadn't known how to copy out the information in his papers, according to which his hair was brown and his eyes gray.

As she moved from country to country, her father's friends came to greet her; like cities on a map, they were dotted across the great distances she had to go. And when she neared the end of her journey, two of them, an uncle and nephew named Hoffmann, took on the local and foreign officials while she stood or sat silent nearby. Sometimes she felt compelled to interrupt, especially as people seemed to keep changing their stories. Her father, she was told, might not have been exactly ill; he might actually have been poisoned – that is, murdered. There was a woman in the case: more than one woman. And that always made for danger.

'This is ridiculous,' she whispered to the Hoffmann uncle. 'My father was used to having all sorts of friendships and so on. He never left anyone feeling resentful or unhappy.'

'Perhaps a man who was a rival?'

'Much more likely to have been a poor cook,' she said. Then, feeling just like Mrs Schuyler, she asked for information about the servants.

His household had loved and admired him. According to them, he'd had a fever. One of them – a superstitious man – suspected that the professor had caught the disease from something he'd found when he was digging up a grave: everyone knew that it was forbidden to disturb the dead.

She asked where her father had been buried. They were shown to a small cemetery for Christian Europeans. The Hoffmanns stood on either side of her, in case the emotion or the climate should prove too much for her. She found it impossible to believe that her father was there, in that space of earth. Could they have buried someone else by mistake? She wanted to ask to see him – just to be sure. But that would be impractical as well as shocking. Everyone agreed that the thing had happened and that he was there. Friends of friends had been at the funeral. She simply found it against the nature of the world as she knew it that he should suddenly not be there for her to talk to or to write to.

On the return journey she began to believe in his death. Everyone she had met going out tried to comfort her on the way back. So many people had loved him. It made her feel closer to him to hear them talk, and yet it also persuaded her to accept the fact that he was dead.

When she got to Switzerland there were two letters waiting for her, from him. They were just like his usual letters, with no hint of bad feeling among his acquaintance or in the household.

She began to go through his papers, which were neatly arranged, as always. She kept herself busy. There were the clothes to be given away, the boxes of papers to be gone through: letters from his colleagues, his friends, and from her. All the letters from her childhood were there – every note she'd sent him from her schools in Egypt, France and Italy.

She used to wake in the night, choking with tears, bawling. Sometimes it was as if she were in the middle of a storm. The first time it happened, her cook, Maria, ran up the stairs to pound on her door. Beatrice shouted for her to go away; the next day she said that she was grateful for the kind thought but that since nothing could help, it was better to ignore these outbursts. She didn't try to stop.

For months she carried on mental talks with him. At times they became so real to her, she sometimes imagined that she could hear his voice. Perhaps if her mother hadn't died early, there would have been another strong influence in her life. As it was, although she had loved her mother dearly and with a particular kind of love that no other person she'd met could evoke from her, her father had always been at the center of her life. He had shaped her interests, passed on his knowledge and talents to her, yet he'd given her the freedom to leave, if she wanted to. Despite the fact that she had remained an unmarried daughter, she led a more liberal life on her own than any married woman she knew, whether happy or not. Her father wouldn't have minded if she'd wanted to travel to a different country, visit friends for long periods, spend her time in some new pursuit, or get married and move away. They'd known each other well enough for him not to have to explain that, as before, he'd speak out against any admirer of hers whom he considered unsuitable; and for her not to have to say that she sometimes felt guilty about

53

her comfortable life, knowing how much he'd have loved to have grandchildren.

She missed him all the time. For years – long after his death – as soon as she thought of him, his presence was with her. She understood how it was that many people became religious after a bereavement: it was because they were impelled by an urge to reach the other person again. In her case, she grew less religious. The act of prayer had become a process of having conversations with herself and her memory of her father. She didn't feel that she was developing eccentric habits – other people told her how they caught themselves thinking of what her father would say to such-and-such, and how dear he still was to them, how clearly recalled. She loved to hear people talk about him, especially if they were old friends who had known him before she was born, or even before he was married.

Sometimes she would remember, with a dreamlike vividness and immediacy, a phrase he used to favor, the way he'd looked at certain times, the sound of his chair scraping back over the floorboards as he stood up from his desk. It was as if in her mind she were once more writing him letters. The ancient Egyptians, he'd told her, used to write letters to the dead. They'd put up a statue of the departed person and inscribe the letter on the front. Usually the survivors wanted the dead to intercede; to help them in some way. Occasionally the letter was an accusation, saying: 'Why are you causing me such bad luck, when I was always good to you?' Unhappiness, they believed, always had a cause. And usually the cause was witchcraft by other people, dead or alive. Beatrice's father had shown her one of the letter-statues when she was still a child. She had immediately realized that the writing was really for the living, not the dead, who couldn't answer. If the dead had been able to do anything, her mother would have spoken to her from wherever she had gone to.

*

One day while she was in Rome on a visit to the Arnoldi family, she looked up Dr Santini. His son had been one of her father's old schoolfriends. At the time of her father's death, the son had

54

written to her; a year afterwards, when the son was killed in an excavation, she had had to write to the old man. She wouldn't have gone to see him, except that his name came up and Signora Arnoldi said, 'I hear he's dying.'

She sent a letter first, and was invited. The professor lived in a part of town she hadn't seen for many years. The house was large, underlit and cold. It had abundant tile decoration, some marble, dark wood paneling and many tarnished silver wall sconces adorned with ugly human figures. Three maids stood in the hallway to greet her. They were dressed in baggy skirts and shawls. For all she knew, they might have been relatives. The one who struggled up the staircase in front of her screamed down to another one near the kitchen entrance to get the tea ready.

The old man was delighted to see her. He said that he remembered her father as a young boy: when he'd come to visit his son, Giorgio, at their cousin's house on the island. The two boys had been up to all sorts of tricks. They were always inventing games and stories; her father, even then, was fascinated by the past. But he was also a boy who liked to play outdoors – not at all the bookworm type. Dr Santini could remember him and Giorgio catching the big, hard-shelled beetles they used to have on the estate: you could pick up any beetle easily while it fed on grapes or flowers – tie a thread around the middle of its body, and walk around with it that way. The beetle would fly at the end of the thread and make a loud, whirring sound like a bumblebee. What the children liked best about the game was the noise the beetles made, but the creatures were also wonderful to look at – black on the underside and on top a bright, emerald green that changed in the sun to gold. He could remember seeing her father and Giorgio – his son, Giorgio – walking down the path side by side, and their beetles flying above on strings. Everyone had loved her father. It was a pleasure when he came to stay.

'And his mother,' the old man continued, 'your grandmother; sometimes we'd see her. She was the most beautiful woman I've ever met. Did you know that?'

Beatrice said no, she hadn't known.

One of the maids brought tea and propped the doctor higher in his bed. He went on to talk about his own childhood and also asked about her life. She told him that at the moment she had to decide what to do with her father's collection. Some of it would go to museums. 'And I ought to sell the rest, I suppose. All those things should be in a place where they can be seen. Where people can learn from them.'

'And you must get married,' he said. 'Don't smile. I can still see well enough to tell what expressions people have.'

'If that's meant to happen – ' she began.

'You shouldn't wait. I waited for too many things. Sometimes there isn't another chance.'

'But sometimes it doesn't matter. I'd rather be the way I am than the way I might have become if I'd married the first man who asked me.'

The doctor shook his head. He said that he'd probably been spoiled: he'd always had a large family around him and of course, he knew, it was the women who had to do the work in the house. But if you outlived all your family, it made you wonder what sense there was in anything. He blamed the French, for not providing adequate supports for the higher trenches on the site, so that when it rained the mudslide came down all in a flash and buried his son. It was a matter of seconds; nothing could be done for him. 'This tea tastes bitter,' he said.

Everything tasted bitter when you were sick. Her father might have voiced the same sort of complaint, and that could have given rise to the rumors about poison.

She stood up, brought the sugar to him and offered to spoon some crystals into his cup. He asked her to take the cup away, which she did. And soon after that – seeing that he was tired and wanted to think about his son – she left.

She went to his funeral. She would have gone anyway out of respect, but the fact that she hadn't been able to attend any last ceremony for her father made her want to be there for her own sake too. Vittoria Arnoldi accompanied her. They, and the maids, were the only women. All the other mourners were old men. Vittoria said she thought that they were probably part of the archaeological faculty of the university; unless, she added casually, they were something it had dug up. Beatrice slapped a handkerchief to her face and exploded into giggles. For several minutes she fought against hysteria. She hadn't known anything like it since her schooldays. Fortunately the handkerchief was large enough so that everyone would assume her to be weeping. Vittoria, having caused the trouble, remained unaffected, and unrepentant afterwards.

The lawyers sent Beatrice a letter to say that the doctor had left her a picture, which she could come to collect. She imagined that it would be something to do with her father or perhaps with the house where he and Giorgio had spent their school holidays. But a note on the package she was handed said: *This is your grandmother. She was more beautiful than her picture.* The portrait was in pen and ink, the face lovely, and the attitude so natural and modern that if it hadn't been for the arrangement of the hair and the set of the rakish little hat – both in the style of another age – it might have been of someone who was still alive. There was no resemblance to her father, nor to anyone else, as far as Beatrice could see. She was so pleased with the picture that for a long while she didn't ask herself how the doctor should have come to have it in his possession. It was possible, of course, that her father had given it to him. And while she was still wondering about that, she thought again how strange it was that, enigmatic as these lives were to her, they were all on one side of the family. She still knew nothing about her mother's people, not even where they had orginally come from. The parent about whom she kept finding out unusual facts was the one she already knew. Her mother, never known, could not be mysterious. Her mother had become a being she recognized emblematically: an unalterable, undifferentiated presence, stationed in another place, reaching her from another time; always the same. Her father had become the mysterious one: more could be known about him; more of his life revealed by other people.

Signora Arnoldi admired the grandmother's portrait so extravagantly that she asked for permission to have it copied. And when the work was done and she held it in her hands, she said jokingly, 'Who would ever have thought it of old Santini?'

'Thought what?' Beatrice asked.

'That he'd nurse a hopeless longing for years. He always seemed such a dry old fellow.'

Beatrice wanted to say that there was no proof of any longing, hopeless or otherwise, on anyone's part and that this was just gossip again; but since Signora Arnoldi had hit on the same suspicion she'd had herself, she let it go.

*

That summer in Switzerland she hired a young student named Ernst to help her with the recataloguing of her father's library. She also made preparations to sell most of the Greek and Roman sculpture and the larger objects from ancient Egypt. Some of them were very large indeed. Even statues smaller than life-size required the kind of lifting gear normally found only among the loading equipment in a harbor town.

She took photographs of everything and was so satisfied by the results that she went on to take pictures of Ernst, his fiancée, Marta, and Marta's parents, who came to visit her one day and were frightened by the statues and helmets, and the vases and jars emblazoned with animal heads. They had never been in a museum before. They thought that everything was slightly sinister. They went down the hallways behind their daughter and said, 'My, how interesting. Think of that.' They held hands and looked as if they were prepared to protect each other if anything strange were to happen.

Beatrice chattered on in an attempt to put them at their ease. She told them about the gods and goddesses represented in the works of art. She described aspects of religion that the couple wouldn't find too shocking. 'I didn't realize how much there was,' she ended. 'I'd never thought about all those boxes out in the old barn. And the things stored at the institute. At least a third of the collection was given to him by his teacher, long ago. I don't suppose there's anyone nowadays who has anything like this – certainly not like the big statues. They really shouldn't be in private hands.'

Marta's parents shook their heads. They agreed: Get rid of the things as soon as possible.

The auction was held eight months later. It went well. Several American museums joined the bidding, which knocked the prices up considerably. Beatrice sold to the United States, Great Britain, Germany, Austro-Hungary, France, Russia and several countries in South America. Private collectors accounted for over fifty per cent of the sales, despite the size of some of the statues. There had been a great demand in recent years for garden statuary of any kind and in any condition. It pained Beatrice to think of the Greek Apollo outdoors in a German winter; the Roman cupid with his pet deer had gone to St Petersburg and the two Etruscan sarcophagi to Vienna. She was glad to hear, however, that most of the Egyptian treasures in the sale had gone back to Cairo, to a bidder named Hassan. She assumed at first that that meant purchase by an institution, but a man on the auctionhouse staff told her that the largest of the Egyptian lots were all going to a private family. 'Oh,' she said, 'to a private museum, like my father's.'

'Well, possibly,' the man said. 'I'd understood it to be a private collector.'

She thought that that couldn't be: she knew what the prices were. For a single family to buy such things might have been possible in North or South America, or in Russia, but the sort of millionaire who might have a weakness for Egyptian statuary didn't live in Cairo. A rich Egyptian collector would be looking for French and Italian paintings, German machinery, South African diamonds; or, at least, small *objets d'art* and *objets de vertu*. The father of one of her schoolfriends in Cairo had had a vast collection of enamel boxes; he'd once said to her that the ancient art of the Pharaohs gave him the shivers – modern life was much more to his taste. He'd also had a passion for sweet liqueurs, Irish racehorses, the operettas of Jacques Offenbach and English tweed jackets. She remembered him as a very agreeable man.

She thought suddenly that there had been many pleasant people in her life with whom she'd fallen out of correspondence. It was possible that they'd moved, or – like her – suffered bereavement. Most of the girls would be married by now, and would have children. Claudia already had three and her American husband, Charlie, was putting on fat and beginning to look important.

As long as the collection had been unbroken, she'd had so much to do that her life was full. Now that most of the pieces were disposed of, she felt that she'd lost her occupation. She sat down at the desk that had been her father's. She wrote to Claudia. As her pen shaped words on the paper, she remembered their schooldays. She felt a longing for the friendship of her childhood and for the family that had seemed to be hers: among whom she was at home, never just a guest.

Claudia wrote back; she was coming to Paris and going on to Florence: Beatrice must stay with her.

They met. On the morning after Beatrice's arrival, Claudia told her, 'You should come to New York. You need something entirely new.'

Beatrice said, automatically, that that was certainly something to consider. Later in the day she did think about the possibility, and asked herself: Why not? Some of the treasures from her father's collection had gone as gifts to museums and some – but only a few – he'd held in trust for archaeological foundations that were looking for places to house them. Most had been his. They had brought her a huge sum. She hadn't yet begun to contemplate what she was going to do with it. She could go anywhere in the world.

'I just might,' she said the next day.

'Good. Come to town for the spring and spend the summer with us at the seashore. And during the winter – we're going back for a visit to Egypt. You've got to come. You can help to cheer up Jack. Did I tell you about Evie?'

'Yes,' Beatrice said. 'Such a simple thing. And so quickly. It's terrible to think about.' Claudia's sister-in-law, Eve, had developed a cold sore on her lip. She'd tried to cover it with powder and some sort of liquid make-up and then it had become infected, either as a result of what she'd put on it or simply because it wouldn't heal. At any rate, the infection had turned septic and it had killed her. She and Jack had two small children. 'He's still knocked sideways,' Claudia said.

Jack met them in Florence and did the museums and galleries with them. Beatrice felt that, after so many years, it was still as though they were her family. She found that she seemed to know Jack just as well as she'd always known Claudia. When Claudia said that she wanted to stay in the hotel one rainy morning, Beatrice and Jack went out together. After that, they'd often go out with each other. He began to court her. It happened so easily, and her response was so wholehearted, that it was as if she'd burst into flame. She knew that he'd loved his wife and undoubtedly still did, and that he was lonely and needed a mother for his children. She also knew that he genuinely wanted her and had always been her friend. She didn't mean to wait an instant: she was afraid of losing her happiness before it had begun. But it wouldn't look right to be in such a hurry, and before his year of mourning was over. 'After Egypt,' he told her.

Claudia said, 'It was my doing, of course. You two didn't stand a chance.'

Beatrice smirked and blushed. She was blushing all day long. She considered it ridiculous for a woman in her early thirties to be overcome by such feelings of maidenliness, but she was also happy. She made plans. She prepared to sell the house in Switzerland.

She arrived in Egypt two days before the others and had time to settle her luggage and unpack her clothes. As soon as the Schuylers joined her, they began a series of parties at the hotel, at friends' houses, at restaurants. All the family was there, including some of the Arnoldis, with in-laws and children. In the daytime they enjoyed the sunshine, at night they ate and drank and danced. Jack presented Beatrice with her engagement ring – an emerald centered between two smaller diamonds.

The next morning an invitation arrived for Beatrice; it was delivered to the hotel by hand. She'd never heard of the people. While she was puzzling over the question of why strangers should ask her to their house, she picked up the envelope again and saw that there was a second piece of paper inside. She pulled it out and read the explanation: the stranger, a Mme Cristo-Marquez, thought that Beatrice might want to see her father's collection in its new surroundings.

'How nice,' she said. 'It's the people who bought Papa's statues.' She read out the name.

'Not them?' Mrs Schuyler exclaimed from her end of the breakfast table.

'Don't you remember?' Claudia said. 'You once told me about meeting the daughter in a shop. There was something unusual about it – I can't remember. She said something to you.'

'No,' Beatrice said. 'I don't remember.'

'Of course you do. In that shop that sold the rugs and the paper. Where I bought my silver bangle. She was going out and she said something that upset you so much that – '

'Oh,' Beatrice said, remembering all at once. The family must belong to the strange-looking girl she'd seen shopping with a servant nearly twenty years before. 'Now I know. What an odd coincidence.'

'One couldn't possibly go there,' Mrs Schuyler said. 'No one could. It's out of bounds. And certainly not at night.'

'Mother, dear,' Claudia said, 'what difference could that make?'

'It makes a difference in that house. The whole of Cairo knows what they get up to at night. I won't tell you what they used to say about that family.'

'Why not?' one of the children said, and was immediately shushed. Beatrice too would have liked an answer, but the interruption had brought the topic to a close.

She accepted the invitation. When the fact came out during a comparison of dinner-dates, Mrs Schuyler expressed such concern that Beatrice began to feel unsure about her decision.

'You mean to say, you accepted?'

'Yes, of course. I thought it would be so lovely to see the collection again. It was thoughtful of them to ask me.'

'They aren't thoughtful people. You can't go, Beatrice.'

'But I've accepted.'

'You'll have to cancel.'

62

'No, I don't do that kind of thing.'

'My dear, this is serious. I should have made it clearer. These people are much more than simply undesirable. They are extremely unsavory. They indulge in practices that – that – I don't quite know what to call it. A great deal more than the ordinary sort of orgy. And the servants join in.'

'I've accepted,' Beatrice said.

'You can become ill at the last moment.'

'As soon as I'm well, they'll ask me again.'

'And you'll still be unable to go, until finally they stop asking.'

'I couldn't do that.'

'Beatrice, it's not a house to go to at all, but if you can't get out of it, at least it's not a house to go to alone. I expect Jack will have to go with you.'

'He isn't invited.'

'If they try to turn him away, you leave with him.'

'But it's for dinner. And I can't bring an extra guest anyway, if I don't even know the people.'

'You can and you'll have to,' Mrs Schuyler said.

Beatrice recalled her schooldays, the incident in the shop and the effect it had had on her. Of course, it had been the old woman, not the girl, who had spoken to her. Even so, she began to sense again the mixture of curiosity and panic the event had aroused in her. The prospect of visiting her father's collection no longer appealed to her. She thought about entering the Cristo-Marquez house. She tried to imagine what it would look like inside, and what the people would be like, but she couldn't. All she could think of was that everything there would be dark. She said, 'Well, I can't say I'm very anxious to go now. I'd be glad if Jack could come along.'

Jack took the affair as a joke. 'That old place,' he told her. 'We used to believe it was haunted. Mother's always distrusted the family. It probably goes back to sometime in the past when they managed to outbid her at an auction. Something like that.'

'Didn't someone mention singing? That they sang at night?'

'Yes. Chanting. Wailing. Religious, I guess.'

'At night?'

'Yes. I used to hear it myself.'

'What was it like?'

'Rather like . . . like what I said: the kind of chanting you'd hear at a religious ceremony.'

'Just the thing to brighten up a dinner table.'

'Should I go armed?'

'That's another thing – don't start me laughing. I'm beginning to feel nervous about it. I'm quite capable of bursting into laughter the moment we get in the door. So don't make jokes.'

He promised, and then told her several terrible old jokes that doubled her up with giggles.

They held hands on the drive to the house. A friend of hers in Switzerland – not a very close friend – had once accused her of being interested in the past because she was afraid of the future. The comment had hurt her deeply; she'd feared that it might be true. Now she knew that it hadn't been true at all. It had simply been a spiteful remark. She loved the past because she was able to imagine it. She could see it clearly. And now, all at once, she saw her own life too, as it was and as it could become.

The driver deposited them outside the railings of the garden fence. He left as soon as he was paid. There was a small, inadequate streetlight above the gates. Jack looked for a bell. There was nothing. Through the open ironwork they could see the path, the trees, the gigantic, partly-lighted house beyond. He pushed the gate, which opened in the middle and gave a loud, wrenching squeal. 'Come on,' he said.

She stumbled along beside him over uneven stones. They went up a flight of steps and stopped at the front door of the house. Again he hunted in the dimness for a bell, and at last found the button. They waited a long time. Just as she was feeling relieved at the delay and thinking that they could leave, the door was thrown open and it was too late.

'Mlle Norbert and Mr Schuyler,' Jack said.

The servant who had opened the door stood back to let them in. As they passed him, Beatrice thought there seemed to be something wrong with his back or shoulders. He held himself stiffly.

The corridors weren't so dark as she'd imagined. On the other hand, they were extremely narrow, without room for decoration or hangings other than the light brackets, and the ceilings were so high that it was like being in some vast, underground cave.

They had to walk in single file, the servant leading, over an old rag carpet; in several places it wasn't securely attached. Twice Jack had to catch Beatrice as she skidded to the side. The floor underneath was stone. And the house was quiet enough so that as they shuffled forward, the only sound other than that of their moving feet was the wheezing of the man in front.

They came out into a space that in another house would have been the hallway by the main door: well-lighted, with plenty of room to stand. There were chairs against the wall and carpets on the wooden floor. A large Venetian mirror hung from a ceiling rail. Beatrice wondered how old the place was. The curiously labyrinthine entranceways might have had something to do with an ancient system of defence.

A butler took their coats and showed them down two steps and through a door, into a reception room filled with people talking and raising glasses to their lips. An Egyptian in his mid-forties came up to them; he introduced himself as Hassan, the son of the house. 'My mother is resting,' he told them. 'But you must meet my sister and my uncle, Constantine.'

Uncle Constantine was a dessicated old gentleman who immediately attached himself to Beatrice and began to tell her about his young days in Paris. She enjoyed his stories, despite the fact that occasionally he'd repeat phrases or ask all at once, 'Where was I?' or, 'What was I saying?' The daughter, Ernestine, was also presented. Beatrice didn't recognize her until a few minutes after they had been introduced; she now wore her hair pulled back into a knot. Her face was thin, the skin dried out, and the light eyes – which had made such a startling effect in her youth – had lost their clear, open look; they seemed sunken into her face and their color no longer appeared remarkable. Her hair was lighter than before. Beatrice suspected that she'd been putting henna on it. That was surprising, but merely a detail. What troubled Beatrice was the greater change that had taken place: from the striking-looking girl to this unsmiling, charmless woman.

Two waiters circulated through the room with trays of wine. Jack engaged Ernestine in conversation. Like all the Schuylers, he could talk to anyone, and on any subject. Beatrice said to Hassan that she hadn't realized there was to be such a large gathering.

'Every week,' he told her. 'They come for the ceremony.'

'Oh?'

'Recitations from the classical texts. My mother started the custom years ago. This is just the usual crowd.' As he finished his drink, one of the waiters whispered to him. 'I'll be back in a moment,' he said to Beatrice.

She could see Jack edging towards her. He waited until Ernestine and Uncle Constantine were drawn into larger groups and then eased himself away from them.

'I recognize the son,' he told her. 'We used to see him at the bank. He's got a reputation for business transactions that go a bit wrong for other people. He always seems to come out of them all right. Quick on his feet. Makes a lot of money and loses a lot, too.'

'Hush,' she said. 'He's coming back.'

Hassan bowed to Beatrice. 'My mother would be very happy to show you the sanctuary now. Will you come this way, please?'

Beatrice and Jack moved forward together. Hassan said that it wasn't necessary for the gentleman to come: he could stay and amuse himself with the other guests, if he so wished.

'I'm looking forward to seeing the statues,' Jack said. 'Immensely.'

Hassan hardly paused. He said that his mother would be delighted. He led them up a staircase, down a long corridor and up another flight of stairs. Beatrice had to stop for a moment to catch her breath. At the end of the hallway two men who looked like bodyguards stood to attention in front of studded double doors.

'Are you not well?' Hassan asked.

66

'Very well, thank you. Too much dancing and champagne this week, I'm afraid. I'll be all right now.'

They moved to the doors, which now seemed to Beatrice like the entrance to a tomb. The guards swung the doors open to reveal a long, high, wide room like the main showroom of a museum. She recognized the sitting hawk and baboon, the two rams, and in the far distance the torso of Tuthmosis the Third. She did not recognize the woman who glided towards them, but felt that she ought to have.

'Mother,' Hassan said, 'this is Mlle Norbert. Mademoiselle, allow me to present my mother: Mme Cristo-Marquez.'

Beatrice stepped forward, smiled and took the woman's hand. She tried not to stare at the long, square-cut, dead-black hair that must have been a wig, or at the extraordinary, flamboyant make-up on the face in front of her. Mme Cristo-Marquez was painted to resemble an ancient Egyptian queen or goddess: the eyes were heavily outlined with black, the lids azure-shaded. The eyes themselves never stopped moving. She greeted Beatrice and Jack, looking at them and away again – at a stone jar, at a blue bead necklace, at Hassan, and at Ernestine and Uncle Constantine, who had followed them in. It took Beatrice a few moments before she realized that the woman was insane.

Mme Cristo-Marquez described an outward arc with one hand. 'He would have wanted me to have them,' she said.

'It's wonderful to see them again,' Beatrice told her. 'But shouldn't they be on the ground floor? The weight – '

'The weight of the past,' Mme Cristo-Marquez said portentously, 'is always with us.'

'They might actually go through the floor. We had a bad accident at home with a granite cat – quite a small statue, but it weighed – '

'It weighs on my mind,' Mme Cristo-Marquez said. She laughed. Beatrice heard Jack draw in his breath. 'Do you see my daughter there? My daughter, Ernestine. She looks like an Arab, doesn't she? And sometimes she looks almost like a Nubian. Do you know why? It's because of our association with the past. With history.' She prowled towards a lidded sarcophagus in the center of the room and turned back without warning. 'It's caused by thought,' she declared.

Beatrice took Jack's arm. She prepared to make an excuse to leave.

'She's your father's daughter,' Mme Cristo-Marquez proclaimed. Ernestine showed no response, nor did her brother, nor the uncle. Beatrice began to feel angry as well as uneasy.

'He loved me,' Mme Cristo-Marquez murmured. She closed her eyes for a moment, displaying the blue color to the full.

'He loved everyone,' Beatrice said. It wasn't quite true. He'd had no time for women who were silly without being beautiful or charming enough to make up for it. He'd never had much patience with posturing and melodrama: he liked people who had some sense.

Mme Cristo-Marquez swept towards the sarcophagus and draped herself against one of its corners. 'I was the only love of his life,' she said.

Beatrice wanted to say: *How long did you last?* She felt herself being overtaken by the indignation of the legitimate. She tried to stop herself from saying anything that would hurt the woman. Mme Cristo-Marquez was repulsive, outrageous and offensive, but she was also ludicrous, pitiable, ill. And the rest of her family knew it. Her painted face, her stories about her daughter's parentage, her collection of objects, were all for nothing. *The things people will do out of despair*, Beatrice thought. *And then afterwards they sit there with a handful of trash, and tell themselves that they're happy.*

'And in the end, he came to me. He came back to Cairo, to seek his final resting place. He died of love.'

A sense of her father's personality came to Beatrice so strongly that it was almost as if he were near her in the way people describe the presence of ghosts. *How he would have detested the impertinence of this woman*, she thought. *How he would have disapproved of all these theatrical trappings. He liked reason, science, logic.* It was impossible that these people could have known him. 'He died,' she said, 'of food-poisoning.'

68

'There are poisons and poisons, you know. Some can work at a distance, and some over a period of time. Love is a poison.'

'Love is a pleasure,' Jack said. 'Always.' Beatrice squeezed his hand.

'Not always,' Mme Cristo-Marquez shrieked. 'But he knows better now. Now he's come home to me.'

'He's buried near Bagdad,' Beatrice stated coldly.

Mme Cristo-Marquez made a snarling noise. She slapped the side of the sarcophagus. 'Here,' she said. The other members of her family still hadn't moved. 'Shall I show you?' she shouted.

Although Beatrice was incensed, the fact that she hadn't seen her father die – that she hadn't even been able to look at the body – suddenly made her fear that there might be something inside the sarcophagus. It was even possible that a crazed woman with enough money could bribe people to dig up a corpse and transport it from one country to another. She said, 'Jack, would you take me back to the hotel, please?'

'Certainly. Will you excuse us? It's been a delightful evening, but a long day. I'm afraid we must be going.' He drew her away, heading towards the doors. Beatrice said, 'Goodnight,' as they turned.

Hassan made a move to follow them. His mother screamed that they were to stay, but he didn't try to stop them. He told Ernestine, 'Stay with her,' and ran ahead of Jack. 'Let me show you the way,' he said.

They went down the staircases in silence, across the carpeted lobbies, down the narrow hallways. In the foyer where the mirror hung, a butler presented Jack with his cape and Beatrice with the velvet cloak she'd bought in Florence. Hassan proceeded to the last, dim corridor and the door to the garden. Jack put his hand on the latch and opened the door before the arthritic servant could move. The cool air came in to them.

Beatrice stepped out so that she was halfway through the door, and turned. She asked Hassan, 'What's in the sarcophagus?'

He shrugged. 'My father or your father – perhaps more than one person. Why should it make a difference to you?'

69

'Do you mean that she'd really go so far as to dig someone up in order to put him in there?'

'And why not? It's what archaeologists do all the time. That's their job: digging up the dead.'

'Their job is to add to the sum of human knowledge,' Beatrice said.

Hassan started to shut the door in her face. He'd forgotten that Jack was still inside. Jack threw him against the wall and pushed his way out of the door. He caught Beatrice by the hand.

They ran down the path to the gate. As soon as they were out on the street, they turned around to look back.

'Those horrible people,' she said. 'Your mother was right. My God, what a nightmare.'

'Not a nightmare. A farce. Listen,' he said, freeing his hand and using both arms to imitate the dramatic movements of Mme Cristo-Marquez, 'there are poisons and poisons.'

Beatrice laughed. From the house, faintly, came a doleful wailing.

'I suppose that's from *The Book of the Dead*?' he said. 'They'll get a surprise when all that masonry comes thundering down on them one of these days. That'll really give them something to moan about.'

He led her to broader streets, more densely populated, bursting with crowds and brightly lit. Every once in a while he made her laugh by leaning to the side and whispering into her ear, 'Love is a poison.'

Somewhere Else

Beth was still working on the crossword puzzle when Alan finished his section of the paper. He reached for the pile of letters that looked like bills and throwaways. There was a time when the mailman delivered letters from living people, not just from organizations and offices. Of course nowadays practically everyone picked up the phone instead of a pen. Beth, and Alan too, preferred the telephone. Unless they had to send a contract somewhere, nearly all their business was done over the phone and by fax. They had answering machines at the office and in the house. The telephone dominated their lives. It was a blessing; and it was a nuisance.

He lifted the heap of catalogues and magazines and dumped them at the right of her coffee cup. 'Clothes, handbags, shoes,' he said. 'Save the environment. One for jigsaws, one for music boxes, one that sells replicas of prehistoric animals. Two book clubs you can join.'

'I don't have time to read anything.'

'Except the catalogues, and that's a real waste of time.' He shuffled through some more bills. She went back to her puzzle.

'Hey,' he said. 'I think I've won a prize.'

'What for?'

'Being good, of course.'

'Oh, ha-ha.'

He held the paper up to her, but she didn't bother to look. She was trying to think of a six-letter word meaning stop. 'Listen to this,' he told her. 'Two thousand dollars if I apply within forty-eight hours of receiving the enclosed. It's got a date and a time-stamp on it. We've got a day more than they say.'

'Desist,' she said. 'Those urgent things are never important. Alan Q. Beasley, you could win a million dollars: remember?'

'This looks okay. No pictures of Colonel Kentucky. No free stamps.'

'Another bonanza from the black-diamond mine,' she said.

The black diamond episode had been about three years before; they'd been carrying on a smoldering quarrel for a couple of months. She'd begun to think that they weren't going to pull out of it – that this time their marriage would end: and she wouldn't have cared a bit if it had. One morning, another of those prize envelopes arrived for Alan. He'd actually sent for it. How dumb could you be, she said. He told her huffily that he'd written back to them just to see if they were crooked. 'And,' he announced, 'I've won a black diamond.' He opened the envelope and took out a little transparent plastic packet, in one corner of which rested a tiny brown ball of something that might possibly have been a piece of low-grade coal. He held it up. They stared at it. Then, both of them burst into laughter. They laughed so hard that they had to hold their heads in their hands. 'A putative diamond,' he shouted. 'An alleged diamond,' she gasped. They stopped for breath and started each other off again. They laughed, uncontrollably, until they ached. And somehow the quarrel had ended.

'Two thousand bucks,' he said, 'if I apply within the time-limit.'

'What's the hitch?'

'You'll never guess. It's got to be used on travel.'

'That's a joke.'

They ran a travel agency. They'd been in the business for six years. It took all their energy and thought. It was the reason why they didn't have children: they kept figuring that next year they'd find time to plan their own lives. But they couldn't even squeeze in the hours to work on future holiday schemes. They only just managed to keep up. Their range of vacation trips was still the same as when they'd started. If your standards were high, you had to spend money. Alan saw it as his job to make the past – from which we ought to be able to learn – usable and habitable in modern terms. There was no point in going to a quaint English village or a picturesque Greek temple if you were going to have to sleep in a place with no running water. That would be ridiculous. Even Beth, who tended to get worked up over authentic atmosphere, agreed with him about that.

'We do need to do some research,' he said. 'Find a couple of new places.'

'We can't spare the time. We'd need lots of . . . we'd need weeks. Can you see Rosa in charge for that long?'

'The Stones might help out for a while.'

'And you know what they'd expect in return. They want our list. If they got their hands on that, we could say goodbye to the business. I don't just mean what they got out of Mr Pettifer.'

'I'm going to put in for it anyway. It can't hurt.'

'That's right. We might win a fun-filled holiday in Butte, Montana.'

'With two thousand extra, you could come, too.'

'Too?'

'Two thousand. That's what it says. What we should really do is go over our itinerary. I wish people would let us know how things went.'

'It's like everything else,' she said. 'Who's going to spend the time on it? People don't like writing letters. Except cranks.'

'If they send the money, would you come along?'

'We can't both leave the office at the same time.'

'For a week, we could. Just.'

'What could we do in a week?'

'We could go over the part of the British tour we never got to. Wouldn't you like that?'

'Well, sure. I guess.'

'Fine,' he said. 'That's settled.'

Beth still wasn't certain, but since she thought nothing was ever going to come of the idea, she didn't say anything.

It was her day to have lunch with Faye. Faye worked in the magazine office a few doors away. Ella, Beth's other lunchtime crony, was at the opposite end of the shopping mall. Beth had

73

once tried to introduce them to each other; everything had seemed to go well, but the next time she suggested a meeting, Ella and Faye complained so much about the distance, the dates, the pressure of work, that she knew it hadn't been a success. So, she saw them separately, which took twice as much time. That was another thing, she realized: she'd been trying to get her two friends together in order to save herself an hour or two.

For three years, until the crisis in Ella's life, Beth used to see her for a coffee break in the afternoons. Ella now needed that time for what she called 'contemplation' and what Alan described as 'goofing off'. Ella's life had been irreversibly altered on the day she'd lost her Filofax. She'd had a breakdown. Her doctor had referred her to a psychiatrist and a time-management consultant, but neither one had been able to help her. Someone – an aunt, or some other relative – had advised her to pray. Ella did better than that; she went on a pilgrimage. She got on a plane to Venice, took the train to Padua and joined the crowd of people waiting to beg St Anthony to find things, or people, they had lost. She moved with the others to the left of the silver altar, filed past the stone carvings that illustrated the miracles worked by the saint in his lifetime, and at last reached out, put her hand on the casket and asked him to get her Filofax back.

When Beth told the story, Alan said, 'I can see it coming: she got home and there it was, right where she'd left it.'

'No, she really had lost it. But when she got home, there was a package waiting for her. Somebody'd found it and mailed it back.'

'St Anthony, no doubt,' he said. He thought Ella was crazed and affected. To Beth, the story seemed a little zany but it made perfect sense. If there were such things as saints, no task could be too enormous for them, no request so silly that it was unimportant: they could do anything.

He said, 'Why would a saint bother about something so trivial?'

'Why not? For a saint, a big favor would be easy. So, a little one wouldn't be any trouble at all. I think you could also count on his tolerance of human folly and petty-mindedness. It wouldn't be

74

any skin off his back to grant something really idiotic. If you accept the basic principle – '

'Well, if you accept that, you're beyond hope to begin with.'

'Maybe,' she said, meaning that she didn't agree. It wasn't surprising to her that ever since Ella had had her Filofax restored to her, she'd been preoccupied by questions of religion; she hadn't gone so far as to take instruction, but she'd begun to spend a lot of time reading, meditating and trying to pray, which – she told Beth – wasn't so easy as you might think. It took discipline. It was hard work. The afternoon break was no good any more. Ella became another lunchtime friend, like Faye.

On three days of the week, Beth would usually stay in the office through the lunch break. Rosa, their secretary, would run around the corner to buy her a sandwich from the delicatessen. Occasionally Beth would say to Rosa that this was going to be a diet day. She never made it past two-thirty. Rosa didn't mind the extra trip; she was on good terms with one of the boys behind the counter.

Their office was in an arcade, one of four that radiated from a central area where trees in tubs surrounded a large fountain. Between the trees there were benches. It was a pleasant spot for people to sit in after they'd done some shopping and were wondering where to go next. It was also a meeting place. The planners of the mall had originally called the center a piazza; when most shoppers were making an effort to get the name right, they'd come up with the word 'pizza', although normally everybody just said, 'By the fountain.'

You were doing all right to have an office in one of the arcades near the fountain. The only trouble with the location was that a customer who tried to find you for the first time could get mixed up between the four arcades, which looked alike: they had been given the names of the four main points of the compass, but who knew one direction from another? Left and right were fairly easy for most people to remember, but you couldn't expect everyone to race outside in order to check where the sun was; and anyway, that depended on something else, too. A mapmaker or a navigator would know about directions. Ordinary shoppers didn't. They got lost. That was how Beth had met Ella, who had ended up at the office after her first morning in the mall. 'Where am I?' she'd said, like someone coming out of a faint.

The great advantages of the mall were for those who worked there. Almost all the people Beth thought of as her friends were her neighbors at work. In fact, it seemed to her that the mall was really the neighborhood where she lived. The house that she and Alan owned was just for sleeping in and for giving parties.

She wouldn't mind getting away from the house for a while. She wouldn't mind leaving everything for a week.

As she picked up her tunafish sandwich, she asked Faye, 'Have you and Hutch had one of those prize envelopes offering you two thousand dollars to travel with?'

'No. Wish we had. What is it – something to do with a rival firm?'

'I don't think so.' She bit in and munched, thinking that she'd have to ask Alan about that: it hadn't occurred to her. 'As far as I know, it's just another one of those win-a-million things.'

'But if you got the money, you'd go, wouldn't you?'

'You bet. I wasn't so sure this morning at breakfast, but I am now. We both need a break. And I need some time to think about things. We just keep going and going.'

'You love it.'

'In a way.'

'In every way. You thrive on it.'

'But it's taken over. I'm beginning to suspect that it's done something bad to me. I think maybe Alan would like to get out, too. At least – well. I don't know. We don't have time to talk about anything at all any more.'

'That sounds like a good time to take a vacation. You two should read some of your little leaflets.'

'Aren't they brilliant?'

'You'll have a great time.'

'We haven't won it yet.'

'Don't wait to win anything. Just go.'

'That's the trouble with you, Faye. You encourage my weaknesses. Act now, think later.'

'It's a good idea, isn't it? You could afford a week off.'

'Afford, sure. It isn't a question of the money. Not really. It's the time, as usual. The thing is – I have the feeling that if I went, I might not come back. I've been feeling that way for a long while.'

'Something wrong at work?'

'Nothing's ever wrong at work. That's the point. The work is always just great. It's a substitute for everything else. I'm beginning to think it's my excuse for not living my life.'

'Oh wow, Elizabeth. Let me write that one down.'

'You know what I mean. It's everything; not just that we don't have kids. Well, that's the main thing. I realized a few months ago, last year: I kind of feel I've left it too late.'

'What are you talking about? You're still in your twenties, aren't you?'

'Well, not quite.' She wasn't prepared to say anything more exact, unless Faye spoke first. From the beginning of their acquaintance it had been obvious that Faye didn't want any questions asked about her age; or, for that matter, about her first husband, her daughter's experience at the boarding school they'd sent her to, or about anything at all connected with Trenton, New Jersey. 'You know what I mean,' Beth told her. 'I've sort of run out of steam. I've put it all into the agency. Now I couldn't start a family unless I gave up work. But that's the one thing that keeps me going. It's fun.'

'It's fun, but it's killing you. I see.'

'I guess I'm what they call a workaholic. Alan's the same.'

'Does he want to go on this trip?'

'He was the one who suggested it. He's sending in the form.'

'Good.'

'You could be right, you know. Maybe some other travel company's doing a promotion. I'd better ask around.'

They said goodbye at the fountain. Beth turned off into her arcade. The clock in the jeweler's window caught her eye. She began to hurry.

As she opened the agency door, Alan came out, saying, 'Where were you? I've got to get over to Meyerson's.' He ran off, not looking back.

She sat down at her desk and reached for the telephone. She didn't stop working until four o'clock, when she asked Rosa to go across the arcade for some coffee. She stretched in her chair and yawned. It had been a good afternoon.

The pleasure she took in describing places was founded on her need to communicate enthusiasm. You couldn't call her exaggeration falsehood; it was a slight emphasis in the process of persuading and convincing someone about the fictions she already believed in. It wouldn't be right to say that her work required her to engage in deliberate acts of dishonesty. She simply tried to get prospective clients into the right mood: to create an atmosphere. If people took off on their holidays with a few skilfully devised impressions in mind, they were pretty well certain to find them justified. That wasn't doing anything wrong. It was smart salesmanship backing a worthwhile product – that was what Alan said.

She picked up the receiver again and punched the buttons for the Stones' number. The Stones were their friends but it was a business friendship, not personal. A personal friendship might be like marriage, whereas this particular business friendship was like having a lover who lied and cheated and was unfaithful with friends and enemies, yet who managed to remain so attractive and charming in other ways, so desirable, that one didn't want to break off the affair. They liked the Stones and they didn't trust them an inch. Several times Pete and Marcie Stone had tried to poach customers away from them. They were, Beth believed, the kind of people her grandmother had once described to her: they'd come to dinner and try to hire your cook out from under you. Once or twice Alan had done things back to them, just to show that he and Beth weren't pushovers. There was no point in ending the friendship, as long as the others kept within bounds; Marcie and Pete had shown that they could be useful people to know. On the other hand, one more outrageous stunt like the one with Mr Pettifer, and Alan and Beth would cut them adrift.

She got Marcie at the other end of the line. They talked about the new airline prices and Beth asked about the two-thousand-dollar offer.

Marcie said, 'It's news to me. But I'll ask around.'

'I was thinking: it might be nice to get away for a week anyhow. We could check out the places they never bother to tell us about.'

'Hey, I got news about that. I had a customer drop in. Two of them – husband and wife.'

'I don't believe it.'

'Honest to God. Five years in the travel business and these are the first people that ever came back to tell us what the trip was like. When you see them again, they never stop to talk – they just ask how much it's going to cost to go somewhere else. Nobody's ever got a spare minute. God, they were so nice. I nearly cried. They said they just wanted to thank us, because they'd had such a good time.'

'I hope you asked them a lot of questions.'

'I certainly did. And there were a few changes I thought I'd pass on to you: opening times at a couple of country houses, restaurant hours – that kind of thing. It was the south of England, including London, and over to Paris and Rome.'

'We'd love any information,' Beth said. She thought Marcie must be feeling guilty about wangling Mr Pettifer's little list away from him.

'Okay. I'll send you a copy of what we've got. And if you're taking a trip, let us know what you find out, hm?'

'Sure,' Beth promised. 'Unless we have such a good time that we just never come back.'

After she'd hung up, she thought, *I've said something like that before: today, at lunch. When I was talking to Faye.*

Rosa brought some hazelnut cookies with the coffee. The delicatessen was giving them away as a special, introductory offer. She had a big bag of them and she was chewing on one as she came in. Beth said, 'Don't let them near me.' Rosa tried to break her down, but she wouldn't be tempted. She concentrated on work until closing time.

*

She sat in the rush-hour traffic with Alan and blanked out a little, while he complained about Meyerson's. They were always

79

having trouble with the brochure, but they never did anything about it. There weren't any other printers around who could do a good job. It was specialized work. Their only consolation was that half of the other agencies in the vicinity used Meyerson's, so they were all in the same boat.

When he'd talked everything out of his system and then done the paraphrase, Beth told him about her afternoon phone call.

He'd been thinking all day about a trip, he said. 'I think we should go anyway. Cassie could take over for a while. She's always said she'd be happy to.'

'But it might not be a good time for her.'

'I don't want Pete and Marcie in there, not for a hundred peace-offerings.'

'Why don't we just close for a week? We could send out a leaflet to everybody.'

Alan thought the idea was impossible. Cassie was related to his brother-in-law and was trustworthy. She and Rosa could keep things running: he thought so until they got through the traffic, reached home and sat down to cocktails. He thought so until well into the first bourbon; but by the end of his second drink, he'd changed his mind. 'We'll wait a week,' he suggested, 'to find out if we've won the prize.'

'Nobody wins those prizes.'

'We'll see.'

He made the airline reservations for two on the transatlantic flight; it left in the evening and arrived in England early in the morning, London time, which would still be night for them. He bought himself a new suitcase. She tapped out a letter on the computer, printed out stacks of copies and gave them to Rosa. Then she had a quick word with the people next door, before running in to town to buy a new raincoat. While she was hanging the coat up in the front hall closet, she saw Alan's suitcase and decided that it was just the kind of thing she needed. The next morning she went out and bought one, to find on her return that he – having admired her new raincoat on its hanger – had gone shopping again and had found a coat just like it for himself. 'We ought to have done everything together,' she told him. 'We'd have saved a lot of time.'

He said, 'I'm looking forward to this. We should have taken a trip a long time ago. I think I was in a rut.'

'And I was in something worse. I didn't realize until a few days back. I'd lost hope.'

'About what?'

'I'll tell you when we're away from everything.'

'Let me take you away from all this,' he said, throwing an arm around her.

The day before they were set to fly out, a check came through from the prize people. There were no stipulations, no strings attached.

'See?' he said. 'I was right.'

The check was issued by an organization called *United Holdings and Travel Co.* They'd never heard of it. Beth picked up the brochure that came with the letter of congratulation. She flipped through the pages, saying, 'I'd like to know who their printers are. Look at the quality of the pictures. Isn't that incredible – color reproduction like that? This is as good as one of those art magazines.' She reached the section where, at last, they found the catch. She read out the passage: *Prizewinners who apply for the Finborg weekend will automatically receive a further one thousand dollars.*

'It's in the letter, too,' Alan said. 'You agree to go there, all the expenses are paid, they give you the round-trip ticket from whatever city you name, and you've got a luxury weekend in this top-notch castle full of swimming pools and gourmet cooking. It's a promotional gimmick. I guess they've just converted it.'

'Our clients aren't in that league. I suppose we wouldn't have to tell anyone that. Just turn up and have a ball.'

'We aren't going to have the time, unless I change the plane tickets. We have to tell these United people right now.'

'For an extra thousand?' she said. 'And it might be interesting. If all the other people they wrote to are travel agents, we could learn a lot.'

'That's a point,' he said. 'Okay.'

*

They stayed up all night, writing memos and leaving messages, taking things out of their suitcases and putting them back again. When, the next evening, they were finally on the plane, they both felt slugged. He wanted to order some drinks, to relax.

'You can't be serious,' she told him. 'That dehydrates you. It'll make you feel terrible. And they say jet-lag hits you a lot worse if you drink. That's what I read in that body book.'

'Well, my body book says a little drink never hurt anyone.' He ordered a double for himself. She stuck to water. They came out nearly equal, because she'd been tired to begin with and she always fretted more than he did.

They landed in the morning, had an hour's sleep, made themselves get up and go sightseeing, and ate their evening meal early. Already they were glad they had come. Beth kept saying, 'Isn't it wonderful? Isn't everything beautiful?' He said yes; he was more interested in seeing what was happening to her than in looking at the sights. He'd been worried about her for a long time. Her friend, Faye, was all right but the other one, Ella, was certifiable: she had a bad influence on Beth. Ella had turned into some sort of religious or ESP fanatic. She'd tried to make Beth believe totally crazy things, such as that it was possible to go through walls by concentrating on an imaginary black dot in front of your eyes. She'd told Beth to meditate and to sing certain notes and melodic phrases and to go on diets. Luckily Beth couldn't prevent herself from nibbling potato chips, wasn't able to carry a tune for long and fell asleep as soon as she relaxed; she hadn't needed all that. One look at her now would have convinced anyone: what she'd needed was a break. She'd even become flirtatious.

'It's like our honeymoon,' she said.

'Without the mosquitoes,' he reminded her.

'But, darling, that was the best part.' She made a face at him. The phrase was from a family joke – something to do with the part of a lobster you weren't supposed to eat because it could kill you.

'The second-best,' he said, leaning over from the other side of the table to catch hold of her hand.

They spent the weekend in London, then they visited the two Devon hotels on their list, looked in at the Stratford guesthouse and did the Stonehenge trip. On the fifth day they felt tired, but that was simply the reaction they called 'traveler's dip': everyone had at least one day of it. After that, you straightened out.

*

The temperature dropped as they boarded the plane. Beth wondered if she should have brought an extra sweater with her; she'd had her shopping-spree clothes sent back home.

'Cold,' Alan said, lifting his head. 'Scandinavia, here we come.' He settled down to read, while Beth shut her eyes and tried to doze. She didn't like flying. What she used to tell her clients was that it was exactly like a bus ride, only safer; but, naturally, that wasn't quite true: even if you could adjust the air-conditioning nozzles so that they didn't shoot jets of air straight on to your head, the pressure made a difference. It did something to the fluid in all the sinus passages. It gave you a headache. That was funny, she thought: the travel agent who didn't like to travel.

She went right under for a few minutes. Alan had to touch her shoulder to wake her up. They were beginning the descent.

She got her handbag from under the seat in front of her, redid her lipstick and combed her hair. She pulled her seat belt tighter. At the same instant the plane braked suddenly, unnaturally; everyone was tossed forward. A steward's voice, omitting the usual, 'Ladies and gentlemen', spoke loudly over the address system, saying, 'Fasten your safety belts, please. We're experiencing some turbulence.' Although there was no indication of what it could be, everyone knew: something had gone seriously wrong. This wasn't a small or incidental disturbance. There were murmurs of distress among the passengers. Several people had been thrown against the seats and had hurt their heads or broken the glasses they were wearing. And they were frightened.

The engines of the plane began to roar. Beth wanted to reach for Alan's hand, but she knew he wouldn't like it. She was relieved and pleased when, without saying anything, he placed his hand lightly over hers.

The noise stopped, but they seemed to be falling fast. All at once they were plunging, rushing. A man's voice, abruptly, announced, 'Attention, all passengers. Prepare for an emergency landing.' The rest of the message was cut off as the plane screamed. Many of the passengers too were shrieking, crying, moaning. Beth and Alan looked at each other. His hand gripped hers. Her lips moved. She said, into the uproar, that she loved him. He said something back, which she couldn't lip-read; it might have been *Thanks for everything, Happy landings*, or *We should have drunk our duty-free bottle*. The plane crashed.

She was still trying to undo her belt while he was up from his seat and out into the aisle, pushing a space clear for both of them. The air was bitter with smoke. Everyone was yelling and fighting. Fire fanned towards them from the rear of the aircraft. She kicked herself free of the seat in front of her. She scrambled to her feet. Alan had gone. The thrashing crowd had carried him away from her. She could just see him, a long way off. He turned back. He was shouting. She tried to get into the aisle, but it was no use. She held her arms out to him. There was an explosion. High flames shot up from the seats near the front exits. Across a wave of fire she saw him, looking back at her. A fierce heat blasted the left side of her face, her shoulder and hand. She jumped back. She couldn't protect herself: the flames were everywhere. She knew it was too late.

She woke up. Alan was standing in the aisle. He was getting the coats down from the overhead locker. They had landed. The other passengers were collecting their belongings.

'Okay?' he said. She nodded, unbuckling her seat belt. She was too shaken to speak. She never wanted to talk about the dream. She didn't even want to go over it in her mind. It had made her feel sick in a way that was worse than anything she could remember, even the nightmares of childhood. She kept herself busy with her flight bag and shoulder bag until everyone began to move down the aisle. Alan said, 'All we have to do now is find that other plane.'

They put their carry-on luggage on a trolley they found in the airport building. Beth stayed with it while Alan went to investigate. Now that she felt calmer, she would have liked to tell him something about the dream – only a hint, to get rid of it herself by sharing it; but she had the feeling that to mention it at all would bring bad luck. It might turn something into a reality that, so far, was only thought.

It would be nice, she thought, to have a long, cool drink; better yet, to wade into a pool of refreshing water. She imagined doing it – stepping in slowly. She could picture the water, pure and effervescent as a drink of bottled mineral water. She thought of the fountain back at the mall, in the center of the meeting place by the arcades, near their office, at home.

Alan was at her side again. He said, 'I've found it. We'll have to walk a long way, but there's plenty of time.'

'Good. I'd love a nice, big drink of spring water.'

'Oh, Beth. Can't it wait?'

'I guess so. I thought we had so much time.'

He started to push the trolley forward. 'We've got time to catch the plane,' he said. 'No customs. They'll look at our passports and cards at the gate.'

She followed him. She wondered if her thirst had been brought on by dreaming of fire; or, it might have been the other way around – that her mind had produced a fire-dream to account for a thirst she'd already felt in her sleep.

They reached a smooth passageway, slightly ramped. Alan raced along it with the trolley. She trotted to keep up. 'I had a terrible dream,' she said.

'So did I.'

'About the plane.'

'Uh-huh. Don't tell me.'

She didn't think he'd had any dream. He simply hoped to stop her talking. There were times when he didn't enjoy keeping up a conversation: when she'd be rattling away on some topic and all at once would notice that he was taking part reluctantly. In the early days of their marriage she'd been hurt by that kind of thing.

Now it didn't bother her. People were different not just in temperament but in their sense of pace. There was no reason why they should be in perfect symmetry every moment of the day and night; it was probably just those incongruities that kept them attached to each other for so long.

They had to wait for two officials to look at their airline tickets and passports, then they were motioned towards another hallway; it led to a waiting room where their bags were taken from them, to be loaded on to the plane.

They studied the other people in the room – four couples, one man on his own and a single woman. The couples seemed to be much like themselves; one of the women was pretty, one had red hair, one was fat. The redhead's husband had a mustache, slicked-back hair and a sharp-featured face. He looked like a bandleader from the thirties. Another husband, standing up, was tall and beefy and was dressed in a frontiersman's outfit: fringed deerskin jacket, stetson and western boots. 'Myron,' his wife called to him. Myron returned to his seat. He put his hands on his knees. His wife – definitely a city type – had on a dark business suit and black patent-leather shoes with very high heels. She handed him a map, which he accepted without interest.

'Look at that woman's shoes,' Beth said to Alan. 'I thought we were all supposed to be travel agents. One of the first things I tell a female client is not to wear exaggerated heels on a plane. She must be incredibly uncomfortable.'

'Maybe they came here by car. It's a short flight, anyway.'

'Well, just the same.'

The single man – tidy, bespectacled and wearing tweeds – resembled a math teacher at the school Alan had gone to the year before highschool. The man reminded him all at once of the whole year: of the street corner where he'd waited for the bus; and the drive out to the school through the suburbs and into what looked almost like real country. There were several nice houses they passed; a park, and streets with big trees on either side. There was one particular part of the ride he'd never forget – a stretch of road lined by tall maple trees that arched over and formed a tunnel: in the fall it was like driving through a land of jewelry, the leaves scarlet and gold. Every morning for about two weeks he was made happy by the sight of that gorgeous avenue. He would have liked to see it going in the other direction too, but in the afternoon the busdriver took a different route. He'd thought then: some places made an impression on you that you never recovered from. They were special. Some of them used to be hard to reach, yet now that air travel was so easy, it was possible to get to countries and landscapes that – only as far back as the last century – couldn't have been visited by anyone but explorers and pilgrims. That was one way in which the world had improved; the convenience of modern travel was wonderful.

At that age, when he was young, he'd wanted to go everywhere, anywhere: after Europe, to Asia, the South Seas, Africa and South America. He'd wanted to get to the Arctic. He'd yearned for places where no one else had ever been. And later, he'd hoped to open up the world to other people; to allow them to be in marvelous places and to see fascinating things. He'd never quite outgrown his adolescent longing, never completely achieved his dream, which was to find himself suddenly, and as if magically, somewhere else. And, as it had turned out, the one place that was the most beautiful for him had been at home: on that ride through the maple trees. They had remained his vision of beauty on earth, of the best from all the world outside the school bus. He hadn't realized it before. He'd forgotten, for years.

'That woman looks like your Aunt Nora,' Beth said.

He looked. The woman was the one he'd decided was unattached. When he'd first noticed her, she'd had her head down and was reading a booklet. Now that she was talking with the tweedy man, he could see what Beth meant, although he didn't agree. 'Sort of,' he told her, 'but not much.'

Two airline officials, a man and a woman, came through the entrance. Their uniforms were immaculate, their smiles toothy. They looked a little like mannikins from a store window – perfectly regular and bland. The woman stood at the microphone and made an announcement: they could board the plane.

Everything was ready. The passengers stood. Beth and Alan joined the group.

They had to duck to get into the small plane, and to crouch as they moved to their seats. The aircraft had fourteen seats, seven on each side.

It was a bumpy ride. The engines made so much noise that conversation was out of the question. Beth tried to sleep. She closed her eyes, but couldn't drift off. She felt as if they'd been traveling for years. It was impossible to imagine going back home. London had vanished from her mind, together with America. The house, work, the office in the mall, were like memories from as long ago as early childhood.

Alan looked across the aisle at her. They were near enough to hold hands without stretching, if they wanted to. He would have liked to reach out to her, but he saw that she was trying to sleep. He had no wish to sleep. He'd had his fill of nightmares. The one he'd had on the plane from London was enough to last him a lifetime; he'd dreamt that they'd crash-landed in flames, that he'd jumped out of his seat to get a place for both of them in the aisle; and as soon as he'd turned around to help pull Beth clear, the other passengers had swept him away. The dream ended as she was holding her hands out after him, the fire roaring towards her, and he was being carried ever farther away.

It was only a cliché, of course – one of the basic dreams; one of the earliest myths: Lot's wife, Orpheus and Euridice. You turned around and she was gone, or dying, or transformed. Or, maybe, just divorced. It was possible that that was his real fear. Years before, for a long time, he'd wanted to leave her. He'd waited for the right moment to talk about it. But time passed, the moment never came and suddenly everything was all right again. Now he was afraid that perhaps what had happened to him could happen to her. One day she might feel that she'd just had enough, and she'd want to get out.

Their landing this time was easy. All the passengers had to stoop, almost to crawl, out of the cramped cabin. It was like emerging from a cocoon or coming up from a tunnel.

The plane sat in the middle of an enormous clearing surrounded by pinewoods. A road ran across one end. Near the road stood a shed with a corrugated metal roof. Boxes were stacked against two of the walls and piled up next to a neighboring shack. A mound of fuel drums had been set some distance away from the buildings and also from the trees. There were no other planes in sight.

Their transportation was waiting. As Alan and Beth stepped down from the narrow ladder, people were already pointing at two old-fashioned, horse-drawn carriages that were heading towards them from the shelter of the woods.

'Not bad,' Beth said. 'Right on time.'

'They probably pulled up back in the trees there,' he told her. 'Otherwise the horses might have been spooked by the plane.' He knew nothing about horses. He was guessing. In the early days of their marriage she'd been in the habit of asking him all kinds of questions, as though he were an authority on everything; and he'd taken to acting like one: if he thought or suspected a thing, he'd say it was true, certain. It gave him confidence in his abilities. His speculation became fact. The odd thing was that so often he turned out to be right. Sometimes he even felt that he had insights of a kind that could be called psychic; he'd know things almost before they happened – not that he really believed in such powers, but belief was part of the phenomenon: her faith in him had made him capable. It might also be true that his unwillingness to concede an equal capacity in her had kept her in a state where she didn't feel that her life was important, or that she had anything special to contribute. He'd taught her to assert herself when she was at the office. Outside business hours, she was unchanged. What she needed, he thought, was just one or two friends who weren't crazy. A woman should have a few women friends, so that they could all get together every week and complain about their husbands and families, not bring everything home to the dinner table.

The robotlike steward and stewardess unloaded suitcases. The carriages stood one beside the other, facing the same way; every so often one of the horses on the inside would swing its head over and try to nip the nearby horse of the other pair.

They joined the rest of their group, who were already getting into the high seats. Alan chose the carriage that had their bags on it. He climbed up and held out a hand to pull Beth after him. They were sitting next to the redhead, Gina, and her bandleader husband, who was called Sonny. Like Beth, Gina worked in her husband's business. 'We met,' she told Beth, 'when we were both operating one-man outfits.'

'She kept cutting my sales down to nothing,' Sonny said. 'I got to thinking: Who is this broad? I figured I'd better go straighten her out, make some kind of a deal with her. So, one day I drop in at the address, I open the door, and – wham, it's just like the songs: there she is sitting there, and Love came and tapped me on the shoulder. That's how we amalgamated.'

Gina said, 'We sure did. We amalgamated in under twenty-four hours.'

The single woman, who had taken her seat in front of them, turned around and smiled. She introduced herself. Her name was Myrtle. She'd been talking to the tweedy man, Horace, who was worried about whether the coachman had packed his bag upright and not sideways. 'I've got a lot of bottles in it,' he explained.

'Don't they have any liquor over here?' Gina asked.

'Oh, it's just aftershave and that kind of thing. But I don't want it to spill all over everything.'

They started off. The fat woman, behind Alan, spoke with approval of the wide, comfortable seats. 'They should build things like this nowadays,' she said.

'Nancy,' her husband told her, 'that's asking too much.'

'Trains, buses, the subway – everything nowadays is plastic. And skimpy.'

'It's the times we live in,' he said.

Beth and Alan turned their heads and said hello. They exchanged names. Nancy's husband was called Ed.

The coach entered the pinewoods. All at once the world was darker, quieter. It was like going from daylight into night. Beth looked at her watch. What it said meant nothing to her. There were time-differences between countries; that could mix you up to begin with. On top of that, you got tired. She asked, 'Does anybody know what time it is?'

Gina said, 'I always lose my sense of time when I'm on vacation.'

'You find another way of measuring it, that's all,' Alan said.

Nancy and Ed told a story about ordering breakfast in Mexico, but because they hadn't specified whether it was to be at a.m. or p.m., the waiter brought it up at eight-thirty in the evening, while they were still drinking their cocktails on the balcony. 'That was a different sense of time, all right,' Ed said.

Beth began to feel strange. She waited until it wouldn't seem that she was spoiling Ed's story, then she asked again if anyone knew what time it was. No one did. 'Relax,' Alan said to her.

The carriage rolled on. The landscape around them seemed without sound. They were the only noise passing through, their chatter foreign to the place, the steady rhythm of the horses' hoofs like the muffled pounding of a machine.

Beth said, 'Maybe this is that famous Scandinavian long night you read about.'

'But this is the wrong time of year for it,' Myrtle said over her shoulder. 'That's in the winters.'

'It feels like winter.'

'I didn't get any information at all on this part of the trip. It's all very mysterious. You know what would be fun? If it's one of those mystery games – know what I mean? They give you characters to play, and then there's a murder and you have to solve it. I had a couple of clients who wanted to go on one, but the price was too steep for them.'

Horace said, 'I heard about one of them they held in Venice. Somebody fell into the canal.'

'We're all tour operators, aren't we?' Alan asked.

From the back seat Ed spoke up. He said, 'What do you mean, Scandinavia? We were booked for Yugoslavia.'

'Austria,' Horace said. 'But it could be a lot of places. It sure looks foreign. That's about all you can say.'

'Well, where are we?'

'Ask the coachman,' Nancy suggested.

The coachman, sitting high up and beyond the barrier of his seat, was too far removed from them to be reached. They called out to him, but he didn't turn around.

They made conversation, stopped, started up again, and waited. At last the carriage came to a halt.

They all got down, although they could see that they hadn't arrived yet. They were at some kind of way-station. There was a small hut and a dim light in it. The passengers from the other carriage joined them.

They tried to get some information out of the two drivers, who didn't speak a language any of them could understand. By signs everyone was told that they were all to keep going.

They got back into their seats and started off again. This time, they felt, they were on the last lap; they'd be welcomed with light and warmth, a drink of something: their host would give them explanations, facts, plans.

They became talkative. As Alan and Beth's carriage moved through the forest, they called out stories to each other, leaning over the seats and saying, 'But this is the best part,' and, 'You aren't going to believe what he said then.' They talked about funny things that had happened in their businesses, swapped anecdotes about cities they'd been in, asked each other to describe the worst and best clients they'd ever had. And they all agreed that the brochure was a problem every year.

The coachmen pulled up again at a spot so like the first one that for a moment the passengers were bewildered. 'Isn't this the same place?' Myrtle asked. 'Do you think that man knows the way?'

'It isn't the same,' Sonny told her. 'I remember there was a log out of line up near the top there.' He raised his arm. 'It does look a lot like it, though.'

Nancy said, 'At the rate we've been traveling, they could have fixed the roof while we were gone.'

Myron, the man in the frontier costume, came over to where they were parked. He suggested that since it was turning out to be such a long drive, they might switch around: that way, they could all be acquainted by the time they got to their destination.

Alan was happy where he was. Somebody in the other carriage, he thought, must be a bore; but there was no polite way out of the invitation. 'Sure,' he said. Behind him, at the same time, Ed said uncertainly, 'Well, I guess so.'

On the third lap of the trip there was plenty of time to get to know Myron and his wife, Cora Bee. And after that, on the fourth stage, Sue and Greg, from Omaha. By the fifth and sixth times around, they all knew each other very well.

They traded family histories, got to know about the children, ex-partners and in-laws. They sang songs, played wordgames, wondered about the existence of God; and they asked themselves whether a unifying set of physical laws in the universe might do just as well as a divine being if you didn't want to take such things personally. They tried to remember lines from poems.

Alan began to lose heart. That was another trouble with travelling: everything was out of your hands. Someone else was behind the information counter and on the telephone and at the controls of the plane. You had to wait, patiently, as if you'd given up being human and had become just a package to be transported. If you were used to doing your own organizing, it was difficult to put up with that. He always felt more confident when he was the one in charge.

They ran out of things to say. Beth began to feel strange again. She whispered to Alan, 'I'm getting a funny feeling about this. It's weird.'

'Just relax, like I told you,' he said, 'and enjoy the scenery.'

She thought: *What scenery?* There was nothing but pine boughs, the darkness and silence, except for the creaking of the wheels and the sound of the horses' hoofs on the dirt track. There were patches of leaves on the ground, then sandy soil and pine needles, but no other variation in the landscape. She tried to think about getting to their destination; her mind went blank. But they had to stop. They had to get somewhere, otherwise nothing made sense. She made a great effort to hold within her mind some picture of the place they were meant to find. If she concentrated hard enough, they might get there.

They stopped again and changed around and started off once

more. Alan looked up at the dark shapes of the trees that passed, in unceasing progression, above and around him. Everyone nowadays worried about conservation and the environment, yet it seemed that the forest they were in was limitlessly huge, its growth encompassing time as well as space – as if they were seeing all the trees that had ever been alive since the beginning of the world. It was – like the journey itself – unending. He changed his mind. He gave up.

The two carriages continued to roll forward. The hoofbeats sounded on the track. The wheels kept turning. Eventually the others began to feel that something was wrong.

'We're never going to get there,' Nancy stated. 'This is it.' Ed told her not to be silly: of course they were going to get there, in the end; it was just taking a long time. And if she started to complain, it was going to seem even longer.

'I think she's right,' Alan said. There was no other outcome he could imagine. They were going to keep traveling, forever. 'You'd be kidding yourself to think anything else.'

'Don't say that,' Beth told him. 'We'll get there pretty soon now. We've got to.' She was too frightened to allow for doubt. There could no longer be any question. She'd come to believe, like her friend, Ella, that all events were a matter of faith. And anyway, she'd decided that this holiday was going to make up for everything else. She'd been looking forward to it too long to let herself be disappointed.

She kept on believing. She never lost hope that if they continued to move ahead, somehow – all at once – they would reach the light. It would come upon them like a revelation of truth, a burst of sunlight. It would be amazing, overwhelming and out of this world – like the coming of spring, or like the sudden appearance of fire in the dream she and Alan had had, a long time ago, when they thought that they were dying in a plane crash.

Sis and Bud

Alma and Bruce were adopted. Their adoptive parents, Elton and Bess, had done the right thing and had told them the history of their adoption when they'd turned fourteen: Bruce first, and Alma the next year. Fourteen was the age the agencies had designated for the long, understanding talk that was to be administered with tact and kindness and which had to include at some point the phrase, 'You know we love you, because we chose you.' Fourteen might not have been the right age for one or the other, or both of them, to learn the facts; nor was it to be supposed that one fourteen-year-old was like another, nor that a girl would have the same attitudes as a boy. But you had to start somewhere.

They each took it differently. Bruce was horrified, infuriated, offended and sickened. Alma was strangely pleased. She began to form the notion that perhaps her mother had been someone very important – maybe even a princess – who hadn't been able to marry her lover for reasons of state, or something like that.

To begin with, they both thought of the true parents as unreal and somehow theatrical or unusual. They didn't feel less warmly towards Bess and Elton: on the contrary, when they'd been told how much their new parents had wanted children, how they'd been disappointed over and over again and how finally they'd been granted the great joy of two such wonderful children, Bruce had been deeply moved. And Alma had cried and had said she couldn't imagine that her biological parents would ever have been so good to her, even if they were actually the real ones: and she was glad that she'd had the luck to be adopted.

But she began to daydream about the people she now thought

of as her real parents: the ones from whose bodies she came in a way that she didn't yet fully understand – the way that was secret, shocking, delicious, immoral, full of pleasures, terrifying and – so everyone kept saying, even though you weren't supposed to do it – natural.

The natural part of parenthood was simply physical. What Bess and Elton had contributed and what their years of patient care had created, was social and cultural. Alma loved them, of course. Yet there was that other element – the mysterious origins that had to do with bodily love and passion. She wondered about the two lost parents: their characters, how long they had known each other. She didn't doubt that they'd been in love. They must have had parents, too; there would be two whole families from whom she had come, not just the two main actors.

As Alma made up stories about this other family of hers, she became increasingly curious about them. Her own imagination supplied the information, as it had invented the questions. She herself was the source and purpose of the drama. In the early stages genuine knowledge would have upset her. She definitely didn't want to find out the truth. There were only two facts that she recognized; the first was that she was now on a different footing with Bess and Elton, so that they seemed more like friends than relatives. And the second was that Bruce was not her real brother, so that therefore there was no reason why they shouldn't get married some day. She'd always loved him. Now she fell in love with him in another way.

Bruce had had a year to think over the subject without her. When Bess and Elton had had the talk with him, they'd asked him not to tell Alma yet. And he didn't tell. He hadn't told her about Santa Claus, either. Unlike so many older brothers who grow up bullying their sisters and being jealous of them, he'd always tried to shield her. The difference in their size might have had something to do with the development of his protective instincts; she'd been a small, elflike child. Another factor in his response could have been Elton, who entertained a high, idealized opinion of womanhood, and had taken care to guide Bruce towards a desire for the same, rigorous certainty. Elton would have thought of it as one of the treasures of his son's upbringing.

During the year in which he had the time to think about his adoption, Bruce decided: his plan came all at once, not piece by piece. It seemed to him that he'd had a shock and that it had pushed him towards the need to force everything back to the way it had been. As far as he was concerned, his purest and most private feelings had been desecrated. And Elton, whom he'd always thought of as his real father, was not only unrelated but had obviously lied to him about women.

After he'd been told that first time, Bruce never raised the topic again. He thought that it might hurt his adoptive parents' feelings to see him express too much curiosity about the others – as if he hoped that the real ones might have been better or more interesting. He also knew what they'd say. If he asked Elton, 'What kind of a woman do you think my real mother was?' what could Elton tell him? That she was the kind of woman who went with a man when she wasn't married: who had had an illegitimate child; and that she was the kind of woman who gave her child away to other people.

Up to the age of fourteen Bruce's best subject in school had been history, which had filled his mind with pictures of romantic adventure. All at once he knew what history really was – not just the battles and buildings and heroes, but all the families and how they felt about each other, and how they carried with them distorted versions of each other's lives. He realized that there was private as well as public history. Only the great names lived in such a way that the two merged, but everyone participated somehow in the large, public sweep of historical event. Everyone was influenced, willing or not. He didn't want to be the passive victim of his own life. If you knew where you stood and what you were doing, he thought, you could direct events yourself. He intended to take action, and to run things.

As soon as Alma too had been told, he felt better. He regarded her as an ally in his struggle to come to terms with history. He didn't want to say anything to make her feel crushed, as he had been, but he couldn't understand her gullibility or her willingness to think well of the people who had reneged on their parenthood.

'We don't know,' she said. 'I guess they could be any kind of people at all.'

'She could have been some drunken whore off the waterfront.'

'Oh no, the adoption agencies are very careful about who they allow in.'

He laughed.

She said, 'I think if the mothers don't fulfill certain conditions, the babies have to go into an institution. We've been pretty lucky, haven't we?'

'The hell we have.'

'But you'll feel just as close to me, won't you? Even though we aren't really brother and sister now?'

'Who knows? How can you be sure we aren't related? We might be, you know. A man that's had one bastard could have thousands.'

'But not a woman.'

'No. They only need to have one. That makes them whores.'

'How can you say that? Especially nowadays. Nowadays that's all changed. Women can keep their children and bring them up. It used to be impossible. For everybody. Maybe she couldn't marry. Maybe he wasn't free. He could have been already married to somebody else, or he could have died before she knew she was going to have a baby.'

'Sure, maybe. Maybe there's icebergs in Africa.'

'And maybe she didn't want to get married – have you thought about that? Maybe she was one of those independent career women who just got caught.'

'Then she could have had an abortion, couldn't she?'

'That might have been against her religion. It's possible. Maybe the idea of an abortion was worse than going through with the birth.'

'No. If you're going to have the baby, you don't give it away.'

'Maybe she couldn't afford to keep it. It costs a lot to bring up a child. And if you don't have a job, or some man to support you – '

'Cut it out,' he said.

'Well, the way I look at it, I just feel they must have been all right.'

'Both of them? Him and her? She might have been some girl your age who was raped by her own father. Or by a whole gang of people.'

'Don't say those things. I don't want to think of her like that. And anyway, what about him?'

'Oh,' he said, 'that doesn't matter.'

Alma was already beginning to incorporate her new knowledge into her life. At Christmas she'd been taken to see a ballet about a transformed maiden, brought up by strangers, who had a sister-double who was her moral opposite. And although Alma was the one who was adopted, she had immediately identified the heroine as a character who must resemble her mother: an innocent beauty, preyed upon by evil influences, but in her heart shining and lovely, like a swan. 'We might as well think nice things about them,' she said, 'since we're never going to know.'

'We can find out.'

'No, we can't. The adoption people never give out information.'

'They don't give it out to the real mother. That's so she can't come back and try to squeeze money out of the new family or upset the child by pulling it both ways. But if you're the child, they let you find out about the mother as soon as you're of age. You've got a right to that information. In the state Bess and Elton went to, and according to the adoption place, the age is eighteen, not twenty-one.'

She didn't think that could be true. If it were possible to find out, it might even be possible to see the real parents. She said, 'Are you sure? Suppose a woman got married afterwards and never told her husband? They couldn't just give you her name and address. You could cause a lot of trouble for her.'

'I'm pretty sure they can. It may not be a law. Maybe it depends on the adoption agency. The one we came from allows it.'

'Did Mom and Dad tell you that?'

'They told me the name and address of the agency because I asked. And then I called up and asked what the policy was. They were a little cagey but they said that if they were satisfied it was a genuine desire to know, they'd tell you. So all we've got to do is wait.'

Alma thought about it. She tried to see herself going to an adoption agency to talk with someone there. What were those places like? Maybe they were like hospitals, or maybe it was a clinic with a kind of office attached: the mother could be at one end, giving birth, and, at the other side of the building, the adopting parents would be waiting anxiously, hoping that the baby they got would be all right.

If a child were born with something wrong with it, did they hand it back and ask for a refund? Alma imagined Elton and Bess sitting on chairs in a waiting room: Bess would be holding a brown paper bag, to take the baby away in.

She didn't want to think in any greater detail about the procedure. Obviously it was a business – that was the reason why some people did it. The mother would have her hospital bills paid. The agency would get something: a percentage. It was strange to think that she might have cost five hundred dollars, or a thousand, or whatever it was. But she didn't want to ask Bess. She could think about the farcical possibilities without further information and she'd dream about the more mysterious, dramatic and possibly tragic side: the love and character of her mother.

For a long time she never even wondered if her mother had gone on living after giving birth. As soon as the question came to her, she passed it on to Bruce. 'You don't think they're dead, do you?' she asked.

'Of course not,' he said. 'Why?'

'We might have been transferred to the adoption people because our mothers died in childbirth and there was nobody to bring us up.'

'I hadn't thought of that, but I don't reckon it's likely. That sounds to me like another case where the orphanage would take over. The kind of place Bess and Elton would go to would be pretty fussy about where they recruited their unmarried mothers from.'

'Not off the waterfront, after all? How can you be sure?'

'I suspect they got the name through some religious organization. Don't you think so? First, prevent them from getting hold of birth control and then sell the babies when somebody knocks them up. Wouldn't you say someone like Reverend Hodges would know quite a few convenient little addresses?'

'Not as many as the doctors.'

'More. Especially in this part of the country.'

'That's another thing: why did they go so far away?'

'Because that's where the adoption place was. And I guess they figured it was a good idea to go to a big city, where they wouldn't run the risk of adopting the child of somebody who could turn out to live right down the road. Both of those women might be there to this day. Or they might have moved away, anywhere: even out of the country.'

Alma started to tell herself another story: the search for the mother. She'd think about it in the daytime and occasionally even have a real dream. The mother was always found after long and painful effort and sometimes Alma would arrive too late, just after her mother had died.

*

Elton and Bess were quieter, more formal, more modest and also older than the parents of any of Alma's or Bruce's classmates. They had had to wait a long time until the adoption agency had found the first baby. Many times before that they'd been disappointed. Bruce was their idol until, so soon afterwards, Alma had arrived. They were glad to notice that the news of the adoption didn't seem to have bothered the children. Bruce had become more serious; but that was undoubtedly just because he was growing up. His schoolwork hadn't fallen back – that would have been a bad sign; on the contrary, it had improved. Alma too appeared as outgoing and alert as ever, although sometimes she looked unhappy. Bess had gone out of her way to say that if there was anything Alma wanted to know – anything at all about, say, being a woman – then she could always come and talk to her, or to Dr Brewster, of course.

'I couldn't talk to a man about anything like that,' Alma had said quickly.

'Well then, maybe you could see my doctor. You're too old to keep going to Dr Brewster now, anyhow.'

'Is your doctor a woman?'

'No dear, but he's a gynecologist, so it's all right.'

Alma said that she'd wait and see. She wouldn't go back to Brewster, who'd been the family pediatrician, and she didn't see why she had to go to anyone anyway, if there wasn't anything wrong with her. However, she finally agreed to accept the name and address of a woman doctor and to have a complete check-up before the beginning of the next school year.

The doctor's name was Morse; she was married to another doctor. They had three children, two secretaries, a nursemaid, a cook, and a cleaningwoman who came twice a week. One of the daughters was in a lower grade at Alma's school. Mrs Morse was intelligent, stylish, a first-rate diagnostician of physical symptoms, and someone you couldn't talk to. Alma said she was fine.

'I can see that,' the doctor said. 'I wish all my patients were so healthy.'

Alma smiled, put on her clothes and headed for the door. She didn't ask any of the questions she might have put to an older woman who was also a doctor, for instance: *If a woman gives up her child voluntarily, do you think she's really loved it? If she didn't love it, why did she carry it for nine months? If all that business is as natural as people say, is it natural to take a baby from its mother for any reason whatever? And is it right that a doctor should be helping to say that a childless couple is able to take care of a baby better than its own mother, just because they've got more money than she has? Do you think she could be pushed into giving it away and then change her mind, so she's been thinking about me, so that maybe she wants me to come look for her after all? Do you think she was bad, and that she got pregnant because she was just no good? Am I bad to want to sleep with Bruce: because we*

102

were brought up as brother and sister, even though we were never really related? And if we did, is it true what they say – does it hurt a lot, can it make you sick if you do it too much: what's it like?

Bruce already knew what it was like. He'd wanted to find out without becoming involved, so he'd asked a friend of a friend and he'd made an appointment at a motel with a call-girl. After the first few times, he'd come to an arrangement with her, to see her once every two weeks. It wasn't enough, but he couldn't afford anything more. He hated her, yet she didn't behave hatefully to him; she was ordinary. He couldn't believe how matter-of-fact she was – almost apathetic. It was as if it meant nothing to her, as they said murder meant nothing to psychopaths.

His real mother might have been just like that.

He had dreams about Alma. In his dreams they made love and it was wonderful. He also, once, dreamt about Bess. But he didn't want to have such dreams. His family was his family; it was important that they should stay the way they were. And it was even more vital that his feelings about them should be of a certain nature: filial or brotherly. If they changed, or if he himself did, the idea of the family itself could be altered.

When everybody at school started going steady, he knew that he'd have to have a date, too. He chose the class tramp from the year above him – a coy, lecherous girl with a gobbling laugh, abundant dyed hair and a weasel-like face. He used a contraceptive, as he always had, from the beginning. He said it was because he'd once had gonorrhea and there was a lot of it around. The real reason was that he wanted to be sure he never got a girl pregnant. She told him to take off the rubber because she'd had everything, so she was immune to all that stuff. Then he said that he really wore it because there was insanity in his family, but it skipped a generation: he was okay, but his kids were going to be crazy; it was sad, but true. She believed him until, apparently, she discussed the matter with somebody else. Then she said: Come on, his Pa was all right, wasn't he, and nobody ever heard of insanity like that anyway, that skipped. He blew up and said, 'Thanks for talking about me with all your friends.' And he told her that the reason why he wore a contraceptive was that at least twenty other guys had warned him: if you go down with her, it's like sticking your prick into the town sewer, so watch out. She screamed and hit him in the face. He picked her up and threw her out of the car so that she had to walk home in the dark. They weren't on speaking terms after that.

Alma started going out with boys, but she was shy with them. She didn't want anyone but Bruce. She developed a friendly, joking manner that discouraged romanticism and if that didn't work, she'd just say that she was old-fashioned and intended to save herself for marriage. She started to believe it, although she listened eagerly to what all the other girls she knew had to say about sex. She made up a story that satisfied them, too: she claimed that she'd had a dream about meeting a man four years after highschool and that he would be the one she married. She said that she'd know straight away, and she also knew that none of the boys at school was the right one.

One of her friends, named Penny, said, 'I don't see how you can be so sure. I mean, even if you find Mr Right like that and you get married in a silver cloud and all, why's it going to stop you having some fun now?'

'It wouldn't be fun if he isn't the right one,' Alma said.

'Sure it would.'

She didn't believe it. She was convinced that you had to be in love. She became moody and short-tempered. She cried a lot. She lost weight and decided that she was going to be a dancer. Bess and Elton agreed to pay for lessons.

*

Bruce took up the violin. He said that he wanted to develop some minor skill that he could use in later life to annoy the neighbors.

'That doesn't sound like a very good reason, dear,' Bess said.

'That's because it's a joke,' he told her patiently.

He'd saved enough to buy a fiddle that he'd seen in a pawnshop. Bess wanted to know what he'd been doing in a part of town where there were pawnshops. She didn't ask where he'd managed to get hold of the money. He always had money. In the winter he shoveled snow, in the summer he mowed lawns. He'd do deliveries, fix things that were broken, feed pets while their owners were away. He always had some job or other, often several. And he found himself a music teacher by looking through the yellow pages and phoning up one number after another: asking questions, until he'd decided which teachers he wanted to talk to. He settled on a man named Schneider.

He took a lesson twice a week. No one in the family ever met Mr Schneider but from the sound of Bruce's practicing at home, he seemed to be able to teach a lot of music in a short time. A long while later, Bruce told Alma that Mr Schneider was a musicology student, only a couple of years older than he was himself – still in his teens. It had amused him to see how everyone, without knowing anything about the man, believed that a music teacher should be ancient, white-haired and, probably, someone who spoke English with a thick accent.

* * *

After school Alma would ride all the way across town to do dance exercises in a small room over an art gallery. There was a bar and nightclub next door, a fact that bothered Elton and Bess. But Alma wasn't afraid. She immersed herself in her afternoon practice the way a novice would sink her personality into the formalities of religious training. When men spoke to her on the street or made more determined attempts to pick her up, she took no notice. They tried frequently; she'd turned into a good-looking girl. And the clothes she wore, the way she did her hair, made her seem older than she was.

What she couldn't discuss with her parents she could talk about directly with Bruce. She told him, 'You know how I feel. I never said it, but you're the one I want. I used to see you going out with that girl and I hated her so much. You could have gone out with me. You like me: I know that.'

'I love you, Alma,' he said.

'To marry? Or, we don't have to get married. We could just sleep together.'

'No.'

'Why not?'

'Because maybe you aren't my sister, but I feel like you are.'

'Isn't it ever going to change?'

'No,' he said.

'And you'd want me to marry somebody else?'

'Yes, of course. Eventually.'

'But I don't want anybody else. I want you.'

'You'll find somebody. Listen, if you just want a guy to screw around with, there's the whole world to choose from. But somebody to understand you and give you support in what you think, and be really close to you – that's different.'

'That's marriage,' Alma said.

'Are you kidding? Marriage is the in-laws and the Thanksgiving dinners and thank-you notes and bringing up the children.'

'But you start with love, and working together as a team.'

'I can work with men. I don't need that kind of thing. What I need is somebody to be my sister.'

'I could be both.'

Bruce said, emphatically, no: it wouldn't work to mix things like that. You had to be one or the other. It could ruin everything.

She thought he was right, but she wanted to be the one who wasn't the sister. It didn't occur to her that the whole question of being a sister or a lover, having a real parent and an adoptive parent, feeling love or desire or friendship, was one that could be with her all her life and to which there might not be an answer.

Her teacher, Merle Singer, told Bess that Alma was her best pupil, although she had started so late, and that if she wanted to, she could make her living as a dancer. Three of her pupils, including Alma, had what she considered the perfect physical proportions for a dancer. Some teachers, she knew, held the opinion that the shape of the body determined the nature of the dance, but she had seen too many exceptions – cases where the shape was not conventionally pleasing but the movement was good. Of all her promising students Alma alone stood out. The two who, according to the rulebook, should have equalled her were ungainly and without musicality. When Alma danced, her smallest gestures were charged with meaning and beauty. You couldn't explain something like that simply on the evidence of measurement and ratio. She had the talent. But – just as important – she had the good health, stamina, will-power and concentration to succeed in competition against other girls who might have had better training.

'If you want to go on,' Bess said to Alma, 'and really try for a career, we'll help you. It means a lot of money at this stage, so think carefully. Merle is sure you can do it, but she talked about the drawbacks too: it's a short working life. You wouldn't have the time or energy for anything else. It's easy to injure yourself – the professional ones sprain and break things all the time. And getting to the top and being famous means a whole series of lucky chances that just might not ever happen. So, you think hard about it.'

Bess was proud of Alma. Bruce had the brains; that was a good thing for a boy, but he could be cold, secretive and unforgiving. Neither she nor Elton knew all the time what he was up to. Alma shared herself. And she'd turned out to be beautiful-looking, Bess thought – just like some kind of foreign actress, but underneath it a really nice, down-to-earth girl. Other mothers had daughters who were drinking hard, who were going to bed with just anybody and were being arrested for dangerous driving and all kinds of wild behavior: they didn't care what they did. Elton said you had to blame the parents, but Bess wasn't so sure that that was all there was to it. Some went the wrong road, no matter what you did and some won through in spite of everything. She and Elton had been lucky. 'You know,' she said to Alma, 'we'll be happy with whatever you choose. It's only a matter of getting the timing right, so you don't spend years working at a thing you're never going to want to use.'

'All right,' Alma said. 'Give me a few days.'

She thought over what Bess had said. She liked dancing. She enjoyed the exercise and needed the expression of movement. But the glamor of the stage had never drawn her. Her place was on the other side of the footlights, following the story – that was what she had always loved. And that was something she could have for the rest of her life. If she felt no sense of dedication as a performer, it would certainly be better to stop now.

She told her parents and Merle that she intended to go on doing her exercises in private and maybe taking a class or two every once in a while, but that she was giving up the dance. She was thankful, she said, that she'd had the opportunity to train for long enough to find out that it wasn't the right thing; some girls, she knew, were thwarted by their parents, so that they had the idea forever afterwards that they might have been great artists if somebody hadn't prevented them. She realized that it wasn't the profession for her, even though she was good at it, because there were other things she wanted to do with her life. A girl who wasn't so good, but for whom dancing was the only interest, could give an audience more.

Everyone understood except Merle. Merle said that she did, but all the time she'd really hoped that Alma would continue; she'd seen her as a star, in the lead role, as the heroine. If she'd known about the family history, she might have fought for her belief and told Alma that the willingness to forsake her talent could well have its beginnings in her conviction that she was not the central character in anything but was, on the contrary, the daughter of a heroine. If you gave dancing lessons to a bunch of clumsy-footed, plain girls who all seemed oddly built and without inborn grace, timing or rhythm, the appearance of a natural champion in their midst was like the arrival of a comet. After one outburst Merle kept quiet, but she couldn't get over the waste of it.

As for Alma, she did what she'd told everyone, occasionally taking a class and continuing to practice on her own. Every two weeks or so she'd drop in on Merle to have a cup of tea or coffee and to chat. It was a while before she realized that it was her lost career that weighed on Merle's mind, and not perhaps the loss of revenue that might mean so much: Merle had two teenage boys and a divorced husband who was always ducking out of the alimony. By the time Alma understood that another person – of an age to be her mother – had had great expectations of her, she was too far away from her decision to feel guilty about causing the disappointment.

Twice a year, around Christmas and just before summer, she went with Merle on a weekend expedition to the big city, where they saw the Saturday matinée and evening performances of a ballet. For the whole day she'd live in a world of princesses and sorcerors, enchanted maidens, magical animals and demons.

She began to think of Bruce's predicament in terms of the stories she'd seen on stage. He too was living under a spell and was unalterably persuaded of the necessity of breaking it. There was a willingness to disbelieve, Alma thought, that could be just as potent a force as the need for faith. Bruce had that. He thought that when he found the real parents, when they were confronted with the outcome of their actions – with the sight of him – they'd disappear. It would be as if they had never been. He would then be like a god: someone who had been brought into the world without the aid of parents. He was willing to waste himself and the whole of his life on his obsession, just as she would waste herself on him.

*

Bruce kept a diary. He'd started it at the age of ten, beginning with descriptions of what had happened during the day, of the food he'd eaten, the clothes people were wearing and the state of the weather. Seasonal phenomena were also noted: ice storms, trees in flower, leaves turning color. That stage didn't last long. He skipped days, then he began to use the diary for ideas that had occurred to him, stories he'd been told, interesting facts he'd read; and, in the end almost exclusively, for his dreams.

When he was fourteen, he wrote in the diary:

If people are really in trouble, even atheists, they call on God. They all know what that means. They say to themselves, 'Oh God, get me out of this. Oh God, help me – save me.' The idea of God comes from deep inside them. It may be caused by their fear, or it may be a wished-for aspect of themselves that would be capable of controlling the hopeless situation as their parents once ordered the world for them. But everyone recognizes what's meant by the idea.

It must have something to do with the catastrophic side of life, which there's no way of avoiding. You have to give it a name.

*

Once the number of her dance classes had been cut down, Alma spent more time with Bess. She asked to learn how to cook, to sew and to knit sweaters. Unlike most schools in larger towns, hers had never had a domestic science course. It was taken for granted that girls would be taught all those accomplishments at home and that boys wouldn't need to know them. The only sewing Alma had ever done was repairwork on her ballet shoes and mending her tights. She'd always bought anything that Bess couldn't supply. Bess, who took pride in her own domestic skills, hadn't wanted to interrupt Alma's life with home chores. She'd thought that Alma could pick up those things when she got married.

For a while the dinner table saw new dishes half-crumbled or partly burned, cakes that looked like sponges and pies that had suffered a cave-in. But Alma was quick to learn. She liked to cook. Soon she was pushing the family to experiment with more exotic foods and flavors. She also enjoyed the evenings when she and Bess sat sewing or knitting and Elton read the papers. Elton could read a paper straight through a conversation, although every once in a while he'd put it down to listen or join in.

Alma used to ask questions about Bess's early life, about the grandparents and other relatives she'd never met because they'd died while she was still too young to remember anything. Bess had a fund of ghost stories too, which Alma loved to hear her tell again and again. Elton knew only two frightening stories, both supposed to be true: one about a man who was struck by lightning, and the other about a howling dog that gave the clue to who had murdered its owner. Elton was impressed by true stories, or rather, the stories he read in the papers. Sometimes he'd laugh, and announce in the middle of talk, 'It says here . . .' and usually he'd end up by asking, 'Would you believe it?' or 'How about that!'

*

Bruce was the class heart-throb at school. He went out with everybody. The phone never stopped ringing for him. 'In my day,' Bess said, 'we didn't chase boys. They don't like it.'

'They love it,' Alma told her. 'They love having a fan club and playing the field. So do girls.'

'Well, you don't.'

'Nope. And just about everyone in my grade thinks there's something wrong with me.'

'Nonsense. You're a nice, old-fashioned girl.'

'They call it frigid.'

'I never heard of such a thing. It wouldn't hurt some of them to get a little frigid for a change. You'll see – you'll be glad when the right man comes along and you didn't throw yourself away.'

Bess didn't bother to give Bruce advice; neither did Elton. They both suspected the sort of thing he might be doing, and knew that he could handle whatever trouble he got into. He was like a grown man, although he was so young. He was ambitious too, in school and out. He'd learned a lot from working with Elton in the hardware store, then he helped out at the garage they went to. He fixed people's cars, radios, TVs, clotheswashers – anything. He'd bought an old car from a junkyard and made it practically like new. He was successful in everything. Even the teachers admired him. But his classmates weren't close to him. If he sometimes led them to believe that they were, his friendliness was merely diplomatic. Nor did his girlfriends touch him at all deeply. He didn't give himself away emotionally. He didn't reveal his true mind. He stood aside.

Elton and Bess often felt shy about talking to him. They used to get Alma to ask him questions they wanted answered or to tell him things 'for his own good'. He'd take anything from Alma.

Alma was now his lieutenant and his right hand, almost his other self. As soon as he'd started to go out with so many girls, she knew that he wasn't going to be interested in any particular one for long. When his dates called up, she'd answer the phone and pretend to be sympathetic. Even the ones who knew that she and Bruce were adopted assumed her to have nothing but a sisterly interest in him. As for him, he'd said to her that all his dating was unimportant. It was like having an itch and scratching it: it made no impression on his feelings or his thought, or anything that made him a person.

She told him that she was glad to hear that, because she didn't see why she shouldn't start going out seriously herself. 'It's different for a girl,' he said quickly. 'I wouldn't want you to get hurt.'

'You wouldn't want me to have fun, even though you don't want me yourself.'

'That isn't true,' he said.

'You're never going to want me, are you? It's worse than being in love with a man who doesn't like women. In your case, there's no reason.'

'I don't think I'm capable of loving too much anyway. It isn't in my temperament. Honestly. I don't understand what people mean by it. And what I think maybe they've got in mind – that strikes me as being totally uninteresting and false.'

'How do you mean?'

'Oh, the usual gooey hearts and flowers stuff.'

'When you were little, you loved all that kind of thing. You were a very tender-hearted little boy.'

'Was I? Well, things have changed. What I want, Alma, is for you to be on my side.'

'Aren't I always?'

'You know what we said: about finding our parents.'

'Oh.'

'Tracking them down.'

'I still think – '

'You promised,' he reminded her.

She said yes, she'd promised. And she repeated the promise: she'd help him. As soon as they were old enough, he'd said, they'd go to the adoption clinic and find out about their parents. He'd get there first, naturally, and she'd go the next year. They'd swear to help each other find the missing parents – that is, the mothers. The fathers, in Bruce's opinion, didn't seem to carry so much blame, even supposing that the women knew who the fathers were.

They'd had a long conversation on the subject about eighteen months before, after she'd refused to see or speak to Bobby Paling. Bruce was the one to answer the phone then. Once Alma had substituted her two surrogate mothers, Bess and Merle, for the friendship of girls her own age, she'd become isolated from part of school life. Her attitude towards boys had further estranged her from schoolfriends, so for a while – just to have someone as an excuse – she'd gone out with two of the class duds. They'd turned out to be even more desperate for sex than the attractive ones. Her standard defense to suggestive maneuverings had always been the reply, 'Why should I?' Bobby Paling's answer to that was, 'Because I want to.' He was nervous, skinny and tripped over his own feet, but his approach to the opposite sex was fearless. Outside school his main interests were building model ships and trying to find someone else who had Victorian lead soldiers from the regiments he was missing. After Alma had said that she never wanted to see him again, the girl at the desk to the left of hers told her that, according to the other boys, he also had a huge collection of pornographic magazines.

Bruce thought the episode was funny. He'd lean back in the front-hall chair and murmur into the phone that his sister had happened to mention that very morning how Bobby reminded her of the rear end of a baboon.

'I thought you'd given that up,' she said.

'Why?'

'I don't know. I thought you'd sort of cooled down. Are you really going to try to find out?'

'You bet I am. Aren't you?'

'I don't think so. Why do you want to?'

'To hunt them down and pay them back.'

'What for?'

'For ruining my life.'

'But they haven't done anything to your life.'

'That's right,' he said. 'That's just the kind of thing I mean.'

'I don't understand it. If someone had done you a wrong, or betrayed you – '

'What greater wrong could there be? What betrayal could be worse?'

'It might have been worse for them than for you. Especially now. You've got a full life without them. But they'll always be wondering about you. At least – maybe not your father. But she would: I'm thinking about your mother.'

'So am I.'

'And I don't think you ought to allow yourself to become so wild about other people and their quarrels. If I were in one of those lawcases people are always pulling on each other, I'd just pay up and get out, no matter how much in the right I was. Otherwise they dominate your thoughts and emotions for years.'

'So, if somebody attacked you in the street, you'd just drop it, would you?'

'I didn't mean that kind of thing. I meant grievances, arguments.'

'Same principle.'

'Why do you want to throw away your life on something that's past? It isn't even your past. It's theirs.'

'It's mine. And it's mine because of them.'

'It's – '

'It's no use talking about it.'

'– like picking a scab.'

'That's right. I can't help it.'

She couldn't talk to him about it. She didn't even understand what he meant, though she was glad that he was willing to confide in her. She'd help him, she said, if that was what he wanted. But for herself – she didn't really think she'd want to know the truth. If she did ever meet her real parents, it would be so much too late for all of them; that was probably why the adoption societies insisted that you had to be legally of age before you could get hold of any information: after a certain point, you were just no longer a child. You'd be more willing to understand. You'd be able to think about things objectively. At least, that would be the general idea. Alma didn't believe that Bruce was going to change his mind. The plan of somehow getting back at his parents had taken root. It wasn't going to vanish. It would grow. You could hear a special tone and emphasis in his voice when he talked about it. He thought of it as a quest.

Once he was talking about it to her and he started to sound so

114

vicious that she said, 'It makes me feel bad to hear you talk like that. It's tearing you up. Maybe you should go see somebody about it.'

'Who?'

'I don't know. A doctor, maybe.'

'Why should I go to a doctor? What's wrong was wrong with them, not me. Did it help you to go to that doctor?'

'I didn't get so wound up about everything.'

'Sure, you did. You only show it in a different way. I'm just fine. Don't come up with any more dumb suggestions like that.'

'I don't like to see you getting upset, that's all. I can listen, but I don't know how to help.'

'You help by listening. That's the whole deal. Don't worry about me.'

'Sometimes I think you want to kill them.'

'Listen,' he said. 'I'm supposed to be writing a history essay at the moment. You know what they tell you – great history is great interpretation. There's no other way to examine it. You can plot it all so intricately, and then there are these sudden upheavals that there's no reason for. You can't even see them coming. You can only start tracing it back and then say to yourself: Well, that was a sign. But that would be the kind of clue you'd get from talking to someone who's insane. It wouldn't help to predict what he's going to do next. It doesn't point out where any future burst of power is going to come from. That's the secret. I can really understand why politicians go crazy for power. It's the urge to be able to change history, to guide it or redirect it. Imagine if you could do that. You'd change the world. If you could get people to follow your ideas, you could reshape the world in your own image. Couldn't you?'

Alma said, 'What would the world be to me, if it was only myself? The world is other people, Bud. It's the outside. It isn't home.'

'Sometimes I just don't feel that I belong here.'

'Of course you do. We all love you.'

'I mean, I don't feel that I belong anywhere. That I belong anywhere on this earth.'

115

'If you're alive, you belong here. Everybody does.'

*

He was the hero of the school playing fields and the star of every class play. He was a good actor, both for serious and comic parts. He also had a fine singing voice. In his junior year he was running the school paper. In the summer he worked hard at different jobs, mainly on construction sites, where he earned a lot of money. Parents who might not have liked his fast reputation with girls approved of his diligence and initiative. When he suggested to Alma that she should come on a tour of hospitals with him to demonstrate dance steps to the patients while he played the violin, the community was astounded by his sense of civic responsibility. No one in town had ever thought of such a scheme. He said that he got the idea from reading about nineteenth-century mental asylums that held regular concerts for their inmates; the music, he'd read, soothed and delighted the audience. Just recently he'd also heard somewhere that hospitals in Scandinavia maintained the practice. The school principal and the board became enthusiastic about his idea. They took the entire school band on a charity tour of hospitals. Meanwhile, once a week, on his own, he played the fiddle while Alma danced and Merle explained the steps to their audiences. In Bruce's last year a boy named Richard was added to their group; he wasn't an especially good dance partner but he was strong enough not to drop Alma and he didn't mind the idea of playing to a roomful of confused, crippled, dying or possibly insane onlookers.

Alma loved the hospital sessions because of Bruce. She knew how the idea had come to him and why: because he recognized the irrationality of his obsession and perhaps feared that there was something in his own inheritance akin to the conditions suffered by many of his listeners. He treated the patients as if they were normal. He was absolutely relaxed with them. She wondered why he'd never thought of becoming a doctor. Bruce laughed at the idea. He didn't want to help anyone, he said: he wanted to have their attention, that was all.

He won a scholarship to the college he'd set his sights on. He told Alma, and no one else, that he'd gambled with a large part of his savings and had won, making so much money that he could travel all over the world, if he had to. That meant that if his real mother turned out to live in China or India or Australia, he'd still be able to get at her.

*

Last night I had a dream that I was sitting at my desk, reading one of my history books: one that I'd never seen before. It was full of colored illustrations, like the books we used to have when we were children. I was turning the pages and looking at scenes from ancient Egypt, from classical Greece and Imperial Rome. And as I looked at them, each page became like a kind of box, inside which a scene of history was being acted out. They were like little theaters that you could look into and, as you watched the plays going on inside, you could listen to them too. While I was turning the pages, the scenes became more and more fascinating and beautiful and real, until suddenly I was in one of them myself.

I was in a medieval castle, where there was eating and drinking and some music playing from the gallery. People were helping me to put on a chain-mail shirt and metal shinguards. Then I was in a courtyard with the other knights. We got on our horses and rode off to battle. The ride was terrific – fast and breathless, and we went thundering through a forest of gold trees. I thought that I'd entered a fairytale, but the man next to me pointed ahead at a large, dark mountain in the distance. As we neared it, I could see that it was coming at us with a speed greater than ours. The man said, 'It's The Tide of History.' As soon as we got close to it, it reared up and went over us like a wave. It was thick and smothering – a horrible kind of mud. But you could cut it with your sword. So we kept hacking all around us, kicking wedges of the stuff away from us. But it was also pulling us down into itself. It was trying to grab hold of me. I got scared. And then I saw that it wasn't mud. It was blood. It was the blood of all the people who had ever been killed and of all the ones who weren't born yet. It was uncontrollable. I wanted to get away from it, but I couldn't. And I woke up, staring into the darkness.

* * *

The adoption agency was housed in a one-story building of municipal brick. It looked as if it could have been a bank, a firestation or even a chapel. He thought it was fitting that everything about the place should appear anonymous.

He'd written ahead and he'd dressed for the part: neat, respectable, mature. He was good at interviews: they gave him a chance to display his acting talents. And he wasn't going to make any mistakes. He'd told himself that if the bastards saw he had a hair out of place, they'd probably refuse him the information, or just lie and say that they didn't have it.

The woman who interviewed him was in her early fifties and not good-looking, although she too had taken care with her appearance, mainly with her hair, which looked almost sculpted. She had his file on the desk in front of her. It crossed his mind that if she really said no, he could knock her out, grab the file and just run. Why not? This was going to be his only chance to get his hands on the records. No court would convict him because a jury would understand a man's need to know the truth about his past. And an adoption agency would be very careful about getting into a tangle with the law, maybe hitting the headlines.

The woman's name was Mrs Whitlow. A sign on her desk said so, as did a plastic card pinned to the cardigan she'd draped over her frilly blouse. 'Well, Bruce,' she said, 'why do you want to find out about your natural parents?'

'Just because of that,' he told her. 'Because no matter what, they are my parents by nature. I guess you could say I feel that things have got to be settled. My parents have been great. If I'd never known, it wouldn't have made any difference to me. But when they did tell me, I knew then that I'd always want to know more about the others.'

'Yes,' she said, 'I see.'

He could tell that he'd made a good impression. She put her hand on the file and turned the cover. His breathing speeded up a little.

'There isn't too much we can tell you,' she said, and stopped. He gritted his teeth and waited. She seemed to be reading. He

118

concentrated on keeping his voice right, and asked, 'Were they married?'

'No.' She looked up. 'I'm afraid we have no information at all about the father.'

'Well,' he said gently, 'anything you can tell me.'

'The mother's name was Joanna Elizabeth Henderson. She was sixteen.'

Despite all the possibilities he'd gone over in his mind so many times, he'd expected to hear that she'd been in her thirties, or possibly late twenties: a woman – someone who could take care of herself and who knew what she was doing. Not a young girl.

Mrs Whitlow continued, 'Fifteen, when her parents first came to us, in 1962. It seems that there was an unsuitable alliance, with a married man. Yes. We talked to the girl. She was hostile but not hysterical. She agreed that adoption was the best course. She knew that without the help of her parents, she'd be in the hands of the courts. Underage, no means of support . . .'

He felt sick for a moment as he wondered if the interview could have taken place in that very room, where the low ceiling added to the sense of claustrophobia. It was certainly possible that other rooms down the corridor held pregnant girls and worried parents, who didn't want to become grandparents. He would have liked to know if anyone in the family had expressed regret about giving the baby away. It wasn't a question for asking eighteen years later.

Mrs Whitlow said, 'That's all I can tell you.'

'If you don't mind, I'd like to know quite a few practical details. Medical history, that kind of thing. Have I inherited anything that I should know about?'

'Everything was perfectly normal, so far as we could tell.'

'On my father's side, too?'

'That we don't know, but we did receive an assurance from the family doctor that there was nothing out of the ordinary in his history.'

'His family doctor? Or hers?'

'It's the same name on both reports.'

'They had the same doctor?'

'So it appears.'

'Then they must have had a record of the name.'

'Yes.' She flipped to a section in the file, looked through a few sheets of paper and turned back the cover again. 'There's nothing here. It does seem strange, but not completely unheard of. There may have been reasons. I just don't know. We have the name of the doctor, but not of the patient. And no medical record, only a statement that the examination showed nothing unusual.'

'Right. Well, in that case, if that's all, I wonder if you could let me have the address she was living at when she came to see you.'

'You're going to try to make contact?'

He smiled one of his dozen best smiles, saying, 'Oh, I don't think so. I told you: my parents are enough. But I really do have the feeling that I'd like to find out about the others. I guess it's because my field is history.'

'Oh,' she said. And after a moment she simply took the file and turned it around so that he could see, and copy out, everything.

He wrote down all the names and addresses: town, parents, daughter, doctor, and so on. His handwriting seemed to him jerky and strange-looking. Mrs Whitlow sorted through some papers of her own while he was busy. When he'd finished, he stood up. He thanked her and said that she'd been a big help. His face and voice were composed as he left the room, went down the hallways and came out of the building.

He walked straight to his car, as if he had somewhere to go. All his movements retained a look of purposeful coordination.

He drove the car around a couple of corners, just to put some distance between himself and the adoption agency. He parked under a tree.

He sat behind the wheel and sweated. He started to shake. He didn't understand what was happening to him. The whole of his face was suddenly wet. He put his hands up to cover his eyes. He couldn't stop.

It lasted for about three minutes. There was a point where he was afraid that he wasn't going to be able to get himself out of it.

He tried to think. He tried to tell himself to relax. It couldn't be. It ought not to be possible: that he, who was always perfectly in control of himself, should fall apart.

When it was over, he felt exhausted. He wished that Alma were with him, right at that moment, sitting on the seat next to him. They could begin the search now. He had all the information he'd needed.

He thought: Maybe Joanna Elizabeth hadn't known the man was married. She could have been taken for a ride. Maybe. There hadn't been anything about religion in the files. That had surprised him. If a fifteen-year-old, middle-class girl went ahead and had a child, you'd think that there would be some religion in the background, especially since the girl hadn't intended to keep the baby. On the other hand, he'd known quite a lot of fifteen-year-old girls himself and not all of them were angels. Some of them had been doing it since they were twelve. Some charged money for it. It was certainly a possibility that she'd gone after this married man and tried to blackmail him, or had done it to spite her parents, or something like that. The man had had the same doctor: that would make it a lot more likely that all these people were known to each other, and that she'd be aware of the fact that he was married. And he wouldn't necessarily have to be her parents' age, either. He could have been under thirty. Still – it shouldn't have happened: for her to have a child and then ditch it.

He started to tap his hand against the steering wheel. 'No,' he muttered. His hand beat down more violently on the wheel, again and again. He wasn't aware of it, nor of his voice repeating the word 'no', until he hit the horn by mistake.

Stop, he told himself. *This is idiotic. Facts first; then start to think about it. Never theorize ahead of the data: that's the rule for historians. It should be the rule for everyone.*

He started the car. The sky was still clear, the trees in leaf, the houses evenly spaced along the road. Nothing was out of place. Given a little luck, anyone ought to be able to find his way in such a well-regulated world.

*

He took Alma out for a meal at her favorite Italian restaurant. They sat in a booth away from the other diners. He purposely didn't order any cocktails or wine. He wanted to keep calm and get everything in the right order.

'It was simple,' he told her. He described Mrs Whitlow. He repeated what he'd discovered. 'Now,' he said, 'we just find out if anybody's living at that address – if they died, if they moved, if they changed their names, and so on. Twenty years ago it wouldn't be so easy. Now everybody's on a computer somewhere.'

'They didn't say anything about your father? No name or anything?'

'No. I don't know why I expected it. Bastards don't usually know the name of their father.'

'Don't keep calling it that.'

'Why not? It's the truth. Anyway, I'm having second thoughts about the married-man story. Maybe she didn't know who it was. Maybe she was just one of nature's whores.'

'Bruce, whatever she was, she was your mother.'

'Uh-huh.'

'She could also have been a girl whose parents disapproved so much, they sort of forgot to tell her about birth control. You know what I mean? There are a lot of them left, even now. And in those days, you couldn't get anything legally, unless you were a man. A doctor would report you to your parents, otherwise he'd get into trouble. It was against the law.'

'Sounds a little far-fetched to me.'

'I don't like it that you've got this feeling of hatred against her.'

'Joanna.'

'You had it before you even went to the agency. It isn't good to think like that, Bruce.'

'You're just nicer than I am. What I feel is that there are some people who always get away with it – always. And they shouldn't be allowed to.'

'Do you really think a woman who's had an illegitimate child has gotten away with anything?'

'She could have stayed with us. With me.'

'Oh, Bud. Way back then? Even nowadays – at the age of fifteen, with her parents about to throw her out of the house?'

'Well, if she couldn't, then she should have had an abortion.'

'I guess in those days they weren't so easy to get. And it would have cost a lot of money. And maybe it would have been too dangerous.'

'I think she was just a bitch, that's all.'

Alma reached across the table and grabbed his hand. 'Stop,' she hissed at him. 'Stop it, right now.'

He laughed. 'Right. It isn't that important.'

'And it was over a long time ago.'

'I'm still going to find out, though. Aren't you?'

'Maybe. I don't know.'

'Well, do what I did: just go there and see what they can tell you. You don't have to do anything about it. You could even think about it for ten years before you follow it up.'

'Is that what you're going to do?'

'I'm starting now. I wouldn't want to leave it and then find out they'd died just the week before I rang the front doorbell.'

'If we'd never been adopted,' Alma said, 'I'd never have met you.'

'Probably not.'

'We could do other things besides look for our parents. We could travel around the world together. We could get married.'

'I told you: I'm not getting married.'

'I bet you will.'

'And I can't start making plans about anything else till I get this out of the way.'

'So, you wouldn't mind if I got married to somebody else?'

'Who?'

'How do I know? I could meet somebody at any minute.'

'Oh. Well, when you're ready to settle down, I guess that'll be up to you. But you promised to help me if I need you to go in and get information for me.'

'Yes,' she said. 'Sure.'

*

In the ballets, Alma thought, it was always the woman at the center of the drama. She was lifted high, carried into the light, put where you could see her displaying herself like a preening bird. But life was the reverse. In love, in marriage, she was supposed to be in the background, coming second. She was waiting by the stove or standing at the front door, tapping her foot and thinking: *Where are you? If you were going to be late, you could have called.* She was the one who loved and he was the one who didn't care. Why wasn't Bruce ever going to love her?

What brought her almost to despair was the thought that if she didn't care so much, he might begin to consider her interesting or romantic: if she were unaffected by him, if she felt nothing. But she'd never be able to pretend that. Her feeling for him was always boiling up in her to the point where it blocked out other people. It spoiled everything. All the wonderful things she had – the good luck, the loving parents, the nice life – weren't enough. The only thing she'd ever wanted was never going to be hers.

And her mother? Her mother had taken one step further. In her case it hadn't been just that the one wanted prize was withheld. No. The one unwanted calamity had come upon her and she'd had to accept it. Even though the evidence had been disposed of.

But perhaps her mother hadn't thought of it like that. Who could tell?

*

He didn't need her at all in the beginning. He only wanted her to listen to him as he reported back the things he'd found out: The Hendersons, his grandparents, were still in the same house. He could go and take a look at them any time, if he wanted to. The daughter, Joanna, had run off to Maryland when she was eighteen and married a man called Raymond Baxter, who was ten years older than she was.

'Well, maybe they're happily married somewhere,' Alma said.

'Maybe she's been divorced and remarried six times by now.'

'And they could have children of their own.'

'What?'

How could his mother have had other children, when she'd thrown away the first one? She'd have no right to do such a thing. He didn't think she'd have the right to be happily married, either. 'Well, we'll see,' he said.

He went away to college. He studied hard. He got top grades. Alma too applied herself to her schoolwork. She didn't see the sense of working at anything, but she knew that if she didn't push herself, she'd give up completely. Every day, from the beginning to the end, she missed Bruce. Time passed without enjoyment for her, so that when she looked back at the year, long stretches of it seemed never to have been.

*

Alma memorized her lines for the school play, *The Importance of Being Earnest*. She had the part of Gwendolen, the sophisticate. The part of Cecily, the sweet, unspoiled girl, had been given to the class flirt, who played it surprisingly well.

After rehearsals she'd rush back home to see how Bess was. Bess had started to have fainting spells; her doctor, Dr Mason, said that they were caused by blood pressure. He'd given her some pills, but she still got tired out and would feel faint. At last Dr Mason referred her to another man, a doctor named Boyd. Elton told Alma that Dr Boyd was a specialist in heart diseases, and that in fact there had been a lot of heart trouble in Bess's family; she'd never mentioned it: she didn't see why she should upset the children. 'But modern medicine,' Elton said: 'They can work wonders. They've even got these little pacemaker gadgets.'

'Oh, my God,' Alma said, 'is it that bad?'

'No, honey. Don't fly off the handle. I'm just telling you: if. You know what heart conditions are like. People can last up into their nineties so long as they take good care of theirselves.'

Or they can go at any minute, Alma thought. She telephoned Bruce. 'I don't want to worry you,' she told him. 'I just wanted to hear your voice, that's all. Dad says I'm getting too worked up about it. Anyway, she's not feeling so good. And that's why.'

Bruce said that he'd be back in two weeks for a visit. He called up the next day to say hello. When Alma came home from school she found Bess pleased and cheerful.

'He'll be here next week,' Bess said.

'That means next month.'

'Well, at least he's keeping in touch.'

'It's the thought that counts,' Alma said.

'That's right.'

'But actions speak louder than words.'

'Alma, you're teasing.'

'I think he could come home a little more often than he does. He can afford it.'

'It makes a big difference in the house. Even when he was so busy with something, and he'd just march right upstairs without saying a word: at least he was here. He said if he couldn't make it, he'd be home for your birthday, definitely.'

*

Bess was well enough to attend the school play. She applauded vigorously. 'Wasn't it just the best thing?' she kept telling everyone: 'Wasn't it fun? You couldn't see anything better on a professional stage.' Elton's enthusiasm almost surpassed hers. He'd loved everything: the story, the laughs, the other players and the costumes. He kept saying how pretty Alma had looked in her dress. He thought that they ought to let her keep it.

Bruce was busy and didn't come. He sent a telegram instead. Alma felt that he'd let her down. He never missed something he really wanted to see.

All the time everyone had been praising and petting her, she'd been looking at the door or listening for the telephone; hoping for him.

After that, she didn't believe that he'd turn up for her birthday.

*

The night before her birthday, she had a dream. In the dream she went to visit Bruce in the hospital. She entered a room where he was sitting up in bed, reading. A long tube like a garden hose came out of his chest and plugged in to a machine that stood by the bed. 'Is it your heart?' she asked him. And he said, 'That's right. The machine replaces what the heart used to do. I'm going to have to be on it for the rest of my life.' She said, 'Aren't I going to see you any more?' 'Of course,' he told her. 'You can come visit me any time you like.'

126

*

Bruce came home, bringing presents for everyone. They had a party for Alma and the day afterward he drove her up to the city for a weekend of shows and celebration.

They went to a play, a musical, two movies; to the zoo and the park. And to the adoption agency. She didn't realize where they were headed until he parked down the street and told her which building it was. He'd made the appointment for her, so everything was fixed. 'If you don't take the trouble to find out now,' he said, 'you never will – I know you. You'll just sit around all your life, wondering about what your mother was like and what she's doing now.' He reached across her and opened the door. He pushed her until she got out. Then he leaned forward and slammed the door behind her. She moved away, not really knowing where she was going. All she could think of was that he shouldn't have sprung it on her like that. He should have given her warning. Now that they were there, she supposed that she'd better go in.

All the way down the sidewalk and up the path to the building, she was nervous. But as soon as she stepped through the doorway, she thought: *He's right. I don't have to do anything with the information but at least I'll have it, just to know. And they can't refuse it to me, because it's my right.*

She saw a different woman from the one Bruce had described. This one was named Roberts; she was plump-faced and sandy-haired and had a businesslike manner. She asked why Alma wanted to find her parents. Alma said she wasn't certain that she did.

'When I was younger,' she explained, 'I was sure I never even wanted to know about them. But I've changed. Now I'm curious. I'd also like to know medical things; every doctor I go to comes up with these questions like: Did my mother have heavy periods? and that kind of thing. The family history. And I do sometimes have the feeling that I'd like to know what my mother looked like. If you've got a photograph? And to have her name and maybe address – then, if I ever did want to meet her, I could

127

write to her first. Or maybe I'd never do anything. But I'd have the choice.'

There was no photograph, and again, as in Bruce's case, no information about the father, except that he'd been young. The pregnancy had been the outcome of a highschool romance. Both sets of parents had apparently discussed the matter and everyone had agreed that the two young people weren't old enough to take on the responsibilities of marriage and children; they were still underage and supported by their families.

'How sad,' Alma said. 'For all of them.'

'It's a story we hear a lot,' Mrs Roberts said, 'even now. Sometimes it's like taking a dare, to show their parents they're grown up. And then they get in too deep and find out it's really too much for them to handle.' She passed a piece of paper across the desk.

Alma took the paper and started to read. Her mother's name was Rose Ellen Parker. The last address the adoption society had was that of her family's house in Connecticut. The medical facts appeared to be straightforward and the birth had been without complications. Everything had been completely usual.

'Except,' Mrs Roberts said, looking down at her papers, 'that afterwards . . . but that's normal, too. There's a certain amount of time you have to allow. For adjustment.'

'Whose adjustment?' Alma said.

'Well, everybody's, actually. The new parents, too.'

'But whose did you mean just now?'

'There's a note here about subsequent interviews with the girl, Rose. She was unhappy with the situation.'

'She wanted me back?'

'I wouldn't read too much into it. A reaction one month later is one thing. Ten years later might be different. She might feel relieved that she'd done the right thing. You see, it isn't easy for anyone involved. We just try to do the best with what we're handed. Our first concern has to be the welfare of the child.'

'Yes,' Alma said. She was glad, all over again, that she'd been brought up in a complete family, with a mother and father and brother, instead of being raised as the illegitimate burden of a single teenager and her disappointed parents.

She folded the paper, put it in her purse and shook hands with Mrs Roberts.

For the short time it took her to walk down the corridor, she continued to feel that something had been settled. But as soon as she stepped out into the sunlight, it seemed to her that nothing had changed.

She walked to the car and got in. 'Well,' she said to Bruce, 'that's that.'

'I'm going to buy you a drink,' he told her. 'I sure as hell needed one afterwards.'

They had the drink, and then a second one, and he took her on to another place, where they ate lunch. Alma told him what she'd found out. He asked if they'd given her the name of her father, too.

'The name, but nothing else. James Ridler, Rickman – something like that. I've got it here.'

'If they were in the same school, it should be easy to trace them both.'

'Would they tell me if she'd kept on trying to get me back? I mean, for years?'

'I doubt it.'

'They should have some organization for adopted people to talk about things with each other. I can't imagine what it would be like on your own.'

'I'm sure they do. Why not? They've got everything else. Just give me the names and addresses and I'll do the rest.'

'What?'

'I'll find out where she is.'

'Have you found yours?'

'Yes. A couple of weeks ago.'

'And?'

'I wasted a lot of time at the start, beginning at the beginning. Her parents are still alive somewhere up in New England. So's the doctor in the case, who was married to her mother's sister. Her father was a different kind of doctor; a bacteriologist. I think it's safe to assume that the parents hired their in-law to hush up the name or the facts, or both. Unless I'm the outcome of one of those dismal family passions you hear about. But I don't think so.'

'You could go see them and find out.'

'I could. But there's no point. I can find out from her. I know where she is. That was the hard part. Joanna Elizabeth. She and her husband started a second-hand car firm, then a garage and a taxi service, then a car showroom. They've branched out into horseracing, stud farms, who knows what else. He's a crook.'

'You can't know that. Second-hand cars aren't always a cheat. And horses – '

'He was in jail.'

'Are you sure?'

'It's on the records.'

'What was it for?'

'Rape. Mummy knows some real nice folks.'

'Maybe it wasn't really – '

'Oh, maybe. Anyway, like I said, she got married to this guy a couple of years later.'

'If he didn't tell her about his past – '

'They've got two daughters: Amanda and Diane.'

'What beautiful names.'

'Very snotsy. Somebody's making up for something they didn't have.'

'I don't see how you get that out of it.'

'What's wrong with Mary or Jane?'

'Maybe they're names that were in the family, like ours. How old are the little girls?'

'Seventeen and sixteen.'

'That's impossible.'

'I was a little surprised about that, too.'

'They're so close to our age. And they're your sisters, Bruce. Your real sisters.'

'As real as real can be. You think your mother's married? Or still single? What do you want to bet? Bet you ten bucks she's got a family.'

'It feels really peculiar to imagine it. I'd always thought about her on her own.'

'Five bucks?'

'Okay. You know, she was just about my age – a few months older. I can't get over it.'

'Didn't you expect that, after I'd been to them?'

'It seems to me,' Alma said, 'I keep expecting the wrong things, so I'm always caught off balance.'

*

After Bruce left, Alma made plans. On the next Saturday she took a bus in to the city, where she bought a pair of shoes with part of her birthday money. Then she went to the library, looked at some books in the dance section for a while and, after that, she walked upstairs. In the alcove off the hall between the coffeeshop and the cafeteria, she found the telephones. She looked through the phone books. Just as Bruce had said, there were societies and clubs for adopted children. In fact, there were several. When she called the number listed under *Hotline Trouble*, the woman who answered took a while to come up with any information. Alma could hear her turning pages, minute after minute, until finally the voice came back with four phone numbers, saying, 'Sorry it's taken so long. We mostly get calls about drugs or suicide or, uh, that kind of thing.'

Alma looked over her shoulder. The corridor leading to the coffeeshop was empty, so was the hallway outside the cafeteria. She dialed the first number on the list. Her request was not the usual one there, either; most people undoubtedly got in touch with such societies in order to talk about their feelings towards both sets of parents – the real and (as Bruce sometimes put it) the unreal.

'Hello,' a woman's voice said.

'Oh, hi,' Alma answered. 'Is this Adop – '

'Yeah. What can I do for you?'

'Well, I just wondered. If I tried to find my real mother, do you think . . .'

'Yes?'

'Do you think it might upset her?'

'I don't know.'

Some advice line you are, Alma thought. *I don't know.*

'Nobody can know that,' the woman said. 'So don't worry about it. Ask yourself how important it is to you, not to her. Okay?'

'Okay. Thanks,' Alma said. She hung up quickly, before anyone could ask her if she wanted to join the society. She felt altogether less confident than before she'd made the call.

During the trip home, she changed her mind. She started to think that the woman on the other end of the line had been right: it was up to her.

*

Bruce sent her a letter that told her everything he'd been able to discover about her mother. After the adoption, Rose E. Parker had gone to Chicago, where she had trained to be a librarian. She'd also taken some courses at a teachers' college. For eighteen months she'd lived with an aunt, then she'd found a job teaching in a small country school in Iowa. She'd stayed there for two years, had taken another job in Washington State, and had met her husband: a man named Thomas Shelton, who was an accountant. After the wedding they'd moved to California and had started to buy a house. They had two children, Jerome and Tobias, aged ten and eight. At the moment, Rose had gone back to teaching. Her husband, Thomas, was working for a large accountancy firm.

Jerome? Alma thought. *And Tobias?* They sounded like the names of old men with beards. She wondered if either Rose or Thomas had joined some kind of religious sect.

She sent Bruce a check for five dollars. And she started to think about all of them – Rose, Thomas, Jerome and Tobias – so frequently that it was like being haunted by the present and the future, rather than by the past.

She began to invent scenes in which she met them. She forced her fantasies to go all different ways: sometimes she'd encounter hostility; once, the mother threw herself at her and demanded that Alma should compensate her for everything else that had gone wrong in her life. In most of her daydreams Alma would

132

remain in hiding. She'd see her mother waiting for a bus or shopping at a supermarket. She'd go up and stand next to her. And that would be enough.

A month before graduation, she talked to Bess about her other family and about the visit to the adoption agency earlier in the year. She didn't mention Bruce's part in the business. If he meant for Bess to know anything, he could tell her himself. Alma never wanted him to feel that she had been disloyal to him over even the smallest thing. He suffered too much already from his obsession about betrayal.

'It's something I've got to settle,' she said. 'I don't need to talk to her, or to know what she's like or what she thinks, or anything. I just have this sort of craving to see what she looks like. Do you understand?'

'Of course,' Bess said. 'It's only natural.'

'I didn't say anything before, because I didn't know how to put it. You know I'm glad you're both my parents, don't you?'

Bess laughed. She said, 'You do just whatever you want to about it, Alma. The only thing I'd ever worry about is if one of you got hurt.'

'Me and this other woman?'

'You or Bruce. You're my family.'

'I thought I'd better tell you now, because that's why I'll be going all the way to California. That's where they live.'

'Oh,' Bess said. 'That's a long way. That's a long way, with both of you gone.'

* * *

After his June exams Bruce asked the college authorities to let him take the next year off, and to be readmitted as a sophomore on his return. He described the need for such a long break as 'family affairs'. They allowed him the time because he was one of their best students.

He moved to Kentucky. In the summer he started work on a newspaper. He also hired himself out as a gardener.

He saw them. He saw him first – the husband: Raymond. That

133

was a week after he'd flimflammed his way into the newspaper office.

He was supposed to be covering a local fair, for which he had a photographer named Wilbur Spinks in tow. Wilbur wanted to get some shots of horses. And since Bruce was always asking, 'Who's that?' or, 'Tell me about such-and-such,' Wilbur told him, unasked, 'Those two over there are Harold Judd and Ray Baxter. Harold's president of the downtown bank.'

'I recognize him,' Bruce said.

'And Ray's a real good man to know if you ever want a car. He's got a lot of businesses: stables, electrical supplies. He just bought the old Tropic Club last year – The Tropic Night. It used to be a kind of nightclub. Big business back in prohibition days. Now it's all wired up for disco stuff.'

Bruce took a long look at the husband. Baxter was standing with his jacket slung over one shoulder and his shirtsleeves rolled up. He wore a pair of lightly tinted glasses against the sun. His hair was black and gray, his body thickset but not fat. He had the appearance of a man who took good care of himself, but he also seemed like someone who hadn't been born with the expensive jacket and sunglasses and the generally easy air of comfort. He looked tough. You wouldn't want to get into a fight with a man like that.

The wife came later: Joanna Elizabeth. Bruce was writing out a deposit slip at the bank. He heard one of the cashiers say, 'Mrs Baxter.' He looked up, seeing her distinctly in three-quarter profile and hearing her voice, although not clearly enough to distinguish the words.

She was as glamorous as a moviestar or a television actress: honey-blonde, slim, in a pale knitted suit and strappy, high-heeled shoes. Her face was hard, pretty and bored. She had her sunglasses in one hand, gesticulating with them. The stones in her rings flashed as she moved her hand. She looked young and sexy, and as if she intended to give that impression. The shoulder-length hair had been artificially streaked, her make-up applied in order to attract. The lines of her figure were easily followed through the material of the clothes she wore. You'd never have thought she had two grown daughters. He looked and looked, as if caught in a ball of fire, consumed by the power of his own eyesight. He would have known she was the one, even if he hadn't heard someone speak her name. *Not two*, he thought: *three. She's had three children.*

*

Alma took two training courses over the summer: teaching and librarianship. While she was studying, she met a man named Ernest Allgood. She told him that she'd just been in a play called *The Importance of Being Earnest*. He said: Yes, he had the perfect name for a villain.

He was in his early thirties, divorced, and had a daughter. The wife had remarried. They'd separated within three years. He told Alma that he still liked his wife; she was a nice girl. The trouble was that they'd both been too young for marriage.

Alma was lonely. She missed Bruce all the time. Now that school was over, she felt as if she'd parted from her parents too, even though she still lived with them. Ernest was easy-going and jovial. She didn't want to lose his company, but there was no way of explaining to him that she just needed a friend. He wanted to sleep with her.

He kept her laughing and made her feel comfortable, and one evening got a couple of drinks into her and took her to his place. She kept saying, 'Don't get me pregnant,' and he kept repeating, 'Don't worry. I'm not going to get you pregnant.' She thought afterwards that she'd probably known – before going home with him – how the evening would turn out, otherwise she'd have told him that she didn't want to see him any more.

She went back to Dr Morse and asked all about birth control. This time she could talk. She even thought of asking how many women, who got pregnant, wanted to. But it was no use asking a thing like that. In any case, she now believed the answer to be unconnected to medical fact: it was a matter of opinion. All people had their opinions. And sometimes they had other people's on loan, either temporarily or because that was the only way they could acquire any of their own. There were lots of things you couldn't find out by asking other people.

Ernest said to her, 'I never knew a girl who was so scared of getting pregnant.'

'It's what happened to my mother.'

'It's what happens to all mothers.'

'I mean my real mother. That's why I'm adopted.'

'Oh.'

'I never understood how it could have happened if she hadn't wanted it. But now I do. Because I did the same thing. I left it up to the man. When you said everything was all right, I believed you.'

'It's true. It's all right.'

'It better be.'

'What would you do if it wasn't?'

'I'd rather be dead.'

'You don't mean that.'

She did mean it. She said so.

'Don't you want children?' he asked.

'Sure, but not yet.' She had discovered that it was possible to live with someone, without love, as long as you were decent to each other. You could still have a good life. But to have the child of a man you didn't love: that would be different. She wondered if that had been her inheritance – if her mother had carried her so unwillingly that every drop of blood going to the womb had helped to produce a creature that would look for ways to make itself miserable.

For the moment, and as long as she didn't get stuck in her thoughts about love and family, everything was all right. She was happy with Ernest. At the end of the summer he asked her to marry him. She said no. He told her that he'd been a fool to take her to bed so soon: if he'd waited, he'd have been able to win her over.

'I could have had you for life,' he said, 'instead of just this summer. You aren't really going way out to California, are you?'

They sat in his kitchen: he talked and she drank coffee. He kept reaching over to take her hand. She couldn't understand how it was that she should feel so queasy about breaking off with a man she didn't love as much as she ought to. If she'd loved him better, she wouldn't be feeling so bad. But, of course, if she'd loved him, she wouldn't be going away. He wanted to know if he'd see her again. She said she hoped so. He told her that he should have gotten her pregnant after all. Even if he had, she thought, it wouldn't have done any good. She was still in love with Bruce.

She left for California at the weekend.

*

She'd spent hours writing letters. *Dear Mrs Shelton. Dear Mother. Dear Rose Ellen. Maybe you don't want to hear from me but . . . I hope you don't mind if I ask you a few questions about yourself, just . . . My name is Alma. My mother's name was Rose Ellen Parker. Do you think we could meet sometime, just to say hello?*

She hadn't been able to finish any of them. She'd asked herself how she'd feel if a letter came to her out of the blue, eighteen years after the event that still must be one of the most dramatic, even if perhaps not the worst, in her life.

Her mother might feel hunted and distressed. She might suspect blackmail, or that Alma was out to pay her back for making her illegitimate. She might hate Alma. Mrs Roberts had said that Rose Ellen went through a bad time after the birth. *Maybe she'd want to hurt me*, Alma thought. *Maybe she'd think I really put her through it. Maybe she'd tried to get an abortion and couldn't.* The fact that Rose had later had two more children – and so, presumably, had been happy to become a mother again – might not contradict what had gone before. People always had room for all the emotions and they could change their minds at any time.

She didn't believe that she had the right to disturb the life her mother had made for herself. She decided not to say anything – just to get to know her for a little, and then move on.

*

Bruce met the two daughters at a dance. He danced with the older one first. She was called Mandy. The younger one was Didi. He didn't feel for a single minute that there was anything sweet or sisterly about them. They were stuck-up, brainless egoists with rich-kid affectations. He hated them.

He talked Mandy into going out with him later that same night, and Didi the week after. He could have laughed at how easy it was. They practically threw themselves at him.

*

Alma saw her mother, Rose, standing with two boys at the door of the school library. She knew that that was who the woman was. The younger child was looking up and holding out his hand while he talked – as if he might, babylike, tug at her clothing to hold her attention. The mother looked down and spoke. Alma saw with a pang that the woman had some gray hair. Surely she was still too young to start going gray. But perhaps it ran in the family. Maybe she too would go gray early. She felt shy in the presence of the two boys. It amazed her to think that they were her brothers. She wanted to back away.

Rose laughed at something the older boy said, and looked up. She caught sight of Alma. She said, 'Hi. Are you here about the Beatrix Potter?'

'I'm here about the job,' Alma said. She moved forward. She held out her hand. They introduced themselves. Rose told her the names of the children, Jerry and Toby, who said, 'Hi,' and ran off. She led the way back into the library. Alma couldn't think of anything except how strange it was that she should be taller than either of her mothers.

A few days later she met the husband, Tom. He walked over to pick up the boys from school. He was working at home that day, their house was only a few blocks away. As he approached, Jerry and Toby were asking Alma to show them how she could do the splits; she'd made a tremendous impression on them by kicking high into the air so that her foot was above her head.

'I'm Tom Shelton,' he said. 'I guess you're Alma, is that right?'

They stood talking while the boys collected their sneakers and notebooks. Toby had to go back into his classroom to find a box of crayons he'd left behind.

Tom was light-eyed and freckled and had a wiry build. His manner was friendly. He couldn't stand still for long but bounced up and down on his toes or shifted his weight from one

138

foot to the other. He looked younger than his wife. Rose had told Alma that he was at a good stage in his work. When things piled up, he got tense: his stomach would begin to bother him and he'd lose weight.

'They're nice boys,' Alma told him.

'Oh, they're great,' he said. 'But Rose always wanted a daughter.'

Was it possible that Rose had never said anything? No. She'd have had to tell her husband. It would be too big a risk if the truth ever came out. And besides, Alma thought, if a man didn't love you enough to want to know that kind of thing about you, there wouldn't be much point in getting married to him, especially after you'd been let down once already.

Rose talked a lot about her family. She didn't chatter – sometimes she wouldn't say anything for a long time. And then she'd tell you something about herself, as if she'd known you for years. *She likes me*, Alma thought.

One day while they were reshelving the nature and biology sections of the library, a floorboard creaked on the upper level, where the gallery was. Rose looked up. She ran her eye around the curve of the balustrade on the second story.

Alma said, 'What is it?'

'It's the ghost. It always makes me nervous.'

'What ghost?'

'I was in here one day, all alone, and I couldn't stand it. I don't believe in those things at all, but I had to leave.'

'What ghost?' Alma said again.

The building they were in, Rose told her, had at one time been a large private house. Late in the last century, at about the turn of the century, the house had been bought by a man from San Francisco, who was newly married to a beautiful young wife. He and the wife had come up from town to move in. They were still on their honeymoon. As soon as they arrived, she started to unpack. She opened one of his suitcases that had a loaded pistol in it and the pistol went off and killed her instantly. Three people connected with the school had seen her ghost, standing up on the balcony in a long, dark dress.

'Do you think it was really an accident?' Alma asked.

'Oh, I'm sure it was. They'd just been married. They were happy. It was a terrible thing.'

'It seems funny to pack a loaded pistol like that.'

'Everybody carried guns in those days. It wouldn't have been so unusual. And they'd always be loaded, in case you needed to use them.'

'When she appears, is she unhappy?'

'No. She's just there. She's drawn to the house.'

'You really believe it?'

'I don't know. I only know I wasn't able to stay here when I heard the boards starting to make noises. It went all the way around, like somebody walking.'

'My mother used to tell me ghost stories,' Alma said.

'But this one is true.'

'They're all supposed to be true.'

'Do you come from a big family?'

'Just the two of us, me and my brother.' Alma went back to the books. She added quickly, 'We're both adopted.' There was a long pause. She kept her head turned away.

Rose asked, 'Do you ever think about your real mother?'

Alma began to feel suffocated. She felt as if she were dying. She said, 'Yes, a lot.'

'Do you hate her?'

'Of course not.' She looked up, but Rose had moved; she was staring down at a book in her hand and her voice sounded muffled. 'I just knew somebody once,' she said, 'who told me that that was how a lot of adopted children felt. They hated the real ones for letting them go. So, they never wanted to meet them.'

'My brother feels that way. Full of hatred. But he's a man. He isn't ever going to get pregnant and not know what to do.'

'But I guess it would be hard to forgive.'

'Not for me.'

She's going to tell me now, Alma thought. But Rose didn't say anything more: she sighed. She gave her attention to the books. All the science sections, she said, were in a mess.

At the end of the day Alma went back to her room and lay down on the bed. She shut her eyes. The moment had been there and she'd missed it. She thought: *I was the one who should have said something. Why didn't I tell her? I ought to have. But I couldn't. I ought to now. But I can't. That was the time. And I let it go.*

*

Bruce had the two girls exactly where he wanted them. They were frustrated and baffled. They'd been used to calling the tune. By the time they realized that he was going out with both of them, and each suspected that he might be sleeping with the other, he was entirely in control of the situation. He denied his complicity, while seeming to enjoy the flattery of accusation. He said, 'Oh, she's exaggerating. She's making it up. She's jealous. I take her out sometimes because she's your sister. I feel sorry for her. She's sort of got an obsession. She says it feels better to talk about it.'

It was like being in a school play again, but doing half a dozen parts at the same time. He had to keep remembering what he'd said to which one.

He was introduced to the parents. Ray made an effort to engage him in conversation about newspaper space and advertising. Joanna looked him up and down and smiled slyly. She flirted with him, though not so openly that her husband could see it. Bruce couldn't make up his mind about whether she'd be an unfaithful wife. He guessed that maybe she would, if she thought she could get away with it, but she might be afraid of her husband. It was possible that Ray too was the type to have somebody else on the side, but if so, it wouldn't be serious; you could see that he was crazy about Joanna. And he was full of plans and schemes and deals that kept him busy. He'd probably never had much time to spare for the daughters; he was proud of the way they both looked, but Bruce didn't think he'd have any idea that they weren't pure as lilies and actually hadn't been that way for a couple of years.

Bruce gave Joanna a sympathetic look as she complained about the state of the garden. He said that if she didn't know what to

do about the laurel bushes at the end of the path by the trees
he'd take a look at them: he wasn't an expert, but he'd picked up
quite a lot of information while he was working on people's
lawns.

'Oh, we have a man for all that,' she said dismissively.

'Well, tell him they're dying, then. It isn't just the weather
The boxwood bushes don't look too hot, either, and they're
American box, aren't they?'

Her eyebrows rose. She looked utterly disdainful. He didn't
know how he'd offended her, but he had. He'd also made her
interested in him, he could tell. So, the other part didn't matter

He smiled pleasantly and said, 'Just a suggestion. It's your
garden.'

*

After closing time Alma went back to the library to look for
letter that she thought she'd left there. She searched all around
the places where she'd been doing the reshelving downstairs
then she walked up to the gallery.

The late afternoon sun threw a pattern of bars down from the
upper railings to the stairs she was climbing. Her footsteps
echoed in the empty building. She thought how strange sound
was: a voice or a step could be soft, yet the effect of it was to touch
everything. Even a breath could be heard, if you were listening
for it, from one end of a building to the other.

The stairs creaked. When she reached the top, she crossed to
the point farthest away from the front door downstairs. From
where she stood, she could see the two staircases leading down
on either side and, beyond them, the opposite wall like the other
half of an egg: built in a curve similar to the one she stood
against. All the wall was lined with book-filled shelves, but in
front of her and on the right-hand side, windows let the sun in
Motes moved soundlessly along the trails of light. Now that
everything had been closed and locked for the night, the
atmosphere was becoming slightly stuffy.

She found it hard to imagine what would have been there
century before. Perhaps there had been a ballroom with

balcony. It seemed unlikely that a private gentleman would have made provision for such an extensive library.

She turned to the wall, where she'd been standing earlier in the day. There were the three stray books she'd meant to check and, under them, the letter from Merle. She pulled the letter out from underneath. As she did so, the floorboards at the far end of the gallery began to squeal. She turned around, the letter in her hand. She stared across at the windows.

There was nothing. But the wood continued to make intermittent, small noises. She put the letter into her pocket and waited. She was about to head for the stairs when the sounds changed from single, isolated noises to a pattern. Clusters of tapping came from the floorboards at the opposite end of the oval; they moved in bunches, like spurts of rain.

Arnie Lodz, who taught science to the seventh graders, had a theory about the library and its ghost. Long before he'd been told what he might expect to see, he'd come across an apparition. Naturally, he wasn't discounting the possibility that indirect influence had prepared him. First of all, he'd heard a regular step that sounded like someone walking in high-heeled boots or shoes. At the same time there had been a rustling and swishing sound as of a long skirt in motion. His explanation of the phenomenon cited temperature, displacement of weight, the drop and warp of timbers. He also suspected the proportions of the solid parts of the structure compared with the spaces in between. Everyone who had ever lived in an old house, he said, knew about the noises you could hear at night from the expansion or contraction of the wood.

Arnie had taken measurements in the gallery, had removed samples of wood and plaster, had noted the temperature at different times of the day and night. He'd studied the moisture level and he'd rigged up an apparatus for detecting any airwaves that might be expelled from the walls or floorboards as changes took place within them. In addition to all that, he'd left a sensitive recorder in the building overnight. But none of his researches bore fruit. He'd never figured out where the manifestation – whatever it was – had its source, nor along what lines it proceeded. And he'd never encountered the ghost again. 'If it weren't for the fact that I'd actually seen the thing myself,' he'd told Alma, 'I'd say the origin of it is that people know it's supposed to be there.'

Her eye traveled from the windows to the floor and back to the extreme end of the gallery. She waited.

The sounds began again. As before, they started next to the far windows, along the floor: the stepping, the whispering rustle and the patter of little creaks. But this time they seemed to be coordinated, so that as she listened, the uneven bursts fell into a forward-winding scheme almost like something that might issue from a slow, uncertain worker at a typewriter, but more akin to lines of music being tapped out with slight variations at every repeat.

She was about to walk forward to investigate, when it was as if she'd been anticipated: the repetitive snapping and creaking moved from the end of the gallery and began to follow the curve of the bannisters along the right side of the oval. As they approached the place where she stood, they grew louder and faster, hammering. She turned her head to the right. She tried to trace the drumming course of the noise along the railing, but her eye was caught by something above – a movement in the air.

It was in a hurry, coming at her fast, but she couldn't understand what it was; it seemed to be a large smear or a wave or a knot of movement, or as if something had gone wrong with her eyes.

Her mouth opened, her hands gripped the edge of the shelf to her right. The noises came straight up to her, almost to her feet and, as they stopped, the wavelike bundle of smudges unraveled and rolled away into nothing. It was as if the air were coming apart.

The light in the library appeared to settle itself at a lower pitch. Everything looked normal. Whatever it was, had gone. And as soon as she realized that it was over, she knew that what had happened was so strange that it was impossible.

God, she thought, *what was it?* It wasn't a person, so it couldn't have been a ghost. It was like seeing an eclipse, if you didn't know what one was; if you didn't realize that it was natural, you'd be frightened.

But perhaps there wasn't any explanation.

* * *

Alma was in the middle of taking the sixth graders through the scrubland behind the science lab, when a senior named Muriel started to shout her name from the paintshop steps. The girls and boys had their notebooks out to write down descriptions of insects and plants; a boy called Roger had even brought a magnifying glass with him, although he and his friends were using it to look into each other's noses and ears; before being warned, they'd tried to light a fire with it.

Alma appointed a bossy girl to look after things. She hurried to Muriel, who said that there was a phone call from her father. She ran.

Elton told her that Bess had had a heart attack and had been taken to the hospital: she'd had another, minor one when she arrived there. He wanted Alma to come home. He also wanted to know if she had Bruce's telephone number, because it didn't seem to be anywhere in the house. She told him that she was coming straight away and that she'd call Bruce for him.

She found Rose, who began to organize the taxi, the packing and the money, so that there would be no need for Alma to waste time by going back to her room.

She telephoned Bruce. He answered, but she didn't recognize his voice. 'I'd like to speak to Mr Manson,' she said. That was the name he'd chosen for his locked mailbox.

'How did you get this number?' he asked. He hadn't recognized her, either. He sounded furious.

'Bud,' she said, 'it's Sissy. It's an emergency.' She told him about Bess and Elton. She said that he'd be able to get home before she could, even if she caught a flight.

'I can't,' he told her.

'You've got to.'

'I just can't, Alma. You go, and hold the fort for me.'

145

'She may die.'

'If she does, there's nothing I can do about it by being there.'

'She's had two heart attacks.'

'I've got to go now,' he said. 'Call me when you get there. Goodbye.' He hung up.

She telephoned the airport. There were cancellations because of fog; what flights there were had been delayed. She wouldn' be able to fly direct in any case: all the seats were booked. She' have to take a bus and try to catch a plane farther along the line At least she'd be on her way, heading east.

Rose put her into a cab and told her not to worry: the library would be all right, the school would hold her salary. 'We'll b thinking of you,' she said.

The moment Alma was on the bus, she took a pill to calm herself down. It didn't work; it didn't even get rid of th headache she had, but after an hour she fell asleep. She dream that she had a quarrel with Bruce. He was sitting next to her in the bus, telling her that she had to make excuses for him because that was her job. She started to cry with hopelessness and vexation. She told him it was bad enough that he didn't love her but to force her to lie to somebody he ought to love, was worse He said, 'You've got to,' and she answered, 'I can't.' Then he tol her, as if in punishment, 'I've got to go now,' and he disap peared. At that moment the bus swung sideways, crashed and turned over. The windows changed into partly emptied spaces o white granules, like cracked sheets of ice. People screamed and coughed. A thick, dark smoke began to fill the tangled interior pouring past her and out of the lacy, fragmented windows Someone tried to climb over her. She hit and kicked, struggling to get ahead, until at last she pulled herself through and fell on t the road. She still had her coat and shoulderbag clutched in on hand.

She ran along the road. All she could think of was that she ha to get to the hospital and now she was late. It was like thos dreams where you thought you were either going to mis something important, or else you wouldn't be able to sto

146

something terrible from happening: you were afraid, all the time, that you wouldn't get there soon enough.

The roadway was in confusion; cars were stopping and traffic was building up. She saw a police car and ran to it. The driver honked the horn at her. He almost drove into her. Both men inside screwed down their windows and started to shout at her, to get out of the way. She yelled back at them, saying that she had to get to the airport because her mother was in the hospital. 'You're blocking the road,' the driver told her. She said that if they didn't get her to the airport, she was never, never going to buy another ticket to the policemen's ball and, besides, she'd taken down the number on their license plate. The one in the passenger seat said, 'I guess you'd better get in, otherwise Murphy here won't have anybody to dance with this year.' He opened the door. She got in. The driver said, 'Christ Jesus, Frank.' His friend told him, 'Have a heart.' He explained to her that they had to stay at the scene of the accident, but they'd call another car for her and it would take her to the airport.

She waited. Then she was in the car; and right after that, at the airport. She stood at the counter. Once again, people tried to get in her way. Some of them kept asking her if she was all right. She told everybody about having to get to the hospital. Finally they let her have the boarding pass. The next thing was a scene where she was standing in front of a mirror. Her blouse was ripped and covered in blood and her face was streaked with dirt. Near the hairline, on a level with her ear, she had a small cut that had bled copiously. A woman in a uniform put a bandage over the cut and cleaned the rest of her face. Alma kept jerking away. 'I have to get to my mother,' she said. She looked into the mirror, where she saw herself getting into the bus that was driving out to the plane. Bruce was still sitting next to her. 'Look,' he said. Right in front of them a plane turned sideways and hit the wing of another plane. *Not again*, she thought. The bus swerved and braked. The driver backed up. He drove out on to the grass and stopped. Alma could see ambulances going past. Bruce said again, 'I have to go now.' She asked, 'Why?' 'They're coming to take me away,' he told her. When she looked, he was gone, just like the other time. She turned back and peered at the window. She was in the plane. The man next to her said, 'You're not very talkative.' She closed her eyes. The man said, 'Not very friendly, are you?'

*

When she landed, she telephoned the hospital. The nurse who answered went and got Elton for her. He said to hurry. She went to the head of the line at the cab rank and said she was sorry, but she had to get to the hospital to see her mother. She was crying. The people who were getting into the next taxi stood back to let her go first, but the ones behind them didn't like having to wait. They began to quarrel. Alma got in. As the driver started up, two of the quarrelling people called something after her.

Elton was waiting at the front doors of the hospital. He gave her a hug. At that moment she realized that she wasn't dreaming. She'd been awake ever since the bus had crashed: that was what had woken her up.

'This way,' he said. He led her to an elevator and afterwards out into a long corridor. A nurse came towards them. She took Alma by the arm.

They turned off to the left and straight into Bess's room. Alma went up to the side of the bed. She leaned down and touched her mother's face. Bess turned her head on the pillow; she opened her eyes. 'Hi, Alma, honey,' she said. She swallowed twice.

'I came as fast as I could.'

'It sure is nice to see you,' Bess said. Her voice wasn't much above a whisper. Alma touched her face again.

Bess sighed. 'Did Bruce come with you?' she asked.

'He'll be coming from Kentucky. I was still in California.'

'That's right. I forgot. I'm all mixed up.'

'Don't worry about it.'

A nurse came from behind one of the screens and murmured, 'Not too long.'

Alma said, 'I guess they want you to rest a little.'

'Where's Bruce?'

'He'll be here soon,' Elton said.

148

'I couldn't get hold of him,' Alma said. 'I'll try again, just as soon as I can get to a phone.'

Bess smiled groggily. *They've probably given her a lot of drugs,* Alma thought. *Because she's in such pain.*

'Maybe you could phone from here,' Elton said.

Alma asked the nurse if she could make a long-distance call. She told her parents, 'I'll be right back.'

Bruce must have been waiting by the phone because he answered before she expected it, saying, 'Yes?'

'Bruce, it's Alma.'

'Where are you?'

'Home. At the hospital.'

'How is she?'

'Not good. You've got to come.'

'I can't, Alma. I can't explain, but I can't come.'

'I came. My bus crashed on the highway and I had to climb over dead bodies to get out, but I did it. This is more important than whatever you're doing. Bruce, if you don't come home now, I'll never forgive you. I mean it. She's asking for you.'

He said again that he couldn't. He hung up. She'd forgive him: she'd have to.

She went back along the corridor. Bess had died while she was out of the room. Elton was sitting with his head down on the body, his arms out.

*

Another dream last night, that I was traveling. Then I arrived at a hotel somewhere in Europe where the people were French-speaking. It might have been Belgium, Switzerland or France. The hotel was a large, fine old place in a spa town. I signed my name in the register at the reception desk, but after I'd done it, the clerk behind the counter said, 'And now, will you sign your real name?' I said, 'What are you talking about?' And he turned the register around to me again, saying, 'We need your real name.' I looked at the name I'd written, and realized that it was an alias because I was an espionage agent, working on a case, and it was very important that I shouldn't give my right name. I said, 'I lost it at the train station when my wallet was stolen, but I should be able to let you have it in a couple of days.' The answer appeared to satisfy him.

149

After Alma came home from the hospital with Elton, she made
some sandwiches and the two of them watched the news on
television. There were pictures of the bus crash she'd been in and
the aircraft accident she'd only just missed.

'That was my bus,' she said.

'Which?'

'That one there.'

'Eight people died.'

'That's how I got the cut in front of my ear. And that plane
crash: I wasn't in it, but we were right near where it was. We
drove by it.' She tried to recall scenes from the past day but she
couldn't get them in sequence. She sat still, her eyes staring
ahead until the program was over.

'I think maybe you ought to get some rest,' Elton suggested.

'Just as soon as I make a couple of phone calls.'

She telephoned California. Tom answered. He sounded
pleased to hear her. He called Rose to the phone.

Rose said, 'We were so worried. There was that bus wreck,
nearly everybody dead, and then a crash at the airport, too. The
boys were going crazy. They kept saying that even if you'd
missed one, you might have been in the other one.'

Alma told her that she'd been in the bus; and that she'd seen
the accident at the airport. She was all right. But her mother had
died, so she was going to stay on for a while. She didn't know for
how long. It might be a week. Or longer.

She phoned Bruce one more time.

As soon as he picked up the phone, he asked, 'What
happened?'

When she told him that Bess was dead, he said he was sorry.
She gave him the date Elton had set for the funeral.

He said, 'I won't be coming.'

'You'd better.'

'How would that help her?'

'It would help us. It would specially help Daddy.'

'He'll be all right. He's got you there.'

'Why did you give me your number, if it wasn't for something like this? What could be worse than this?'

'Jesus, Alma, don't fold up on me now. I gave it to you so you could tell me what was going on.'

'Well, I'm telling you. Come on home.'

'No, I can't,' he said, and hung up again.

After that, she went to pieces. She cried for four minutes without stopping, and then collapsed on the front hall floor. Elton got Dr Mason over straight away; he told him about Bess's death, the bus crash, everything. Dr Mason said it was possible that Alma was suffering from delayed shock, but as far as he could tell at the moment, she was actually just asleep.

They carried her up to her room, took off her shoes and put a blanket over her. Elton asked the doctor to stay and have a drink. Dr Mason looked at his watch and said: Yes, sure, there was time for a beer. They sat and talked for twenty minutes or so.

*

I dreamt that I was getting married to Alma. We were standing in front of the preacher and he said, 'Do you, Bruce,' and so on. And I said, 'I don't have to. We're already married.' And then I remembered that we'd been married for about two years. Alma said, 'That's right. We're just doing it to get the piece of paper.' We went through the ceremony and, at the end, a man in an usher's uniform came out of a back room and handed Alma a piece of paper that was just that: a tiny, little torn scrap about an inch long. But she seemed very happy with it. She put it down the front of her dress to keep it safe.

*

Alma slept for fifteen hours. When she woke up, she remembered seeing blood and smoke, hearing children screaming. She saw the faces of the people she'd hit and kicked in order to get out of the bus first. In order to get to the mother who wasn't her true mother, she'd been willing to kill innocent people, who were in the same trouble she was in. And when she'd managed to fight her way home, she'd found out that her mother was only really interested in seeing Bruce.

But that was the way it had always been. She shouldn't be

151

disappointed or surprised any longer. She should accept things. She closed her eyes, but didn't sleep. She was busy thinking. She thought and thought, and couldn't remember what she was supposed to be thinking about. After a while she got up and went downstairs.

Elton met her at the foot of the stairs. He didn't want to talk about the future, or even about the past. He had a cousin who could come visit him; and Bess had a widowed sister-in-law. There were other cousins, too.

'I'll stay as long as you like,' she offered. 'It's only a job. I told them a week, just to let them know I'd be away.'

'A week is fine.'

'I don't have to go back to California at all.'

'I appreciate it, Alma. But I'd like to be alone for a while. To get things straight in my mind. Do some thinking.'

'Who's going to cook for you?'

'Oh, I can handle that. Maybe if you could do some of the packing up – clothes, and that kind of thing.'

'Of course.'

'It's hit me pretty hard,' he said.

*

I was in the hospital and Alma was with me. She was holding my hand. I'd just had one operation, but they were going to do a second one.

I said, 'I miss my fiddle. I'd like to hear somebody right now, playing "Hearts and Flowers" as I go down the drain.'

Alma said, 'You aren't going to get out of things so easy.'

I said, 'I'm dying.'

'Oh, I don't think so,' she told me. 'Modern medicine is pretty good. You've got plenty of years left.'

'Jesus, I hope not,' I said.

They wheeled me away, into the operating theater. Blood filled my lungs, my throat, my mouth. The doctor looked down at me and said, 'It's the tide of history.'

The nurse standing next to him asked, 'Is it twenty to, or twenty past? They go out with the tide, like ships. The moon causes it. It sets the cycle of blood in women. It controls conception, birth, madness and death. It's the heavenly body of lunatics. How can we hope to rule the world when the most important influences in our lives are faceless, nameless, hidden?'

The doctor said, *'There's no way to stop the bleeding.'*

I wanted to see Alma. *'Where is she?' I asked them. 'I want Alma.'* But nobody could hear me.

*

On the plane to California Alma wrote three letters. The first was to Merle. The second was to the state police, to thank the two officers who had helped her. She'd found their names, with the number of their patrol car, in the notebook she carried in her shoulderbag. She still had no memory of writing down anything during her journey to the hospital. In a p.s. she said that she'd been asleep when the bus accident had happened, and that she'd been in shock when she saw the plane crash at the airport, but if they wanted to ask her any questions about what she remembered, they could find her at the school where she worked.

The third letter was supposed to be for Bruce, but she couldn't finish the first sentence. After a while she came to the conclusion that it would be no use trying to say anything; she was too angry. She thought: *What was so important that you couldn't come to your own mother's funeral? What have you done to your father by staying away? And what have you done to yourself? There's no way you can get back that time and do it over. That was your time and you refused it.*

She slept. She ate part of the airline meal. When the lights were turned down, she got out her pad of paper again. She wrote to Bruce. She described to him the crash she'd been in. She said that it could have been some other kind of disaster – not a catastrophe that threatened physical danger and death, but an emotional calamity. It might not have had to harm her in any way, simply to make her think. *The way I feel*, she wrote, *is that I've survived and that it isn't worthwhile or right to hang on to petty things. I don't think you should nurse a sense of injury and vengeance against these other people. It can't be good for you to be tormenting yourself so. It's hurting you much more than you'll ever be able to hurt them. Let it go. Let people live their own lives and forget what you think they did to you. I won't say anything else about not coming home for the funeral, except that it's important for people to participate in death when it's a death in the*

153

family. Dad and I are very sad and grieving, but that's part of it. She's with us and she's gone. But what's happening in your heart? You know I love you. We all love you. Why don't you love anybody back? Couldn't you go home and stay with Dad for a while? And then come to California – or I can come to you. I feel like we could lose each other.

She mailed the letters as soon as she landed. Bruce answered quickly: he must have written the moment he got the letter. *Don't worry about losing me*, he told her. *Of course I love you back. I'll go see Dad when all this business is finished and then I'll come see you.* He'd crossed out a sentence that had begun *Maybe we can*, and another that had started out, *As soon as I'm free of*, and below that he'd just written the word 'love', and signed his name.

*

We can shape history to a certain extent. The course of it follows a pattern of the human mind – or, maybe it's just that we think it does because that's how we interpret events.

Even though some causes or ideals seem wrong to us, as far as history is concerned, the right one is the one that wins. Victory is only for a while, anyway. Everything could all come back: the Dark Ages, the wars for a hundred years. If you've got a chance of winning, isn't it better to fight for a hundred years, rather than go under?

*

Rose was careful not to ask Alma too many direct questions. She asked around the edges: was there someone to look after Alma's father, would she need to take a break to go home again fairly soon, could any of them do anything? No, Alma answered; everything was fine. The two boys, Jerry and Toby, broke the ice: they wanted to hear all about the bus crash. They wanted to see Alma's cut, which had almost healed. Their interest in the scope of the death and mutilations was intense and ghoulish. She was amused, but she told them something of what it had really been like. She didn't include too many details; despite his pleading for gory incident, Toby still had nightmares after seeing monster movies.

Alma thought that she was getting over it; that she was easing herself back into a routine again. But one afternoon in the library, when the two of them were alone at the desk, Rose said something about a mother being a real mother even if, as Alma had told her, she was adopted; and Alma began to cry.

'That's just it,' she sobbed. 'He didn't come. He wouldn't even come to her funeral. He wanted us to make this pact a long time ago: about how we'd go to the adoption agency to find out about our real parents and then we'd hunt them down. He wanted to get back at them some way. But I never felt like that. I figured it was better to forget everything and just think how lucky we were to be here at all and have a good mother and father: even if we were adopted and they weren't the real ones. He wouldn't even come to her funeral. She was the only mother we had all our lives. And she loved us, even though she wasn't my real mother.' She stopped, to catch her breath. She wiped her hands across her face. Rose put her arm around her and patted her back.

Alma got out a kleenex. She blew her nose. She took a deep breath. 'You're my real mother,' she said. 'That's why I came out here. That's why I got this job. I wanted to see you.'

'Oh,' Rose said. 'My goodness.' She looked at Alma as if trying to recognize someone who was standing a long way off. 'Oh,' she said again. Her eyes filled with tears.

Alma steered her into a chair. 'Let me go get you a glass of water,' she said. But Rose caught hold of her hand and wouldn't release it. Alma pulled up a second chair. She sat down. 'I wasn't going to tell you,' she said. 'I thought it might upset you. I shouldn't have said anything.'

'It's my dream come true. I've just been thinking about you for too long. My little girl. Do you have another one of those kleenexes? I've thought about this moment so many times.'

'Me, too,' Alma said. She pulled a kleenex out of her pocket and handed it to Rose.

*

History is only what other people say about you after you're dead, or – if you're lucky – what you get to say about yourself, as long as you're holding the reins. None of it matters at the time, only afterwards.

*

Over the next few days Rose began to tell Alma about her own

155

parents, about her highschool boyfriend and his family: they all still lived in the same town; she'd even seen him again. For a long time she'd hated him, but she'd come to realize that he'd just been young, as she had been. He had a family himself now and she felt nothing against him, or for him. She still couldn't forgive her parents. That was another reason why Tom and the boys meant so much to her. Tom knew the whole story; she'd told him before they were married.

Alma asked all the questions she'd been storing up for years.

'Right at the beginning,' Rose said, 'I was horrified. I couldn't believe it had happened. I wanted so much for it not to be true. I thought of getting rid of it, I really did. If I'd known a little more, I'm sure I would have. But I didn't know what to do. I told him and he told his parents, and they told mine, and they all got together. I still feel bitter about that, to this day. That's why I don't have much to do with my family any more. They were trying to do their best for me. They said so. I've just never been able to believe that again, not completely. Maybe they wanted to think that was true at the time. It's hard to face the disapproval of a whole town. I wouldn't want to, myself. But if it was a question of my child's future or the town's opinion, I'd get up and go. If I could. I guess it was my father who decided that they couldn't. Anyway, I'm sorry I never met your mother. I could have. When it was getting near the time of the birth, I wanted to. And the agency said it would be all right. But my parents wouldn't allow it. They were afraid of it coming back on them later in some way.'

'I wish you'd met her,' Alma said.

'So do I. I really do. But you can tell me about her. Did she name you after a relative in her family?'

'Yes. One of her grandmothers.'

'It's strange to think of you being called Alma. I never knew anybody named Alma.'

'You had another name for me.'

'Yes. It was –'

'Don't tell me what it was. Please. I'm the way I am now. I can't be somebody else.'

'No, of course. You're right.'

156

'You could meet my father.'

'If he'd like to.'

'Good. I'll talk to him about it.'

They went for a long walk together late one afternoon while the boys were playing over at a neighbor's house. Alma said, 'I think it's inhuman that they never let you see me.'

'It wasn't the society's policy in those days. Maybe it still isn't. They didn't want the mothers to change their minds. They thought it was better to knock you out in the delivery room and then you'd come to, and all the problems would be over. Everyone was very nice to me. They made me feel as if they thought that there had been a mistake, but it wasn't my fault, and that if I went along with all their advice, I'd be proving how sensible I was; how much character I had. They hardly mentioned the baby once. They just kept saying that there was nothing to worry about. They did tell me it was a girl, that's all. One of the nurses told me; I don't think she was supposed to: she let it slip. You know, while I was carrying you, before I even knew if I was going to have a girl or a boy – I was so mixed up about everything. Sometimes I hated it. Sometimes I had this feeling of hope, of buoyancy – I didn't know what it was: like happiness. It was only later, about ten days after the birth, that I knew how much I loved you. I tried everything to get you back. They told me I'd change. They said it was part of the reaction and I'd get over it. But I didn't. I got worse. I was desperate. They gave me pills and they told me that I had to think about the future: I should ask myself if I wanted it to go down on my record that I was unstable. I might never be able to get a job. So I gave up writing the letters and making the phone calls. I think my mother started to have a bad conscience about me then. But it was too late. I felt that something had been done to me that could never be put right, ever.'

'And now I'm here,' Alma said.

'All grown up.'

'We'll settle down with it. We like each other already, so it'll be all right.'

'What if you hadn't liked me?'

'I don't know,' Alma said. 'I think I'd just have moved on in a couple of weeks.'

'It frightens me to think of it.'

'I bet it happens. There must be a lot of kids who get a summer job someplace, to look at their parents, and that's all they want to do, whether they like them or not: they just take that one look and go away. That's what Bruce should do.'

'Tell me some more about him.'

'I wouldn't know where to begin. I hope you'll meet him, too, some day. Then you can see for yourself.'

'It's hard to describe people.'

'It gets harder, the closer you are to them.'

'I've got some pictures from my highschool days. Everything's in a box. I haven't opened it since the adoption. I used to think about throwing it all away, but I never did. There's a photograph of Jim. Do you know something: when we were at school, he was a very good athlete but what he was really wonderful at was – he was the most beautiful dancer you ever saw. I guess that's something you inherited from him.'

Alma thought about a teenage boy, a marvelous dancer and younger than she was now. He was no longer anonymous. Something that was hers had once belonged to him, too. There was a way in which he and she were the same. Now that she knew, she couldn't forget it. She saw a time coming when curiosity would draw her to the place where he lived, not to meet him but just to catch sight of him for an instant.

At the moment, she didn't want to. From having no relatives, she'd gone to having too many. They were beginning to confuse her. She needed to sit down for a long talk with Bruce.

* * *

Joanna telephoned him early in the morning. The call came through on his second phone. He'd decided only the day before that he'd give her a ring himself that afternoon.

She said that she was afraid he'd been right about those laurel bushes, and most of the other things in the garden as well: could he come over tomorrow afternoon and talk about it? The girls would both be away on the school glee club weekend. And her husband was going to be looking over somebody's horses all day long. 'So, we'll have plenty of time to talk,' she told him. 'About the garden.' Her voice sounded low and purring, as if she'd be smiling. He said: Sure, he'd see her around two-thirty.

That night he went to a movie theater and sat through a double feature. One film was a low-budget light comedy about insurance fraud investigators; it starred a TV actress he liked. The second told the story of a city cop who tried to buck the system, was thrown out of the force and ended up saving the whole of New York single-handed, after shooting thirty-six people.

When he got home he wasn't sleepy. He took a walk.

Back in his highschool years he used to enjoy walking around alone at night in the late spring and early summer; he'd be feeling restless and he'd start out fairly fast, but as the light went he'd calm down until he was moving lazily from street to street, the trees around him growing massive and shaggy with darkness. He used to love walking all through the night. That was another town of white picket fences and neat lawns. At one time he'd detested everything about it. Now he thought of it with the longing of homesickness, and of his youth and childhood that were over forever.

He walked for hours. He tried not to think ahead, not to plan; just to walk from one shadow to the next.

*

He got the afternoon off by doing a deal with a man at work. He'd arranged it the day before, so he had nothing hanging over him. Everything was going smoothly.

He took his time getting to the house, parked, and sat in the car for a while. The trees were only just beginning to turn. The blue sky had a few bright, puffy clouds in it; the air was mild and stirred by the constant movement of small breezes. He wanted to relax into the beauty of what he was looking at, but instead of giving him rest, the loveliness of the day excited him. Everything he looked at seemed invested with immense significance. He wondered if the strange heightening of emotion – apparent in the world outside as well as within him – meant that he was going to end up killing her.

When he tried to think ahead, it was as if he'd gone blind: as if his mind had entered a kind of night. Things distant and near were equally incomprehensible to him, as were the past and the future, the home that was gone and the one that had never been. He thought that he might have come to the end of his life. He didn't know what he was going to do. He seemed to have forgotten his way.

He knew that the solution to everything would come to him at the right moment, but he ought to have had a plan. What he'd imagined at the beginning was that he'd start with the two daughters. But they'd been too experienced to be damaged, too shallow to be hurt. All he'd done was to prove that they were worthless, and he'd already known that. They had cheated him of his revenge. They were fighting and full of spite against each other, but that wasn't enough. He had to do something to Joanna herself. Maybe he could cause a break between her and her husband. Or – more than that; he might be able to persuade her to run away with him. That would be best of all.

This was the day for it: the culmination. Everything was going to work. Maybe he still didn't know how, but that wasn't important.

He got out of the car and walked down the street to the house. She opened the door before he had a chance to ring the bell. She had a glass in her hand. She smiled as if posing for a photograph, and said, 'Hi. Come on in. Have a drink.'

'Fine,' he said.

She swished away in front of him, across the hall, down two steps, over the living-room rug and to the screened-in porch that looked out on to the garden.

The sliding glass doors were closed; no one would be able to hear them from across the lawn. And the slatted bamboo blinds were drawn on two sides: without a good pair of field glasses, nobody could see them, either. She'd set everything up. All he had to do was to let her fall into it.

She was wearing a silky, wrap-around dress that had appeared to be flowing like water while she walked. Now that she was stretched out on one of the sofas, the material pulled tight so that he could see the lines of a tiny pair of bikini pants underneath and, above the belt at her waist, the shape of her breasts and nipples almost as exactly as if she'd been naked.

'What can I offer you?' she said, in the same voice she'd used over the telephone.

Right, he thought. *I'll make you work for it*. 'How about a gin and tonic to start with?'

She got up, mixed him a drink, bent over his chair to hand it to him, dumped some more bourbon into her own glass and repositioned herself on the sofa. She'd made sure that he'd been able to see down her dress. This wasn't going to be the day to examine the shrubs for mildew and leaf rot.

She said, 'Why don't you bring that erection over here and let it say hello?'

'I might,' he said. He lifted his glass and swirled the ice cubes around. 'Why don't you tell me something about yourself first?'

'Like what?'

'Oh, your unspoiled girlhood, how you ended up with a man who's got a jail record – that kind of thing.'

'How do you know about that?'

'If you work on a paper, you've got access to a lot of information. I was curious about you.'

'Why?'

'Why not?'

'My two girls are both crazy about you.'

'Oh?'

'I guess you think you know a lot about girls.'

'Uh-huh. And you know about men. So that makes us even.'

She moved her leg. Her dress fell open at the side, showing her thigh nearly up to the hipbone.

'Tell me about yourself,' he said. 'Where did you grow up?'

'In a small town. Full of small people with small minds.' She drained her glass and banged it down on the table next to her.

'A lot of them live in big towns too, and in the suburbs.'

161

'But you can get away from them easier there. This town I grew up in – if you were seen talking with somebody on the way home from school, five people would have mentioned it to your mother before you got in the door. That's how I met Ray. He was working on the road. I was on my way to the bus stop. Nobody else used to walk that route; all the girls in my grade were like their mothers – they'd disassociated themselves from me because I'd been out with a boy in the senior class who had a bad reputation. They were all saying I'd been sleeping with him, which I had, of course. You bet your boots. And didn't they wish they had, too. He was the real McCoy, all right. He had what it takes.' She reached for her glass, tried to drink from it and realized that it was empty.

Bruce stood up and took the glass from her. He poured her a drink of water with a fistful of ice cubes in it. As he put some more tonic into his own glass, he said, 'Go on.'

'Sure. I thought he was pretty cute. He's gotten a little beefy now, but you should have seen him when he was twenty-five – Jesus. A little like you, matter of fact, but darker. It was early spring. We had a freak heat-wave. He'd be there with his shirt off and they'd call things out to me – not the usual dirty stuff: jokes, to make me laugh. It was mainly him. I got to doing it back, just for fun.'

He gave her the drink of water, pulled his chair nearer and sat down again. He didn't want to get too drunk to see the right moment when it came. He wanted the news of who he was to be devastating. She was pretending to be drunker than she was; she'd be able to take it in when he told her. 'Go on,' he said.

'Then one day he waited around the corner for me. Asked me out. So I said yes, and from then on we were just screwing each other to death. You can't imagine what he was like. Me, too. I needed it all the time. When you're that age, it's like being insane. All the time.'

'And then?'

'They found out about it, of course. Big scenes. Lower-class thug and how could I demean myself and so on: I was doing it to shock, I didn't really have any interest in him, so on, so forth, trying to make him look bad. I thought I was supposed to have a whiskey here. What is this – gin?'

'It's a light whiskey.'

'Brucie, this is so light, it could pass for white in Alabama. Put something in it.'

'So what happened?'

'I thought I was so smart. We both did. You know how the legal age for marriage varies from state to state? In Arkansas it's something like fourteen for the girl and sixteen for the boy, but if you've got your parents' consent, it's about twelve and fourteen. South Carolina, too. I think so.'

'That was supposed to be the Church's answer to the illegitimacy rate: if you let them get married young, at least all the children would be legal.'

'I thought if I got pregnant, they couldn't object. I got a copy of my birth certificate and just waited. Where's that drink?'

'Him?' he said, suddenly understanding. 'It was the same guy you're married to?'

'What about that drink, bartender?'

He took her glass, poured out more water and handed it to her. As he sat back down in the chair, his hand brushed against her bare leg.

'So what happened?'

'Pretty dumb. I'd underestimated how much they hated me. Some parents do. They're forced to have kids because of the social conventions – it's something they need, like a car or a house, to show they've made it. But they don't want them. Maybe I was doing it back, too. Anyway, I waited for it to show, and then they laid it on the line: I was no better than a whore, my moral behavior reflected on them, but I was underage and they were in charge of me and if I didn't agree to have the baby adopted, they'd call the police and have Ray arrested for statutory rape. That's what they can do to a man who screws around with a girl who's – '

'Under eighteen, I know. You should have gotten to the next state before you broke the law.'

'Oh, what I should have done. They'd have caught us under

163

the Mann Act, or something else. You can't win against people like that. They'd locked me in my room. I wanted that baby so bad. I couldn't believe they'd be able to do it to me. I figured, if I could just get away, get to Ray, I could give birth by myself and it would be okay. I looked old enough, so we could pass for man and wife. I – ' She sat up, with her hands to her cheeks.

'Yes?' he said. He thought she was going to choke, but she started to cry, and to scream, and to shout the rest of her story.

'Those bastards,' she shrieked. 'Doing that to their own child. Took me in to that adoption place and I fought all the way. Told me how many years he could get behind bars if I didn't cooperate. Till finally, I gave in. I thought – well, we could get married in two and a half years – in a lot of states. And then we could sue, get the baby back, and it would be better than him going to jail. The other girls sitting there in the waiting room – my God. I can still remember them: Cheryl and Pat. Cheryl engaged to a boy who was just making his way up the office ladder; they were supposed to have their wedding the next April. But his parents and her parents decided that a baby just then would come at the wrong time for everybody. And Pat – she'd had one boyfriend who'd run out on her and another one that said he'd marry her if she got rid of the baby the first one left her with. I really wonder how that place could have pretended it was helping people. I know what they were doing: they were selling merchandise. They got me into their operating theater and I fought. Everybody was screaming, including me. All those papers they have on their walls, to say how they'll heal the sick and be as good as Jesus Christ – you should have seen the whole gang of them on top of me, sticking their needles into me like I was a pin cushion. When I woke up, it was all over. The baby was gone. They were nice enough to tell me it was a boy; that was the only decent thing they did: imagine going through all that, and never even knowing? Anyway, I was too weak to put up much resistance afterwards. I kept passing out and crying. My parents got the doctors to tell me that if I didn't pull myself together, I'd be in the hands of the psychiatrists for the rest of my life. I could even be committed. You know, if you've got the money, you can buy a doctor like anything else. That's what they were afraid of, see – that Ray was after their money. My mother kept saying, "You're doing it on purpose, I know you are." I guess she was scared people would find out how they'd treated me. I was on the edge of going crazy: I could feel it right next to me. And I was scared, too. But I finally reached a point where I could think. It was like being one step away, and if you got too near, you'd be standing in the shadow. I knew that if I could get my health back, and just keep living, in a couple of years I'd be in the clear: I'd be with Ray, and we'd get the baby back, and we'd have a lot of others, too. It was a good thing I didn't find out till later what they'd really done. They'd had him arrested, of course. He was there in jail, all the time, paying his debt to society. Nice, huh?'

'Perfect. How did you get back at them?'

'I used to think about that a lot. It started to take me over. I couldn't think about anything else. I had less and less of my own life left: they covered everything. Then he got out of jail. He said to forget it; we'd just leave and get married and start our family.' She sniffed. He handed her his handkerchief. She said, 'You know, it's funny: in a way they were right. I mean, I love him, but he's kind of a lunkhead. And I don't even know if he's always on the right side of the law. We don't have anything in common. Honest to God, I'm lonely as hell sometimes.' She started to sob again. She sat up from the sofa, tried to pour out some bourbon and sloshed it over the table and floor. She fell on top of him. He grabbed her around the waist, to keep her from sliding to the floor. She tried to kiss him. Then she tried to hit him in the face. She yelled, 'For Christ's sake, are you going to sit there all day like a store dummy? Aren't you going to take me to bed?'

He got a firm grip on her and stood up, holding her in his arms. The chair fell over backwards behind him. The glass slipped out of his left hand on to the floor, and broke. He said, 'Okay.'

He carried her out of the porch, through the living room and into the hallway. He knew where all the rooms were. It would have been best, and appropriate, to take her to the room she and Ray slept in, but that was upstairs and too far away. He lugged

165

her towards one of the downstairs guest rooms and lurched across the threshold with her.

He almost stumbled, hitting the door with the side of his arm. 'Whoops,' she cried gaily. He left the door open. It didn't matter; there was no one else at home. As he turned around to drop her on top of the bedspread, her wrist caught the lamp on the night table and knocked it over with a crash.

She was out of her dress in seconds, tugging at his clothes. Twenty minutes later they were still making love when Ray ran into the room and started to shout at them. They turned and broke apart.

Ray was looking at them down the barrel of a shotgun. He fired at Bruce, who fell – deafened, blinded and bleeding – down the side of the bed. Joanna screamed at him to stop, but Ray pulled the trigger again. The blast shot half her face away.

Bruce clenched his jaws against the pain, trying not to make a noise. His hands clutched the blankets down on the floor. Everything was wet. Everything smelled like blood. He heard Ray cursing, and another cartridge going into the barrel. He tried not to breathe. But he had no reason to be afraid: Ray turned the gun around, put the barrel into his mouth and blew the top of his head off.

It took Bruce several minutes to crawl to the telephone. He was sure, all the way, that he'd bleed to death before he got there.

*

It made the papers in a big way. The county hadn't had such a crime of passion for years. The two daughters came back from their school trip to find both parents dead, their lover in the hospital and the police telling them that he'd been discovered in bed with their mother.

The younger girl, Didi, slashed her wrists but, being ignorant about the correct method, only managed to make two shallow cuts with a breadknife across the backs of her hands, which she then held up dramatically, declaring that she wanted to die and, look: she'd cut her wrists. Her older sister, Mandy, had more intelligence. She loaded one of her father's pistols and went to the hospital, gunning for Bruce. The policeman on duty there

166

stopped her before she got to his room. The nurses gave her a sedative.

The sheriff himself arrived to ask Bruce for his story. It was one of those things, Bruce told him weakly: they'd started drinking heavily and before they knew it, they were in bed and her husband was standing in the doorway.

Alma came to see him. She sat in the chair and held his hand. His voice was faint and he spoke slowly, but he kept her fingers in a tight grip. 'So many transfusions,' he said. 'Blood. The source of all my troubles. I keep bleeding and they keep pouring it into me. Comes in those jars. Looks dark. Looks brown, like my dream. Could be mud.'

'I'm sorry you were shot,' she told him, 'but I'm not sorry you've got the time to think. Something had to stop you.'

'I guess. Didn't stop me soon enough. I was in bed with her.'

She said, 'I'm glad Mom isn't alive.' She could see as she raised her eyes that it was the only thing anyone had ever said – except perhaps the news of his adoption – that had hurt him. 'How could you do such a thing?'

'Well,' he said, 'I felt sorry for her.' He looked away and yawned, as if bored. 'It seemed like the natural thing to do. She'd been through so much. What her parents did to her: nobody has the right. They took everything away from her at the beginning. Then she fought her way through, and found out she didn't have a very good marriage, after all. I think she started to drink when she realized she didn't love him any more, so it had all been for nothing. She kept talking about her lost child. Well, I just couldn't tell her. I couldn't say: *I'm it and I've been screwing both of your daughters*. Could I?'

'The daughters?'

'Nothing special. Neither was she. Except at the end, of course. That was pretty special.'

'I think they want to give you some more blood,' Alma said. 'Don't go.'

'It's all right,' one of the nurses told her. 'You can stay.'

'Violent man,' Bruce whispered. 'That's what he was like. Maybe that's what I'm like, too.'

167

'Don't make excuses for yourself.'

'Why not? It's true what you said. I've destroyed myself.'

'And a lot of other people.'

'Yes,' he admitted. He turned his face to the side, looking towards the door. She thought that his mind had wandered to something else, but after a while he came back to the subject. He said, 'But they don't matter.'

'Don't you feel any sorrow for them?'

He caught his breath and swallowed in a way that reminded her of when she'd seen Bess for the last time. 'Isn't this enough?' he said.

The nurses began to wheel a table into the room.

'I'm the one you should have slept with,' she said.

'Brother and sister?'

'Not by blood.'

'Psychologically.'

'So much the better. In spite of everything, we're your real family. The others are still nothing to you.' She wanted to say he should have been able to figure that out a long time ago. But he looked too tired and he'd never been able to stand criticism. 'Try and get well,' she told him. 'You're the only one I can't spare.'

'You always loved me, Alma.'

'Always. And if you hadn't been so scared of it, we'd have been all right.'

'Think so?' he said.

The nurses advanced with their bottles and jars and rubber tubing. His eyes dilated. He held her hand harder.

Alma said, 'I had a dream about you. And in the dream, you lived.'

'I wouldn't bank on it. I just saw the doctor walk down the hall. Same son of a bitch that did the other operation on me: the one that didn't work. Why don't they let me die?'

Alma said, 'Stop talking like that. You aren't going to die. I'll be thinking of you every minute you're in there. I'll be praying so hard, helping you. You're going to pull through just fine. And then you'll get well.'

A nurse came up to the bed, saying, 'Miss – '

168

Alma wouldn't pay attention to her. She leaned forward, to catch what Bruce was trying to tell her.

*

I had a dream that I was in the hospital and Alma came to see me. My time was running out. I could feel it trickling away from me, all my time.

She said, 'You aren't going to get out of this so easy. You're going to keep on living.'

I was so tired that I wanted to sleep. They were going to do an operation on me. I thought I might sleep through that, too.

A nurse came into the room. Alma said, 'I'm not leaving,' but I said to her, just like the tough guys in the movies, 'Kiss me goodbye, Alma.'

She kissed me on the cheek. And I said, 'Not like that. That's for strangers.' So she kissed me again.

Be My Guest

Sandra and her boyfriend, Bert, worked for the same firm. She knew that that was a mistake. She'd known it from the beginning, but mixing business with pleasure was something everybody did. It was just because everyone did it that there were so many warnings against it. Where she and Bert worked, everybody certainly did it all the time. It was convenient. Of course, it was more convenient for people who were married, especially for the men. Bert wasn't married, but somehow he acted as if he were – as if he had other commitments that she didn't have the right to question him about.

On Thursday night they had a quarrel because, having planned – and promised – to take her on a weekend trip, he'd changed his mind and decided to go fishing or hunting, or something like that. He said that he'd be with three other men he'd known from college days. She didn't believe that, or at least she said she didn't, because she didn't want him to break his word to her. If he were really going to trade in a weekend with her for one that meant getting drunk and swapping stories with the boys, then that showed just what he thought she was worth.

On Friday morning she waited to see if he'd back down and tell her that he wanted to be with her, after all. He didn't. He took the flightbag and the smaller tan suitcase and he went off to work, without another word to her, as if she'd agreed to it the night before and as if she hadn't told him, 'If you do, I'll know how much you care about me.' Why had she said that? It made the outcome seem inevitable. She could have waited, quietly, to see what would happen. But anyway, what she'd said only made the matter appear final for her, not for him. He wouldn't give it a thought. Maybe she'd better spend the weekend mulling over how much it really did matter to her whether he cared, and – if he did or didn't – whether she ought to get out of the affair. Perhaps she should do another kind of thing everyone else did, too: let things slide and start going out with somebody else on the side.

When she got home from the office in the evening, she didn't want to do the laundry or get into the bathtub: Bert might telephone. She walked back and forth, willing the phone to ring, until she couldn't stand the tension. She made herself a cup of coffee, sat down in the easy chair and turned on the television.

She watched a comedy serial, two short westerns and an old black-and-white movie from the thirties. She was thinking of switching the set off when a second film followed – a romantic adventure, shot in lush color and set on a tropical island. From the instant the music began, you could tell what kind of story it would be: just her kind. She burrowed more comfortably into the chair.

At first the film presented a map of the South Seas. Then the printed names and numbers faded, turning into a real picture: a boat, off in the distance. Meanwhile, a mysterious-sounding voice said, *Legend tells us that among the atolls of these vast, uncharted seas there lies an island named Mona Zima, the place of the jewel. So potent is the lure of its fame that, though none return from the quest, it continues to draw to it men of passion and daring. Such a one was Joshua Bridgewater in the year 1908.* At last, young Captain Bridgewater himself was shown, standing masterfully at the wheel of his ship, *The Dauntless*, while the ocean grew stormy. His men came up to ask him questions and he barked back orders. The sea became wild and tumultuous. Sandra took two large gulps of coffee.

As the captain's plight became steadily more dangerous, the voice went on to tell the story: One of the volcanic islands in a little-known and as yet unmapped chain was populated by members of a secret religious cult. Its worshippers sacrificed to an idol that was inlaid with many jewels, all set around one fabulous diamond: an enormous stone (bigger than a fist) of perfect purity. It would have made more sense for the inhabitants of a tropical island to revere a giant pearl and not a diamond, but that was explained; the jewel had been brought to the place by an Indian prince, who was fleeing from his brother's army. Just as the maharajah's ships reached the treacherous reefs, a storm blew up and the seas pounded everything to splinters. All the people were drowned. Nothing survived but a small, ornamental casket that was shaped like a boat and therefore, captainless, floated into calmer waters until it gained the shore. Inside was the diamond. From the moment of its arrival it was considered sacred, not simply on account of its great beauty, but because of the seemingly magical way it had steered itself – as if by conscious will – to a place of safety.

The cult worshippers thought that the large and still-active volcano on their island could be pacified by the light of the jewel. They also believed that the diamond would bring them good luck in general, that they were meant to guard and protect it and that all strangers wished to steal it. Any foreigner who expressed interest in it was told that it didn't exist: it was just a story. If he managed to discover the idol and see it for himself, he was killed.

Captain Bridgewater had started out as a freebooter, but his travels had changed him. He'd been moderately chastened by his ordeal in the storm, although through the exercise of his superb seamanship he'd managed to save his vessel. And as soon as he landed on the island – as the sole survivor of his ship's company – he became a better man: he fell in love. The girl who won his heart was a curvaceous strawberry blonde: she caught his eye as she was about to be sacrificed to the idol. The diamond – so she told him haltingly, in her newly learned English – was angry. It had to be appeased. She had been chosen for the job on the basis of her unusual appearance and perhaps also because her parents had been foreign; they had died many years ago when she was still a baby. No one would tell her how they met their fate, but she guessed that the jewel had claimed them. She herself had never been persecuted. She'd been treated as an honored guest. Now she wondered if, all along, the priesthood hadn't been saving her for this moment.

As soon as the commercials began again, Sandra ran to the bathroom and then to the kitchen. There wasn't time to make another cup of coffee. She settled for a glass of water. She sipped slowly as the movie continued.

The hero, as she might have suspected, was captured. But, since he'd done a good deed earlier in the story when he'd rescued two men from execution, he had helpers in the community. So hope was not completely lost, in spite of the fact that he was tied up in ropes when the girl was being led off to the place of sacrifice. As the camera switched back and forth between the hero in his bonds and the heroine, being dragged towards a bed of coals, the helpers struggled with the hundreds of knots and Sandra – not daring to swallow the last drops of water in case she missed something – whispered, 'Hurry, hurry up.'

The ending used the same back-and-forth device: although the captain was now freed, he had to get to the girl in time. He raced across the island, while she – surrounded by a muttering mob of fanatic acolytes – gained a few minutes of life; the high priest had to chant the right words over her before she could be thrown into the fiery pit. Close by her stretched a long, burning track of live coals. That was the testing place for liars. You were supposed to have an even chance of getting to the other side if you were telling the truth. But three people had already burst into flames halfway to the finishline and Sandra knew, from the way things were shown, that they'd been telling the truth. Of course, that kind of thing wouldn't work. It was like those penalties for witches: if they sank, they were innocent; if they floated, they were in league with the devil. But at least on the coals you'd have the possibility of escape. If you were in the pit, you stayed there until you burned to a crisp.

The hero ran, the heroine wriggled and screamed, the high priest intoned gloatingly. Behind and above him the perfect diamond sparkled with light. It seemed like an object from another world. The mob – louder and more restive by the minute – kept looking up at it. The priest droned, the heroine moaned, the hero raced. And at last, just as the captain broke onto the scene, another element was added: a sudden, deep rumbling.

Way off in the background, smoke began to rise from the volcano. The sky darkened, the grumbling was like thunder, the earth shook. Everyone screamed, even the two hulking guards who were holding the girl. The hero ran up and took her by the hand. But the high priest, seeing him, pointed and shouted to his priestly warriors. They moved forward, their spears ready. The escape route was cut off. The only way out was to go through the fire.

Sandra leaned over to put her glass down on the floor without taking her eyes from the screen. The volcano erupted, showering sparks and ashes everywhere. Hero and heroine dashed through the mob and reached the fiery walkway, which – miraculously – they negotiated without harm, although parts of their clothing exploded into a bright, gassy cloud around them. They reached the far side and stepped out on to the ground. That was the kind of thing true love enabled you to do. The high priest was in fits. He ordered people to go after them. A few started out, but the fire engulfed them. And suddenly everybody realized that the priest wasn't helping. In fact, he was spending most of his time sending other people to their death. What was left of the mob advanced on him. His bodyguards tried to protect him but when they saw that the maddened crowd was backing them into a corner with him, they quit worrying about their leader and tried to save themselves.

The phone rang. Sandra knocked over a stack of cassette tapes to get to it fast; she thought it would be Bert, repentant and sentimental, ready to propose something really nice, to make up.

It was her Aunt Marion. They didn't see each other very often. Aunt Marion had always been independent. But in the past three years six of her friends had died and once more her family had become a necessity to her, though she still didn't like them much.

'Is something wrong?' Sandra asked.

'Nothing bad, dear. No, just inconvenient. I'm supposed to be away for the weekend, but now the only day the men can deliver the window is Saturday. They can't even take it to McHutchin's, because he's in Bangor for his son's wedding. And I couldn't cancel my outing with Elsie.' Elsie was one of the two surviving friends. 'I don't suppose you could let them in for me, could you?'

'I guess I could.' So far, Aunt Marion had proved to be someone who appreciated and returned favors, not a person who took acts of kindness to mean encouragement towards further – and possibly, unending – imposition. 'What time did they say they'd deliver the thing?'

'In the afternoon. "Sometime after noon," they said. You know how they are.'

'What time are you leaving?'

'Oh, early. As early as possible. But you could get the key from, um, the usual place, you know.'

Sandra knew. One of the reasons why her aunt had singled her out was that she was quick to pick up that sort of hint. There were other members of the family who were more cheerful or obliging, but some of them were pretty dense. 'I remember,' she said. 'I won't repeat it over the phone. Yes, sure. I can be there about ten o'clock.'

'How kind of you, Sandra. That really is a relief. If that window doesn't go in soon, I can see myself waiting all winter for it. You're an angel.'

'As a matter of fact, it could work out very well. I've got a lot to think about over the next couple of days.'

'A boyfriend?' Aunt Marion too was fairly quick on the draw. 'I hope it's something nice.'

Sandra laughed. She said she wasn't sure: she probably wouldn't know about that until she'd done the thinking.

'I'll make up the bed in the guest room,' her aunt said. 'The second on the left, at the top of the stairs. And there's plenty of food in the icebox.'

'I'll be there,' Sandra told her. 'And if you leave a phone number, I'll call you.'

Aunt Marion said that that would be perfect and Sandra was truly a friend in need. She hung up.

As soon as she put the receiver down, Sandra began to think it was possible that all the time she'd been talking to her aunt, Bert

175

might have tried to get in touch with her. Maybe she should call him up, to find out: to see if he'd changed his mind. He could come with her to Aunt Marion's; spend the weekend. She'd have to ask first.

She lifted the receiver and immediately put it down again. That would be weak and silly. And if she felt angry at herself, it was – naturally – his fault. He was the one she should be mad at.

The adventure movie still rampaged across the television screen. She stepped back into the living room. The mob yelled and brandished spears, while fire shot up into the sky like celebration rockets. She sat back down in her chair.

The hero and heroine made a rush for the cool jungle and the sea beyond, where his boat was waiting. In the background you could see the priest being thrown into the burning pit, his two guards following him. The sound of their screams was covered by the roaring of flames, the crack and crashing of the volcano. Sparks rained from the sky. Hero and heroine speeded up, but things didn't look good. As they entered the tall foliage, the earth was shaken by new rumblings, the idol shuddered on its pedestal. The crowd groaned and the statue split, sending the diamond vaulting high into the air, projected like a shooting star over the heads of the embroiled mob.

It fell right in front of the escaping lovers. The heroine gasped. She bent down to where it lay nested in a halo of light, its outlines almost hidden by the twinkling sparkles of its radiance. Her hand opened towards it. But the hero pulled her back. He kicked the jewel out of the way and dragged her forward. They crashed through the trees. Behind them the vegetation became an incandescent river of writhing flames and whizzing fireballs. They reached the shore, plunged into the water, swam to the boat. And the last anyone saw of them was their embracing forms against the white sail of *The Dauntless*. The boat slipped quickly away from the burning island. Every sail was full, straining towards freedom. And large letters spelled out the words, 'The End', over the two faces as they approached each other from left and right for a central clinch – the ecstatic kiss that was to be both conclusion and beginning. Sandra sighed. She relaxed. Right up to the end, she'd been worried that something would go wrong.

There were other shows to watch afterwards, but she'd had enough. He wasn't going to call.

She took the bath she'd been putting off. Then she brushed her teeth. If he'd tried to phone, that was too bad.

She sat propped up in bed with a magazine open on her lap. She read for a while, but she lost interest. Her mind kept going back to the South Sea island in the movie: the exotic jungle, the pagan crowds baying for blood, the idol that guarded its shimmering diamond, the escape of the two lovers as the island went up like a torch. That was what she loved about the movies – they gave you everything like a dream. It wasn't just that she liked them, even though they weren't true: she liked them precisely because they weren't. In real life, what would have happened to the hero and heroine? That would have been a different kind of human sacrifice. She could imagine it: eight years later, the two of them trying to make a living in an American city somewhere; the heroine would look back and say to herself, *I had a fortune right in front of me and he kicked it away. What kind of a fool would do that? We could have lived like kings.* And he'd be thinking, *If only I'd gone for the diamond and not the girl. I'd be happy now, have new women whenever I liked, and my own boat again – my own island, if I wanted it; freedom for the rest of my days, and a good life for all my children, even if I had hundreds of them.*

And what would have happened to the diamond? It would be all right, even if the island sank to the bottom of the sea. It was not, like human love, vulnerable to change. That was the trick to real life: you could walk through fire for each other and still end up wishing you'd never married.

She put the magazine on the night table and turned out the light.

*

The next morning she packed a nightgown, the summer sandals she wore as bedroom slippers, the book she'd been intending for months to read straight through. She set out early enough to miss the traffic in town.

It was a cloudy fall day but the sky looked as if the weather might clear up later. It had been a bad year for trees. The long drought in June and July – maybe even the strange spring weather before that – had done something to their leaves: instead of turning color, they'd just dried up and gone brown. Halloween was less than a week away and still there had been no beautiful trees to look at. Everyone felt disappointed. It was like seeing a spring when the fruit trees failed to blossom.

All night long she'd expected the call from Bert. Now she was glad that she knew how things were. She was also happy to get away from the city for a few days. She drove fast. Before she arrived, the sun came out. She hummed a little tune as she entered the neat, picturebook suburb in which Aunt Marion had a medium-sized frame house surrounded by flowerbeds, lawn, picket fence and everything else her neighbors had too. It seemed a nice place to live – peaceful and pretty, and not – as she used to think of such districts – dull, houseproud and undoubtedly full of bigots.

Aunt Marion had left a note by the telephone. There were instructions about the stove, the lights, how to double-lock the front door and what to do to the handle of the guest-room toilet if the water kept running. A long list of foods followed – all the delicacies Sandra could and should help herself to. And then there was the information about the window. Sandra had trouble reading the name of the delivery firm, but she got as far as Lo-something. She put the note into her pocket and went to the kitchen. She inspected the icebox crammed with food. It almost looked as though her aunt had spent the night cooking meals for her: a fish casserole, puddings, cold chicken and ham. There were glass containers of peas and rice. And in the cold room were two cakes, several full jars of cookies, fudge and walnut brownies. Unless Aunt Marion had made a lot of new friends recently, she must have been holding bridge parties at her house, or entertaining people from the garden club she belonged to.

Sandra walked back to the dining room and on to the living room. It had been several months since she'd been in the house, yet everything seemed to be exactly as when she'd last seen it. She took her suitcase upstairs. Most of her visits to Aunt Marion had been for the day. She hadn't spent the night in one of the guest rooms since her childhood. And it had been years since she'd stayed long enough to explore the neighborhood.

She unpacked. After that, she wandered downstairs again. The house was beginning to feel strange. It was an odd thing about empty houses; this one felt quiet in a way that wasn't restful. It was as if the absence of the owner had brought on a parallel absence within the house: as if the air had died.

She got out her book. As she read, the sun outside brightened and warmed the room around the big, high-backed chair she'd chosen. She sank deep into the story. It was about a southern belle who was falling in love with a scoundrel; he wanted to take over her family's plantation. The heroine was struggling hard against her feelings and wondering whether she ought to let him dance with her at the cotillion, when the doorbell rang. Sandra jumped.

She opened the door without bothering to look first. It could have been anyone, but in a suburb like this it would be ridiculous to suspect the kind of attack that happened in big cities. Life wasn't like that here.

Three hefty workmen stood on her aunt's gray-and-white painted porch. One of them – the one in charge – had rung the bell. The two others held between them a large pane of glass in a frame; they had rested it where it was just about to dig into one of the strategically placed potted geraniums that made the porch look so cheerful and welcoming, or – as Sandra had once believed – so maddeningly tidy. All three men wore white overalls. The leader had removed his cap.

She welcomed them with a smile, showed them through the house and opened a door next to the pantry, where Aunt Marion had said the window should go. Gardening equipment and vases had been pushed back to make room. When the time came to slide the window into its space, the man in authority lent a hand. 'Over to the right,' he told the others. 'Don't let her down yet. Look out for the edge there, Jake.' It all went smoothly.

Nothing was broken or knocked over. Everyone seemed pleased. Sandra thanked the men profusely. She told them how delighted her aunt would be. They said they were glad to help out: you needed the windows to be right, now that the cold was coming on. The one named Jake gave her a little wave and all three trooped out.

She closed the door behind them. She hadn't offered a tip, since Aunt Marion's note had expressly cautioned her not to let the men have anything. *I've given them plenty already*, she had written, *and this window is late*.

She waited until the workmen had driven away, then her city habits forced her back to the front door. She put the chain on and turned the lock.

All the rest of the morning she read. She made herself a sandwich and salad lunch, listened to some music on the radio and went out for a walk. She could have driven to another town, gone to a museum or tried to get into an afternoon show somewhere, but she felt that she was responsible for keeping an eye on the house. She didn't think that she should get too far away. If the year and the trees had been better, she'd have cruised around the countryside and looked at the fall colors.

While she walked, she thought about Bert, about how she was going to start regular exercise at the Y this year – swimming or aerobics; about whether she could afford to go away in the spring and, if so, where she should go. She realized all at once that if she could get together the money for a really nice trip somewhere, she wouldn't want to take it with Bert. If he were with her, her time would be spent in paying attention to him, not absorbing new sights and thoughts. Maybe he'd felt the same way. That could be the reason why he hadn't wanted to spend the weekend with her.

She'd been out walking around the neighborhood with her aunt twice before: once when she was about eight years old, and once again three years before her Great-Aunt Constance had died. On that visit they'd gone to look at a nearby memorial – a bronze statue erected to a woman who had dressed as a soldier in order to follow her husband into battle during the time of the

Revolution. Sandra remembered the statue as pretty and looking rather like the portrait of a musician, although – perhaps because of the ponytail hairstyle – too obviously a woman.

She walked until she realized that as far as the statue went, she was lost. It wasn't to be found in the direction she'd taken. She turned back, trying not to feel upset. Just lately – no doubt because of Bert – whenever anything didn't pan out, she'd add it to her list of what wasn't going right for her.

She would have liked to see the memorial for reasons other than its prettiness. She'd have liked to see the visible corroboration of the woman's story. Of course, it was a famous theme: the loyal wife. And she remembered that there was a folksong, supposedly based on fact, about another woman from farther south, who had also tried to join her husband at the war but hadn't been able to get across the river at one stage; she'd had to follow the river for miles, all the way up north. It had taken her about three years, until nearly the end of the fighting.

She couldn't remember if the woman had found her husband in the end. Probably, for the song to make sense, she must have, although in a way that didn't matter. It was the effort that counted. Some women were just brave: they would try. Where did they find the reserves of courage – was it simply necessity that brought out noble action in people? That couldn't be all there was to it. You had to be pretty good to begin with. The woman in the folksong had had children: sometimes motherhood made timid women strong. But often it worked the other way – it wore them down. And was it a sign of strength to leave your children in times of trouble, or was it better to stay with them? There really were no rules for behavior. Half the time she didn't even understand her own actions. But she knew that nothing would have persuaded her to pick up a gun and go off to the wars dressed like the young Mozart. She'd have crawled into a hole somewhere and waited till the action was over. Perhaps it was an appreciation of her cowardice that made her admire these decisive, revolutionary women; she wasn't particularly impressed by men who were of the same, heroic type. Men were supposed to be like that. Men of action were nothing special.

They liked it. It was a biological compulsion, or so she'd been led to believe.

It was still light when she got back to the house. She had time to make herself a cup of tea, sit down again with her book and get through the villain's seduction of the heroine's cousin, before she had to turn on a lamp.

She was somewhere among the arguments about what the Dredd-Scott Decision had done to influence ordinary people's lives, when the doorbell rang again. She switched on more lights, including the one outside on the porch. It was quite likely that the delivery men had just discovered that they'd brought her the wrong thing earlier in the day.

This time she looked, leaning to the side and peering at the gauze-covered panel windows to the left and right of the door. She saw no delivery men. She saw a child: a small boy of about ten, who was dressed in a jacket and tie, as if he were going to a party. She assumed that he was one of the children whose parents had decided to set Halloween on the weekend, rather than on Monday.

She undid the chain, opened the door and said hello.

'Um, good evening,' he said. He stood there smiling and nervous, and as if he couldn't think of anything else to say.

'I'm afraid I wasn't expecting any Halloween callers tonight,' she told him. 'And besides, why aren't you wearing a costume?'

'Halloween's Monday,' he said. 'It's not about that. Ah. I need help.'

'Are you lost?' Few children got lost after the age of six or seven, but it was an explanation she was always ready to accept. She got lost all the time herself.

'Yes,' he said. 'That's right. I'm lost.'

'Well, you'd better come in, I guess.' She held the door open. He walked in after her. She led the way to the living room and to the hallway where the telephone sat on its table. 'We can call your parents,' she said.

'Oh no, that's just the trouble. I can't.' He sat down in a chair quickly, as if he'd be safer there. He held on tight to his knees. His look of discomfort seemed to be based on something other than the fact that he was too small for the chair. 'It's a long story,' he said. 'And it sounds weird.'

She sat down in the chair facing his. 'Well, you just tell me,' she said. She'd never been the mainstay and comfort of a child before. She felt like a fake. She'd always imagined that motherly talents came naturally after childbirth and probably had something to do with hormones.

'It sounds impossible,' he began. 'But I didn't want to go to the police.'

'Why not?'

'Well, you know what the cops are like. They've got their hands full already. They won't want to take care of some kid who's off his rocker. They'd put me in a psychiatric ward.' As he began to talk, he stopped looking so jittery. And his gestures, his facial expressions, were like those of an adult: matter-of-fact and easy.

'Would they?' she asked.

'Sure.'

'What's your name?'

'Roy,' he said. He added absently, 'It means king.'

'I'm Sandra.'

Roy held out his hand, shook her hand, said, 'How do you do?' and sat back in his chair again, like a businessman who was ready to begin a discussion. 'Do you believe in magic?' he asked.

'Taking rabbits out of hats? Making things disappear?'

'No, no. Not the stuff you can see in a show. Like the fairytales. Making things change. Turning somebody into a stone. Or into – something else, maybe.'

'A prince turning into a frog, you mean? Or the other way around?'

'That's right. You think it's possible?'

'Does this have something to do with Halloween?'

'No. At least, I don't think so. But I hadn't thought of that. I guess we're coming up to that time of the year, aren't we? Is it the equinox or the solstice? I always forget.'

'The equinox. Daylight Saving is tomorrow. And Halloween is on Monday. Like you said.'

'Um. You'd think if that had anything to do with it, it would have happened right on the day. Not one or two days before.'

'Just tell me, Roy. What's happened?'

'Okay. I'll tell it to you like a story. There's this eleven-year-old kid. His father got divorced over a year and a half ago.'

'Yes.'

'And she married somebody else. Some guy with two kids of his own. And they didn't like this boy. So, he kept saying to his father that it was no good – he wanted to live with him.'

'Yes,' Sandra said. She'd lost track of how many people were in the cast of characters and which 'he' was at the center of the action.

'So this boy,' he went on, 'got to live with his father. And he wouldn't let him alone for a minute, so the father never got to go out with any women: he was going crazy. Then this kid saw some kind of show on TV – I don't know what it was; and he got all interested in magic. He asked for a couple of books, and he'd sit in his room doing things like – oh, incantations, I guess. And then this morning I woke up, and look at me.'

'Yes?'

'How old do you think I am?'

She didn't want to offend him by guessing too young. He might be small for his age. 'I'm not very good at judging how old people are,' she said.

'I look about eleven, don't I?'

'About that.'

'I'm thirty-four. It's my son who's eleven.'

He waited for her to take in what he'd said. She stared at him. He shrugged finally, and looked down at the floor. When she still didn't say anything, he muttered, 'I told you, it sounds weird.'

She pushed herself forward in her chair. 'Would you like a cup of tea?' she asked. 'I was just about to make another one when you rang the bell.'

'What I'd really like is a good, stiff drink, but I don't know if I could take it. Maybe a coke, or something.'

184

'How about a Sprite?' She couldn't remember if there were any Coca-Colas in the icebox.

'Fine. I'm not out of my mind, you know.'

'You don't seem to be. But I've got to get used to the idea. Let me think a little. I'll get things ready.' She got up and walked into the kitchen.

First, she put the kettle on. Then, she opened the icebox and took out a bottle of Sprite. It wasn't until she started to look for the icecubes that she began to feel incensed. It was a joke, of course: a kind of pre-Halloween prank, or possibly the date was coincidental and he was just trying this out for fun, to see how people would take it. There were really only two questions to consider: did he know what he was doing, or was he lost in some other way, so that he was driven to throw himself on the mercy of strangers? After all, he was only a child, even though he appeared to be extremely self-possessed.

She thought he must know what he was doing. That might not mean that he was wholly malicious. It would probably be the usual thing: unhappy at home. If that were the answer, his father would seem to be the main culprit; no matter what background story the boy had told, the central theme was concerned with his father.

She took the glass into the living room and handed it to him. 'There you go,' she said. Behind her in the kitchen the kettle started to whistle. She ran back.

There was also the problem of whether this game of fooling the neighbors was a first attempt or a regular practice. If it were the first time, her reactions could be crucial to his future emotional state. That might also hold true if this were a habit. He was definitely a very smart little boy. He'd managed to make up a story that would prevent her from wanting to return him to a parent and that, at the same time, would make her think twice about getting in touch with the police.

Well, she thought, *poor thing*. Her own upbringing had been distinctly old-fashioned, boringly solid: no divorce, no embattled couples or extramarital allegiances. She hadn't liked her childhood, but she'd always known where she stood. Children nowadays sometimes couldn't figure out what they were supposed to be. They ended up being given more advice and information by television programs than by their parents. Come to think of it, she'd once seen a movie on TV about this very subject: a comedy about a father and son who changed places. The transformation had had something to do with an object that had occult powers, like the magic lamp in *Aladdin*; one of the characters, either father or son, had made a wish. And the wish had switched them both around. This little boy, Roy, had probably seen some similar comedy episode. He'd simply altered it to suit his needs; that was what grown people did all the time, only they learned to tone down their fictions. The sheer outrageousness of his story was a sign of innocence.

She carried the teacup carefully. As she approached her chair, she said, 'I shouldn't have filled this so full.' She was always doing that and because she couldn't drink anything too hot she'd have to leave it full and then she'd spill some. This time her hand was steady. She got the saucer on to the table and sat down. 'So,' she said, 'what am I going to do with you?'

'You don't believe me.'

'I guess I can't understand how you could change a person from one body into another. I mean, just to begin with: the mind is part of the body. They grow together. So, if you had a different body, you'd be a different person. See what I mean?'

'I don't understand it, either. But it happened.'

'What I do believe is that you're in some kind of trouble.'

'I haven't done anything. If you call the police, I'll run away again. They'd take me back to him. And I don't know what he'd do. He might even kill me. He could do it. He's bigger than I am now. And stronger. All that time I spent at the gym – Jesus.'

'Am I the first person you came to for help?'

'I tried two others. The first one lived right down the road. She actually called my son. My father. You know. I realize it sounds crazy. What am I supposed to do?'

'That's the problem. And what am I supposed to do? That's another one. I can't keep you here. Nobody can just let you stay.

And if you're stuck that way, what are you going to do about our job?'

'Oh, he'll do that. He's going to be better at it than I was.'

'Really? What's your line of work?'

'I do the advertising for a big firm of toy manufacturers.'

'Isn't that very specialized? You deal with accounts and presentation and all that?'

He waved his hand. 'He's a natural,' he said.

She almost burst out laughing. To pretend to be his father, who was describing him in praiseworthy terms, must be making him feel good in several ways at once. *It's like the theater*, she thought. *And I'm the audience.* 'What about your mother?' she asked. 'That is: your ex-wife; wouldn't she understand?'

'Her? Are you kidding?'

'You don't think it's worth a try?'

'She didn't even understand when everything was normal.'

'Well, sometimes that's the way it is. You don't see other people's worries until they're brought to your attention.'

'She wouldn't be interested. She wants her own life.'

'You're still part of her life, aren't you? You're part of a family.'

'No, listen. She wouldn't believe me. She'd think I was doing it to get a rise out of her. Let's stop talking about her.'

'All right. What about your son?'

'What about him?'

'The way this thing works, he looks like you now and you look like him – is that right?'

'That's right. He's got my body. And my face and voice and the car keys and the bank balance and the woman I've been going out with for the past couple of weeks; except, I don't think he knows about that yet. But I guess he'll find out.'

'He can't use the car, though.'

'Oh, he can drive. I taught him last summer.'

'Well.'

'Uh-huh.'

'When did all this happen?'

'Thursday.'

'When was the exact moment?'

187

'I was trying to get him to go to bed and he wouldn't. He used every trick he knew, distracting and delaying. But eventually he got into bed and I turned out the light and went downstairs. I was a little drunk. You know, you finally get out and have a nice meal with somebody and come back, pay the babysitter, and you think that's the end. And then he starts up again. I could hear him working on his computer. He does that a lot. By the time I get up the stairs, he's back in bed again, pretending to be asleep. Then, he lies. He says the machine works on its own sometimes.'

'Do you think that could be true?'

'What?'

'That the machine has something to do with whatever happened?'

'Oh, no. It's him.'

'And the babysitter?'

'Karen. She's fine. She's a girl from our neighborhood. Not like that other one he found for last night: Debbie. The minute he was out of the door, she started pulling all my clothes off – I couldn't believe it. She carried me to the bathroom – she carried me. She was huge. I couldn't do anything. I was kicking and yelling and everything. It was like she was deaf. I mean, she was like a robot. She threw me into the bathtub and started to scrub me raw. It was awful. I was humiliated. I guess she thought that was what babysitters were supposed to do. Unless she was crazy. She didn't make me brush my teeth. I actually had to ask to do that. Jees. I bet he did it on purpose.'

Sandra stood up and snapped on the ceiling light and two of the lower lamps. The more he talked, the more she thought that she really shouldn't have invited him in. Now that he was there, she had to listen. And then what? She couldn't send him away in the dark. And she didn't like the idea of turning him in to the police. To hand a child over to the state's official body of law enforcement would be a gross act of betrayal. Children weren't criminals just because they ran away.

There had been a story in the news once, a few years ago, about a boy who had run away from his parents; he'd managed all on his own to get to his grandmother's house, some two hundred and fifty miles away. And when he'd arrived, his grandmother had immediately phoned the police. Whenever Sandra thought about that story, she was filled with outrage. Everyone she knew had agreed with her at the time: it was a horrible thing to do. How could a child trust anyone after that?

She said, 'Do you think maybe something he did with the computer was what started it all?'

'I don't understand how it could have. But I don't see how any of this could happen from any other cause, either.'

'You heard the computer from downstairs.'

'That's right. And I ran up again to shut it off. I was ready to wipe the whole thing. He's got games and all kinds of things in storage. He knows a lot more than I do. He was always winning prizes at those children's clubs he belonged to. And then later, he'd win all the games you can plug into.'

'Would you say he's smarter than you are?'

'Oh, he thinks so.'

'You don't?'

'I think he's crazy. He's sick. You can't call somebody intelligent if he's not . . . well, listen: a couple of years ago he had a pet hamster. He called it Schizo. It died. I don't think he was feeding it the right stuff. Or maybe he was doing nutritional experiments on it – that's what he said he did to the goldfish. Anyway, after it died, he wanted us to call him Schizo, instead of Eric. We found out he'd gotten all his friends at school to do it. One day Ginette answered the phone and there was this kid on the other end of the line, saying, "I'd like to speak to Schizo, please." Now, that's too much, isn't it? That's over the edge.'

'If you're unhappy, nothing's beyond the limit. He was trying to keep the memory of his pet alive, wasn't he? And I guess he's unhappy about the divorce, too.'

'Oh, the divorce puts him in a perfect position. He can have power over all of us. The hamster business was something else. That had to do with a thing called atavars, or avatars, I forget which. I wouldn't be surprised if he'd killed it as part of a ritual. He doesn't feel affection, you know. He likes to have the upper hand.'

189

He likes to rule, Sandra thought. *Roy means king*. She couldn't figure out whether the story he was telling about his family was the way he'd meant to outline it, or whether her sympathetic reaction had caused him to change some masterplan he'd tried out before. He'd already talked to other people: that was what he said, although that too might be a lie.

'What's his name again?'

'Eric.'

'Was that the only time he asked you to call him by a different name?'

'What scares me,' he said, 'is that he's getting better at it. The first time, it only lasted a few minutes.'

'What?'

'The switch-around. And the second time was for three hours. I just hid in the room till it was over.'

'It happened before? This is – '

'The third time.'

'Okay. I see. There's probably a pattern that'll help to show how it operates.'

'I don't think so. The first two times, it happened while I was asleep. I woke up different. Changed. First time, in the morning. And the second time was in the afternoon – I'd just dropped off, having a nap. This time, I ran up the stairs, opened his door and got the lightswitch, and that did it. The light – it was as if the light caused it. I thought I'd been electrocuted. But there I was, all of a sudden: him. And he was sitting up in bed, saying, "Hi, Schizo." '

'What clothes did you have on?'

'Why?'

'When you turned on the light, you changed size. What happened to the clothes?'

'Oh, yes. That was funny. I had on this huge suit.'

'And the shoes?'

'Same thing. I had to step out of them.'

'What about Eric? He was sitting up in bed and he'd just been changed, too. So, he was full-sized. Whose pajamas was he wearing?'

'He doesn't. He won't wear pajamas.'

His answer wasn't quite quick enough. These things always broke down on the detail, like theories of life after death.

Something was going on. There was no way she could know exactly what, but that didn't matter. She'd caught the gist of it: that this undersized child felt an overwhelming need to take over the position of father, so that he would no longer be helpless. To pretend that his father had become a child would be paying him back for all sorts of things, including the divorce. But he hadn't worked out the finer points of his story.

He'd made a mistake in talking too much. He'd over-explained. He should just have told her that his parents were mean to him. If he'd left it simple like that, she might never have moved away from her initial feeling of pity. But she was being asked for too much. It seemed to her now that he was quite strange and rather creepy. She'd give him something to eat and then call up a rescue squad. She ought to have done that straight away. She sensed herself edging towards betrayal, telling herself that she wasn't qualified to deal with a child who was obviously so disturbed: that this was a job for professionals. She'd telephone somebody. She'd have to. While they'd been talking, while the light had grown less and had at last disappeared, he'd become her responsibility.

'Are you hungry?' she asked. 'I think I'll fix myself something to eat. Come on into the kitchen.' She got up and walked ahead of him.

*

As soon as he saw what was in the icebox, he went to work. Without asking her what she wanted to save or how much he was being offered, he pulled out dishes, bowls and jars. He dropped bread into the toaster and asked where the plates were. He'd just put the finishing touches on a toasted club sandwich when the telephone rang. He froze, his hand covering the food as if he'd stolen it.

'It's probably my aunt,' she told him. She walked into the hall and picked up the receiver.

'Sandra?' Aunt Marion said. 'Did Lomax & Kidder send the men?'

'Oh yes, that's fine. I mean, it seems to be. I haven't measured it, but I'm sure it's okay. It looks the right size.'

Aunt Marion was pleased. She asked in a general way if Sandra was all right; if she needed anything. All the arrangements were just fine, Sandra said: they'd see each other soon. She hung up. She'd forgotten to ask about directions for finding the statue of the Revolutionary heroine. She'd been thinking all the time about the boy in the kitchen.

He was halfway through his sandwich when she got back. She put two more slices of bread into the toaster.

'Was that your boyfriend?' he said.

'That was my aunt. My great-aunt. She wanted to know about the storm window.'

'Why?'

She wasn't going to explain everything to him, to tell him that it wasn't her house and that she was a guest almost as much as he was. She snatched the hot toast out of the machine and threw it on to her plate. 'Why not?' she asked.

'Just asking. You aren't married, are you?'

'No.'

'Is your boyfriend coming back tonight?'

'Maybe. Why?'

'Well, if he's away or something, maybe I could stay over.'

'No.'

'Just for tonight. It would make a big difference. It would mean he couldn't find me.'

'I can't let you stay here. That's definite.'

'You don't know what he's like.'

'Don't you have any ideas about what I can do with you? I don't want to hand you over to the police, but what else can I do?'

'You can keep me right here.'

'Would you rather go to a kind of shelter place, or to a hospital, or to the social workers?'

192

'I don't want to go to any of those places. They'd just send me back to him.'

'I don't think so. Not if you really made a fuss.'

'They wouldn't believe me.'

'Well, don't tell them everything. Just tell them that he treats you badly and you're scared of him and you don't want to go back.'

'They wouldn't care. They'd all start persuading. People talk and talk at you, till you lose hope. And then you just agree to what they decide.'

'Some of those places give you a lawyer.'

She sat down at the kitchen table to eat her sandwich. She'd cut it into four sections. As she picked one of them up, he asked, 'Can I have some of your sandwich?'

She pushed the plate towards him.

They ate in silence for a while, then he said, 'If Jesus Christ came back now, what do you think would happen to him?'

She chewed. Did he think of himself as a misunderstood Messiah – was he aiming that high? 'He'd be a rock star,' she said. 'He'd capture the audience and then he'd get born again and try to take everybody with him.'

'I don't think so. I think he'd be betrayed again. I know it always happens, sooner or later. They just can't believe you.'

She waited. He bit into his quarter of the sandwich. At any minute he might claim to be The Second Coming. Or maybe he'd go for broke and announce that he was an alien.

*

He might just want some sympathy. Or he might be out of his mind. The mentally ill came in all shapes and all ages. So did con artists. And you could see anything on television nowadays: you could be excited by the idea of trying out something you'd seen. This might be a practice run, like a rehearsal. It would take a lot of nerve, or course. There couldn't be many children who would engage strange grown-ups in conversation – that was a thing they were always being warned against. Even if they weren't scared, they'd expect an unfavorable response. But a lonely boy, without brothers and sisters at home or friends at school, might be driven to make contact with other people: this meeting with a stranger might be a way of asking for advice. It could also, just as easily, be a joke he'd cooked up with his friends. If a joke, how harmless was it? And who else was in on it? She was all alone in the house. Maybe she'd better think about that.

She also began to wonder to what extent their acquaintance was a matter of chance. Had he picked her out at random, or had he chosen her specially? It was possible that he'd seen her out walking earlier in the day, and had followed her to see where she lived. That wasn't a nice thought. The picture of a lost and sad little boy didn't agree with such predatory action.

He said, 'If Jesus Christ was alive today, they'd say he was loony.'

'They'd probably just say he was a Communist, unless he started boasting about who his father was. He'd have to keep a low profile.'

'What does that mean?'

'Keep his head down, so nobody could see him against the skyline. But you're assuming that all those miracles and things are true.'

'If Jesus Christ was alive today,' he said again, 'his own mother would turn him over to the cops.'

Not his mother, Sandra thought, *nor his wife. They don't. You can read in the newspapers about maniacs and murderers or rapists, and almost always they have families; they're married. The wives and mothers have to know some of what's going on. Part of them doesn't know, part of them does. But they never say anything. The unspoken, unacknowledged evil in families, society, in politics, isn't condemned because – if once recognized – something would have to be done about it. And then our world would come to an end. Our world is the one where we don't do it ourselves, but we can see the advantages to be gained by keeping quiet about it.*

'His mother wouldn't,' she said, 'but the neighbors might.'

She was beginning to feel as if that kind of traditional neighborly interference might make sense. No matter what they were like or what might have happened between them, his father and mother would be worried to death. She had only his word for it that they were even divorced. She ought to turn him in to somebody who could deal with him.

But not against his will. At the moment he seemed relaxed. It was insidiously agreeable to imagine that he considered her a sympathetic listener and therefore, by inference, a better parent than either of his real ones. There was no denying that he was odd but something about him, from the beginning, had appealed to her. Why had he chosen her to unburden himself to – to put on this performance? Why did people choose each other?

'How did all this begin?' she asked.

'I told you. With the computer.'

'I mean: when did you notice that things were going wrong between you?' *I sound like the advertisements in a* True Romance *magazine*, she thought: *When was it that you first spotted those telltale signs that his love was waning?*

'It all goes back to six years ago,' he said. 'At Christmas.'

'Was that when the marriage split up?'

'No, that was less than two years ago. It wasn't anything to do with that. This was just him. It began with his Christmas present. He'd asked for a magic wand. Nothing else. He said afterwards that he figured he wouldn't have to ask for anything else, because once he had the wand, he could get whatever he made a wish for. That was a disaster. He was so disappointed, he cried. He kept saying, "It doesn't work." And he blamed it on us. He couldn't see why we'd lie to him like that.'

'Didn't you warn him? That it wouldn't really be magic?'

'Of course not. That's silly. Everybody knows that.'

'I can remember seeing one of those tricks at the circus. I thought it really was magic, but I was pretty sure it wasn't the wand that caused it. Or the cloak and hat, or anything like that. I thought it was the person. I thought he was using something like electricity.'

'He thought it was the wand.' He wasn't interested in her childhood memories. 'You think I could have another sandwich?' he said.

'Sure.'

She sat with her elbow bent and her chin in her hand, while he made himself another large sandwich. He'd dropped his guard. All his physical actions seemed comfortable. He was no longer pretending to be a man who had suddenly found himself half the size he was used to being. He must have come to the conclusion that he could count on her allegiance; whereas she, on the contrary, had suddenly had enough. He was too peculiar. Although his story, and the way he was presenting it to her, had its touching and amusing aspects, to hear someone talking about himself in the third person was beginning to annoy her. She remembered with amazement that he, a child, had managed to put her in a position where she was eager to believe that an utterly impossible, supernatural event had taken place. She was right – it wasn't the wand, it was the electricity.

As he unloaded plates and jars from the icebox, he started up again. 'You know how it is,' he said, 'when you want something really bad. You think about it so hard, for so long. You think: nothing could ever make you want it less. But then you get nervous about losing it before you get to it. And then people – they don't actually try to talk you out of it, but they tell you to turn your attention to something else while you're waiting. So you do. And then somehow, you just forget it. You forget how much it meant. The importance is gone.'

'Yes,' she said. That was desire: there was a time-limit attached to it. To be grown up wasn't so marvelous, once you were there. It could only seem wonderful to a child. She hadn't understood that when she was younger. But he did. He already knew about desire.

'This might be building up,' he said. 'That could happen to me. I could just forget my life.'

'I don't think so.'

'It's possible. It happens to people.'

'Amnesia?'

'I meant: forget that I'm me, so that everybody thinks he's me. But I guess I could get amnesia, too.'

'I got interested in amnesia once. It's sort of scary to think about. But it usually only happens after a shock or if you get hit on the head, like concussion or something. Sometimes a big

196

mental shock will start it, but then it only happens to a certain kind of person.'

'What kind?'

'The kind that can't face things.'

'I didn't put enough mayonnaise in this one,' he told her. 'It's good but it needs just a little – '

'I'll get it,' she said. She stood up, took a few steps over to the icebox and had her fingers on the doorhandle when the front doorbell rang.

He jumped up. She got the mayonnaise out and handed it to him. He held on to it as if it were some kind of protection. 'Don't let anybody in,' he said.

'It's all right. I'll just go see who it is. You finish your sandwich.'

*

She walked back through the dining room, the hall, and past the living room. A young man stood outside the front door. He looked like an executive type, not the sort of person to be selling anything door to door or to know her Aunt Marion. A step up from Bert, anyway. Perhaps something had gone wrong with his car or his telephone. Or maybe he was another one who was lost. The knowledge that one other person was in the house – even though underage and possibly not right in the head – made her feel safe against intruders. She opened the door.

He smiled. He said that he was sorry to disturb her.

'That's all right.'

'I wonder if you've seen a boy, about eleven: my son.' He raised a hand as if to indicate a flood level, and added, 'About this high. Hair kind of, um, more or less like mine. Eyes . . .'

He was better-looking than his son, though it was impossible to tell how eleven-year-olds were going to turn out, especially in the matter of looks. He seemed completely all right and normal, not a cruel father or a man who was claiming to be something he wasn't.

'I did see a boy when I was out walking this afternoon,' she said. 'He was coming from the direction of town, over there, and I passed him on my way back here. Has something happened?'

'What did he look like?'

'He was on the other side of the street. He just looked like a schoolboy. You know. Except that he was all dressed up.'

'That's right. He was supposed to be going to a party, but he didn't. He skipped out of it.'

'Is he in some kind of trouble?'

'No, no. This happens periodically. He runs off for a while. Anything he doesn't want to do.'

'It might have been some other boy. I don't know. If I see him again, should I phone the police?'

'No, don't do that. Here. I'll give you my phone number.' He took a notebook and a pen out of his breast pocket. From inside the book he produced a business card, which he handed to her. 'And I wonder if you'd mind giving me your name. I'm Roy Martinson: it's on the card. My son's called Eric. And this is number – ?' He stepped back. His eyes went to the doorframe and the brass numbers on it. 'Twenty-three.'

'Sandra,' she said.

'And do you have a phone number?'

If the house or the telephone had been hers, she would have hesitated. The thought didn't occur to her that by giving out the phone number she might be subjecting her Aunt Marion to a spate of unpleasant anonymous calls. She told him the number.

'I've been running around for hours,' he said, 'and you're the first person I've met who might have seen him beyond Hillside Avenue. Plenty of people saw him at the Perrys', when he was walking out of the party, but they know him in that neighborhood. So, I think I'm going to knock off for a while. Go back home. He might be there already, waiting for me.'

'I hope so,' she said. Everyone did that: told lies and hypocrisies because they wanted to change things, but couldn't. They wanted to appear helpful and comforting, even when their actions were obstructive. They needed to be liked. She hoped that everything would be all right for him. She wanted him to be happy. But she didn't tell him that his son was in the kitchen.

He thanked her and turned away. She closed the door. She

went back to the kitchen, where Eric was sitting behind a pile of jars and plates, his face rigid, his eyes large.

'Well,' she said. 'I said that I'd seen a boy, just some boy not specified, going in the opposite direction. But I think maybe I ought to call up and get you back home.'

'You're a real fool, aren't you?' he said. His tone was so assured, adult and nasty that it stopped her in her tracks. He had a look to go with it. Where did an expression like that come from – from the attractive father?

'Why's that?' she said.

'I know a lot about this house now.'

'And I know your father's phone number.'

'And I know yours. I think I'll stay. Got some videos we can watch?'

'No.'

'Try and make me go.'

'That's easy. I pick up the phone and say you arrived just after your father asked about you.'

'He isn't my father,' the boy screamed. He raised the knife he was holding, until it pointed towards her at a definitely deliberate, offensive angle. Luckily it was one of the kitchen table knives – not a carving knife, but the sharper ones weren't far away. 'You'd better not,' he shouted at her.

For some reason she wasn't afraid. She didn't believe he could hurt her with a blunt knife. And she was bigger than he was. She stepped up and took the knife away from him. 'Don't be silly,' she said.

The situation was too much for her. He was too much. Suddenly she just didn't want him in the house. 'He seemed,' she said, 'like a nice man.'

'Oh, yeah. Women like him.'

They liked him because he made a good impression, even if you didn't count the looks, which made a big difference to begin with. The son made a bad impression, although he'd figured out how to overcome other people's reluctance; he'd kept her talking for hours, persuaded her to invite him to a meal, made her feel guilty about him.

'I like him too,' she said. 'But if you really don't want to go back to him, I won't call him up. I'll phone the police instead.'

'No.'

'Then, your mother.'

'No, no.'

'You choose,' she told him. 'It's up to you.' Three impossible choices – that was freedom. Her own childhood had been like that. She'd never understood why children had to be subjected to that kind of cheating. Now she knew – it was simple; because otherwise, you couldn't get them to do what you wanted them to.

She took out the calling card and went to the phone. She dialed the number.

He didn't move. The phone rang and rang.

She thought that she might have to hang up: the father hadn't had time to get home yet, or he'd gone out again.

There was a click. A man's voice said, 'Hello.' The voice was a little different, but Sandra recognized it. 'Hello,' she said. 'It's Sandra Beale from Number 23, Wheaten Road. You were asking about your son.'

'Is he there?'

'Yes, but he doesn't want – '

'I'll be right over,' he said, and hung up. She put the receiver down.

From the kitchen doorway Eric said, 'That's not fair. I told you not to.'

'That's what you told me,' she said, 'but sometimes people say things they don't really mean, because it's a way of playing for time. You know that you've got to settle things with him. He's the one you live with. If you really don't want to stay with him, there's your mother.'

'I don't want to live with anybody. I want to live all alone. Like you.'

'Well, that's no problem. You'll just have to wait. Till you're grown up. Then you can do it. Do what you like.'

'It's too far away,' he said miserably.

His father, the real Roy, was at the house in a few minutes. His face was serious. The boy couldn't look at him.

'Come on,' he said.

Eric shuffled forward. Roy put an arm around him. 'That's right,' he said. He moved a step back and opened the door. Over Eric's head he said, 'Thank you,' to her, and left. She nodded. She'd done the right thing, but she'd betrayed someone in order to do it; someone who was weaker than she was.

She closed the door after them. She stood there a long while before locking up and putting the chain on.

*

She went back to the kitchen and sat down at the table. The evidence of Eric's hunger was everywhere in front of her: jars, open boxes, bottles. She stood up again to put the mayonnaise into the icebox. She was beginning to feel bad.

She cleared up the table, put things back where they were supposed to be, washed the dishes and got out the dustpan and brush. She felt a little better. What was either of them to do with her? They were strangers.

She took a long time cleaning up in the kitchen. To keep herself company, and to stop herself thinking about Eric and Roy, she turned on the radio. She worked until everything was spotless but she was almost ready to start the job all over again. It wasn't so much that her aunt's high standards of housekeeping urged her towards imitation; rather, that she was in the sort of mood that was drawing her deeper into itself.

She cleaned the sink, the counters and tabletop, the floor. Then she made sure that the back door was locked, looked at the windows to see that the catches were on, and turned out some of the lights. She hadn't thought about Bert for hours. It was time to give serious attention to the subject. She'd planned to use some of her time over the weekend doing just that. *Right*, she thought: *Bert. What am I going to do about it?* Nothing came to her. She didn't have anything in common with him, he took her for granted, she'd never believed that he loved her; and as a matter of fact, she didn't like him enough, either. The hell with him.

She made herself a cup of coffee and took it around the corner into the alcove between the hall and the dining room, where the television set was. Aunt Marion maintained that she looked at the news and nothing else, but Sandra suspected that she watched a couple of quiz shows too, every once in a while. A capacious, stiff-backed armchair was positioned in front of the set. A small table stood to the right of the chair, a footstool in front. In the seat, and against the back, several cushions had been bunched into a second, inner shape. Sandra pulled the chair back a few feet, pushed the pillows around and tried them out in different ways.

She looked at a documentary about an Indian landowner who had made his family property into a nature reserve. Among his many schemes for maintaining the natural balance of plants and animals was one that would restore the original wildlife to the numbers on record before drought, famine, flood and – worst of all – hunters had disrupted the populations. Tigers had died out of the area, but one of the workers in the reserve had brought him a female leopard cub. The film was about how he trained the leopard to go back to the wild.

She watched to the end of the program and then for a little while longer, through the start of a comedy, until she began to yawn. She turned off the machine, checked the doors and windows once again, looked around the kitchen and went upstairs.

She took her book with her. Aunt Marion read a lot, mostly biographies and history books; if she had a few minutes of extra time, she'd pick up her embroidery or her knitting. She was a real person, full of information and practical experience: someone you could take seriously. When she died, she would leave behind many useful things that she'd made herself and given to other people. Her character too was generous. She sometimes dispensed advice, although usually only when asked for it, but all the time – in a transaction as easy as breathing in and out – she gave understanding. Whenever Sandra was with her for a few hours, she could feel herself taking on the way Aunt Marion looked at things. For all her traditionally spinsterish ways, Aunt Marion was a woman whose type was that of a mother. She would know what to do about a runaway child. *Never mind*, Sandra thought. *It's all settled.*

When she was ready for bed, she no longer felt like reading. She left the book on the night table and turned out the light.

She dreamt that she was standing on the outer stairs of a grand plantation mansion. The steps she stood on, the columns at either side, the building behind her, were all white, like the dress she was wearing. She could actually feel the dress, in which she stood as if captured: the skirt went out and down from the waist like the sides of a balloon and she was lashed into the center of its many lacy spheres. As the dream began, she'd been looking outward, evidently expecting someone to arrive, but there wasn't anyone there.

The next thing she knew, she was standing inside the house. She was still waiting, but now she had no view of the outside, nor of the front entrance leading to it. Several men appeared suddenly, carrying something. Of course, she thought: Aunt Marion had told her to let the workmen in. She went forward into another room and met the gang of men. She started to give them directions about where to put the window; she now knew exactly where it was to be. As she pointed to a wall in front of her, there – as if it had been there all along, and not made up by her on the spur of the moment – was the empty space where the window was to fit.

The men went to work. The window was in place. She was alone again. But once more she could see – looking through the newly installed window to the front of the house – the steps, the carriageway and the garden beyond. The window became a door. A man walked up the steps and rang the bell. She could see through: it was Eric's father, Roy. He said, as before, 'I hope I'm not disturbing you.' She let him in.

They went into a large room, also white. They stood there for a few minutes while he told her something about what had gone wrong in his son's life. Then he put his hand on her breast. They made love. They talked about getting married. Aunt Marion came in with a wedding dress and veil. She was accompanied by deliverymen who carried flowers. The house changed into a church: the wedding was about to begin. But Roy wasn't there. In his place stood his child, Eric. Aunt Marion was at her side; she seemed to think everything was normal. So did everybody else. And she, Sandra, was the bride – she was there to get married. She took Eric's hand. She said, 'I do.' He said, 'Sure, I guess so.' Then they were going back down the aisle together. Everyone else was happy; some of them were even applauding. But she felt defrauded. She didn't see why she hadn't been able to get the one she'd wanted. 'Where is he?' she asked her aunt, who said, 'He's on a tropical island.'

* * *

The next morning was a sunny day. A light, springlike breeze fluttered across the neighborhood gardens and twirled back on itself, playing. She felt it on her face when she opened the front door to take in the newspaper.

She made herself some real coffee and had a large, thick piece of toast with butter and honey. The bread was from a homebaked loaf – the kind of thing that was probably as fattening as cake. She put extra milk in her coffee. She didn't turn on the radio or the television, or bother to open the paper. The only sounds to be heard were of her chewing and swallowing. It seemed as if the rest of the world had disappeared. She wondered suddenly why her aunt didn't have a pet. Dogs could be too much trouble: you had to walk them and they pined if you left them. But a cat wouldn't mind being left on its own, or being fed and patted by strangers. She thought that she might give her aunt a kitten. She'd have to find out first, whether it would be a good idea. There were many people, more than you'd think, who didn't like pets, and who believed that life with a pet carried the same demands and responsibilities as life with another person.

She went for a walk. She stepped out of the door and into a world that seemed to be abandoned by the human race. The birds were still there and a lone dog trotted purposefully, tail-up, in the distance. But no people came into view, not even children. Everyone must have listened to the weather report, considered it believable, and decided to drive away to other places: to see friends, to visit relatives, to search for the more beautifully leaved trees that must be somewhere, although no one had seen them that year: any place, different but the same.

She started out in the direction of the pioneer statue. Her feet, her whole body felt light and unusually flexible. A wonderful day could really be better than people.

The road she was walking along led her through a neighborhood where the houses were small, as were their front yards, but there was no indication of poverty. On the contrary, houses and gardens alike were well tended. Aunt Marion would have lived in such an area if she'd moved into a house forty years later than she had. When she'd married, these houses wouldn't have been where they were. They came after the days of large families.

Two turnings brought her down to the end of a long road that, as far as she could guess, curved back towards where she'd hoped – the day before – to find the statue. When she got to the point where she expected to see the beginnings of the road she remembered, there were three branches: one kept on, the other turned off down a hill and the third seemed to go back in the right direction, but uphill and at an angle that, if unchanged, might lead her eventually to the other side of town. She was lost again. She was also getting tired.

Where had she made the mistake? Or had she taken more than one wrong turning? She stood still for a minute, thinking that there was no way of guessing which way the roads went, especially for someone with such a poor sense of direction.

As she was looking ahead and to the right, she noticed smoke coming from somewhere. At least one person was at home and out in the gardens around her, burning leaves. The smell was faint, and gone away, back again and then lost. It might be coming from a long way off. At that moment a man appeared in the road that ran from the top of the hill. She turned around. She decided to retrace her steps. It wasn't exactly that she felt nervous, but she didn't know the neighborhood, nobody else was nearby, and the locality from which the stranger came was unknown; he was therefore to be avoided, whereas if she had seen a man raking leaves in a yard, she'd have gone up to him and asked how to get back to the street her aunt's house was on. A man standing by his own house was fixed, identifiable and as safe as if he were wearing a nametag. Strangers could come from anywhere. She forgot that she too was a stranger.

She was almost at the end of the row of houses and approaching to another fork in the road – hoping that she'd remember it – when she heard someone calling her name from behind her. She turned. The man from the top of the hill was coming up to her at a slow run. She didn't recognize him until he called her name again and waved. It was Roy, Eric's father, from the night before. He looked different. He was wearing a pullover and a pair of chinos. He might have been a student or even a teenager.

'Hi,' he said. 'I waved at you from back there.'

'I didn't see,' she said. 'I was trying to figure out what road to take. I'm lost.'

'This one goes back to your house.'

'I wanted to get to the statue of the pioneer woman.'

'Oh. Sure. Wilhelmina.'

'Is that her name?'

'No, that's just what we call her.'

We? Did that mean him and his son, or him and the wife he was divorced from? Or a new girl he was going out with?

'It's a long walk up the hill,' he said, 'or back to Trellis Road, and then you jog left.'

'That's where I went wrong.'

'I'll walk you back.' He started to move forward, putting his hand on her arm for a moment as he did so. She fell into step beside him.

'It's a beautiful day,' she said.

'One of the few. It's been a lousy year. Even now: I hear it's still raining just about everyplace else.'

'Well, I guess we need it, after the drought. The trees look so sad.'

'Yes. Everything looks wrong.'

They passed a yard where someone had been burning a pile of leaves. Whoever it was had gone back inside.

'How's Eric?' she said.

'He's okay. Quiet. It follows a pattern. I guess you've seen him around here before. He's been going off like this for – oh, a year and some. Usually he comes home of his own accord.'

'Oh?'

'It's hard to know what to do. I keep hoping he'll grow out of it.'

'Have you asked a doctor about it?'

'He doesn't need a doctor. He needs a mother.'

'Well,' she said, 'he's got one, hasn't he?'

'What he had was worse than having nothing.'

'There's something I ought to tell you.'

'Yes?'

'He threatened me with a knife.'

'Oh, God. I've always thought most of what he does is for show. And a lot of talk.'

'I don't know how serious it was. The knife was just an ordinary table knife. But it could have been a sharper one. He yelled at me not to phone you and he held it like this. Right? I couldn't tell if he meant to do anything, because I don't know him. But it's a bad sign. Especially since – well, at the moment he's too young to be dangerous. But what's going to happen later? He's smart and he doesn't like people.'

'He likes you.'

'Oh? But I'm the one who betrayed him. I handed him over to you.'

'I guess you made him realize that it was necessary.'

They came to the point where the neighborhood changed. She saw that there was a road running around to the back of one of the houses; she hadn't noticed it and, if she had, she'd have assumed it to be a private driveway. Now that she was seeing from another angle, she remembered that it was the road to the statue. 'We're here,' she said. 'This is it.'

'Do you want to go see it?'

She looked at her watch. 'I'd like to,' she said, 'but I don't know what time my aunt – she said she'd be back on Sunday afternoon. That could mean one minute past twelve.'

'That's a long way off.'

'Yes. Okay, sure. I'd like to.' They walked up the road she'd missed. He talked about the neighborhood: he'd moved there around the time when he was at college. He said, 'So you live with your family? That's nice. Hardly anyone does any more.'

'Oh, I don't, either. I live in town. I'm only keeping an eye on my aunt's house while she's away for the weekend.'

'In that case, it was incredibly lucky that you were there.'

'I don't know about that.'

'Oh yes – definitely. Ricky doesn't respond to everyone. In fact, he'll hardly speak to anyone. I think he sort of opened up to you. He keeps talking about you.'

'What does he say?'

'How nice you are.'

'Well. I was just thinking last night that my great-aunt would have handled the whole thing a lot better. I don't know much about children.'

'Christ, who does? They seem to do certain things at set ages, so there's a general standard you can measure their behavior against, but that only works if you've got one of those so-called average children. I'll tell you one thing: the worst advice you can get about them comes from people who are supposed to make their living out of it. Teachers and those behavior people. Especially when they're faced with a boy like Ricky. Aside from everything else, he's simply a lot more intelligent than any of his teachers. And the ones who can see it, don't like that. Most of them are too dumb to register. They've got a format that somebody's handed them, and they go ahead and shove until every child's been squeezed into it. They tried to do the same with me. Of course, he's not helping things. I think about a year ago he figured out that there's just about nothing they can do to you, if you refuse to cooperate. I wasn't smart enough to get that far until I was in my teens. And by that time I wanted all the things I was being bribed with. He doesn't want anything. He's got nothing to lose. Oh, hell. I'm sorry to dump all this on you, especially on such a fantastic day. Look at that.'

They'd reached the top of the hill, from which further wooded

208

lands – in front and to the sides – stretched away. If the trees had been in their normal autumn colors the sight would have been staggering. Even as it was, the air glittered, houses to the far distance were picked out crisply; you could see right back to the next town, miles away.

'Not bad,' he said.

'It's wonderful. I only saw it like this once before, when I was in school.' She looked down on the roadways ahead. They were laid out as clearly as if on a map. Although she couldn't see the statue, she could make out the spot where it stood, among evergreens. When she turned back to him she knew that while she'd been absorbed in the view, he'd been looking at her. On his face she caught the last of the expression that had been there: concentrated, possessive. It made her self-conscious; she wanted to move on. 'It's over there, isn't it?' she said.

He nodded. They began to stroll to the fork in the road.

'Maybe,' she said, 'you could find one of those schools for gifted children, where he'd be able to meet other kids and teachers that didn't make him feel so bored and out of step.'

'I could. It would mean sending him away. I don't want to do that. Unless he starts asking about it himself. That might happen in a few years. That would be great. But so far, I figure: he's been rejected by one parent – I don't want him to get the idea that the one he's got left is trying to get rid of him, too. Poor little squirt. I was just the same at his age.'

'You?' She couldn't believe that a man who looked so open, athletic, handsome and successful, had ever been anything other than a miniature version of what he was at the moment.

'Just exactly,' he said. 'I thought they started off, right at the beginning, thinking I was a freak. It didn't seem to me that they were doing anything to help. Or that they wanted to. It takes a long while to understand that there's not really much you can do when a child's unhappiness is caused by not fitting in. You've either got to grow out of it, or move away.'

They came to a second turning. The road started to go downhill. Soon they were surrounded by fir trees. She said, 'He could become a member of one of those groups for people with high IQs.'

'He's done that already. They all have endless games with each other. Playing chess on the computer and doing those wargames where you conquer the world.'

'He likes those computer things?'

'Sure. So do I. It's part of my work.'

'Oh? He said your job was doing the advertising for toys.'

He stopped walking, and laughed. He said, 'That's one way of putting it, I suppose. I'm in aeronautics. What else did he say?'

'Oh, lots of things.'

'Such as?'

'Maybe he wouldn't like it if I repeated them.'

'You're kidding. I'm his father.'

'I'll tell you something: I can remember a family Christmas, when I was about five, and one of my grown-up relatives teased me about something I'd put on my letter to Santa Claus. I was just mortified. Everybody else was fine – they didn't say a thing. But it only takes one. So, I know that children can be funny, but sometimes they just don't hide what they think. And that's not really funny. It's – '

'It's just artless. Without guile.'

'Right. So to get together and laugh about something that might be a secret dream somebody told you in private – you see what I mean?'

'Of course,' he said.

'You're laughing.'

'I'm wondering what you asked for.'

To the left, beyond him, she saw the break in the trees. She skipped towards it. He followed. The statue stood at the end of a narrow path lined with plants that had flowered earlier in the year. Only the green showed now. She hadn't remembered them, nor the enclosing height of the pines and hemlocks, nor the fact that the statue itself, up on a plinth, was so small.

'It looks different,' she said. 'I don't remember those lines of flowers or anything.'

'How old were you the last time you saw it?'

'The only time. About eleven, nearly twelve.'

210

'That might explain it.'

'But I was almost as tall as I am now.'

'Well, the flowers have been there for six years. And the trees would have grown. And you only saw it once.'

'Oh, I like it just as much now, but I don't like the idea that I could remember something all wrong. Why should that be?'

'You've fitted it in with the other things you've seen since.'

'I see.' The statue hadn't changed; she had. She liked that idea even less than the thought of being wrong. If you weren't what you were, what were you? Who were you?

'It's a pretty little statue,' he said.

'Yes. And I like the story. It's supposed to be true, too, although I never heard if she got back to her family afterwards, or even whether or not she found her husband.'

'That's not important. In all those stories the main thing is the endeavor. If you're going to wonder about reality, none of it makes sense.'

'Why not?'

'I bet they'd have given her a rough time in the locker rooms.'

'She wouldn't have had to be in a regiment. And they wouldn't have been in barracks, anyway. They were all out in the woods.'

'Until she got to some kind of a town where she could get information about her husband. As soon as she came into contact with other people, she'd be eating with them and washing with them.'

'They always leave that out of the history books.'

'Because it's assumed. That's like not making a movie that's got people taking a leak all the time. You know they do, but there's no reason to put it in unless that's your favorite part of the story.'

'Why do you call her Wilhelmina?'

'I can't even remember. Had enough?'

'Yes. Thank you for showing me how to get here.'

'My pleasure. I'll walk you home.'

They walked back slowly. She asked him about his work. He wanted to know if she'd seen a play he'd read about; and, if not, would she like to go to it with him? She said that she would. She wrote down the address and phone number of her place in town. She asked what day of the week he had in mind. 'Tomorrow,' he said.

*

Aunt Marion didn't arrive till nightfall. She was loaded down with packages and was full of apologies for her lateness. 'It was such a beautiful day,' she said.

'How was Elsie?'

'Much better – almost transformed. We had a lovely day. We talked all about old times. You know, it makes such a difference, when you reach my age, to know people who remember you the way you were as a child. And they remember your parents and grandparents, too. I used to think that remark of Will Rogers' was so stupid, but sometimes nowadays I wonder if it mightn't be true, as long as you had enough time to get to know the person. Time does seem to give you the truth in ways that are hard to explain. I think about it a lot.'

'What's all the shopping?'

'Bargains, dear. I've spent a fortune. Elsie decided that we'd go out as soon as I got there. I didn't think she looked well at all. I thought we ought to stay at home. But she wouldn't take no for an answer. A very stubborn woman when she wants to be. She took me out to one of those enormous shopping malls. But it wasn't like any one I've ever seen. The quality of the merchandise – I was bowled over. And they had a sale on. We ripped through that place like nobody's business. Wait till I show you.'

'Aunt Marion, I had a strange thing happen while you were away.'

'Not the pipes?'

'No, it – '

'Or something electrical?'

'Nothing like that. The house is fine. And so is the windowpane they delivered. And everything else. No. It was a little boy, who rang the doorbell and seemed to be lost. I asked him in and he started telling me all kinds of wild stories. And then he asked me if there was anything to eat, so I took him into the kitchen.

And I'm afraid he's eaten up just about everything in the refrigerator.'

'Good. That's what it was for.'

'I thought I was never going to get rid of him, but then his father came looking for him and the boy finally agreed to go back. They live around here; I wonder if you know them? His name's Roy Martinson. The Roy stands for Conroy.'

'Oh,' Aunt Marion said. 'It rings a bell. Faintly. You'll have to let me think. I've been back in my schooldays all weekend.' She bustled around, found some bread and a few cookies that Eric hadn't discovered, and made tea. Over their meal she showed Sandra the haul from her shopping binge: shoes, gloves, a tweed skirt, yards of summer materials. 'I never used to like shopping,' she said. 'It was always a duty – a necessity. And I had to be careful with the pennies. I used to walk miles to find something that cost a little less. That was a long time ago. The world has changed for the better in that way. Money has changed. These credit cards . . . Of course, we were brought up to think that that sort of thing was immoral: to be in debt. And I'd never dream of letting it mount up – I send my check off straight away. But it's nice to go on a spree with an old friend.'

'To buy things you don't really need, but you want them like crazy because they're pretty.'

'Yes. And even to spend a while looking at things that you'd never bother with. We went to a camera store. That was very interesting. I thought that – for what they were – the prices were quite reasonable. I've still got Hudson's old camera, but he used to make it sound so complicated that I was sort of tempted by these new ones. They do everything for you. Ordinary people never used to be able to work mechanical gadgets without a lot of training. Nowadays you just buy a box and push the buttons and out comes something – like magic. We went into a typewriter shop too, because Elsie wanted to sit down and I thought I'd like to find out about word processors. It's so embarrassing to say that you only came in because you couldn't walk another step. They were very kind. They found Elsie a chair straight away and a nice young man explained the machines to me. And then he let

213

me type a letter and we printed it out. Naturally I wouldn't have taken up his time if they'd been busy in there, but everyone else seemed to be down at the china reject shop. They had a clearance sale on.'

'But you didn't buy any?'

'We didn't want to carry anything heavy. And besides, what would I do with one more earthenware pot or a willow-pattern coffee cup? Most of my things just stay in the cupboard until the bridge-club meetings. No. We thought about going into the garden center, but by that time we were getting hungry, so we stopped for lunch. My, the different restaurants they have: there's a whole place just for desserts. It's called "Sweet Stuff". They serve everything you can name. Then there's a restaurant for breakfast, and a teashop and all kinds of international food: Chinese, Indian, Malayan, Swiss, Italian, Hungarian. Well, we couldn't make up our minds. We went into the nearest one.'

'Aunt Marion, I think you've hit on a new system for fun shopping: only go into a store if you have to sit down.'

'It worked very well, I must admit. They gave us a really nice luncheon.'

'What did you have?'

'A salad full of radish sprouts. And for dessert, a peanutbutter waffle with something called Dreme Whip. Delicious. It almost convinced me that I ought to buy myself a waffle iron. But I wouldn't use it enough. Do you have one?'

'No. For the same reason. We had one at home. It just sat there, except for about once a year. We used to get it out around Christmastime. I think nobody ever wanted to have to clean it afterwards.'

'And Elsie had a most intriguing soup: carrot soup with cardamum, ginger and a bit of cream. I meant to write that down.'

Sandra stood up. She crossed the kitchen and picked a pencil out of the flat straw basket on the windowsill behind the sink. She tore a piece of paper off the notepad next to the basket.

'Thank you, dear,' her aunt said. 'I owe one or two people a good recipe. That spinach and cottage cheese casserole was the last surefire thing I had to trade with. I hope it wasn't too dull for you here.'

'No. There was that little boy.'

'Oh, yes. Of course.'

'And I went for a couple of walks and watched a nature movie on TV. And then I did a lot of thinking about that boyfriend. You know.'

'And?'

'I decided that I've got to break it off. I don't know why I let it go on so long. He's always going away on those hunting weekends or taking a trip to see some team play a game. The only time we're together is when we're eating or going to the movies.'

'Men do have their particular interests, you know. They like to get together every once in a while, to drink and tell stories. It's like my bridge meetings. I'd miss them dreadfully.'

'That isn't all of it. I'm not having any fun. And he doesn't even know I'm there.' He just wanted someone to sleep with. She didn't think her aunt would care to hear that; it would make plain what Sandra's relationship with men was, and the idea would offend her. Aunt Marion undoubtedly knew all those things in any case, but she appreciated a certain amount of tact: they weren't actually to be mentioned.

'If you don't enjoy his company,' Aunt Marion said, 'then I'd do what they recommend on the stockmarket. I'd cut my losses.'

'That's what I'm going to do.'

'Well, then. I'm glad to hear that your weekend hasn't been a waste.'

'On the contrary. I really think I needed a little time away from things.'

She went upstairs and checked that she'd packed everything. She put on her jacket and brought her bag down. At the door she kissed her aunt goodbye, stepped out and turned around again, to smile and wave.

The old woman stood holding the door. Her face was thoughtful. She told Sandra to have a good trip back to town, and to drive carefully. Then she said, 'Oh. I know what it was: Conroy Martinson. I remember now. He's the one who killed his wife.'

Somehow, although Aunt Marion seldom got things wrong, she must have mixed up one story with another. Sandra was so sure of it that she hadn't contradicted her, nor did she remember, until she was well into the weekend's homecoming rush of cars, that there was evidence to back up her conviction: both father and son had spoken of the ex-wife in the present tense. She was certainly still alive. Sandra put the matter from her mind and concentrated on the increasing traffic.

When she got home, she was later than she'd thought she would be. She dropped her bag inside the door. She looked around. Not even a new coat of paint would cheer the place up. She'd lived there too long and she'd never liked it.

Her eye fell on one of Bert's knapsacks. His hockey stick and fishing rod were in the closet, the iceskates and baseball bat in the cupboard under the window. It was just luck that everyone in the building had been issued a new set of keys after the Huxtables had had the burglary; and that she hadn't yet made copies for Bert. She gathered all his clothes and equipment into a pile near the door. Then she climbed into bed and finished reading her novel.

In the morning, she bundled Bert's possessions into the car. She drove to work early so that she could dump everything with his secretary before he came in.

The moment she walked away from his office, she felt elated. She crossed to the other side of the building, took the elevator down and went to her desk. She picked up the phone and made an appointment to get her hair done during her lunch hour. On the dot of one she left her desk, beating her friend, Maureen, to the doorway into the hall.

At the hairdresser's they gave her a sandwich and a cup of coffee. While she was trying to balance the cup and get it up to her mouth without hitting the hood of the dryer, she noticed that another woman was having the same sort of trouble, but worse: she hadn't figured out that she should leave the saucer and spoon behind.

On her way back to the office she ran into Bert. 'Sandra. Hi,' he said.

'Hi,' she answered. She kept walking.

'Where are you going?'

'Back to work.'

'I thought we'd go out to lunch.'

'I've just had lunch.'

'I mean: I did think. Where were you?'

'Hairdresser. Bert, I'm going to be late.'

'I thought maybe we could have a talk.'

'About what?'

'I'll drop by tonight, okay?'

'No, not tonight.'

'Why not?'

'Because I can't. Come on, Bert. What do you want to tell me?'

'Well, I've been thinking: Maybe we should cool it for a while.'

'That's not enough.'

'What?'

'We've got to admit that it's no good, and say goodbye.'

'I didn't mean anything drastic like that.'

'Well, I do. That's why I left all your stuff with your secretary. Didn't she tell you?'

'Oh. She did mention something. I thought it must have been those spiked running shoes I asked you to get fixed.'

'I'll phone you at the weekend,' she said.

'Hell, Sandra, you know I can't this weekend.'

'Okay. Next weekend.'

'What's wrong with tomorrow night?'

'I can't. I could see you some day for lunch, I guess.'

He pulled out an appointment book. She started to walk ahead. She got as far as the steps in front of the glass doors. 'How about Thursday?' he called after her. She nodded, waved and went inside. She had no intention of keeping the date. She still felt irritated, which was silly. There was no point in being angry because she'd let things between them go on too long. Now she begrudged him the time she'd spent in his company, yet that wasn't his fault. It was hers. Everything would be different when she went to the theater with Roy.

That afternoon she was out of the office in record time and on her way home to get ready for the evening.

*

He arrived on the dot of six. And he was driving the kind of car that looked like the ones you could see in races. It was red. He said, 'I hope you don't mind riding low to the ground.'

'As long as we don't drive under a truck,' she said. She buckled up her seatbelt. She felt as if she were in a fighter plane, next to the controls.

On their way in to town they passed small groups of children dressed up as witches, ghosts and goblins. A few of the gangs included a grown woman: a mother who was too worried about her children to allow them out trick-or-treating even if they were surrounded by friends. When Sandra had been at school, they hadn't allowed that kind of thing. If anyone tried to bring a mother along, or even an older brother or sister, the original crowd would go into a huddle, plan out what moves to make and then, at a signal, run out on the sissy and the protector.

He drove to an underground parking lot that belonged to a hotel up the road from the theater. The attendant knew him; he also knew the car: an expression of intense compassion poured over his face as he got behind the wheel to park it.

They went into the building at a side entrance. There didn't seem to be any guests, and only a few of the staff were working. Over at the reception desk a white-haired man was reading a ledger. Roy walked her across the lobbies and into a waiting room. 'I love this place,' he said. 'It used to be a grand old hotel back in the nineties. Everybody used to come here. Then – I don't know what happened. Maybe they didn't modernize the bathrooms, or something. I've never stayed here, so I don't know what it's like upstairs. People used to come here in the thirties for a while. That was the last time it was fashionable. It's a shame. When I was at college across the river, it was just as empty as it is tonight. I used to bring my friends over for cocktails. But

218

erybody was trying to be casual then: eating hamburgers and
earing sneakers. It never caught on with anyone else.'

He took her into the bar and introduced her to a gnomelike old
rtender whose name was Perkins. He and Perkins talked about
e hotel, the staff and old clients, while Sandra gazed around
e room, taking in the immensely high ceiling, the marble
oors, the thick, flower-patterned rugs, the old furniture that
as solid but elegant.

'Nice?' Roy asked her.

She nodded. Already she liked the things he liked.

They had two of Perkins' secret-recipe cocktails. Sandra would
ave liked a third, or even more. She'd have liked to sit there for
ours. But Roy looked at his watch. It was time to go.

They caught a cab to the theater and arrived in time to look
rough the program. 'I haven't been to see a play in years,' she
id.

'At the last play I went to, I was surrounded by people who
ept whispering to each other all the time.'

'That's because of television. It gets to be automatic.'

'I was ready to start hitting them over the head.'

'They wouldn't have noticed. They're those people who turn
n the machine and talk over it all day long.'

The light dimmed slowly. The chattering of the audience gave
ay to a hush. As the house lights went out altogether, the
urtain rose on a scene set in a psychoanalyst's office. The
nalyst was pretending to listen to a patient, yet all the while he
as doing everything in his power to prevent a woman, hidden
ehind his chair, from stepping out and revealing herself. She
as trying to leave the office. And she was also attempting to put
n the rest of her clothes. The patient talked about how he
ought that his wife might be seeing another man.

The next scene was set in the office of a female analyst. She had
nce been married to the first analyst and now she was taking
otes while she listened to one of her patients.

Each new scene allowed the audience to see that the characters
ho confessed their infidelities or doubts were giving infor-

219

mation to the very people who were involved in their betrayal
Not only that: after the initial misunderstandings had beer
shown, they were followed by variations; the characters who
appeared to be the conscious manipulators of the first scenes
became the unwitting victims of those that followed. And after
the second act the pace quickened: people were rushing through
doors and dashing behind sofas so fast that every person or
stage was suffering from at least four mistaken ideas. But it al
worked out in the end: by the time the final curtain came down
all the couples – even the two analysts – were reunited, and
everything was serene and reasonable, with only a slight loose
end announcing that perhaps a gentle tweak at the plot could
start the whole mix-up all over again.

Sandra and Roy turned to smile at each other while they
applauded. Before the last curtain call he took her hand and led
her out of her seat to follow the couple next to him, who were
heading down the center aisle.

They were out on the street, with their coats on, and climbing
into a taxi before the main crowd had left the auditorium. And
soon they were sitting at a table for two, in a restaurant where the
lighting was only slightly dimmed and the waiters and the other
customers were lively enough to make the place fun.

They talked about the play: how delightful it had been and
how cleverly it managed to string the audience along from one
point to the next. The action had been like clockwork – like one of
those watches where you could look in and see the wheels going
around. Cause and effect had been so clearly demonstrated: you
began to think that if only you could pin down the sources of
your own mistakes and confusions, they too would be explained
and, consequently, solved.

They ate and drank and looked into each other's eyes. He told
her stories about where he'd grown up. She talked – because he
asked her – about Aunt Marion and then about the rest of her
relatives: her attractive, pig-headed sister, her maddening and
sometimes unkind, yet irresistible mother, her adorable, absent-
minded father, who was the peacemaker of the family.

All at once she realized that she'd had a lot to drink. She didn want to spoil things; she put her glass down. 'This is a nice place,' she said.

'Yes, it's not bad. At least the food's all right. And you can see what you're eating. And nobody's playing a piano right in your ear.'

'Is Eric out in a costume tonight?'

'He said he didn't want to. He said he'd decided that Hallow-een was for the younger kids.'

'I always loved it. I was very upset when it all stopped. Who's with him?'

'Somebody named Karen.'

'Not the one who gives him a bath?'

'He told you about that?'

'She didn't sound like a very good babysitter.'

'No, but she's a great cook. That's what I hired her for. Her name's Debbie.'

'Oh. He didn't say she worked for you. I got the idea that she came in from outside.'

'That's Ricky. He'll take something that's basically true, extract the part that made the impression on him and rework it so that it's completely different. Something's there that's similar to what was in the actual event, but even if you dig for it, the emphasis is all wrong.'

'I sort of figured that out while he was talking to me. But I think most people do all that anyway, don't you? I do it. To make myself more interesting, or to impress. Most of the time I'm not really aware of doing it.'

'He's fully aware of what he's doing, I can tell you that. Don't ever underestimate his intelligence.'

'He needs some friends,' she said. She cleared her throat and added, 'At least, that's the way it seemed to me.'

'Uh-huh.'

'Because he needed to talk.'

'I don't think it's because the other kids avoid him. But I don't know what comes first: he's standoffish with them. And a snob. They call him names. And then he says something back, full of five-syllable words they can't find in the dictionary because they don't know how to spell them. That's how the business with Schizo began: because he used the term "schizophrenic" in class. It was one of the words he was showing off with; he'd even named his pet hamster Schizo, because of the way it ran around. The hamster – that was horrible. Of course he didn't mean to do it. And it taught him something he'll always remember, but still – I'll never forget that moment when he came screaming down the stairs, all covered in blood.'

'What happened?'

'Oh, he . . . he's so smart, you know. It's hard to remember that sometimes he just doesn't see things any idiot can understand.'

'What happened?' she said again.

'He cut it open, to see what was inside.'

'Oh, no.' She put down her fork.

'I don't think the blood bothered him at all. It was when the hamster started to squeak. Then he was terrified.'

She put a hand over her face. She couldn't get rid of the picture; Eric and his hamster: cutting it open with a razor blade, or something less grown-up – a pair of scissors, maybe.

'He was so upset about it that he cried for hours. We held a funeral for it and everything. Buried it in a shoebox, underneath a lilac bush in the back yard. I was just beginning to believe that he'd recovered, when he started to talk about how some people were vegetarians because they thought it was wrong to kill animals. I worked for days on explaining the difference between a domestic pet and an animal bred for consumption.'

'Is there a difference?'

'Of course there is. That's why farmers eat the animals their neighbors sell, and let them buy the ones they've raised. It's the emotion you invest in them.'

'It isn't the act of killing?'

'You're not a vegetarian.'

'No. But if I had to kill the animals, I would be. So would a lot of people.'

'Not me.'

'And Eric? Ricky?'

'I think he'd agree with you. On the other hand, if it were for something like medical research, I have a feeling he'd be able to kill anything or anybody without giving a thought to how much it hurt. He's good at putting things in different compartments. That's another reason why I have such a hard time keeping up with him. He's always got something new.'

'Well, he's still growing.' She changed the subject back to the play. They had coffee and a liqueur.

It was still fairly warm outside, in spite of the late hour and the time of year. They walked back to the hotel. As he started the car he said, 'I've always wanted to check in here for the night sometime, just for fun.' He looked at her as he said it.

'I can see why,' she said quickly, brushing aside the suggestion he'd put in front of her. She knew it was intended and he knew that she knew, but she had to act as if she hadn't seen what he'd meant. The whole thing was ridiculous but they were supposed to follow a prescribed set of moves in the correct order, otherwise the result would be like a painting-by-number game where no one had obeyed the instructions. Unlike her meeting with Eric, there was a particular, formulated method according to which this encounter was meant to proceed, and to finish.

'It's a great hotel,' she said. 'It's one of those places you know you'll want to go back to.'

At the street entrance of the building she lived in he said, 'I'll see you to your door.'

At the door he kissed her. It wasn't an ordinary kiss. She was ready to give him everything right then, but she'd never said yes on the first date, not even when she'd been a little drunk. She pulled away. He whispered, 'No?'

'It isn't that I don't want to,' she said.

'Can I see you tomorrow? Same time, same place?'

'All right. Yes,' she said.

She closed the door slowly. If they went out the next night and came back to the apartment afterwards . . . She suddenly thought: It was going to take her all night to clean the place up.

She put the books and papers into neat stacks, dragged the second table back to where it was supposed to be and hid the

223

laundrybags behind the bathroom door. She was dusting the top shelf of the bookcase when the downstairs doorbell rang.

She picked up the receiver of the entryphone and said hello. There was no answer. She said hello again. A man's voice, not easy to recognize, said, 'I forgot something.' It was Bert. It had to be, even though it didn't sound like his voice.

'It's late,' she said. 'Phone me tomorrow. Goodnight.' She hung up. She put the chain on the door.

The bell went again. She ignored it. She went back to cleaning the apartment. The bell rang steadily, and insistently, for nearly a minute; then there was silence. She finished everything but the vacuuming, working fast, and got ready for bed. Before she turned in for the night she took out the phone book and telephoned the twenty-four-hour locksmiths. She asked them to come change a lock for her at six in the morning.

She dropped into bed. It seemed to her afterwards that she had many dark and fragmented dreams but she couldn't remember any of them. She felt that the alarm had rung just a little before it was quite fair. When the locksmith arrived she was already dressed and drinking coffee.

He didn't tell her his name. Over the entryphone he just said, 'Locksmith,' and at her door he told her, 'From Lockett's Locks.'

She offered him a cup of coffee; he said that that was okay, it wouldn't take long. 'Been burgled?' he asked.

'No.'

'Well, that's something, anyways.'

'Um.'

'Lost your keys?'

'No, I lent a set to somebody. And now it sort of makes me nervous.'

'Better be safe,' he told her.

'Right. I guess most of your work is for people who've had their keys stolen.'

'All kinds of reasons. Divorce – we get a lot of that. And some people change their keys every time they get the workmen in to fix something. It's a never-ending job. Twenty-four hours, like the ad says.' When he'd finished, he gave her two keys.

She put one of the keys in the bottom desk drawer and the other on her keychain. She threw the old key into the waste-basket, so that she wouldn't mix it up with one of the others.

Twenty minutes after the locksmith had left, Bert was outside the door. He'd persuaded, or tricked, some other tenant into buzzing the street door for him. He was trying to work the lock with his old key.

She stepped up to the door, put the chain back on and said, 'Who is it?'

'It's me.'

She opened the door as far as the chain allowed. She said, 'Go away, Bert. I've had the lock changed.'

'Who was that guy?' he asked.

'What guy?'

'I saw you go out with him last night. You know. The one with the incredible car.'

'What do you want, Bert?'

'I want to talk to you. Is he in there? Come on, Sandra. Open up.'

'Nobody's here, Bert. Will you please go away?'

'I'm not going anywhere till you let me in.'

'No. I won't. And why should I? If you don't let me close this door, I'll phone the police. I mean it.'

'All right,' he said. 'All right.' He took his foot away. 'What the hell? What do you think I'm going to do to you? If there wasn't anybody here last night, why wouldn't you let me in?'

'If I'd let you in, I'd never have been able to get you to go away again.'

'Oh, I'd have gone. I'm not one of those violent types. You know me.'

'I know how much you weigh. And I could just see you flopping down on the couch and talking at me for six hours about how I should have second thoughts. If you didn't want to leave, I wouldn't be able to throw you out.'

'Oh, come on.'

'I've got to go,' she told him. She closed the door.

She had time to do the vacuuming, wash two pairs of tights and get a load of laundry hung up over the bathtub before she went to work.

There was a note on her desk to say that she was supposed to get in touch with Bert as soon as she got in. She didn't. Fifteen minutes later, when she was about to go to her first meeting, his secretary called. Sandra was ready with an excuse, but he came in on the line before she could get it out.

'You can't keep this up,' he told her. 'I've got work to do. I'll see you for lunch.'

'I don't want lunch,' she said. 'I'm out for dinner tonight.' He'd already hung up.

Five minutes before she was due to go to lunch, she scooted around to the back of the building, took the janitor's elevator and went out one of the emergency doors. The only difficulty left was the open stretch between the front of the building and the main road. If she hurried, she could walk all around the block and try to approach the shops from the far side. Of course she didn't need to buy herself any lunch at all. There was a coffee and sandwich machine down the hall from her office. There were lots of them, all through the building. But if she stayed at her desk, Bert would probably come in and make some big outburst – or, at the least, a loud complaint – right there.

As soon as she'd crossed the double main road, she thought that she was in the clear. Everything was going to be fine. She slowed down and looked around: another nice day. She wondered where he'd take her tonight. Perhaps nothing would happen. But if it did? And maybe the dark blue taffeta wasn't right. She'd have to iron the grey dress.

As she turned in to the alleyway between the row of shops where the hairdresser was and the arcade that she was headed for, Bert grabbed her elbow. He said, 'Look, we've got to talk about this. You can't just start going out with somebody else. What am I supposed to do?'

She pulled her arm back. 'I don't know,' she said. 'That's up to you. I told you yesterday: there's nothing to talk about. No fuss, no bother, no more Sandra. I should have done it a long time ago, but I was under the impression that we were engaged. I can't believe it now.'

'But we are. I mean, we're going to get married, aren't we?'

'You've never mentioned it. And the only time I ever tried to get you to say something about it, you told me we shouldn't rush things.'

'Well, I always sort of assumed that it was going to happen. I mean, we love each other and everything.'

'Bert, you don't even like me.'

'What the hell is that supposed to mean?'

'No. You want to go out with your friends and have a good time. And somebody like your mother will be back at home, waiting to clean the mud off your hiking boots. It isn't just that we've got different interests.'

'You could come along whenever you like. Why don't you?'

'I guess I would have if you'd ever asked me. You've always made me feel that I'd spoil things if I went along and slowed you down. Maybe I would have. But we could have done other things. We could just have taken a walk together every once in a while.'

'Where are you going? It's this way. I made a reservation at Francesco's.'

'I'm just going to have a sandwich someplace.'

'You can fit in a plate of spaghetti. Come on. I'm hungry.'

'Well, I'm not. I'm out to dinner tonight, with lots of food and wine. I don't want a hot lunch.'

'You're going out to some big candlelit seduction scene? Jesus, Sandra. What are you trying to do to me?'

'I'm saying goodbye. Why can't you admit that you don't really mind?'

'That's not true.'

'You mind that I've done it first, that's all.'

He started to wave his arms and talk about how she'd never given him any sign – not one, not a hint – that she'd been unhappy with the way things were. And this just wasn't fair.

She'd tried, she said, she honestly had. Every time she'd opened her mouth to tell him, he was in the middle of watching a football game, or ice hockey or baseball or basketball. All she'd ever been able to get out of him was uh-huh and uh-uh. And now her lunch hour was nearly over and she was starving.

She turned right around and ran. As fast as she could, she raced down the alleyway, out to the sidewalk, across the street, along the arcade and into the little sandwich shop where she sometimes went with Maureen. She sat down at the first empty table she could see. A waitress came up to her straight away. Sandra said, 'A tunafish sandwich on rye, please.'

'With lettuce?'

Over the girl's shoulder Sandra saw Bert come bolting in through the door. 'With lettuce,' she said, 'but I think maybe I'd better make that an order to go.'

'We don't do food to go.'

'Okay. In that case, could you make it fast, please?'

Bert yanked away one of the empty chairs and sat down next to her. 'I'm not leaving it like this,' he announced. Three people turned to look.

'Are you together?' the waitress asked.

'No,' Sandra answered.

Bert said yes.

'What can I get you?'

'Roast beef, rare. Sliced thin. White bread. Mustard, pickles.'

'You want that with potato chips?'

'Sure.'

Sandra started to slide out of her chair. If she made a dash for it, she might be able to get out on to the street before he'd understood her actions.

She took a quick step forward. He shot to his feet and grabbed her around the waist. 'You stay right there,' he ordered. Everyone was looking now.

He pushed her back down into her chair. 'And two black coffees,' he told the waitress.

'I'll have some milk in mine,' Sandra muttered.

'Oh yeah, I forgot.'

Her eyes moistened with anger and affection: he still couldn't remember anything about her – what she liked or didn't like,

228

where her parents went in the summer, what her sister's name was. But he was sweet; insensitive, but straightforward. And he was willing to follow her into a strange, small place and make an embarrassing show of himself in order to stop her from leaving him. If she'd crawled under one of the tables, he'd have gone after her. Of course she was still fond of him. That was undeniable. She wasn't going to forget him. But she wouldn't be able to stand living with him for the rest of her life.

She put her hand on his arm, and said, 'I don't want to argue. I've got somebody else, that's all.' She looked at him steadily.

He said, 'But it isn't serious. It can't be.'

She nodded. She took away her hand.

'Well,' he said. 'Well.'

They sat there in silence for a few moments. She'd lost her appetite. She wanted to get out.

The waitress came with their food. Bert lifted his sandwich. He said, 'Maybe you need some time to think about things.'

'Bert, I have thought.'

'Get it out of your system, sort of. That kind of idea. I guess I took a lot of things for granted.'

'You want me to try it out with somebody else and then come back if it doesn't work?'

'Well, I don't like it. But if it's what you need? You'll find out: he doesn't love you.'

'You don't know anything about it.'

'I'm the one who loves you.'

'Bert – '

'Have a potato chip?'

She shut her eyes. Tears rolled down her cheeks.

He took out his handkerchief and started to wipe it over her face. 'Eat up,' he told her. 'You'll need your strength. Remember: you've got a big seduction ahead of you.'

'Don't.'

'Why not?'

She pushed her plate away and threw her crumpled napkin beside it. She shoved her chair back. He put his hand over her wrist. 'Stay a little while,' he said. 'I've missed you.'

She shook her head; she was going to get to the door if she had to drag him after her. She tottered to her feet. He took away his hand and let her go. 'I'll be in touch,' he said.

*

As before, he rang the bell when the clock showed the precise moment they had named. This time he brought her some flowers. She asked him in and took his coat. She apologized for the state of the room, which was neater than it had been at any time since she'd started going out with Bert.

He followed her in to the tiny kitchen. She reached up to the cupboard where she kept the vases: one big, the other small with a chip at the base. She brought down the large one and started to spread the flowers out on the counter.

'I think my son is in love with you,' he said.

'He's too young for that kind of thing.'

'Oh, I don't know. Anyway, he can't stop talking about you.'

'Well, I hope he's saying nice things.'

'Sure. But that wasn't what struck me so much. It's that he's obsessive. Can't stop. Just like me.'

She laughed, but the mention of Eric brought him unpleasantly into her mind. She remembered the strange dream she'd had that night when she'd stayed at her aunt's house. 'Do you dream a lot?' she asked.

'Not a lot. Sometimes. I dreamt about you the night I met you.'

'You did? That's amazing. I dreamt about you, too.'

'What was your dream?'

'You first.'

'Oh, I just dreamt it the way I wanted it. I rang the doorbell, but when you answered it you were wearing one of those nightgowns you can see through. Filmy. You opened the door, you invited me in and then you took off the nightgown and we got down to business for hours and hours. It was a wonderful dream. What was yours like?'

'Part of it was mixed up with a book I'd been reading. But there was a scene in it that was more or less like yours.'

'All that sex? Really?'

230

'Except that we weren't in the same house.' And it hadn't gone on forever, without changing; but she didn't want to tell the rest of the dream.

He said, 'I used to have a repeating dream when I was a child. A nightmare. That's what I think is going on with Ricky. He has these fears, but he doesn't restrict them to the hours when he's asleep. He tries to get into them consciously and change them around.'

'What was your nightmare?'

'I'd dream that I was in my room, lying in my bed. The realistic detail, you see. And I'd look over at the window, where I'd suddenly notice a black shape.'

'What kind of a shape?'

'That's what was so frightening. It was just like darkness. It had no . . . There wasn't really any form to it. And it was coming to get me. I used to wake up screaming.'

'How old were you?'

'Seven. About then. That's when they started.'

'It was a dream about death. I used to get them around that age: being chased by fire, or about to drown, or falling.'

'Or flying. It's all supposed to be about sex.'

'Not when you're a child.'

'Don't be too sure. But children grow out of those dreams. And so did I. Then one afternoon – when I was in college – it came back. I must have been studying for exams or working too hard, or something. I got through college by working nights, taking all kinds of jobs. Anyway, I fell asleep for a while one afternoon. And when I woke up, it was nearly evening. I looked over at the window and – there it was, in my life again, my real life: the black shape, coming to get me. That was the worst dream I've ever had. It was so bad that I haven't thought about it again till now. I didn't want to remind myself. I was afraid that it might come back.'

'It might not ever come back, now that you've talked about it.'

'What I don't understand is that in the dream, I set myself up. I engineered something horrible for myself: I made myself believe that I wasn't having a dream. I changed the setting from my childhood bedroom to a college dorm. That was meant to convince me that the threat was real. Why?'

'I don't know. All I can think of is that you were afraid of something again and that your dream plugged you back into the old story, but it updated your surroundings to fit with your grown-up life. Has it ever come back since then?'

'No. But after the double whammy, I don't know what else it can do to me. Of course that's what I thought before, too.'

She dropped one of the flowers. He bent down to get it. She leaned over at the same time. He got the flower and kissed her while she was still off balance. 'Are you nervous?' he asked. 'Maybe we should go to bed now and worry about dinner afterwards.'

'Maybe we should finish doing the flowers.'

'Maybe not,' he said.

She hadn't imagined such a quick bypassing of all the stages usually considered necessary before a first night that wouldn't be the only one they'd spend together. But she had already established the fact that she was a nice girl; this was no longer the first date, she'd cleaned the apartment and changed the sheets and towels and she was hoping that the evening would end in the bedroom. That was what she was prepared for. So did it really matter if they skipped two or three hours?

Of course it didn't matter. However, since she'd been keyed up to begin with, the rearrangement of all her plans and thoughts flustered her so much that she just dropped everything and let him take over. She left the flowers scattered around the kitchen and she forgot to put the chain on the hall door.

*

While they were still in bed, wondering whether they should get up and go out to dinner, or wait a while longer, the phone rang. That was another thing she'd forgotten: to unplug the bedroom extension.

She said, 'Let it ring.'

He reached over, picked up the receiver and waited. There was a click that they both heard, and then the dial tone.

'Wrong number?' he asked her.

'Wrong man,' she said. 'I've told him it's over. I kept on telling him, but he's checking on me. At least, I think so. I don't know who else would be calling. Especially like that, just to see if somebody's in.'

'Burglars?'

'Not around here. We've only ever had daytime break-ins, on the ground floor. Nothing at night.'

He didn't seem to mind the thought that she'd recently been attached to another man. According to his son, he'd been going out with someone else himself for the past couple of weeks. Perhaps he hadn't even broken it off yet. Or maybe Eric had been making the whole thing up.

He got up to phone the restaurant from the living room. While they were putting their clothes on, he asked her to marry him. She said, 'You don't think we should spend a little more time getting to know each other?'

'Would it help?'

'Well, otherwise – if we're living together and if we don't really understand each other's moods and what you could find irritating and everything – '

'We'd find that out as we went along. Isn't that how it works?'

'I don't know. I don't know how it works.' He did: he'd been married before. She'd have liked to know whether his first marriage had been settled with such speed and boldness.

He said, 'Are you telling me that you don't want me?'

'Of course I want you.'

'Then you will?'

'Well, yes.'

'What a great answer: well, yes. I love it.'

'When?' she said.

'If you can get off work the day after tomorrow, we'll go to the Town Hall and register. They're closed tomorrow. After that, it's a little while – I think maybe two weeks.'

'But that's so fast.'

'Why not?'

'Oh, everything. I mean, my family, my job, um.'

'You want one of those long engagements?'

'Wouldn't it be better?'

'No. Why wait? I went through a long engagement once. All it does is make you restless and impatient. And the honeymoon's even worse. We could take a spring vacation somewhere, instead. How about that?'

'Venice,' she said quickly.

'Oh? You do have it all mapped out, after all.'

'I've just always wanted to go there.'

'Fine. So, it's yes?'

Yes, she said: it was yes.

During dinner they hardly spoke. And afterwards he said that if she didn't mind, he'd leave early in the morning because he didn't like the idea of Ricky waking up and finding that he wasn't in the house. 'In fact,' he said, 'if you can get off a little early tomorrow, I could pick you up and you could come home with me. We could all have tea together. Ricky keeps asking to see you again.'

'Okay. Sure. That would be nice.'

'And on Saturday – would you mind coming down to my ex-wife's place? She's got the right to see him on Saturdays. You might as well meet them. The vipers. They got away with a large chunk of money they weren't entitled to, and one-seventh of my son's life that they also have no right to. He won't speak to them. He takes a book. But every Saturday he has to get in the car and go. At least the two boys won't be there. Ordway was married before, too. This time should be relatively okay. They usually send somebody to pick Ricky up. But every once in a while I do the chauffeuring, just to check that things are all right there. Would you mind?'

'Not at all,' she said. 'That's fine.' Already she was jealous. She wanted to know what his ex-wife looked like. She wanted to know everything about her, especially if it was derogatory.

In the morning, after he'd gone, the phone rang. She hesitated before answering. If Bert were at the other end, she didn't want to talk to him. But the call might be from Roy, to tell her something he'd forgotten or to change the time, or the place, for that afternoon.

She picked up the receiver and said hello.

Her Aunt Marion's voice said, 'Sandra? I'm so sorry to bother you. I didn't wake you up, did I?'

'No, I was up already. Has something happened?'

'Oh, it's stupid. I'm always so careful. But yesterday morning the newsboy didn't get the paper on to the doorstep – it landed on the path. So I walked down the steps and I didn't notice that there was a little patch of damp leaves on one of them.'

'Are you hurt?'

'I fractured my kneecap. It's still in one piece, but they're going to operate: they'll put pins in it, to stop it from pulling apart.'

'Are you still at home?'

'I'm in the hospital. They thought it would be better to keep me here – less uncomfortable. Everyone's very pleasant. And the food is quite nice. Fortunately I'm insured for absolutely everything. But it does annoy me.'

'Can I do anything for you, Aunt Marion?'

'I was just about to ask. If it's no trouble, it would be a big help. But there's no hurry. Any time before Tuesday will do.'

'How about Sunday?'

'That would be perfect, dear. Let me get my list.' She told Sandra the name of the ward she was in, gave her directions for driving to the hospital and read out a list of the things she'd need from home. When she had finished, Sandra remembered the phone call from the night before; maybe it hadn't been from Bert, after all. She asked, 'Did you try to get hold of me last night?' Aunt Marion said no, she'd been sleeping like a log all night long because of some medicine they were giving her. 'To stop the pain,' she explained. 'It doesn't really work. I mean, it just puts me to sleep.'

* * *

She hadn't realized until she saw him that she'd been apprehensive about meeting Eric again. She'd been thinking that he'd blame her. Although his manner was subdued and well-mannered, she felt that she ought to give him some kind of

235

apology before the afternoon was over. He didn't seem nervous himself. On the contrary, after saying hello, he asked her politely and confidently, 'Would you like to see my room?'

They started up a wide, curving staircase. Like the rest of the house, it was bigger and more important-looking than anything she was used to.

'I'm sorry about the other night,' she said. 'I felt badly about turning you in, but I didn't see what else I could do.'

'Yeah, I know,' he told her. 'It's okay.' He headed towards a door that gave off the landing, saying, 'It's this one.' He stood back for her. She walked in.

It wasn't like a child's room, nor like a place where a young boy lived. The furniture, the colors of the materials, the curtains, all looked as if they had come from the room of an adult. Even the bed was an adult's single bed with a carved headboard. Many of the objects and pieces of furniture had the appearance of expensive, well-cared-for things. They might have been antiques.

Over the small desk hung a religious painting. As her eyes went to it, he said, 'That's St Catherine.'

The picture too looked old, as did the little desk with its green leather top that had a floral pattern stamped in gold around the edges. She took a step forward.

There were three people in the painting: two women and a baby. One woman held the baby, while the other one stretched out her hand towards it. The baby, with a little help from its mother, was putting a ring on a finger of the extended hand.

'Mary and Jesus,' he added. 'It's called *The Mystic Marriage*. It's sort of like, ah, you know when nuns get married to God?'

'What?'

'They're given a wedding ring.'

'Uh-huh. Are you all religious? All the family?'

'Nobody in the family. I saw this when my father was buying a set of chairs and I asked him to get it for me, for my birthday.'

'That must have been a pretty big present.'

'He said it would have been cheaper to buy me a car. He thought it was a waste of money.'

'Because he didn't think it was beautiful, or because you don't go to church?'

'What I like about religion are the stories. They're pretty weird, but it's surprising how they can have an application to everyday life.'

'I don't know. What I never liked about Sunday School was that they told you all that stuff that wasn't true.'

'If it has an application, it's still got some truth.'

'I guess I mean the thing you start out with.'

'That would be a composite.'

'Oh. Like how do you mean?'

'A myth or a folktale.'

'Exactly. Not true events.'

'But they could be.'

'But they aren't. They're just made up.'

'They're only made up in that they're typical. They're typical of certain wishes held by the people who tell the stories. Since we all still think the same way, those stories still typify something true.'

'Like what?'

'Revenge, murder, miracles and all that sex stuff.'

'Well,' she said, at a loss how to go on, 'I never thought of it that way before.'

'It's a very interesting subject. I'm also interested in those preachers that get everybody to give them money to save their souls and then have to go into a psychiatric hospital when they're found out.'

'Those people are frauds.'

'They want to be demagogues.'

'Yes.'

'But they're using the wrong propaganda. The real power is in the secular branch.'

'Absolutely,' she said. 'And besides, they let you keep the money afterwards.'

'Right. And even if you get sent up the river, you can write a bestseller about it.'

She started to laugh. He joined in. It was going to be all right, she thought. He didn't hold her betrayal against her.

He sat down in a straight-backed chair at the side. As he did so, he motioned towards the modern swivel chair at the desk. She sat down in it. She gave it a little swing, first one side, then the other. It was fun. The chair must have been another thing he'd asked for.

He said, 'Are you his girlfriend now?'

'I guess I am.'

'I told you so, didn't I? I said he'd be able to take over everything without any trouble.'

'It doesn't mean I don't like you too. You're the one I met first.'

When Eric reached the age of twenty-one, she thought, she'd be thirty-one and Roy would be about forty-five. She was closer in age to the boy who would be her stepson than the man who was to become her husband. That was a strange fact. It made her imagine that the odd tale with which Eric had introduced himself to her – the story about a body-swap – could become true at some future date: that at a certain age she might say to herself that her husband was immature, whereas his son was more like a grown man.

'Is something wrong?' he asked.

'No. Why?'

'You look like you're having trouble remembering a phone number.'

'I was trying to figure something out. But it won't ever happen, so I guess there isn't any point wondering about it.'

'Oh, I think those are some of the most interesting thoughts of all. You know: what would happen if a meteor collided with the moon; or how would you react if you found an escaped tiger in your living room: was it that kind of thing?'

'Not so wild, but that's the general idea. Maybe everything's like that until it happens. If you're thinking about something you have no experience of.'

They had tea in a smaller room off the large, high-ceilinged dining room. By the time they sat down it was dark outside. Roy accepted a cup, but didn't drink it. He sat watching her and Eric

he way a man might relax to the sound of music. Sometimes he
ined in the conversation, but he didn't try to guide it. Eric was
he host; he told a succession of jokes and puns. She countered
ith her cousin's story about the hat and the Dalmatian. And
fter that they got on to the subject of movies.

She met Debbie, who came out of the kitchen to shake hands.
ric looked on with an expression of resignation. He didn't
ppear either frightened or desperate. Everything still seemed to
e all right.

In the car Roy said, 'You have an amazing effect on him.'

'Let's hope it lasts.'

'What did you think of his room?'

'It's beautiful.'

'But peculiar. Like a museum. Everything antique, except for
is computer over in the corner. Most of it was his mother's. He
ught tooth and nail for it during the divorce.'

'The swivel chair's modern.'

'He didn't let you sit in it, did he?'

'Sure.'

'Jesus. He won't even let me sit in it. It's his thinking chair.
hat did you talk about?'

'About religion. We were looking at the painting above the
esk.'

'The girl marrying the baby? Christ, yes. That horrible thing.
's worth a fortune now. When I bought it for him they thought
 was workshop of John Doe and now it's supposed to be the guy
imself. But I guess they could change their minds again. I told
im he should sell it before the price drops back down. And he
oked at me like I'd suggested using chemical warfare on a
aternity ward.'

'He loves it.'

'He could love a photograph of it just as much, and invest the
oney he got from the original.'

'A photograph wouldn't mean the same. A copy wouldn't
ther. From the way he looks at it you can tell that he really
preciates everything about it. I think it's like a person to him.
e sits at the desk and sort of communes.'

239

'My God, now I've got two of you,' he said. 'I'm out-numbered.'

*

The next day, Thursday, they went to the Town Hall. On the way back he dropped her at the office, where she handed in her notice to quit, told Maureen the news and got ready to go out to lunch.

'Have lunch with me,' Maureen ordered. 'I'm paying.'

They were outside, walking quickly in the cold air, when Bert came running up behind them. He caught hold of Sandra's arm. 'We've got a date,' he told her.

'No.'

'Yes. I asked you Monday when you could make lunch and you said Thursday was all right.'

She was about to deny it but suddenly she recalled the sight of Bert looking through his appointment book to find a free day. She'd made the date just to get rid of him.

'Want me to go on ahead?' Maureen said.

Sandra nodded. She turned back to Bert. 'I'm sorry,' she said. 'I forgot. I can't. Let's say goodbye, please. Don't keep going on and on like this.'

'This guy – the one with the car? I asked about him and he's bad news. He did something – '

'What?'

'I don't know, but everybody says he's just no good.'

How childish he was, she thought. Everybody was. Was it likely that he'd approve of the man she was planning to leave him for? But that was why divorcing couples always considered each other emotionally ill, insane, possibly genetically warped – that explained the unacceptable, which was that people changed: nothing was for long. Life itself didn't last and the changeableness was natural, like death.

'I don't want to lose you,' he said. 'I get this terrible feeling in bed, that I've got to have you holding me. And then you aren't there. And nothing feels right.'

She started to cry. He meant more to her, now that they were breaking up, than he had for all the months that they'd been together. There had been many times when – offended and bitter

240

– she'd wanted the power to make him feel bad, even to hurt him seriously. Now she had it and she didn't want it. She didn't want to hurt anyone like this, least of all him.

He held out his hand to her but she pushed it away. She said, 'I can't. I've told you. I told you every nice way I could. We're getting married. We've already decided when. We've been to the Town Hall and everything. We've set the date.'

'When?' he asked.

'In a few days.'

'When?'

'Look, Bert, there's no point in this. I don't want you to get the idea that you're going to show up at the ceremony or something.'

'Me?'

Of course that was what he'd be planning. She tore herself away from him, ran to the corner and crossed the streeet. She didn't look back and she didn't slow up, although she sensed that he wouldn't be following her. He'd be standing where she had left him, watching, while she kept on running.

Maureen didn't ask about Bert directly. She just leaned across the table and said, 'Okay, shoot. The uncondensed version, please.'

As Sandra talked, she started to think that everything was going to be easy. Maureen seemed to believe that the whirlwind romance was just fine – that the speed with which Sandra was being carried towards the altar was a sign of true love, and that the best news of all was that she'd be getting rid of Bert, who'd always taken her for granted and never treated her very well, especially that time when he'd had the affair with Melanie what's-her-name in accounting. Sandra agreed. She pretended to be in control of all her actions and feelings. She hadn't known about Melanie or any other girl. Maybe there had been more than one. It didn't matter now.

'Have you met his family?' Maureen asked.

'Oh, yes. Well, part of it. I'm meeting the ex-family on Saturday.'

'Right. One of those. Are there any kids?'

'One. A boy. He lives with his father.'

'Wow. I don't know how I'd handle something like that.'

'You never know. It's only when things happen: then you find out. That was the trouble with Bert. Nothing was ever going to happen. I always thought he was nice, but it wouldn't have worked. He just wasn't the right one. Now that I've made the decision – God, I don't know how I stood it for so long. I should have gotten out of the job, too. This place: don't you feel it? It's hard to find anybody in that building who isn't one level lower than a computer.'

'I love it. I'd go crazy living with people who only wanted to talk about the weather and the kids. I like things fizzy.'

'So do I. I never felt that way about the office, though.'

'I feel that way about all offices. That's why you're getting married and I'm not. Some girls grow up dreaming about making hubby his breakfast and bouncing the baby in its basinette; I always had this craving for filing cabinets and typewriters.'

'You're kidding.'

'The great thing about offices is: there's no mess, no clutter, no smell of boiled cabbage, no cockroaches and – best of all – the people there don't yell at each other all day long. Wall-to-wall carpets, warm in the winter, cool in the summer, somebody else does the cleaning, everyone's friendly and polite, they like the way you do things, they give you money: there's a lot to be said for it.'

'But not all marriages – '

'You can never count on things for long. And it's always easier to leave a job than to walk out on a marriage.'

'But if you love each other – '

'Sure. That's what they say: it makes all the difference. That's the part I left out.'

*

She let everyone else in the office know that she'd be leaving. Most of them didn't need to be told: Maureen had been spreading the word. She telephoned her sister and then her parents, who sounded stunned, as if she'd done something alarming. Their reaction upset her. Didn't they think she was ever going to get married? The girls in the office had the right

242

idea: they approved. They seemed to feel that getting married was in the same category as winning a million dollars in the sweepstakes. Even Maureen, who didn't have much to say for married life, thought that it was the right thing for Sandra.

Her parents asked her how long she'd known him. They didn't like her answer. Her sister, too, kept saying, 'Are you sure?' and then added, 'What happened to that nice boy you were sort of living with for a while? The Ivy League type. Bert.'

'That was a long time ago,' she said.

*

Early on Saturday morning she drove to Roy's house. His car was outside. Eric was sitting in the front seat, behind the wheel. She parked in back of him, got out and walked over. She leaned towards the window. 'Are you driving?' she asked.

'Not yet. He's on the phone. He told me to stay outside.'

'I'll just let him know I'm here,' she said.

She found Roy standing in the hall. He was holding the telephone receiver to his ear and saying, 'Yes, yes.'

She whispered, 'Do you want me to wait in the car?' He nodded and made a kiss at her. She went back outdoors.

They had a pretty, sunny day for the trip. It even seemed to be a bit warmer. Everything they'd missed in the spring was coming to them now. She got into the passenger seat next to Eric. He was wearing a shirt and sweater: on the back seat lay a folded jacket with a hood. It struck her that every time she'd seen him, he'd been wearing different clothes. That was the way rich people lived, even the children. But for a child to dress that way meant that someone else must choose his clothing. Did Roy do that, dragging his son along on shopping expeditions?

'That's in case we go for a walk,' he said. 'We probably will. My father likes to get out of the house as fast as he can. The beach is okay.'

'Do you two go shopping for your clothes together?'

'Why?'

'I was always taken shopping by my mother. She'd grab a lot of things off the racks and push me into a dressing room with them. I guess she had a very good eye. Usually they all looked fine, so

243

then she'd just ask me which one I liked best and she'd buy that one for me. But my sister couldn't stand going with her. They used to have fights. She didn't like any of the clothes my mother chose. She wanted to wear silver jackets in the daytime and that kind of thing.'

'That's what I'm going to do as soon as I'm sixteen. He says I have to wait till then. Sometimes he makes me come along with him. About once a year, mainly for shoes. You have to try them on. Everything else I pick out of catalogues. Once you know your size, it's easy. Then I show him the picture and most of the time he says yes. I know the kind of thing he's going to want me to get.'

'That's the first step.'

'Is your sister grown up now?'

'Oh, yes. She's a couple of years older than I am.'

'What does she wear?'

'Pants and a turtleneck, mostly. And black eye make-up around her eyes; no lipstick, long hair. And she won't wear shoes in the house: she doesn't like them. But that's as far as it goes.'

'How do you mean?'

'She's not really a rebel. She doesn't want to be anti-social and break things up. She just couldn't stand to have somebody else making decisions about what she was going to wear and how she was going to look: anything about her appearance. She has to be the one to decide.'

'Well, that's the way I think, too. Don't you?'

'Not really. I don't always mind when other people decide for me. Sometimes it saves a lot of trouble. There are loads of things don't care about one way or the other.'

'I always care.'

She laughed. 'I know you do,' she said. 'Listen. Do I call you Eric now, or should I call you Ricky?'

'They're both no good, specially Eric. They called me that because when I was born, I had red hair, so they thought: wow, Eric the Red. And they named me after that.'

'But it's a good name.'

'It's a twerp name. Your name's okay. I bet you weren't named for a joke.'

'It's all right now, but my real name is longer. It's Alexandra.'

'Alexandra? Jees, are you lucky. That's great.'

'It's too long.'

'It sounds like the name of a princess.'

'It probably was. My mother was reading some novel around that time. She told me she got it out of a book. We all have to put up with things like that.'

'But you got a good one.'

'So did you. If you ever go to Scandinavia, you'll be surrounded by Eriks. Over there it's like the name Richard. And meantime, you can call yourself Rick. Like *Rick's Bar*, you know.'

'What's that?'

'It's from a movie. There's a nightclub owner in it named Rick. He's the hero. He wears a white tuxedo and he's a cool customer.'

'Oh?'

She looked up as Roy came out of the front door and down the path. 'Who gets to sit in front?' she asked. 'Or can we all squeeze in together?'

'Not in this car. It's only got seatbelts for two in the front seat. You stay there.' He got out and climbed in to the back. Roy took his place behind the wheel.

*

The house they pulled up at was a new, low-slung beach cottage on the outskirts of town. Many glass windows and doors allowed for the maximum incursion of light. The beach wasn't in sight, but you could hear it.

Sandra made an immediate move to ingratiate herself with the ex-wife, Ginette. 'What a light room,' she said, looking around as if pleased. She already felt relieved by Ginette's appearance: bleached hair, tight skin and an expression of casual toughness.

'I like things clean, with plenty of light,' Ginette said, looking at Roy. 'No dark corners.'

Sandra said, 'My grandparents lived in a house that was so dark, it was hard for more than one person to read the newspapers in the dining room. I used to think it was gloomy but I started to appreciate it later on, when I was working with computers and my eyes began to hurt. I guess all they really needed was better electricity.'

The husband, Ordway, was introduced: an agreeable, sloppy middle-aged man who wore thick glasses. He seemed perfectly happy to have guests. He greeted his wife's ex-husband without concern and appeared to be undismayed by Eric's atrocious manners.

Eric wouldn't look at, or speak to, either the wife or husband. He took his book over to a chair by one of the windows.

'Still not on speaking terms?' Ginette called after him. 'That's a long time to sulk, kiddo. A couple more years of that and you'll be batting even with your father.' She turned to Roy, saying, 'Want a drink?'

'No, thanks. I'm driving.'

'Not even one little drink?'

'Tonic water?' Ordway suggested. 'Ginger ale? Orange juice?'

'Tonic water,' Roy decided.

'My,' Ginette said. 'A reformed character. And you?' she asked Sandra.

Sandra asked for a light gin and tonic. Ordway mixed the drinks and did the serving. He took a ginger ale to Eric, who – without raising his eyes from the page – extended a hand to have the glass inserted between his fingers; the operation went so smoothly that it looked like an established ritual.

How would I act, Sandra thought, *if he ever treated me that way? I wouldn't be able to stand it. And his own mother: what did she do to make him hate her so much? She left. Maybe that's all it was. She wanted out, so now he's showing her that he can do it back, even when they're in the same room.*

'Such marvelous manners,' Ginette said.

Roy slapped his drink down on the table and stood up. He said, 'I think I'll stretch my legs.' He started to move towards the doors that led out on to the terrace.

Ginette turned to Sandra. 'Have you had any experience with children?' she asked.

'Babies?'

'No, a little older. Eric, for instance. How well do you know Eric?'

Sandra paused for a second, not wanting to say anything that would hurt the boy. 'About as well as I know his father,' she said. 'How well do you know him?'

Another moment passed before she realized that she'd said something brilliant that didn't necessarily have to be taken as an insult. Eric looked up from his book for the first time since he'd sat down. He laughed. And Roy was grinning.

Ginette didn't try to hide her displeasure. She said, 'Better than you, I think. But you'll find out.'

Roy said, 'Coming with me, Ricky?'

Eric looked back down at his book.

'Well? Are you?'

'Rick,' Sandra prompted under her breath.

'Coming, Rick?'

Eric shut the book and put it aside. 'Sure,' he said. He walked to the doors.

Sandra watched father and son step out on to the terrace and begin to walk away. There was no polite way of getting up and following them. She was stuck.

'I know what it looks like,' Ginette said. 'It isn't the way you think. I did my best, God knows. I knocked myself out, trying to help. But that boy is a demon.' She set her drink down on the table in front of her. 'Just like his father,' she added.

She's still in love with him, Sandra thought.

Ordway looked over at her glass. 'Another drink?' he asked. Sandra shook her head. He reached for Ginette's glass. She put her hand over the top of it. 'I'll see about lunch,' he said.

He walked around to the side of the bookcase, opened a door there and left the room.

Sandra hung on to her glass tightly.

Ginette said, 'So. How long have you two known each other?'

'Not long at all.'

'Yeah. Well, you're taking on a bundle, I can tell you.'

Sandra looked towards the windows. She could see Eric, far away. He seemed to be throwing something at a point that was beyond her range of vision. As she watched him, Roy came into sight. Looking at both of them, she thought that there was nothing to worry about. She felt fine about them. What bothered her was simply the idea of marriage at such short notice: it was like stepping off a cliff and hoping that something would be out there in front of you.

'Let me tell you a story,' Ginette said. 'I've got a cousin whose sister-in-law studied to be a forest ranger. They do a lot of botany, looking at things under microscopes and so on. And then they go through the woods and make reports. She had an assignment to record growth patterns in a certain section of forest. It meant measuring the treetrunks; they did that regularly all the time to check the rate of growth and line it up with what they knew about rainfall and sunshine and temperature averages. And the way you do it, if you're making a routine survey, is to put your arms around the trunk of the tree. That gives you an approximate figure. Well, she was doing that for a while, taking notes, moving from tree to tree and she didn't notice, but – somebody else was there too, because all of a sudden she put her arms around the next treetrunk: and from the other side of the tree someone grabbed her wrists and started to pull. They pulled her right up against the trunk and pulled and pulled until it felt like her arms were going to come out of their sockets. And then, just as she thought she was going to pass out with the pain, whoever it was let go and ran away. Luckily. She was so exhausted that she wouldn't have been able to defend herself in any way. She just dropped down on the ground and shook all over. She didn't see who it was. She didn't think of trying to look. Her arms hurt her for weeks.'

'And she didn't have any idea who it could have been – a stranger, or somebody who might have followed her?'

'No idea, except that it was a man, of course. A woman wouldn't have had the strength. It's a funny story: she was just minding her own business, going along as usual, and – wham.'

'It's a horrible story.'

'That's what can happen, even when you're not expecting it.

That's what men are like. Not all of them. Ordway's a sweetie. But most of them. In fact, I really used to wonder about Roy and his first wife. Don't you?'

'I thought you were his first wife.'

'No, honey. I was his second wife.'

'Who – '

'The one that was Eric's mother. The millionairess who was twice Roy's age. And she died in such mysterious circumstances.'

'Oh?'

'Oh, did she ever. Ask him about it. If he won't tell you, you can find out by looking up the records. It was in all the papers.'

From the distance Roy and Eric ran towards the terrace. The wind blew their clothes and their hair.

Ordway put his head around the bookcase corner. 'Soon?' he said.

'I can see them coming,' Ginette told him.

During the meal Eric kept his head down and ate. Sandra led the conversation. She hadn't meant to, but the first bite she took drew her to comment; the words burst from her like a blunder. 'My God,' she said, 'this is amazing. I've never tasted anything like it. What wonderful food.' She looked at Ginette, who said, 'Not me. Ordway's in charge of the kitchen.'

Sandra turned to him. His smile showed such pleasure at her appreciation that it was as if all at once they were alone together, two friends at a table of strangers. She said, 'This is much more delicious than just good cooking. Have you studied somewhere?'

'You could call it private tuition, I guess. My grandfather was a famous chef. I never realized how much he was teaching us when we were children. We were all supposed to grow up to be something on Wall Street. But when I think back, he did have us organized like a team of apprentices and he'd vary the menu all the time. We were building up a repertoire without knowing it.'

'Was he French?'

'Polish.'

'You never told me that,' Ginette said.

Ordway shrugged. There was a slight pause. Sandra was afraid that it might turn into an unbreakable silence. She asked Ginette to tell her something about the house.

Ginette began to talk, at first lazily, then with gusto and at last rhapsodically, about the dream she'd always had of living in that part of the world. She'd been on a school visit to the other side of the bay and she'd never forgotten it. She'd always wanted to have a summer cottage there. And later on, she'd begun to look for a place, but nothing matched the dream she'd had of the perfect house. Then, one day, she was browsing through the magazines in her dentist's waiting room and she saw an article on modern American architects. There was a picture in it of a house that she liked. Everything started from there. She knew at that moment that she'd have to begin from scratch: buy the land and hire that architect to design the house she wanted.

The story of the building, with its setbacks, triumphs and surprises, lasted till after dessert. They were back in the living room with coffee before anyone thought of changing the subject.

Roy had remained silent throughout the catalogue of dramatic events. *He's remembering the divorce settlement*, Sandra thought, *and he's telling himself, 'They did all this building and buying on my money.'*

Roy said, 'We'll be getting home early, if you don't mind. There's a lot to do.'

'Could we take a little walk on the beach first?' Sandra asked.

'Sure,' Ginette said. 'We'll all go.'

Sandra tied a scarf over her head and put on the gloves she'd brought. The wind had picked up, the sun was going behind clouds. Eric ran ahead of everyone. Ordway took Ginette's hand. He led her straight out from the house, towards the water. Roy hung back.

Sandra said, 'They've gone off to compare notes about us. And now we're going to talk about them.'

'What's she been saying to you? When we came in before lunch, you looked like you'd been hit by a truck. What was it?'

'Why didn't you tell me that he isn't her son?'

'Oh. I didn't?'

'You know you didn't. Why?'

'I guess I thought you'd figure it out. You're somebody I don't have to give explanations to.'

'But if she's got part-custody, of course I assumed that she was his mother. I could have said something terrible.'

'But you didn't. You've played everything fine.'

'But I could have.' She didn't understand why he'd let her go on thinking something wrong. Had it been a test? Or had it been like a joke – the kind of thing Eric had worked out when he rang the doorbell at her aunt's house?

'What else did she say?' he asked.

'She said I should ask you about your first wife.'

'Uh-huh.'

I'm asking, she thought. Why had he done this to her? He must have known how important it would be to her. Perhaps he hadn't been able to tell her himself; he'd arranged things so that she'd have to ask. Or wasn't it that complicated?

'Okay,' he said. 'I'll tell you later.'

He'd have to tell her soon. She didn't like the thought that some day her suspicions would drive her to the public library, where she'd sit at a table and turn over page after page of old newspapers, seeing his face looking out at her. Maybe there were photographs that showed him trying to cover his eyes with his arm, or putting his head down as two policemen hustled him through the crowds. *It doesn't matter*, she told herself. *It happened, but now it's over.*

She breathed in and turned her face to the sea. 'I really like the beach,' she said.

'Me, too. So does Ricky. If it weren't for those two, he'd be having a good time here.'

'Maybe he'll look back on it later and think it wasn't so bad.'

'Not a chance. One thing I can tell you right now: as soon as we're married, we can drop old Ginette from our list of social engagements. The reason she got what she got was that her hot-shot lawyer made a case for a child needing a steady, maternal influence in his life.'

'That's me, huh?'

251

'You got it. Oh, and there's some bad news, I'm afraid. Ricky's dug in his heels about the wedding. He wants to be best man, you know. So apparently – I don't know whether it's the clothes or what, but he's insisting on a church wedding.'

'You're joking.'

'No.'

'My God. Which church? I haven't been inside a church for years.'

'I don't think I've ever been in one, at least not for the reasons you're supposed to. My father was a devout atheist. Whenever anyone brought up the subject of religion, he'd say, "It's a bunch of crap." It was his favorite expression. I can still hear him saying it.'

'And your mother?'

'Oh, she did what he wanted. You know.'

She remembered the painting of St Catherine in Eric's room. She asked, 'Does this mean we've got to go through some kind of embracing-the-faith thing?'

'Hell, no. We just get some laid-back preacher to let us use his church for the party.'

'From what I picked up when we were looking at the paintings in his room, he might like a lot of authentic stuff: a Mass in Latin and – '

'There are limits. He can have the church ceremony, but that's as far as it goes. If you don't mind, that is. Does your family go to church?'

'Not any more. My mother's family were Congregationalists, I think.'

'Okay. Are you game?'

'I guess so. I'd rather not.'

'We can pretend it's like being in a play. I think we're going to have to go to rehearsals for it.'

'Are they going to ask us if we believe in God?'

'Probably. You just say, "You betcha." '

'That's what I'm saying when they ask me if I take you for my lawfully wedded husband.'

'That's what I like to hear. We'll sail right through it.'

During the drive back Eric was talkative. It was as if he had to make up for his long silence. He wanted to play word games, to ask riddles, to talk about the lemurs of Madagascar; he'd read a long article about them in the *National Geographic* and he'd heard somewhere else that people were supposed to be descended from lemurs, not monkeys.

Sandra was interested. That was a good sign, she thought. If he didn't irritate her after a day of nervous anticipation, that was an indication of future compatibility.

It was dark long before they reached the house. She drove her own car home. Two hours later Roy arrived to take her out for the evening. They went to a seafood restaurant where there was a dancefloor and a band that played the kind of music people used to dance to: foxtrots, waltzes, tangos and the Charleston. They didn't speak about the afternoon until they were sitting in the car, outside her apartment block.

He said, 'Ricky's completely changed. He's like a different boy. You know, it wouldn't matter if he didn't, but I can't tell you what a relief it is to me that he likes you so much. He's taken to you like . . . it's like magic.'

'You've said something like that before.'

'Can't say it too often.'

'It's beginning to make me a little nervous. I already don't want it to change. It's still such a short time since we met.'

'That's not important. It's getting better and better. Here, let me show you something: this is how the state foresters measure trees. What's wrong?'

'That was the other thing Ginette told me while you and Rick were out walking. The story about the girl who was going through the woods and had her wrists grabbed.'

'I think it's a story that has some special significance for her. She didn't tell it to me till about a year after we were married. But you got it the first day. And that fuddy-duddy, Ordway – you practically galvanized him. Both of them, spouting away on their pet subjects. I think they were even having a good time.'

'So was I, looking back on it. At the time I was too panicked to have fun.'

'You should have been in public relations. People open up to you. Don't they? Just like flowers.'

'Not usually. And not the other way around, either. It's because I'm in love.'

'You weren't in love when Ricky made friends with you.'

'But I'd just seen a very romantic movie the night before. And I was reading one of those love stories where they're all wearing costumes.'

'I see. That explains it. The girl who absorbed romance. It should be a headline.'

'But I meant what I said this afternoon. I liked Ordway a lot. I think it's a good thing he got out of his old job. He's an artist. And I certainly admire what Ginette did with that house.'

'That god-awful futuristic thing?'

'It's good.'

'Post-fifties Americana – lots of style and no character. Wouldn't you rather have one of those ramshackle wooden houses with a shingle roof?'

'Oh, I would for myself. But that doesn't mean that there shouldn't be other types of houses around. I wouldn't want to live in the Empire State building either, but I think it's great. And it isn't just the house. It's the fact that she had a dream about doing something and she carried it out.'

'That's Ginette, all right. A schemer.'

'I admire people who are well-organized and good at planning. Rick's like that. Whatever else is going on inside him, he's able to make a clear plan and then act on it.'

'Sometimes his plans are a little crazy, that's all.'

'I'm no good at planning. Everything in my life has just happened to me.'

'Then I guess it's not a bad thing that somebody else is going to be in charge of the wedding arrangements.'

'That's true enough. I don't even know how it all works: bridesmaids and invitations and – God, everything. Even the dress. My sister had a registry office wedding. So did my cousins. Nobody in my generation . . . Well, I guess my mother would know.'

'If you don't mind, Ricky's sort of set his heart on running the show. The whole thing.'

'Are you kidding? I thought you sort of hired people.'

'He's going to do all that. He's even got a fixed idea about the kind of wedding dress you should have. He showed me a picture.'

'Oh, boy.'

'Do you care? It would mean so much to him.'

'Okay, sure. If he wants to make all the arrangements, that's fine. I'd kind of like to see that picture first.'

'I think I've got it with me. Wait a minute.' He turned on the ceiling light. He looked through his wallet. The picture wasn't there. He reached into his breast pocket and pulled out a paper. 'There,' he said. 'That's it.'

She unfolded the paper. She'd expected to be handed a glossy photograph out of a fashion magazine. What she saw was a pencil sketch of the head-dress and veil from the portrait of St Catherine.

She handed the paper back to him. 'It's from the painting in his room,' she said. 'Don't you recognize it?'

He frowned at the picture. 'I think you're right. I hadn't noticed. It isn't bad, though, is it?'

'Not at all. It's beautiful.'

'Good. You'll just be kind of medieval. He made an appointment for you to have the first fitting on Monday morning. And he wants a list of guests. And what about bridesmaids?'

'There's my friend, Maureen, from the office. And my niece and nephew; they're still tiny, but they could hold up the train, or whatever they do – carry some flowers around.'

'Don't forget to invite that old aunt of yours. She's our fairy godmother.'

She thought that before they kissed goodnight, he'd tell her what he'd promised earlier in the day. But they went up to her apartment and went to bed. He was getting ready to go back to his house, still with no intention of saying anything, when she realized that unless she made a move, he'd never do anything about it.

'Please,' she said, 'tell me now. You've got to, sometime. I don't want other people hinting at me. Tell me yourself. Tell me about your first wife.'

'I just don't want to think about it.'

'Good. Neither do I. All you have to do is tell me, and then we won't either of us have to think about it again.'

'Okay. Right. Well, most of my immediate family succeeded in killing themselves while I was young: in car crashes, getting sick, looking for fights and getting beaten up, suicide – that was only one. I was put in the care of . . . it's not important.'

'That's all right. I want to hear everything.'

'I guess it was an act of kindness. Maybe that was why I resented it so much. The community thought it would be a nice idea for one of its decent citizens to give me shelter for a while. So the local optician took me in. But by that time it was too late: I had a grudge against everybody. I didn't like the way they'd always treated my family. I was very busy biting the hands that fed me. So he took me in and I took him in. I seduced his wife. That would have been all right up to a point. Mutual advantages. But when I won the scholarship and was on my way to the station, she staged a terrific farewell scene. She was a lady of great, suppressed dramatic talents. Threw herself down on the ground and confessed all in terms that would have embarrassed Casanova. The doctor got out his pistol. He managed to shoot a hole in a little glass-shaded lamp they had and she was all over him, screaming, "Oh, don't hurt him, don't hurt him." And I ran for it. The only reason this is of any interest is that later on, when I needed as many character references as I could scrape up, the good doctor made it his mission in life to try to send me up the river without a paddle. He got into a plane and came all that way voluntarily just to tell the jury what a conniving, cold-hearted rascal I was. And it didn't do me any good.'

'She must have suffered a lot after you left.'

'Don't you believe it. She had a good time with me. And after I'd served my purpose, she had the supreme pleasure of throwing it in his face. You could see why she wanted to, too. He wasn't the kind to forget an injury, or an oversight, or a misunderstanding, or a mistake, or a badly ironed collar. Anyway, I had the scholarship. I was working nights and looking for weekend jobs. I bought a second-hand pick-up truck and I used to move furniture for people, fix their washing machines, clear the leaves out of their gutters, put the storm windows on, mow the grass – anything. That's how I met Harriet. Something had gone wrong with her gardener's back. He needed some extra help with lifting things. In other words, he'd talked her into hiring another man to do his work, while he stood there and gave his mouth a lot of exercise. But we got along all right. I worked there for a long time. It was one of my best places. And I got to know her. She was famous. She owned art collections and gave charity balls and all that. She had millions. You wouldn't have thought it; she looked like an ordinary woman, nobody special. She was forty-three when I met her. I was almost twenty.'

'What did she look like?'

'Medium height and build, short brown hair, going gray. She liked golf and tennis. When she was younger, she used to ride. And she had a pilot's license. Her family was unbelievably moral and upright for people who'd made millions. She'd been brought up in some old-style ideal of Christian service that made her feel uplifted about life. She was a good sport. Good company, even thought she was teetotal – that was another of their things: no liquor, tobacco, coffee.

'One day there was a fire in the kitchen. We got it out, but when I took a look at the place, I could see it was the wiring. The whole house needed to be rehauled.'

'Go on.'

'I'm late. I should be getting back.'

'Not till you tell me. Please.'

'Right. She'd never had a lover. It's hard to believe that people still live like that, but some do. I asked her to marry me and she said yes. We were fine together; she was fun. I liked her. She wanted to get married fast, so we did. When I met the rest of them, I understood why. You've never seen such a gallery of stuffed shirts. Of course they hated me. And they thought I was a fortune-hunter, which wasn't entirely untrue.'

'But you didn't marry her for her money.'

'Not entirely. But partly, yes. Of course. Why not? It wasn't as if I was planning to walk out on her. I thought we'd be on friendly terms forever. And things went very well. The family had to admit that I made her happy. And then, four years later, when nobody was expecting such a thing, she got pregnant. That was when I began to feel regret – remorse – for the way I'd behaved, because the doctors were all horrified. They didn't think she stood a chance. They said that the baby was sure to be mongoloid or deformed, or that something would go wrong because of her age. According to them, she shouldn't have considered pregnancy after the age of thirty-five. A couple of them suggested an abortion.

'She just swept all the advice aside and said that she felt well and happy, and she was looking forward to bringing up a child. I was scared. I didn't think she'd make it. She was forty-seven. Even after it was too late for anyone to have done anything about it, they kept telling me how dangerous it was for her. But she was laughing. And when Ricky was born, we were both laughing. When she made me hold him in my arms, I was just over-whelmed; all the years I'd stopped feeling any kind of sentiment: and suddenly it caught up with me. He was smaller than I'd imagined he'd be. And he had a lot of wild red hair. That was when I started to love her.

'She turned out to be one of those natural mothers, who take it all in their stride and enjoy it. But of course I was seeing other women, off and on. I was also working hard, going up in the world, making a name for myself, making money. Once I'd made enough, people stopped thinking I'd married her for mercenary reasons. And then: the night of the accident. She'd invited about a dozen people for dinner, maybe a few more. About fifteen. For the past year she'd been giving fantastic dinners where she'd have the table decorated like a kind of bower, or a temple, or a bandstand. I don't know what it was supposed to add to the evening; I'd come home from work and find myself sitting down to a meal where I had to keep batting rosebuds out of my soup or wondering if a white dove might fall off its perch and land in the salad. Most of these evenings were given over to fundraising for charities, so I guess maybe there was an element of showmanship to them. Harriet used to hire all sorts of designers and interior decorators to help her.

'On this particular evening, she'd had a glass pipeline laid down the table and overhead. It curled up, all over the place. The pipes were filled with water. Colored tropical fish swam through them and they were illuminated by a series of lights that were made to look pretty rather than functional. There was a fountain in the middle of everything and a lot more of the lights. The overall effect was intended to be one of an under-sea treasure-cave.

'Well, I got home early but I went straight upstairs. I looked in on Ricky, took a shower and when I came downstairs, the guests were already arriving. So, the first I saw of this Disneyland table arrangement was when I went in to dinner with everybody else. And the first thing I said was that it looked very nice, but was it safe? "Oh, yes," she said.

'I started to check it – all you needed was one loose connection and a little spilled water, and the whole house could be alive. I was still fussing around at my end of the table when I heard her say, "Just this little wire," and then she screamed. Half the other people there started screaming too. For a minute it was hard to tell what was going on.'

'She was electrocuted?'

'That's right. It's a wonder we weren't all incinerated. Apparently the only bit of metal casing that could be dangerous was right in front of Harriet's place at the table, where she was bound to notice it. The people who'd been responsible for setting up the equipment said that everything had been completely safe but that I had degrees in all sorts of things and, since I'd been in the house for hours, I could have tampered with it. Well, the police thought that that sounded reasonable. I was under arrest and hiring lawyers. There were two hundred reporters camped outside the doorstep. They wouldn't even leave Ricky alone. And then, the trial: dear old Dr Danforth getting his chance to dump all over me; I really wished I'd taken the opportunity of laughing in his face before I made my getaway from under his roof. They all thought I'd done it but they couldn't prove anything, so they had to acquit me. For months afterwards I got letters, telling me that I'd gotten away with murder but that everyone knew I'd done it just the same. Do you believe me?'

There was something in the story, some part of it, that wasn't true. She'd been waiting so hard to find out how the wife had died, that she couldn't remember where the moment had come, when she'd heard it in his voice, and had thought: *He's lying*.

But did it matter? She didn't really believe that he'd done anything, merely that he might have wanted to. The important question, she thought, was not what terrible things people did, but whether you loved them or not. Since she did love him, he might have done anything at all and it wouldn't change things for her because her love was like faith: it wouldn't allow her to accept any other truth. Only the loss of that certainty could make her believe that he'd killed someone. What he wanted to know was whether she loved him.

'Yes,' she said. 'Of course.'

*

Her car whizzed along the beltway with the outbound traffic. Every once in a while she looked at the speedometer. Bert had always let himself be pulled in to a faster pace, without realizing what he was doing, especially if he was thinking about something else. He'd switch his mind off and follow the crowd; and she'd sit there, not saying anything, but wanting to.

She thought about a church wedding. Maybe the idea wouldn't have thrown her so much if she'd been given a little preparation. Everything was going fast; that was the way she wanted it, but it seemed dangerous. Years ago, when she'd been trying to choose between two apartments, she'd felt the same mixture of exhilaration and dread. It was as if the more certain she became, the more there was bound to be something wrong with the place. Why was it like that? It didn't make sense. It ought to be the other way around. All doubt should vanish, once you knew.

She reached Aunt Marion's house early, let herself in and packed up a tote bag with the things on her list. Before setting off again, she went into the living room. She sat down in the chair where, just a few days ago, she'd been reading: when the doorbell had rung and there outside had stood a small boy in a suit and tie. It was unbelievable. But after it had happened, it was a fact. And after that it was normal, although possibly still crazy. She should relax. Lots of people did the wrong thing and it turned out all right anyway.

She checked the house, locked up, hid the key, carried the bag to the car and drove out to the hospital.

Aunt Marion looked different; she didn't like being in a hospital, yet she approved wholeheartedly of the nurses and doctors who, she said, 'couldn't have been kinder'. Already she knew all about them: their hopes, their dreams, their families. She seemed inordinately pleased and touched that Sandra had taken the time to come to see her.

'I'd have come before,' Sandra explained, 'but you said that there wasn't any hurry, and I've been so busy with all kinds of things. Aunt Marion, I've got some news. I'm getting married.'

'My dear, how exciting,' she said. 'Was that what you had to think over while you looked after the house for me? After you crossed the other one off your list?'

'In a way it was connected with that. I had to decide what I felt about the man I was turning down. It's so strange – just as I made up my mind, my future husband appeared. He's the father of that little boy who was lost – the one who ate up everything in your kitchen.'

'Wait now, just a minute. Don't say anything more for the moment. I'm a bit scatterbrained nowadays.' She rang the bell by her bed. 'Let me settle down. I'm supposed to have a cup of tea at about this time. Will you join me?'

Two nurses looked into the room. Aunt Marion ordered tea from them as if she were in a restaurant. They chatted and joked with her. She was evidently a favorite patient, despite her old-fashioned ways. She introduced Sandra. The nurses were named Carroll and Reba. Carroll had a high, twittering voice and giggled a lot. Reba was tall, ironic, and she gave the impression that she wouldn't stand for any nonsense. 'You're slipping down again,' she said. Aunt Marion leaned forward to let her plump up the pillows.

'Sugar and cream?' Carroll asked.

'Sugar and milk,' Reba told her. 'She already said. And a slice of lemon. Okay. Anything else you need?'

Aunt Marion said no, and thanked them. The nurses left. Sandra still felt like an outsider, as she had from the moment when the two had entered the room.

'I can't understand it,' Aunt Marion said.

'What's that?'

'You've known this man for no more than a week?'

'That's right. But that's enough to tell.'

'And this is the man whose first wife died in that hideous way? Everyone thinks he murdered her, you know.'

'What everyone thinks isn't always true and it doesn't matter anyway.'

'It doesn't matter?'

'It isn't important what people think. They don't know anything about it except what the yellow press puts out to boost their circulation.'

'Oh, no. It was in the real papers. The big ones.'

'I love him,' Sandra said.

'I don't doubt that. But in any marriage there's also the question of suitability, particularly after the initial infatuation wears off.'

'It isn't going to wear off. It's going to become deeper and stronger and more wonderful.'

'With a lot of work on your part. Men never try to make a marriage go. It's unfair to expect them to. They have other interests. They like comfort, but they also like novelty. Almost as fickle as boys: suddenly they're off and away to something new. Even though Hudson was always good as gold, I was glad that I had the foresight to keep an old admirer of mine up my sleeve. It didn't mean anything, naturally, but if I'd ever needed something to tease Hudson with, it was there.'

'Aunt Marion, those are such sexist ideas.'

'Yes, dear. I expect that's just why they work.'

Sandra tried to laugh. She said, 'You sound as if you disapprove of marriage.'

'Not at all. On the contrary. I simply think it's a mistake to hope that it's going to be something it couldn't possibly be. It isn't heaven; it's merely a way of life.'

'Surely it's heaven to spend your life with someone you love.'

'If you're not suited, that life together can destroy the love.'

'But how do you find out if you're suited? You get married.'

'Sandra, you mustn't think I'm against you when I say these things. I'm very worried for you.'

'There's no need to be.'

'You've known him barely a week.'

'Yes. I hope you'll be able to come to the wedding.'

'That depends on when it is.'

'As soon as possible.'

'The child – what's his name?'

'Rick. Eric.'

'Do you think he's a jealous boy?'

'No. He's accepted the marriage. In fact, he seems to be delighted by it.'

'I meant – when you have children; how do you think he'd take that?'

He might cut them up to see what was inside.

'I don't know. I don't really know how I'd take it myself. I've put off thinking about a lot of things. I'm just going to have to worry about that later.'

'I have an idea that they may keep me in here for a time after the operation. After that, I could be in a wheelchair or maybe on crutches, with a cast. All very awkward. But you'd understand if I didn't come, wouldn't you? Everything can be such an effort when you're not feeling well, even if you're looking forward to it.'

'Of course. But I'd miss you.'

'Well. What would you like for a wedding present?'

'I can't think. I've got everything I want.'

'Yes, that's one good thing: you won't have money troubles. She was fabulously rich. They say that's what he killed her for.'

'Oh, Aunt Marion, how can you? He's a brilliant man. He's made more money on his own than she ever had.'

'Starting from what she left, and using that to back his ideas.'

'He could have asked any big corporation to put up funds for him.'

'Perhaps.'

'Definitely. Anyway, if he's supposed to have killed his first wife for money, I shouldn't be in any danger. He's the one who's rich. I don't have much of anything except my car, and that's all beat up.'

'Yes, that's a blessing. But you might quarrel about something. About other women, for instance.'

'Really? Why would we do that?'

'Because that was part of the story. He even invited the other woman to the dinner where it happened. I suppose he felt obliged to marry her afterwards. But she wasn't the only one.'

'He didn't murder her either, did he?'

'It's possible that she held something that might be used against him.'

'Oh, for heaven's sake. Well, in that case, it's also possible, isn't it, that she was the one who killed the first wife?'

'No. She didn't have the technical skill.'

'She could know enough to take the insulation off a wire.'

'Ah. So you have read up about it, after all. Why did you do that, if you were completely sure?'

'I didn't. I asked him about it and he told me: it was an accident.'

'I see.'

'If you wanted to give me a present, what I'd really like is something you've made yourself. When you've got time. Something to wear, or something for the house.'

'Oh. All right. That's easy.'

'I was thinking last week that I might give you something, but I forgot to ask you about it. Aunt Marion, have you ever wanted a cat? A kitten?'

'Oh, not after Catarina. You never knew her, did you? I'm afraid I'm a one-cat woman. And at my age, I really don't want the worry. No pets whatsoever, please. Not even a guppy.'

There were footsteps in the hall. The door opened and Reba announced, 'Teatime, ladies.' Carroll followed her with a tray that she set up on the bed. Sandra pulled her chair forward.

Aunt Marion said, 'Thank you, girls. That looks just fine.' She told Sandra, 'Reba's getting married, too.'

Reba said, 'That's right.'

'Are you nervous?' Sandra asked.

'The way I look at it, if you never take a risk, you might as well be dead. Got to take a chance sometime.'

'That's what I think, too. And if it doesn't turn out to be what you thought, you can deal with that later.'

'Right.'

'Nothing's ever exactly what you expect, anyway.'

'You're telling me.' Reba gave the pillows one last push and turned to go out with Carroll. 'Chip off the old block, your niece, ain't she?' she said. 'You'll be okay, honey.'

'Good luck,' Sandra told her.

'Uh-huh. Likewise.'

Aunt Marion said, 'It's not the kind of tea I like, but it's not too bad.'

'It's nice that there's one person at least who agrees with me.'

'That's entirely different. Any man who tried to kick up a fuss with Reba would find himself in the emergency ward before he knew what hit him. She's no shrinking violet.'

'Am I?'

'Oh darling, of course. Stars in your eyes, head in a whirl after one week. It's heartbreaking.'

'It's what I want.'

'I had gathered that. And I do appreciate the invitation. Sandra dear, I wish you many, many years of happiness.'

'Thank you, Aunt Marion.'

'But if it doesn't make you happy, please feel free to come and cry on my shoulder at any time. I'll try hard not to say, "I told you so," even though it's always such a temptation.'

'I might be the one to say it to you.'

'Now that's a much better idea. That would please me enormously. You're the only younger person in the family who seems to be even partly recognizable as a member of the human race. I mean – well, you know what I mean. Is your sister still doing that thing to her eyes?'

'The kohl?'

'Last time I saw her, I thought she'd walked into a door.'

'I like it. I think it brings out the color in her eyes. And it makes them look bigger.'

'And she doesn't wear any lipstick at all. She's too pale.'

'She hates lipstick. Aunt Marion, she has her own style.'

'Well, we all have that.'

'And some of us have enough for two,' Sandra said, putting her cup back on the tray.

Aunt Marion laughed lightly. She held out her arms for Sandra to kiss her goodbye.

*

As her panic grew, the formal pattern of events helped her to look at them as if they were normal. Things were proceeding as they were supposed to: she invited her bridesmaids, spent hours talking over the telephone, shopped, put her apartment up for sale. The burden of emotion might have been heavier if she'd had to deal with her own family interfering on the spot, but her parents didn't think that they'd be able to fly in until the very last minute and her sister gave the impression that the wedding couldn't have come at a worse time. 'How much would it matter to you if I didn't show?' she asked.

'It wouldn't matter at all to me. Mom and Dad are the ones who'd hit the roof.'

'Well, that's nothing new. I just wouldn't want you to feel bad.'

Sandra said again that she wouldn't mind.

If her sister did turn up, her mother would find an opportunity of criticizing whatever she'd chosen to wear. There might be open hostilities. At a time when every detail had to be right, it would undoubtedly be better not to have both of them together.

She tried on her wedding dress, in which – despite the unusual design – she felt extremely bridal. As she stood in the center of the floor with her arms up, the dressmaker and her assistants worked deftly over the sleeves, back and neck. She turned around, put her arms down, moved to the left and to the right. They knelt on the floor. While two remained busy near her, the third would go farther back in order to judge the effect. It was like watching people trying to hang a painting; this time, she was the picture. All three of them were amazed by the quality of the materials they'd been given to work with. You couldn't find lace like that any more, they told her – not anywhere. And the veil, they said, was beyond belief.

When the last pins were out, the last stitches in, one of the girls said, 'Oh, you look just like a swan,' and another one added, 'You can't have even one extra spoonful of cottage cheese between now and the big day. Those seams stay where they are.'

On the morning of the first fitting Roy asked her if she'd like a new car. At first she said no, but when she saw how much he wanted to give her one, she remembered what trouble she'd always had with the old rattletrap she'd been driving for years. She'd bought it second-hand and she'd never owned another car. She said yes. The excitement and pleasure of this new toy drove many other things from her mind. She forgot, for instance, about the ring; that is, about the engagement ring. The wedding rings were already being sized.

'Would you like something brand new?' he asked her. 'Or antique? From an estate jewelry collection – that kind of thing? Or would you like to see a ring that's been in the family?'

He'd already described his parents as the sort of people who'd never had much of anything. If there were rings in the family, they'd have belonged to his first wife, Harriet, and now – presumably – to Eric. She said, 'If we had enough time, we could try everything. But if you have something in mind already, maybe you could show it to me now. It might save us a trip in town.'

'That's what I thought. That's why I had it made the right size when we were choosing the other rings.' From his jacket pocket he took a box, opened it and handed it to her.

She took the ring out of its box. The elaborately carved gold was set with three diamonds: two matching stones that flanked a center one of slightly larger dimensions. Wherever the light hit them, they played it back.

'Do you like it?' he asked.

'I've never seen anything so beautiful.'

'They're not as bright as modern diamonds because they're the old cut – not so many facets. But the stones are tops.'

'They look plenty sparkly to me. Would you put it on for me?'

She handed the ring to him. He put it on her finger. They both looked at it. It was obviously the right ring. He kissed her.

She asked, 'Was it Harriet's? I don't mind. I'd just like to know.'

'It belonged to one of her aunts. It's not very old: about 1910. But Ricky thought it was the prettiest one and he made a big point of how practical it would be, because it wasn't too big, so you could wear it in the daytime and not think that somebody was going to mug you for it.'

'I love it,' she said.

*

Although – as Roy said and as Eric had told him – the ring wasn't too large or too showy to wear every day, she was conscious of it all the time. She kept looking at it. When the stones were hit by direct sunlight, they blazed. Under artificial light they sizzled and glittered as if generating brilliance and color, unaided, from within. She was fascinated by them. Her mother's engagement ring had never caught the light like that, nor had her grandmother's.

All the girls at the office loved the ring, too. At the party they gave for her, one of the secretaries yelled above the babble of voices, 'Hey, Maureen says you're marrying a billionaire. Does he have any brothers?'

'No brothers,' she said. 'And if he had any, they wouldn't be anywhere special. He's a self-made man.' She smiled, as if she'd been paid a compliment.

'Gee,' the girl said.

She'd been waiting for someone to mention the money. Bert hadn't said anything, but Bert would know that the money wouldn't be important to her. Now, for the first time, she wondered how true that really was. It would certainly make everything easier. She would have her own space, lots of it; and physical comfort and all the freedoms people didn't have when they were forced to limit their spending. That easiness would become a way of living. 'It's just luck,' she said. 'I'm glad about it, but I'd want to marry him no matter what.'

'Yeah,' the girl said, 'that's better than money. But it's never lasted with me. Six weeks and it's like you can't believe you were so dumb.'

'It's different when it's for keeps,' she said, adding graciously, 'You'll see, when it happens to you.'

*

She went to the church with Roy and Eric. The officiating clergyman for their service was to be a Reverend Eustace: a large, plump man whose air of primness was offset by good humor and a tidy-minded efficiency that broke down periodically as he forgot where he'd put things. The most troublesome article he owned was his pair of reading glasses. He'd never needed spectacles until a few months ago, he explained to Roy. Now he had them and he couldn't find them.

'This never used to happen to me,' he said. 'I've always thought of increasing age as a time of aches and pains, but in my case it seems to be this ridiculous forgetfulness. It started with the glasses and it's spreading to other things. I keep finding myself over in a part of the room and I can't remember why I got up to go there, or what I was looking for. The glasses used to be a real problem until I discovered those ordinary magnifying glasses they sell in drugstores: they're almost as good. So now I have four pairs. But there are days when I can't put my hand on any of them.'

Eric was sent off to check the places where the flower

arrangements were to be set up. He also wanted to ask some questions about baptism and funeral services. A dark-suited man named Bates took him in tow.

Reverend Eustace ushered Sandra and Roy into his study. He sat them down and gave them a short speech that left enough margin for them to express approval about the goodness of man without having to lay claim to any specific brand of religion.

It came as a relief to Sandra that she wasn't going to have to lie. Despite the Reverend's appearance, he was on home ground now and, once the door had been closed, it was – she felt – a little like being called to the principal's office. She didn't have either the effrontery of Roy, who was prepared to say anything in order to get what he wanted, or the honesty of someone like her sister, who had once told an interviewer that she wanted the job because she needed the money.

If asked, she was going to express regrets about her lapse from churchgoing. And if she tried, she could convince herself that that was true. She would have liked to believe.

The chair she sat in faced a windowframe that had been given a shape she recognized as religious. The books in the bookshelves, the cross on the wall, even the Reverend Eustace, put her in mind of the way she'd felt about religion as a child. It had seemed to her, a long time ago, that there was a special sweetness – a rightness – in adherence to a certain way of life and a lovely perfection in its precepts, which you could aspire to but never fully live up to.

Reverend Eustace offered them each a sherry and poured one for himself. 'I'm sure everything will go exactly as planned,' he said, 'although if it doesn't, there's nothing to worry about. If there's a hitch, just remain calm and wait. I've seen people catch their clothes on the door, get their heels stuck or slip on the carpet and fall over. The children can wander off. If there's a baby in the audience, you can bet it's going to cry. Someone drops the ring. And so forth. All perfectly normal. The important thing is that the bond should be made, the words should be spoken and understood and that the union should be consecrated by a man of the cloth in God's presence.'

'Of course,' Roy said. He knocked back his sherry without changing expression. Sandra knew that it wouldn't be dry enough for him. She and the Reverend had a taste for sweet things.

'But some quite extraordinary things can happen,' Reverend Eustace murmured.

'Like people getting up to complain,' Sandra said, 'when you ask them if anyone objects: "Speak now or forever hold your peace?" ' Suddenly she thought about Bert. She imagined him shouting out for everyone to hear: *This woman once spent three days in bed with me and we weren't reading the Bible to each other, either.* Memory, combined with the alcohol, rushed the blood up into her face.

'It's interesting that you should mention just that place in the ceremony,' Reverend Eustace said.

'Well, it's the one everyone waits for. You think it's going to be like the end of *Perry Mason*, where somebody stands up in the courtroom and says, "I did it." '

'As a matter of fact, there was a story going around last year about a case where the proceedings were interrupted at that very point. It happened in a church down south. Everything was going according to the schedule until the minister said those words. There was a silence – you know, you have to leave a little pause – and then he was about to go on, when the bride herself spoke up. She said, "I have something to say." She turned around to face the congregation and she said, "I'd like to thank all the people who've worked so hard to make this moment possible: my mother, who organized the food; my aunt, who arranged the flowers; my sisters, who helped with the catering; and my bridesmaids." She stopped and the preacher was about to continue, when she took a breath and kept going. She said, "I'd like to thank all my friends and relatives who've come here today, some of them from far away, to wish me luck." She stopped again. And once again the minister was about to resume, but she turned around a third time, and said, "But what shall I say of my matron of honor, who went through school with me, and who spent the summers with us all through college, who's been just like one of the family all these years: and who slept with my bridegroom last night?" And then she picked up her skirts and marched right out of the church.'

Roy said, 'I bet that was a bad moment for the matron of honor's husband.'

'And the mother,' Sandra said. 'All that food, waiting for the guests. I hope she stood up and said, "Never mind, everybody. The party's still on." '

'Ah,' the Reverend said. 'That's what I really like about that story. Everyone has a different point of view about it. Some wonder what happened to the bride afterwards, others want to know if the groom tried to go after her.'

'And you?' Sandra asked.

'When I heard the story last summer, my first thought was for the clergyman, of course. Such a dreadful thing to happen in your own church. In God's house.'

'If He made us,' Sandra said, 'He must know how badly we can behave.'

'You can know a thing and yet not want to have it aired in public.'

'That's right. We're the ones who mind, not God.'

'We mind because of Him.'

Roy said, 'My fiancée forgot to tell me she was an expert on theology.'

The Reverend Eustace smiled smugly. He was the expert.

Sandra laughed. She put up her hands in a gesture of capitulation. She still thought that she was right.

Mr Bates was summoned. Eric walked into the room after him. Everyone was supposed to memorize the moves and the timing, and to remember where each person was to stand. Reverend Eustace gave Sandra a piece of paper on which her cues were written.

They went through the questions and answers. Eric said, 'I didn't bring the ring. I didn't think we'd need it today.'

'That's all right,' Reverend Eustace told him. 'Just make sure that you know when we're going to ask for it.'

'I know that already.'

Sandra gave Eric a wink. He didn't like being told things in the tone the Reverend had used to him. He'd decided that the man was a dimwit.

'And now,' Reverend Eustace continued, 'George isn't here today, but I think that Mr Bates can let us have a few notes on the organ. If the bride would wait outside?'

Sandra walked to the door. Eric fell in beside her but the Reverend called after him, 'You're needed back here, young man.'

Eric slouched back towards the others. Roy put out an arm and pulled him close.

Sandra sat down in a pew at the back of the church, where they'd left their coats. The others followed later, gathering together up near the altar. She was glad of the chance to observe without taking part. She especially liked watching Roy and Eric together. They looked happy, she thought.

She was blasted out of her reverie by a roar from the organ. As more musical notes followed, Eric walked away from the others. He came down the aisle to where she sat. She couldn't hear him above the noise. She cupped her hand behind her ear. He gestured towards the door. They picked up their coats from over the back of the pew, opened the door and went out.

They walked down the path and to the sidewalk.

'I don't think that guy is very well organized,' Eric said. 'Do you? He spends a lot of time telling you things you don't need to know.'

'He told us a terrific story while you were looking around the place with Mr Bates.'

'Typical. He waited till I was out of the room.'

'First of all, he wanted to talk to us about how serious it was to get married and what it meant. Um, the spiritual side of it.'

'Oh. Okay.'

'The story came up because it was about a wedding that went wrong.'

'That's great. He thought it was going to make you feel good to hear that?'

'I think so. Because it happened to somebody else.'

'What was the story?'

She told him, changing the wording at the end, so that the bride accused the matron-of-honor of 'fooling around' with her bridegroom. Eric was impressed. He said, 'Do you think it's true? That really happened?'

'I think so. Something pretty close to that.'

'There's something I want to tell you. You know, when I rang your doorbell?'

'Yes.'

'It happened like I said, that day. But I started doing it the year before, when he was going out all the time with all those women. See, I knew that he'd get married again and I thought it would be the same as last time: he'd get a divorce and I'd be stuck with the ex-wife and her husband. I saw you out walking that day. You didn't notice me. You were looking down. You were thinking about something else.'

Bert.

'You took your hand out of your pocket to push your hair back, like this. So I saw you didn't have a ring on. I thought you looked nice. My father . . . He never went out with anybody nice. I thought if I got to know you – well, then maybe I could ask you over. And we could all have lunch together on Sunday. Or something like that. That's all. I thought I'd better tell you, in case people said I was always going around to strange houses and acting weird. I mean, there's no point in doing it any more. I'm not a crackpot.'

'I know that,' she said.

'And it's okay, isn't it?'

'It's perfect,' she said. 'It's almost what you could call providential.'

'I knew it would be okay.'

'Yes,' she said, smiling. 'And if it isn't, it's a big house, so we can all go sulk in our own rooms.'

He thought that was so funny that he had to do a little dance as he laughed.

The Reverend came up behind them, his forward movement

274

seeming to be powered by the swell of his important belly under the clerical garb. 'A time for rejoicing, eh?' he said.

'We were wondering,' Eric told him, 'what would happen if you forgot your lines.'

'My goodness, I hope there won't be any need to worry about that. We might have to do it all over again.'

*

There was no time left. She'd spend an hour thinking, *I'm getting through everything so well, with such businesslike capability, that I'm going to have plenty of time left over*. At the end of that hour she'd wonder if she was ever going to make it.

Her family arrived. The first thing her mother said to her sister was, 'Couldn't you find another hat?' Her sister turned right around and left the hotel room, slamming the door as she went. Her father said, 'Oh, dear.' He said it frequently in the following days. As the wedding ceremony approached, his nervousness took the form of a furious and abnormal need to shake hands: everyone he met was pumped by the arm not simply at the moment of introduction but whenever he felt friendly, which was often, as he was also, unusually, drinking a lot. He remained charming while he became slow, sleepy and slightly hard to understand. 'He looks like a mounted fish,' her mother said.

Her sister helped to dress her on the wedding day. 'You look fantastic,' she said.

'I feel really out of it.'

'Did you drink too much last night?'

'I didn't drink anything. I didn't dare. I keep worrying that I'm going to fall over. God, I wish we'd held out for the registry office.'

'You're actually going to renounce the devil and all his pomps?'

'I think that one's in the baptism.'

'I'd go for the pomps every time, sweetie.'

'But you didn't.'

'That's only because it wasn't among the choices being offered.'

No, Sandra thought, *you wouldn't anyway*. As she watched her sister holding up the veil, carefully brushing the edges straight, she felt very proud of her stubborn, independent spirit, her stoicism and the way she chose to live her life by principles that she wouldn't even bother to discuss; she had married a man her parents disapproved of, lived in obvious bohemian squalor and seemed happy with him and their children.

Sandra asked, 'Did you have any doubts before your wedding?'

'None. But I had all that massive family outrage to keep me steady. It's harder for you. They think he's wonderful.'

That was the way it looked, certainly; everyone except Aunt Marion. Aunt Marion's knee hadn't healed quite so quickly as the doctors had hoped. She wouldn't be at the church after all. Sandra had known that somehow, at the last minute, her aunt wouldn't be able to attend: she didn't want to. After a certain age you had the right to keep away from what you didn't want to do and to save your strength for things that were fun.

'How about the kid?' her sister said.

'What about him?'

'You think that's going to be okay?'

'It's fine,' she said. 'In fact, it's all great. If only I can get through today.'

'I'm glad you're doing it all the right way. It makes up for how disappointed they are in me.'

'It's only Mother who feels that way. And the reason she does is that she expected so much more of you. She never thought was worth bothering about. It's true. And the reason she gets so mad is that she envies you. She'd have liked to live like you, but she never dared. She's always been frustrated. You showed her that it would have been possible, if only she'd had the guts.'

'You're kidding.'

'That's the way it always seemed to me. You're the one she admires. Anyway, she's getting a little better.'

'I hadn't noticed. Did you hear what she said about the hat?'

'I hope you're going to wear it.'

'I'm not sure.'

'There's nothing wrong with it except that it's ahead of its time.'

'That's enough.'

'I like it,' she said.

The preparations, the nerves, the waiting and worrying were beginning to remind Sandra of the time leading up to a long plane flight. She kept running to the bathroom and at the same time feeling thirsty. She was drinking one glass of water after another.

When at last she stood outside the church, with her veil down and her hand on her father's arm, she was so dizzy with anticipation that she was close to fainting. Her knees felt as if they weren't going to work. Her happiness became almost indistinguishable from terror. As she thought of Roy, who would be standing by the altar with Eric, she couldn't remember what he looked like. A wave of sickness passed over her. She was marrying a man she didn't know; this was like the weddings in other parts of the world, where the couple were committed and married to each other before they were fully acquainted.

She was even a stranger to the ground she stood on. She'd been inside the building – a place for ceremony and public spectacle – only twice before. She was wearing a dress that seemed less like clothing than like a theatrical costume or a kind of location in which she was hiding, disguised from anyone who might be looking for her.

A silence fell. Then the organ started up again. Heads turned around to look. Her father patted her hand. 'Easy does it,' he said. She squeezed his arm. They began the long, slow walk down the aisle.

On both sides people leaned forward to look. She was grateful for the veil; although it might not hide her face completely, at least it formed a space between her and the rest of the world. Her cheeks felt tight and burning; they might almost be on fire. Her father sauntered along as if he were out for a ramble in the country. She was filled with affection for him. She regretted the fact that she hadn't gone home more often after moving away to

277

join the office. And now she'd be married and her time wouldn't be her own.

As she passed by, she saw everyone without being able to understand what she was looking at. The only people she seemed to recognize were her mother and sister, who were sitting with their arms around each other. Both of them were crying and her sister was wearing the hat.

They reached the others. She was looking at Roy. Her father handed her over to him. All at once she was glad of everything: the strangeness of the dress, the presence of the crowd behind her, the fact that her friends and family were there to see the moment when her life joined with other lives to begin a new family. And, above all, she was happy that she was being married in a church. Religion was forever: everything else was only temporary.

Reverend Eustace began to speak. All the stages of the ceremony went as they had rehearsed it. When she was supposed to respond, she was pleased at how firm and audible her voice sounded.

The time came for the business with the ring. Her head turned. Was Eric going to drop it? Had he lost it? No. He stepped forward smartly, like a little soldier on parade, presented the ring and retreated. The blessing came next. And another handover. Roy had the ring: he took her hand. She knew that her hands would be slightly hot and swollen, but she had already mentioned that that might happen. If she just relaxed, there was no reason why the ring shouldn't fit. She looked down until it had slid over the first joint of her finger, then her eye was caught by Eric. He had moved from where he was supposed to be. He was craning his neck to see everything. On his face was an emotion she found – from behind the veil – hard to decipher, although it seemed familiar. His eyes were lowered, his posture was one of someone who waits, not patiently nor with excited expectancy, but with mesmerized satisfaction. A little smile had begun to move across his lips, changing his expression by imperceptibly accelerating degrees from the ordinary to the extraordinary, so that as she felt

the ring pushed fully on, she was aware of him standing now
nearly in front of her, his concentration directed wholly at her
and an almost sightless look on his face: rapt, transcendant,
sublime.